The Boy in the Book

NATHAN PENLINGTON

headline

First published in 2014
by HEADLINE PUBLISHING GROUP
First published in paperback in 2015
by HEADLINE PUBLISHING GROUP

1

Cataloguing in Publication Data is available from the British Library

Trade paperback ISBN 978 0 7553 6570 8

Typeset in Berling by Palimpsest Book Production Ltd, Falkirk, Stirlingshire
Printed and bound in Great Britain by Clays Ltd, St Ives plc

Headline's policy is to use papers that are natural, renewable and recyclable products and
made from wood grown in well-managed forests and other controlled sources. The logging and
manufacturing processes are expected to conform to the environmental regulations of the
country of origin.

HEADLINE PUBLISHING GROUP
An Hachette UK Company
338 Euston Road
London NW1 3BH

www.headline.co.uk
www.hachette.co.uk

For Terence Prendergast

Contents

Prologue

I never expected to find adventure by placing a bid on eBay. I had bought a hundred and six second-hand *Choose Your Own Adventure* books simply to relive my favourite childhood stories. A few days after placing the winning bid, they arrived in a huge parcel, the books' distinctive red-and-white covers instantly transporting me back to when I obsessively read and re-read them as a child.

Scrawled at the front of each one in sloping letters written in blue biro was the name of the boy who had once owned the books – Terence John Prendergast. As I continued to flick through I began to notice other annotations, jokes scribbled in margins, notes for future readers and time travellers. Whoever Terence John Prendergast might be, he was in love with these stories in the same way I had been.

As I reached for *The Cave of Time* out fluttered four small sheets of paper, which seemed to be from an old diary. Those pages contained the most heartbreaking lines I have ever read:

Posture - walk properly, when slim
No friends
laugh - practice laugh

Stole money from parents, bought airline ticket, ran away to Scotland,

came back next day.
Saturday detention x 8
Left school with intention to kill myself

This child, growing up in the 1980s, was lonely, unhappy, with no self-esteem and, as he saw it, no future.

I became obsessed with Terence Prendergast's diary, the obsession haunted my sleep, hung over my days. I had a gnawing need to find out the truth behind those entries. I needed to know that Terence, who would now be a man about the same age as I am, overcame the difficulties and emotions that had threatened to overwhelm him as a teenager.

It was almost as if the child I used to be responded to those diary pages as I would have done to a letter in a bottle – but was I twenty years too late? Who is the boy in the book? Is he even still alive?

Chapter 1 – Obsession

There would be no story if it wasn't for the fact I'm an obsessive by nature, a collector and a completist.

A person with an untrained eye could make the mistake of calling me a hoarder, but they'd be wrong. I don't keep everything. I like to think of myself as a curator of a museum – the museum isn't open to anyone else, but if it was, most of the collections would be met with confusion. At times, they make no sense to me either – the gift shop, however, is great.

We are all collectors to some degree. We all have something we covet or hoard. There would be no society without collecting. Everywhere you look someone is collecting something – refuse, tax, tickets, information. Some people's collections are purely social – friends, contacts or compliments. Some collections are made for nostalgic reasons, allowing people to relive their childhood or buy themselves a piece of history, to keep time from eroding, to keep the past present. Most of us collect memories and experiences by splashing out on a night out, holidays, or trips around the world. Other people don't like to waste money by collecting anything, so just allow it to accumulate in a savings account and collect interest instead.

We take pleasure from both our collections and the act of collecting itself. There is nothing as exquisite as the delight of finding the most sought-after piece for your most treasured collection. It's a physical and psychological joy unlike any other. The opposite end of this short-lived feeling of triumph and success is the collector's holy trinity of bad feelings – envy, frustration and despair. All collectors are permanently caught between these two extremes – the ideal of completeness and the anxiety of incompleteness.

The male bowerbird, found in Australia and Papua New Guinea, obsessively amasses and artistically displays his collections around his intricately thatched nest – flowers, fruit, shiny discarded beetle shells, leaves, feathers from other birds. He seizes anything that catches his eye, and more importantly, might catch the eye of a potential mate. The bowerbird makes the legendary, shiny-object-collecting tendencies of the magpie seem tame. He's a cabinet-of-curiosity curator of the natural world. Try saying that three times while holding a bountiful bunch of berries in your beak.

Like the bowerbird, each of us has a unique set of objects and passions that reflect, dazzle and beguile us to want to possess them, also quite often in the hope of attracting a like-minded mate. Whether our collection is primarily concerned with the rarity of exceptional craftsmanship, precious materials and accompanying prestige, or with novelty and amusement, or whether it fulfils another more esoteric or overt psychological function, it reflects our individual taste.

However, we are judged not only on what we collect, but on our collection's perceived completeness. As hard as it can be to know when you've completed a collection, it's even more difficult to know when a collection begins. The first object might be picked up or bought at random because it looks interesting or intriguing. The second might be picked up because it's similar to the first, but two objects are not a collection. If you're lucky and the second object is similar enough to the first, it might be considered a pair. So when does the collection begin? With the third object? The seventh? Tenth?

Mark Setteducati, designer of toys and games, and a magician, is also a collector of pens. At the last count he had over 10,000 different pens, each one distinctive in some way – not just with a slight variation in a design element, such as colour or size, but mechanically or conceptually unique. The pens are stored in neatly labelled plastic boxes, and sorted into a taxonomy of type, including pens that stamp and squirt, frog pens, 'screeching dolphin type pens' (a surprising number of them) and pens whose barrels feature a scene that changes when you turn the pen upside-down – a gondola floats down a Venice canal, a London bus passes the statue of Eros in Piccadilly Circus, a semi-naked, well-built man loses his boxer shorts. Although the last example also belongs in a box labelled 'erotic', next to a box labelled 'erotic (hard core)'.

Mark's collection started when he was lecturing students on creativity. He wanted to demonstrate how the same simple object can be taken in an infinite, and surprising, number of ways. Mark sees his pen collection as a metaphor for creativity, a research library and a constant source of inspiration. Amazingly, he knows when he comes across a pen that isn't already in his collection. In an interview in *M.U.M.* magazine (the Society of American Magicians' weirdly titled publication – it stands for Magic, Unity, Might) he states: 'It is important to actually commit yourself to collecting, to actually buy something. If I'd seen all those pens but hadn't bought them, they wouldn't have gone inside of me as deeply as they have.' He's expressing a truth about collecting – it becomes deeply ingrained in your psyche, your way of being in the world.

Habit, like collecting, is a branch of obsession. Habit is the unthinking routine that makes life possible; otherwise we'd be hindered by the hundreds of decisions we need to make in an average waking hour. Obsession is rationally unnecessary. Obsession is sneaky, it rationalises itself through the mind's need to control, to collect, to know. Obsession itself isn't dangerous; it's how far a person is willing to go in pursuit of an obsession that's dangerous – stalking, addiction and murder are at the dangerous end of the spectrum. At the other end are things like going to the gym every day, train spotting and stamp collecting. I wouldn't like to say where I fall on that spectrum.

Obsessive Compulsive Disorder, or OCD, is the medical diagnosis of a pathological condition in which compulsive behaviours interfere with the quality of life – the condition commonly shows itself in obsessive cleaning, counting and other traits that distress the sufferer. It is the inability to stop those obsessive compulsions from interfering with everyday life – for example, repeatedly locking and unlocking a door, or ritual hand washing – that causes so much suffering and anguish. Obsessive personalities on the other hand generally lead happy lives, the obsessive traits being channelled into one or two areas of compulsion that don't interfere with living a normal life.

It is impossible to know where the obsessional elements of my personality come from, but a lot can be said for it being a product of turning inward, of examining minutely my thoughts, fears and worries during a period of time in my childhood when I was acutely ill. Perhaps this story really begins here, in my own childhood.

With no disrespect at all to my parents, I had a distinctly average upbringing. I was born and brought up in Rhyl, North Wales, a decaying Victorian seaside town halfway between Chester and Bangor. My dad was a postman, and for a long time my mum was a professional housewife before studying health and safety as a mature student. I'm the awkward middle child in a family of three. My brother is two and half years older than I am, and my sister is five years younger. All five of us shared a three-bedroomed 1930s semi in a small cul-de-sac. I like to think our parents raised us well; we went to school, we did our homework, we played out, we watched TV, we rode bikes, we read, we argued, we had fun. These are the facts of a normal, average childhood. And without sounding too dramatic, all that changed when I was ten years old.

During the last year of primary school I became ill with a flu-like virus. Up to that point I'd been a fairly healthy child – the usual knocks and scrapes, but nothing serious. I'd even managed to avoid breaking any bones. But this was a virus I couldn't shake, and my condition deteriorated from there. For years I spent hour after hour on my own. At my worst, I was unable to do anything. The smallest of everyday tasks took intense concentration and effort.

My obsessional traits could also be said to come from having to keep myself occupied, of not allowing myself to become bored. With limited resources, the easiest way of doing that is to explore every facet, read every page, watch every episode. I have never felt that an obsession is something caused *by* me, but something that happens *to* me. I feel like I'm the soft bit of Velcro, and all it takes is for an idea or an object to come close enough to grip its hooks into me. I'm exactly the same way now. Once an idea has stuck itself to me, it's impossible to shake off.

You can't be obsessive without having a clear sense of the normal, or what you are not obsessed with. But we live in a time when we are encouraged to focus and specialise to such a degree that we can all claim to be obsessive about something. And if you can't claim that, perhaps it's you who isn't normal. So then, to draw an obsessional circle back to the start of the argument, being normal is down to what you are obsessive about. And me? Well, I'm now obsessive about many things, including watching darts, the music of Jonathan Richman, and literature and film featuring conjoined twins. I'm obsessive about how things are done – the dishwasher has to be filled in a certain way, I have to read or watch until the end of something even if I hate every minute, when nervously fidgeting I tend to align things in equally spaced patterns. I also have a lot of collections, most of them, apart from some rare books, inherently worthless to other people.

In my mid-twenties I found myself starting to collect Kinder Egg toys, the chocolate egg with the little yellow capsule inside that contains either a plastic model to build or a painted figure. Kinder Eggs are the worst kind of collection to an obsessive personality, because they are readily available and they form an infinite series that will end only when the Ferrero company stop producing them. So the question is, once you've started such a collection, what do you actually do with it? Kinder Egg toys take up too much room to display individually, and are too fiddly, and essentially worthless, to want to dust. I decided to put them in a glass-fronted box, and forced myself to promise that when the box was full I would stop collecting. True to the rules of this particular obsession, I did, and since then I have never eaten another Kinder Egg. The box now hangs on the wall in my office, a gaudy collage of replica vehicles, glow in the dark faces and plastic body parts. If I had to name this work of art, it would be called simply, like all good contemporary art, 'Untitled' followed in brackets by '(The Death of an Obsession)'.

One of my largest collections is of the merchandise of Uri Geller. Uri is world famous for his ability to bend spoons with the aid of his mind, an ability that propelled him to superstar status, and to becoming one of the biggest brands of the 1970s and an enduring cultural icon. As a kid I was obsessed with trying to emulate his feats with spoons stolen from the kitchen, and over the years I've amassed a huge collection of his merchandise range. Since his rise to fame, Uri has produced an exhaustive series of board games, an impressive folding bike, over fourteen fiction and non-fiction books, a line of jewellery produced exclusively for the home-shopping channel QVC, a collection of psychically energised teddy bears, a limited-edition range of porcelain plates and crystal decanters, and a pop album.

A few years ago, as a writer and performer, I thought it was time to share my obsession with the world by writing a stand-up show in which the audience duplicated Uri Geller's psychic feats – telekinesis, clairvoyance, telepathy. As miraculous as these tricks were I didn't predict Uri Geller himself would come to see the first performance. He brought along his wife, his manager and two lawyers. As Uri is famously litigious, I was convinced that, in the worst case scenario, I would be made bankrupt by a long-drawn-out court case, and even in the best case scenario his solicitors would squash the show. From behind the curtains I could see Uri sat in the middle of the front row, flanked by his entourage. As the lights went up on stage, I had never been so scared in my life. I performed the show barely daring to look in his direction, but accidently caught his eye during a section in which I recounted the story of how Uri received his special powers from an alien being when he was three. Uri's body language and facial expression didn't give anything away – a professional mask of composure.

What followed astounded me. The next week Uri Geller invited me to his multi-million-pound mansion for lunch. And what a lunch. We ate nachos, custard creams and fruit cake. Uri gave me two board games I didn't already own, versions of his books in Japanese, posters from when his live show had visited my home town, and eleven silk shirts he had worn in the 1970s, including the one he wore when he met Salvador Dali in 1975. If you were asked to invent a dream involving Uri Geller and a Uri Geller obsessive, it would read like that last sentence. I was living that dream.

Uri came to watch the show again. My obsession had taken a turn for the weird. It seemed like Uri had started to become obsessed with me being obsessed with him. It was almost impossible to know who was collecting what. But that is another story.

As a child I was obsessed with *Choose Your Own Adventure* books, the literary phenomena of the 1980s. The format turned the notion of fiction on its head. No longer were you just a reader on the outside observing the actions of characters. You were actually placed into the book as the main protagonist, reading a page of the story before being offered a decision that affected the outcome of the narrative.

For example, in *The Cave of Time* you are hiking one afternoon through Snake Canyon, a place you've hiked many times, but on this occasion you come across an entrance to a cave you've never seen before. You explore the cave for a little while, but when you leave to carry on with your hike, you suddenly discover it's dark outside, and the steep and rocky trail is lit only by the pale silver of the moon.

You are given two options. Do you start back home and risk losing your footing in the dark? If so, you turn to page 4 and continue reading. Or do you decide to wait until dawn? If so, you turn to page 5 and carry on from there. The decision you make at this point, although seemingly simple, is the beginning of a series of choices that affect the outcome of the whole story.

Choose Your Own Adventure books rewarded you for honesty, courage and patience, but, as in life, things aren't always that straightforward and if you made a bad decision and chose to turn to the wrong page, you could just as easily be punished by failure, or worse – death.

The *Choose Your Own Adventure* format is an amazing idea that could be said to have been independently created by a few different authors, mainly as a literary curiosity at the fringes of experimental fiction. The real honour for creating the phenomenon belongs to Edward Packard. He came up with what would become the *Choose Your Own Adventure* series back in 1968 while telling bedtime stories to his children. He would make up stories involving various characters and at certain points ask his children, 'What would you do next?' Ten years later, after countless rejections from publishers, and almost giving in and shutting his manuscript in a drawer forever, Edward Packard sent *Sugarcane Island* to a small press who were interested in innovative children's fiction and, to cut a short story shorter, history was made. The series, starting with *The Cave of Time* published in 1979, went on to sell over 250 million books in America alone, and was translated into thirty-six languages.

My introduction to *Choose Your Own Adventure* started in 1984 with the back of a cereal box. In the 1980s the back of the cereal box was an exciting place. It either promised the immediate reward of a small plastic thing between the box and the inside bag, or, most excitingly, inside the bag of cereal itself – such as the chicken-shaped reflectors that clipped to the spokes of your bike wheels, given away free with Corn Flakes. Sometimes they advertised a special offer that demanded a more long-term commitment to breakfast in order to collect the required number of tokens to claim your gift. A Weetabix promotion for two different *Choose Your Own Adventure* books must have sparked something in my imagination, because I've always hated breakfast and detest Weetabix.

In the 1980s the Weetabix marketing team were trying to appeal to children by using a gang of five cartoon skinhead characters whose heads and bodies were formed from single Weetabix biscuits wearing matching blue jeans, white T-shirts, braces and Dr Martens boots. You could tell them apart by their accessories, their different personalities reflected by their names – the not-so-bright Brian, Brains the brains, Crunch the hard man, Bixie the token girl, and their leader, Dunk. The first adverts for the *Choose Your Own Adventure* promotion show Dunk pushing the other Weetabix Neet Weet Gang members out of the way. They look visibly shocked. 'Where are you going?' asks Bixie, hands over mouth in astonishment. 'I'm going to read a BOOK!!' replies Dunk. The last frame shows them all reading a book together, as Dunk decides which page to turn to next. It must have been an effective marketing campaign, at least to me.

You had to collect eight tokens for each book and on a box of twenty-four Weetabix there were only two tokens. Even at the recommended two Weetabix every serving that still equals ninety-six breakfasts to claim both books. There were five of us in our family. My mum has never eaten cereal of any kind, my brother preferred toast, and my sister has always had a thing for Frosties. My dad, however, was a Weetabix kind of man, and the bribe of obtaining the *Choose Your Own Adventure* books compelled me, temporarily, to become one, too. So the two of us ate nothing but Weetabix for breakfast for six weeks and six days before I'd managed to collect enough tokens for both *The Horror of High Ridge* and *Mountain Survival.*

After the excruciating 'Please allow up to twenty-eight days for delivery' wait, the books finally arrived. I read and re-read them avidly. I became obsessed with trying to experience every twist and turn, every happy ending, every dead-end, every death. I loved them. I bought and read more books in the series, turning down the corners of the pages, so if I hit a dead-end, I could go back and try again. Falling through the fifth dimension in *Hyperspace* and meeting the author Edward Packard inside his own book, breaking the rules *Inside UFO 54-40* and finding Ultima the planet of paradise, being trapped in a time-loop on *Sugarcane Island* with an old man who repeatedly keeps looming over you – these are all moments from parallel fictional worlds that I remember as vividly as my own.

The simple mechanic of choosing where the story would go next, and which page to turn to, redefined storytelling for a whole generation. As readers we became responsible not only for the outcome of the story, but for the journey. *Choose Your Own Adventure* books neatly illustrated that our own lives are a tangle of narrative possibility. Reading *Choose Your Own Adventure* books allowed me to see that situations might be out of my control but that life was a series of choices with the potential for endless adventure. I might be on one path, but at some point in the future my story would turn a corner, and up ahead would be possibilities I hadn't even begun to imagine. That is powerful stuff for an eight-year-old.

I've still got the *Choose Your Own Adventure* books I had when I was a child. I took them with me when I left home to go to university, where they sat between James Joyce and Samuel Beckett as examples of the greatest twentieth century experimental fiction, and they've moved house with me ever since. I loved them, and I still love them, so much so that I've collected books in the same format from second-hand shops ever since. The huge success of *Choose Your Own Adventure* spawned hundreds of imitators and innovators, so they are easy to find, but constantly surprising in their variety.

One of the most famous was the British series *Fighting Fantasy*, which started with *The Warlock of Firetop Mountain*. This book was the first to introduce a dice-rolling, monster-fighting element to the page-turning mechanic. I remember persuading my mum to buy me a copy from Woolworths to keep me occupied while we were spending a wet week holidaying in a chalet on Rhyl beach. I don't know what was worse, fighting orcs and dwarfs using a dice and a pencil or the fact we actually lived in Rhyl at the time.

One unique book offered you the chance to hate humanity by becoming the biggest orc of all, the loathed British Prime Minister Margaret Thatcher, in the nightmarishly titled *You are Maggie Thatcher: A dole playing game* written by Hunt Emerson and Pat Mills. You, the reader, are physically turned into Maggie by the Tory ad agency, on a divine mission to lead Britain into the light, before your hard-hitting satirical adventure begins. The same team also wrote a special edition of the *Diceman* series of comics called *You are Ronald Reagan*, the equally nightmarish American political equivalent.

And if that is not bad enough, another book offers you the opportunity to be there in the Bible and, as it says on the cover, 'have different adventures with your favourite Bible heroes each time you open the book'. Unfortunately, Pontius Pilate isn't one of them.

A *Choose Your Own Adventure* Bible story has one huge three-letter problem: God. Every action you choose to make is futile against the desire of an omnipresent being whose will is to be done. Any decision you take can't change the outcome of the story – it is not possible to offer Mary and Joseph a hotel room, you're not able to say you don't like apples – which is somewhat missing the point of being able to decide what happens next.

As a side note, I don't know if my aversion to religion is due to the fact that there is no God, or because I was punched in the face by Simon Roberts in the middle of an RE lesson because I wouldn't let him write on my pencil-shaped pencil case.

One religious *Choose Your Own Adventure* style series even went as far as offering you the chance to *Escape from the Holocaust*. You'll be pleased to know that if you do manage to survive the most horrific racial extermination in history, your life always turns out well – for example, spending the rest of your days teaching in a Jewish school in America. And while the book is a completely admirable way of teaching children about the horrors of history, it doesn't go far enough. No ending has you waking up screaming every time you close your eyes.

Religious groups weren't the only ones to write moralizing *Choose Your Own Adventure* style books. The *It's Your Choice* series presented you with a whole range of temptations. In *Danny's Dilemma* 'a teenager experiments with tobacco'. 'What will he do?' is the question on the cover. 'It's up to you!' is the response.

But if you think Danny has got a tough decision, it's nothing compared with *Serena's Secret* – 'A teenager experiments with alcohol . . . What will she do? It's up to you!' And it's a downward slope from here as Christy is offered the chance to 'experiment with marijuana . . . What will she do?' The familiar question is accompanied by an illustration of Christy smiling pleadingly across a pool table. 'It's up to you!'

Once you've started smoking, drinking and taking drugs, the next question you will inevitably find yourself asking is *Too Soon For Sex?* 'Serena [obviously she's been drinking a bit based on her previous exploits] and James are in love and thinking about having sex. What will they do?' You've guessed it. 'It's up to you!'

Those are just a few of my favourites from my collection, but I've also acquired *Choose Your Own Adventure* style spin-offs from cult films, such as *Star Wars*, the *Indiana Jones* series and *Ghostbusters*, and TV programmes, including *The A-Team*, *Knightmare*, and *Dr Who*; and I've got some featuring Marvel comic heroes, such as The Amazing Spiderman and Superman, and computer-games characters, such as the Mario Brothers, Sonic the Hedgehog and the Lemmings. It's a bookshelf that reads like a *Who's Who* of 1980s popular culture.

Other books revisit famous literary characters. Sherlock Holmes, Tarzan, the Famous Five, the inhabitants of Narnia, and Elizabeth Bennet from Jane Austen's *Pride and Prejudice* have all had the *Choose Your Own* treatment. Some amazingly inventive series are more familiar to those born in the 1980s – such as R.L. Stine's phenomenally successful *Give Yourself Goosebumps*. There are piles of fantasy series with masculine leather-and-sword sounding names, like *Lone Wolf* and *Grailquest*. Then there are the strictly adult only, badly written, erotic adventures that allow you to take the role of either a man or woman in a series of sexual fantasies, and the generally appalling, unimaginative spoofs set in boring temping jobs. Audio adventures on CD allow you to choose which track to play next, and animated DVD games let you decide what happens by pressing a button on your remote control. And it could be said that it all started because of that one story told by Edward Packard to his children.

I'm constantly running out of space for my growing collection, but I'd never even been close to owning a complete set of *Choose Your Own Adventure* novels. So, because I am an obsessive nerd, you can imagine my excitement when I found someone on eBay selling the first hundred and six *Choose Your Own Adventure* books from *The Cave of Time* right through to *Hijacked!*

Let me say that again – one hundred and six *Choose Your Own Adventure* books in one lot. My obsession compelled me to put in a bid.

Bidding ended at 9.28 p.m. on a Sunday night in May. For the last half an hour of the auction I clicked refresh every ten seconds, the price rising by a few pounds every few minutes. I calculated my maximum tactical bid, took a risk, waited and placed my bid in the final minute. Anxiously, I watched the seconds counting down, the computer mouse slick with sweat. With only ten seconds remaining, someone put in a counter bid, immediately becoming my nemesis; eBay raised my bid on my behalf, my faceless enemy raised theirs, I clicked refresh, my screen froze, I screamed.

Moments after the auction finished I received this email:

Congratulations 2manynathans!

Dear 2manynathans,

You have agreed to purchase the following eBay item from littlejim75 (J. Costello – United Kingdom) on 23 May 21:28:55 BST:

CHOOSE YOUR OWN ADVENTURE NUMBERS 1 TO 106 – Item #4213774452

I'd won! I'd won!

Part of the traditional excitement of collecting is the thrill of the hunt – never knowing what you will find, or when you will find it. eBay takes that away and replaces it with the adrenalin-fuelled excitement of the auction. My body was pumped with chemicals that would take weeks to work from my system.

I paid a total of £41.01, just under 39p per book. That tactical extra 1p won me the auction. If I'd made a different decision the rest of this story wouldn't exist.

A few days later I was woken by the postman ringing the doorbell. At his feet sat a large green box wrapped with brown parcel tape. It looked as if it had been wrapped securely but carelessly. Through the gaps in the tape could clearly be seen the letters WA ERS RIS. My brain jumped to fill in the gaps between them, spelling out a leading brand of crisps in a flavour I didn't like. I signed for the parcel using the chewed biro offered to me. I've always hated using ballpoint pens, my writing has been spidery and hard to read for as long as I can remember, almost like an abstract shape of the word rather than the word itself. But with my name approximated, the box on the doorstep was now mine.

It was Saturday morning at my parents' house. I'd recently come out of an awkward flat-share with an ex-girlfriend; it was a hard break-up. We'd been incredibly close, had more nicknames for each other than fingers to hold hands, loved and supported each other, and allowed for things that perhaps should have led to arguments. We'd become best friends, and then I became ill again. It was the first time I'd become seriously ill as an adult, and I wasn't really prepared for the added pressures and demands that puts on a relationship, and my girlfriend wasn't ready for the additional responsibilities of having to be a part-time carer. That is not to say she didn't care, because she did, a great deal, but she wanted to be a lover, not just a friend. And at that time, being a friend was all I could offer. My illness was the death of our relationship. I was having a tough time coming to terms with focusing on getting better, and trying not to feel frustrated and worried that it would happen again if I ever started a new relationship.

My parents had come to my rescue yet again, offering me their spare room until I'd got myself on my feet, but that time had turned into a couple of months longer than was really comfortable for any of us. And filling the spare room with a hundred and six books that someone else had just got rid of wasn't going to help the situation.

'Who was that at the door?' my mum yelled over the racket of the food processor from the kitchen. She was on a new diet, something that clearly involved grinding something that shouldn't be ground and then mulching something soft into it.

'No one, just the postman,' I shouted back as I struggled to carry the box into the spare room.

My mum and dad's spare room is just big enough for a tiny wardrobe, a small computer desk, and a single bed. Now that there was a box of *Choose Your Own Adventure* books on the bed it felt like a time machine – I'd hijacked the fundamental laws of the universe and I was a child again.

I cut through the tape, ripped back the flaps and began pulling out books, a tumble of titles that ranged from the prosaic *Mystery of the Secret Room* through the genre-defying *Space Vampire* to the suggestively ambiguous *The Trumpet of Terror.* The familiar covers of the books I'd obsessed over as a child brought back memories of leaving the light on and reading when I wasn't supposed to, of folding down corners so if I hit a dead-end, I could turn back and choose a different path, the mystery of multiple adventures mapping themselves out before me. Now here I was, almost twenty years later, a grown man staying with my parents. Somehow, I was compelled to run excitedly into the lounge to show my mum and dad what had arrived in the post, finding it impossible to keep it a secret. They didn't seem that interested.

Luckily, they were on their way out to do some shopping, so I had room to lay out the books on the floor in numerical order – a feat that took up all the space between the couch and the fireplace and reached as far as the dining table.

For fellow obsessives reading this book, here are the titles of all one hundred and six books:

1. The Cave of Time
2. Journey Under the Sea
3. By Balloon to the Sahara
4. Space and Beyond
5. The Mystery of Chimney Rock
6. Your Code Name is Jonah
7. The Third Planet from Altair
8. Deadwood City
9. Who Killed Harlowe Thrombey?
10. The Lost Jewels of Nabooti
11. Mystery of the Maya
12. Inside UFO 54-40
13. The Abominable Snowman
14. The Forbidden Castle
15. House of Danger
16. Survival at Sea
17. The Race Forever
18. Underground Kingdom
19. Secret of the Pyramids
20. Escape
21. Hyperspace
22. Space Patrol
23. The Lost Tribe
24. Lost on the Amazon
25. Prisoner of the Ant People

26. The Phantom Submarine
27. The Horror of High Ridge
28. Mountain Survival
29. Trouble on Planet Earth
30. The Curse of Batterslea Hall
31. Vampire Express
32. Treasure Diver
33. The Dragons' Den
34. The Mystery of the Highland Crest
35. Journey to Stonehenge
36. The Secret Treasure of Tibet
37. War with the Evil Power Master
38. Sabotage
39. Supercomputer
40. The Throne of Zeus
41. Search for the Mountain Gorillas
42. The Mystery of Echo Lodge
43. Grand Canyon Odyssey
44. The Mystery of Ura Senke
45. You Are a Shark
46. The Deadly Shadow
47. Outlaws of Sherwood Forest
48. Spy for George Washington
49. Danger at Anchor Mine
50. Return to the Cave of Time
51. The Magic of the Unicorn
52. Ghost Hunter
53. The Case of the Silk King
54. Forest of Fear
55. The Trumpet of Terror
56. The Enchanted Kingdom
57. The Antimatter Formula
58. Statue of Liberty Adventure
59. Terror Island
60. Vanished!
61. Beyond Escape!
62. Sugarcane Island
63. Mystery of the Secret Room
64. Volcano!
65. The Mardi Gras Mystery
66. Secret of the Ninja
67. Seaside Mystery
68. Secret of the Sun God
69. Rock and Roll Mystery
70. Invaders of the Planet Earth

71. Space Vampire
72. The Brilliant Dr.Wogan
73. Beyond the Great Wall
74. Longhorn Territory
75. Planet of the Dragons
76. The Mona Lisa is Missing!
77. The First Olympics
78. Return to Atlantis
79. Mystery of the Sacred Stones
80. The Perfect Planet
81. Terror in Australia
82. Hurricane!
83. Track of the Bear
84. You Are a Monster
85. Inca Gold
86. Knights of the Round Table
87. Exiled to Earth
88. Master of Kung Fu
89. South Pole Sabotage
90. Mutiny in Space
91. You Are a Superstar
92. Return of the Ninja
93. Captive!
94. Blood on the Handle
95. You Are a Genius
96. Stock Car Champion
97. Through the Black Hole
98. You Are a Millionaire
99. Revenge of the Russian Ghost
100. The Worst Day of Your Life
101. Alien, Go Home!
102. Master of Tae Kwon Do
103. Grave Robbers
104. The Cobra Connection
105. The Treasure of the Onyx Dragon
106. Hijacked!

As I laid each one on the floor I examined the covers in turn, montages of adventures I'd yet to experience, yellow ant men and old professors, treacherous cliff faces and spectral native Americans, phantom submarines and mysterious temples.

It was only once I'd laid out all of the books that I began flicking through them. It seemed that they had belonged to one child. He had written his name across the top of the first page of every book.

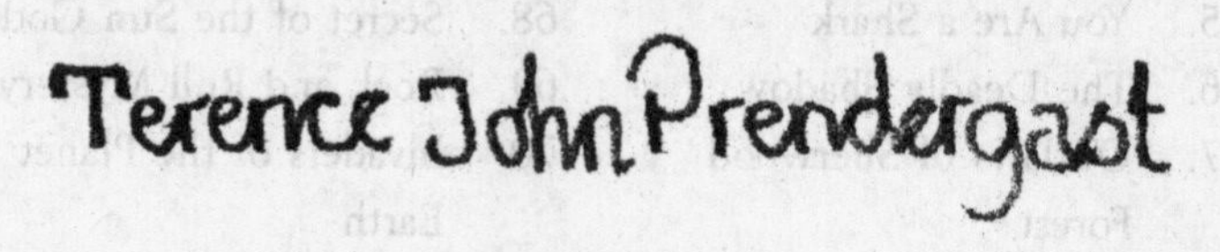

By writing his name he was claiming the book was his, ensuring his ownership would never be in dispute, and perhaps hoping that if the book was found, the person would be impressed that it was his. I certainly was. Unfortunately for Terence, though, the books were now mine.

But as well as writing his name on the first page, he'd also written other things in the books, not graffitiing them but almost personalising them – scribbling out a dedication to address it to himself, grading the books in a system of his own devising with a G or B.

Inside the cover of number 22 *Space Patrol* I found:

Telbot's book

Dimples is a fat
prune

I carried on flicking through book after book, looking for more scribblings by Terence Prendergast, pausing only to read a few of *Choose Your Own Adventure*'s infamous untimely demises. You run hurriedly down the spiral staircase of the Statue of Liberty, miss your footing and bang your head on the iron banister. You are told unequivocally that is the last thing you'll see of America, or anything else. You and your friend Nick are eating berries when mutant alien bears attack you from behind. You might have enjoyed eating those berries but, as the book says, 'not as much as the bear creatures will enjoy eating you'. You are alone on a spaceship hundreds of years from the nearest planet, with nothing to look forward to but old age and a slow lonely death – a bleak existential future for a nine year old.

Like the books, Terence also clearly had a sense of humour when it came to death. Number 45 *You Are a Shark* introduces children to the concept of reincarnation through an old monk who forces you to live the lives of three different animals before you can return to human form. The introduction to every *Choose Your Own Adventure* book always ends with Edward Packard, or the author of the book, wishing you 'Good luck!' for the adventure ahead, but in *You Are a Shark* underneath the words 'Good luck!' Terence has written:

Bad luck
I hope you die

That perfectly illustrates Terence's sense of humour – the book is about reincarnation, and so you can't die.

On the first page of number 29 *Trouble on Planet Earth* Terence does that thing that boys tend to do more than girls – write your address in relationship to the solar system. After he's written his street address Terence ends it with a cosmic flourish.

Birmingham, Englad
PLANET EARTH, 3rd Planet from the Sun

Maybe he was hoping that if the book was lost, a kindly inter-galactic traveller would know where to return it, or perhaps it was simply a statement that in this vast expanding universe there is a boy in bed in Birmingham with a book and a biro. Almost directly in answer to that question, on the following page he wrote:

Terence in bed 9:13am
Sat. 14 Jan 1989
in bed

Underneath, written down the side of the same page, there is a separate entry.

Terence sitting
on bed 12:24am
Mon 6 July 1992
Thinking about
St James
and
my
old mates who I never
see any more

Four years after he first read the book, Terence was reading *Trouble on Planet Earth* again and feeling the empty ache that we all face at different times in our lives.

Who was this lonely child who seemed to have loved these books even more than I did? I began to think of my childhood and the moments I felt lonely and isolated, and wondered if we would have been friends. Were the books a way to escape his surroundings, find adventure, test himself? Is that what they were for me? In those moments, I didn't realise that these questions were going to haunt me for years.

I started to gather the books up from the lounge floor before my mum and dad came home, putting them back in the box in reverse order. I'm not sure what aspect of my childhood I was hoping to relive by buying these books. Perhaps it was only a retreat into a childish escape from my current situation, nostalgia as a way to take stock of the present and a way to move forward.

I reached for the last book on the floor, book number one, *The Cave of Time*. As I carelessly flicked through it, out fluttered four small sheets of paper. It was only as I grabbed them that I realised they weren't pages from the book but pages from what seemed to be an old diary.

A diary belonging to Terence Prendergast.

Chapter 2 - The diary of Terence Prendergast

The diary of Terence Prendergast is small, just four folded pages pulled out of a larger diary. It is not dated, and the week contains just five days, Monday to Friday, and a place for notes, like something you'd be given at school to keep track of your homework or exams. The pages are covered with neatly written biro entries. The entries are the most heartbreaking thing I've ever read.

Week Commencing

MONDAY

1975	born	
1980	reception	1
81	Infant 2	2
82	Infant 3	3
83	Junior 1 met gang	10
84	Junior 2	7
85	Junior 3 (St Bedes)	11
86	Junior 4	6
87	1st Year	9
88	2nd Year	8
89	3rd Year	5
Jan 90	3rd Year	4

TUESDAY

WEDNESDAY

On the first page of the diary is a list of years, 1975 to 1990. A catalogue of schooling that seems to have been marked out of eleven according to some unknown system of preference.

I don't know if eleven or one is the best, but whichever way the scale runs, as only January has been lived through, 1990 might still have had the potential to be better or worse than four. And who or what is the gang?

On the next page is information about the speed of light.

Week Commencing

MONDAY

Light travels at 186,282 miles per second
1 light year is equal to distance travelled
by light in 1 year
Distance to nearest star =
70,000,000,000 light years=
4.2^{24} miles = 420000000000000000000000

TUESDAY

00000 miles

WEDNESDAY

It is not unusual for a child to be obsessed with the mysteries of space and time, and the speed of light is an incredible thing to contemplate – just to think that a star could by extinct by the time its light reaches earth's night sky. Judging by the dates he wrote in the diary, Terence is of a similar age to me, and as a kid I was obsessed by similar kinds of things too – the distance to the corner shop measured by the number of lampposts, how few Weetabix it would take to dry up all the milk on earth, the impossibility of imagining the vastness of the universe. But what makes the calculation especially strange is reading it alongside the entries on the other pages. It's almost as if the purpose is to work out the fastest possible speed to travel, to get away, to escape.

I also used to scribble down my thoughts, mark things out of ten, make plans and write lists. I, too, would write my address in relationship to the solar system, and sometimes imagine the fastest possible way out of the world I found myself in.

But it is the final two pages in Terence's diary that have haunted and obsessed me for the past few years. One of the pages is an incredibly poignant list of things that Terence wanted to improve about himself.

THURSDAY

Fat Carry on exercise, don't eat cake etc
Brace - Voice Practice speaking
Stutter " "
Posture Walk properly, when slim
No Friends
Hair

FRIDAY Shy

Self-Conscious
P.E. If I get slim, do it
Karen
laugh Practice laugh
'being left out'
No knowledge of Science & CDT

Notes Mirror

Report

The list is a punishingly critical examination of areas Terence believes he should improve in order to gain control of his life. The cumulative effect of this list is the image of a child deeply unhappy with himself, how he looks, how others perceive him, and how he fits in. The line I find most heartbreaking is 'laugh practice laugh'. Genuine laughter is one thing you can't practise. The acute self-reflection only increases the ambiguity of words that don't seem to belong on the list – 'Karen', 'mirror' and 'report'.

If the list is about Terence himself, the big question is who is Karen?

The next page is a list of years. Alongside each of those years are moments Terence considers significant enough to catalogue.

81 THURSDAY Met Ada
83 Got smacked by Coulson 2x, Communion
83/84 Wet pants 2x, realised about Confession
back of knee
85/86 Bullied by Kenny, crouched 3x
PE worse
87 Confirmation
87 FRIDAY WRGS, Karen ran away
89 Skived day 4x, loads of PE & Canoe
Smoking, Caught 1st day after Easter, 2 days
before Summer holiday. Stole money
from parents, bought airline ticket,
ran away to Scotland, came back
next day. Sat det. 2x, left
Notes school with intention to kill
myself, stole, suspended +
expelled. Stopped smoking, languag
90 Slimmed, more likable, skive day
x1 PE every lesson, Karen –
drugs. Guns

When I first read the diary my brain couldn't take it all in. If my maths was right, this was the writing of a 15-year-old – a lot of 15-year-olds have those kind of thoughts at a time when it can be difficult to make sense of the world, and if you are being bullied, it can seem impossible to find a way out of it. Some of those sentences are incredibly vague and their vagueness is incredibly evocative. What does 'realised about back of knee' mean? Did Terence really run away to Scotland on an airplane and fly back to Birmingham the next day? And the last three words drop like badly skimmed stones – 'Karen, drugs, guns'.

Terence's diary pages contain the most emotional lines I have ever read, and they pulled me in, posing questions that demanded answers. The diary contains the thoughts of a child growing up the 1980s, a child who has been bullied, has no self-esteem, and, even though he loved *Choose Your Own Adventure*, does not think of his own life in terms of possibility and choice.

I began desperately to try to make sense of it all, asking myself question after question:

Who were those pages written for?

Had Terence written them only for himself, and if so, why?

What happened to the rest of the diary?

Why are those moments catalogued rather than others?

Why was it so cryptic?

Was it intended as a kind of message-in-a-bottle, a summons, a cry for help?

What was the message trying to say?

Who was in the gang? And who was Ada?

Who were Kenny and Coulson? What are they doing now? As I pored over the pages, my heart burned. I wanted to find out who those bullies were and if they were still bullies.

Who was Karen? Why was she mentioned on the list of things to improve? What did she have to do with drugs and guns? Had Terence seen something he should not have seen?

And, more importantly, who was Terence Prendergast? What had he been doing for the past twenty-one years?

And, the thought I found most difficult to articulate, was Terence Prendergast still alive? Or had he already met a terrible end, worse than those in any *Choose Your Own Adventure*, perhaps even at his own hands?

That night I was kept awake thinking about the diary in a confusion of worry and sleeplessness, and something else, something I wasn't yet ready to admit to myself. Hours passed in heavy restlessness before I gave in, turned on the light, got up and tiptoed quietly to the bathroom, hoping that I wouldn't wake my parents. I ran the hot tap at half speed for a minute, splashed my face with water, then reached out and groped around for a towel. Even though I'd been there for months I was still getting used to my parents' flat, the idiosyncratic layout and placement of things that weren't where I would put them and where I'd expect them to be, and in the middle of the night without my glasses on it often became a guessing game. I gave up after knocking over the tower of toilet rolls, and dried my face on the bottom of my dressing gown.

If this was a novel, I would say the face in the mirror startled me, but that would be a lie. It didn't. If it had, I'd have had bigger problems to worry about. It didn't surprise me, either. I just looked a little older than I thought I did. The boyishness that I felt I had was still there, but, like a balloon a week after a birthday party, everything was just a little softer, a little more wrinkled around the ends. Maybe it was just the five o'clock in the morning shadows, or perhaps other people's mirrors are more inclined to show you the truth.

In the days and weeks that followed, I tried to dismiss the diary from my mind – I put it back between the pages of the book where I'd found it, and put the book back in the box. As the old saying goes, 'out of sight, out of mind'.

At last, I moved out of my parents' house and the books moved with me to a small flat of my own back in my old East London stomping ground, an area full of Turkish bakeries and pie and mash shops. Yet, throughout the months that followed, the diary continued to haunt me. I would look at the row of red-and-white spines belonging to Terence's *Choose Your Own Adventure* books, I'd pull down the copy of *The Cave of Time,* and read his diary over and over to myself. The obsession already had its hooks in the soft loops of my brain.

I started trying to piece things together. I compared the list of school years with the list of significant events to see if there was a correlation between the numbers one to eleven and what happened to Terence in those years. I read through all of the hundred and six *Choose Your Own Adventure* books to see if I could find any more notes, or scribbles, or anything that would help shine a light on Terence's distressing and dark set of writings. I was hoping for facts. I wanted facts that I could separate from the emotion I felt, and that would tell me who Terence is and that he was OK.

These are the facts I could state for certain:

- He was born Terence John Prendergast in 1975.
- He was brought up in the Birmingham area.
- He was raised a Catholic, or went to a Catholic primary school where he was bullied.
- He started high school in 1987. He had difficulty fitting in, bullied perhaps because of his size, and as a result was shy, lonely and self-conscious.
- At 14 he suffered from suicidal thoughts.
- The pages must have been written in January 1990, meaning Terence would have been 15 at the time he wrote the diary.

While compiling the list of things I could take to be true, I kept notes of assumptions – things that were quite likely to be true but had no factual evidence to back them up, a notebook of hunches.

- Karen is someone significant to Terence. Her appearance on his list of personal things to improve could mean his relationship with her. Perhaps a sister, or more likely she was a girl at school he had a crush on but was too shy to talk to.
- Terence was clearly a loner.

- The section about stealing money and running away seems like the story of a fantasist – somehow it doesn't quite seem real. And if that's not true, what else is not true?
- Terence might not be alive.
- The opposite assumption would be that Terence left school highly motivated to succeed, and now has a successful career and children of his own.

The walls of my lounge slowly became wallpapered in Post-it notes, over a hundred sunshine yellow squares scrawled with questions and assumptions, facts and dates, some with just a word or two written in thick black marker pen – WRGS? Knee? St Becks. Heat rising from the radiator made them flutter like anxious moths around my obsession.

To the uninitiated my lounge began to resemble the opening scene in a twisty Hollywood crime thriller, where you weren't sure who was the hero and who was the victim, and if any of it was even true. Thankfully, you couldn't see into my lounge from the street or my neighbours would definitely have called the police.

I started talking about the diary a lot, telling anyone who would listen. I'd begun carrying *The Cave of Time* with me wherever I went, the diary tucked securely inside. I don't really know why, but it was almost as if sharing Terence's problems helped other people. They confided in me their own worst thoughts, their own sadnesses and memories of childhood.

One night I met my friends Pete and Alex for a drink, they'd invited their friend Sarah along too. I'd met Sarah a couple of times before. She seemed kind of shy, but intense, intelligent and funny.

It wasn't long before I was pulling *The Cave of Time* out of my bag, and talking about finding the diary. Sarah asked for the full story. I was more than happy to oblige. She seemed curious, intrigued, full of empathy for Terence and understanding of my obsession.

Talking to Sarah recently, she said about that conversation, 'It was hard to know if the diary was a real thing, but my instinct was that it was something you'd invented. It just seemed too perfect to be something that you'd found by chance.'

'You thought I'd made it up! Why?' I asked, surprised.

'It was like you were testing people by showing them. I didn't know you very well, and I thought you wanted to know if you could dupe people.'

'Dupe people! Why would I do that? And in what way would I be testing people?' I was still incredulous, like Alice on the other side of the Wonderland mirror where everything was the opposite of what I thought reality was.

'To see if they bought it, or if they'd be like, "Hang on . . . you've made this up!" I'd seen you perform a couple of times, and I kind of knew what you did. I thought showing the diary was quite mischievous.'

'In what way did it seem I'd made it up?' I still hadn't learnt my lesson – you should never ask what people actually thought during a previous conversation. You are never going to like hearing the truth.

'It's not every day you pick up a random book and find a piece of writing that's interesting or exciting hidden inside. It was like something straight out of a novel. I felt really sad for how lonely Terence had been as a kid, if only in that typically teenaged, romanticised way. There was something that hit so hard about Terence's social isolation – like a Carson McCullers book,' Sarah replied. 'I remember I wanted to read through the pages of the diary myself and you wouldn't let me take them away from you, which was suspicious, endearing and childlike in equal measure. But my initial thought that you'd made it up didn't last that long. I wouldn't think that at all now. When I got to know you better, I understood that your nature was to pick up lots of these kind of found writings, because you collect, you're thorough, you look into things in a lot more detail than most people do.'

I guess what Sarah was referring to was how other things that have started out as writing or performance projects have leaked over into my real life, like the show I made about my obsession with Uri Geller. When I began on the long road of my obsession it was only a dream that one day I would actually become his friend and eat custard creams in his multi-million-pound mansion.

Time moves forwards in unpredictable bursts. If you feel your days are dragging, and you're not careful, you'll turn around and years will have passed. The inverse is also true – if it feels like time is speeding past, it probably is.

That first conversation with Sarah about the diary seems like only yesterday, but it's now two years ago. Sarah has also said about that first conversation that she was intrigued, not only by the diary, and because it was such an odd topic of conversation, but by me, too – what kind of man would be so obsessed about an old diary? Sarah is now the person who I share my life – in a way, you could say the diary of Terence Prendergast helped to bring us together.

My cat Kook and I moved into Sarah's flat. I had to downsize a few of my collections, and throw away the Post-it notes, but the *Choose Your Own Adventure* books found pride of place in the lounge. I would still try to show people the diary, but all of my friends had already heard the story. It seemed that talking about it had diminished its magic, somehow lessened its power.

But a new life wasn't enough. I was carrying Terence Prendergast around with me like some totem of old. Unknown to Sarah, I'd made a copy of his diary that I kept in my wallet. I still had the nagging, obsessive thought that I didn't know the truth. I didn't know who Terence was, where he was, or what had happened to him all those years ago. I didn't know if he was still alive. When I was being honest with myself, I had to admit I was scared of finding out that my worst fears for Terence were correct. If that was the case, it would mean that sometimes problems are too big to be overcome – and, in the context of my own life, that was knowledge I did not want to face. But scared as I was to find out the truth, I desperately wanted to know that Terence was OK. Although life is hard and unpredictable,

I wanted everything to have turned out well for him in the end. If I'm being honest with myself, I actually wanted a fairytale for the teenage boy I had been.

I saw elements of myself in the Terence I'd constructed from the diary, the child I used to be – painfully shy and self-conscious, and at times a loner. I've worked hard to be the person I am today. I've had to overcome a series of difficulties in my own childhood – the health problems that kept me from school for years on end, with nobody for company, my only refuge the adventures of my own imagination and the fantasy lives I could have through reading. Those experiences, despite being so long ago, have helped make me who I am, and there are worse people to be in the world.

I'm now plunging headlong into middle-age. I'm at the point on an ancient map where the land ends, and all that lies beyond is the unknown and the warning 'Here be dragons'. And that makes the world a little bit frightening again. I've never been married and I've never had children. I have a close relationship with my mum, dad and sister, and an estranged one with my brother. I have a girlfriend and a cat. I have a few good friends I'd do anything for and I love strangers. Absurdity and kindness make me smile. I'm driven by curiosity and creativity. I hate stupidity and old bullies in small towns. I sought affirmation in Terence's diary, and now I sought another kind of confirmation – that among all the adverts and articles and TV shows telling me that by my time in life I should have one failed marriage behind me, I should go skiing every year, I should eat organic and have a yearly gym membership, and a hundred other things I should have done with my life but haven't, I'm not the only one who doesn't really know where life is heading. I was hoping that, once again, Terence was not entirely unlike me.

My obsession and the preservation of my sanity left me no choice. I was going to have to go on an adventure of my own – a quest to find Terence Prendergast.

Chapter 3 – Feeling lucky

Four years had passed between finding the diary and making the decision to find Terence, and in him the secrets of the past, and perhaps the secrets of childhood itself. In all that time, Terence had not left my side; I wore him like a birthmark, or as creepy as it sounds, like the ghost of a dead twin.

Once I'd made the decision to overcome the fear and face whatever may be the truth, I felt strangely free. Now I'm on a *Choose Your Own Adventure* of my own, and just like the books, it is a quest in the permanent present tense. Now I have a lot of lost time to make up for.

The most obvious place to start the search for Terence Prendergast is with the person I bought the books from on eBay. I'd already fantasised about where the books came from. Had they been drifting around, a complete collection, for more than twenty years? Did the seller pick them up at a house clearance? Would that confirm that Terence is dead? Or just that the Prendergasts had moved house? The seller might remember where he got the books originally, and that could lead me to who sold them – maybe a member of Terence's family. I feel as if I'm a detective who has his first lead. It might be an obvious lead, but as Sherlock Holmes, the world's greatest detective, said to Dr Watson in *The Sign of the Four*, 'Eliminate all other factors, and the one which remains must be the truth.'

eBay only keeps a detailed record of purchases for a few months, but thanks to the collector in me, I still have the original invoice for the books, lurking deep within my email inbox. The seller's username is littlejim75, and next to it are his initial and surname: J. Costello. Jim, Jimmy, Jamie, James. Certainly not Terence. In the books Terence had written his full name. His middle name is John, not James, but he *was* born in 1975. Was littlejim75 born the same year? Is he a friend of Terence's? Like the TV detectives I'd spent so much of my childhood watching, I flounder trying to find a hint, a digital fingerprint of littlejim75's real identity behind his electronic one.

I search for littlejim75's eBay account, but all that comes up is the dreaded message: 'User ID not found'. My first lead and my first *Choose Your Own Adventure* style dead-end. I send an email to the address on the original invoice, but that bounces back with another error message: 'email address not known on this server.' littlejim75 has simply disappeared.

Perhaps littlejim75 was a pseudonym created just to sell things on eBay, but why anybody would have taken such extreme measures to cover their tracks simply to offload a collection of *Choose Your Own Adventure* books, I have no idea. With my best hope for a direct connection to Terence gone, I now have to face the vast tangled expanse of the internet.

The best place to search for a person is Facebook. More than 955 million people use the social network on a regular basis, 30 million of them in the UK, which is just over half the population. I'm not very good at maths but I can see that, if Terence is alive, there's a pretty good chance he has a Facebook account.

I log in with shaking hands, and type his name into Facebook's search bar. I instantly get the result I don't want – there are no Terence Prendergasts. I'm a little disheartened but there is no adventure without some disappointment. Taking inspiration from littlejim75's name shortening, I drop a few letters from Terence's full name and try searching for Terry.

There are seven entries for Terry Prendergast, which is certainly more promising.

At the top of the list is Terry Prendergast in Hawaii. His profile picture shows him with Patty, probably his wife, at The Valley of the Gods in Colorado Springs. The photo was taken on 21 August 2009 on a return trip from the huge granite carvings of the four American presidents at Mount Rushmore. In his hand Terry is holding a carrier bag from Garden of the Gods gift shop. I can feel the grip of my obsession tightening, as I'm desperate to know what Terry has bought from the gift shop. I look up the Garden of the Gods website. It says they're renowned for their homemade fudge. Terry looks like a fudge kind of guy. In another photo Terry and Patty are sitting on a rock, arms around each other. Terry is wearing a really nice parrot T-shirt. Although he's in his sixties and smiling, he looks tough and tender. He's definitely not my Terence. I catch myself – *my* Terence. That's the way I've already started to think of him. My Terence.

Second on the list is Terry Prendergast whose cover photo is 'The Skiff' by Renoir. Painted in 1875, it shows two figures rowing an orange boat on a river of blue brush strokes, a prime example of French Impressionism.

Underneath the picture Terry says: 'My fav Renoir, got to see it a few years back in Ottawa.' His friend, Scott Pennington, has commented underneath: 'I figured you for an Elvis on black velvet man.' This is not the Terry I'm looking for, either. From his profile picture I put him in his sixties, too, but seeing the friendly exchange between someone with a surname one letter different from mine with another Terry Prendergast instantly makes me jealous. If I can find the right Terry Prendergast, I wonder if we could become friends too.

The next Terry Prendergast has no photo, just the default Facebook grey blank male avatar with a perfectly symmetrical head and sculpted quiff. He has three friends. There is no other information. It could be the Terence I'm looking for, or he could be a spambot looking for company. Either way, I send him a short message. I have nothing to lose.

Hi Terry,

I'm looking for Terence Prendergast, originally from the Birmingham area, who used to collect *Choose Your Own Adventure* books as a child. I am wondering if this is you? If so, I have something to return to you that you have lost.

If you have a spare moment, please let me know either way if you are the right Terence Prendergast or not.

Thanks for your time.

Look forward to hearing from you,

All the best,

Nathan

The fourth Terry Prendergast is standing in front of a Lake Eyre National Park sign in the middle of South Australia. Behind the sign is a sandy wasteland – not the most photogenic of landscapes. Terry looks happy, though, and pleased to be there. He's wearing a Kyoto Public Transport System T-shirt, slightly sunburned, of large build, with a goatee and sunglasses. It's hard to tell how old he is. He could be anywhere between mid-thirties and mid-fifties. His profile says he lives in Melbourne, Australia, and that he is interested in women. His only other interest is Practical Shooting Videos. He has twenty-one friends, none of which are Prendergasts or called James. I send him the same message as Terry number three.

Terry the fifth also has no photos, no posts, no info and no friends. I send him the same message. I don't hold out much hope for a reply.

The sixth Terry looks promising – he doesn't have a profile picture but he lives in London, and his only like is Amazon Kindle, which might mean he is a keen reader. Any child who read and collected over a hundred and six books must still like reading as an adult. Terry has thirty-three friends, two of which are Prendergasts. I send him a message. I have a good feeling about this Terry. Not only does he seem the most likely, but if he is a fan of reading, we already have something in common.

The final Terry Prendergast is a teenage girl. She is wearing a sweatshirt that reads 'My brother . . . one of the few, the proud, a Marine'. She is hugging a boy in military uniform. In a way I can't account for, the photo makes me feel incredibly sad.

I've exhausted Facebook, but Google's web bots have indexed nearly 40 billion web pages. If Terence Prendergast has used the internet under his real name, even in a tiny way, or if he's commented on a forum, bought something from Amazon and said he likes it, if he's on the electoral roll, if he has uploaded a photo, trolled a YouTube video, or worked for a company that profiles its staff, it should be enough to point me in the right direction.

The measure of a man is what he Googles when no one is looking. I look over my shoulder just to make sure, take a deep breath, and in that pristine blue narrow rectangle under the children's magic show coloured Google, I type those letters that collectively haunt my sleep. T E R. Am I feeling lucky? I've never used that right-hand button before. E N C E. I remember reading some research that said if you don't believe in luck, you are less likely to actually be lucky. P R E N D E R. My hand wavers over the right-hand box. G A S T. Yes, yes, I *am* feeling lucky.

No, no, I'm not. My misguided faith in luck has brought me to the Wikipedia page for Terrence Prendergast – Terence with an extra 'r' – the Archbishop of Ottawa, born in 1944. Archbishop Prendergast is a teacher, writer and retreat provider. His hobbies include squash, cycling, skating, foreign films and Italian cooking.

I can't help but wonder what my Terence's hobbies are. He could still be interested in the fantasy genre – maybe playing role-playing or computer games. Real ale? Pub quizzes? He could be a keen traveller, looking for adventure and quests of his own. Or perhaps I'm just constructing a persona for him from another series of clichés, creating a phantom out of shadows.

I try searching Google again, this time without luck to hinder me. It pulls up a list of pages that mention Terence Prendergast. At the top of the page is a sponsored link for Prendergast Caravan Park:

Prendergast Caravan Park is beautifully situated in a sheltered valley in the Pembrokeshire Coast National Park and is perfect for caravan holidays.

It is a small, select family run park, walking distance from the sea, mid-way between the harbour town of Fishguard and the tiny Cathedral City of St Davids.

I'd love to stay in a static caravan, especially on the Pembroke coast, a beautiful part of Wales, but now is not the time to think about a holiday. I add the page to my bookmark list for future reference.

The second result leads me to IMDb, the world's most used database for film and TV programmes. Hidden among the reviews of this summer's blockbusters and celebrity gossip is an entry that makes my heart stop for a moment:

Terence Prendergast
Art department
Filmography – 'Journey to the Centre of the Earth'

This is him! It has to be. A Terence Prendergast, spelt the right way, who is into the fantasy genre! I'm immediately on my feet, walking around the room, talking to myself, my heart pounding. Thankfully, Sarah is at work so there is no one here to see how excited I am. I pick up the cat and hug her. I know this is ridiculous – I'm a grown man, hunting for another grown man who wrote a diary as a teenager – but I can't help it. I try to calm down enough to sit back at the desk, and click the link for more information.

Journey to the Centre of the Earth is a remake of Jules Verne's classic novel in which adventurers seek a mysterious hidden land at the centre of the earth, a land populated with prehistoric flora and fauna. It stars Treat Williams and Bryan Brown. I've no idea who they are. It seems to be a made-for-TV mini-series produced in 1999 rather than a film, but who cares? For there, in the full credits list, in the Art Department, is Property Assistant Terence Prendergast.

As I click on his name I imagine his career path – slowly working his way up the special-effects ladder, moving from TV mini-series to larger productions, finally working on the huge Hollywood sci-fi epics of recent years. I scroll down the page.

Terence Prendergast – Assistant standby props
Credits:
'Journey to the Centre of the Earth' – 1999
'On the Beach' – 2000

I click refresh to make sure my internet connection hasn't timed out. But no, that's it. Two entries. Not exactly the career path I'd hoped that Terence had followed, but as short as it is, it is finally a path I can trace.

On the Beach is another made-for-TV film. The year is 2006. A nuclear war has devastated civilisation. Only two small pockets of human life remain – the crew of a US Navy submarine, and most of Australia. As they face the end of humanity, will the commander of the submarine remain loyal to his crew or pass his final hours in the arms of his new-found love? Can it be dragged out for 198 minutes? 'Humankind's finest hour may be its last' reads the tag line. I don't care how terrible the plot sounds, I'm helpless against my compulsion to watch the complete works of Terence Prendergast. Both films are in my Amazon basket before I can question my sanity. I choose express delivery, which is nine times the cost of the DVDs. This is unrestrained obsession.

As my payment is confirmed I make the logical connection I should have made sooner. Both films were produced in Australia, which means Facebook's fourth Terry Prendergast is a likely candidate to be the prop maker. He might not be successful, but in his profile picture he looks happy. He likes to share his enthusiasm for efficient transport systems with pride. I'm pleased he managed to get out of Birmingham, a place he clearly wanted to escape from, follow his passions, and go out into the world and make new friends and a new life.

* * *

There might not be much information about the former Australian props assistant on Facebook, but the abandoned social-network and music-sharing site Myspace might be more revealing. Visit Myspace today and it really seems like an end of the world scenario. It's as if the world stopped abruptly one Tuesday afternoon in 2009. Years from now the status updates will be dug up to reveal an archaeology of the end of the first decade of the twenty-first century – people frozen in time rather than buried under a mudslide or lava flow, perpetually mundanely looking forward to leaving work and eating pizza.

There are no search results for Terence Prendergast, but one for Terry Prendergast – male, Australia! I'm so close! All I need is an email address and I can make direct contact. I click on his profile. Nothing. No photos, no information, no friends – no friends apart from Tom Anderson, the founder of Myspace and the default friend everyone got when signing up. Tom still uses the same awkward profile picture, looking over his half-turned shoulder, smiling. It must be a lonely party if your 11,774,718 virtual friends are electronic ghosts.

But I'm not giving up on Myspace yet. What if Terence Prendergast formed a band? A lot of angst-ridden teenagers channel their anger and frustration into making music, which helps them come to terms with their emotions. Some bands have made seminal albums in the process – Nirvana, Rage Against The Machine, S Club 7. Again, I type Prendergast in the Myspace search bar to make sure the search hasn't missed anyone, a band member, a nickname or initials I might not have thought of. At the top of the list is PRENDERGAST! There is actually a band called PRENDERGAST!

The band's biography certainly reflects the same kind of feeling I get from reading Terence's diary, biography born of frustration:

FUCK THE SCENE - FUCK THE SCENE - FUCK THE SCENE -
FUCK THE SCENE - FUCK THE SCENE - FUCK THE SCENE -
FUCK THE SCENE - FUCK THE SCENE - FUCK THE SCENE -

FUCK THE SCENE - FUCK THE SCENE - FUCK THE SCENE -
FUCK THE SCENE - FUCK THE SCENE - FUCK THE SCENE -
FUCK THE SCENE - FUCK THE SCENE - FUCK THE SCENE -
FUCK THE SCENE - FUCK THE SCENE - FUCK THE SCENE -
FUCK THE SCENE - FUCK THE SCENE - FUCK THE SCENE -
FUCK THE SCENE - FUCK THE SCENE - FUCK THE SCENE -
FUCK THE SCENE - FUCK THE SCENE - FUCK THE SCENE -
FUCK THE SCENE - FUCK THE SCENE - FUCK THE SCENE -
FUCK THE SCENE - FUCK THE SCENE

You get the idea.

The title of the first song on their playlist is 'Hate You'. I turn the speakers up full and hit play.

Kook jumps and knocks my tea cup from the coffee table. Despite claiming their style is Afrobeat, and citing the former *Baywatch* actor David Hasselhoff as an influence, a distorted, chugging, heavy metal guitar and a punk drum rhythm throbs from the speakers. Then the singing starts, a cross between a scream of pain and shout of anger. I can't make out any words apart from the odd 'fuck you', 'I hate you' and 'you suck' – it's like being in a one-sided argument with 'Gordon Ramsay: The Musical'.

I click on the next track, the irremediably positively titled 'Well It's A New Day'. It starts with what seems like a sample from a film, a voice saying, 'You forgot the briefcase, you forgot the briefcase', before segueing into bongo drum, barking dog and what sounds like a shop bell, then the words, 'I'm going home'. As the guitar starts I can't help thinking I'm missing some important reference that would lift the veil on my incomprehension. PRENDERGAST haven't logged on to Myspace for four years, coincidentally or not, around the time I found the diary. Not logging on might mean that perhaps the band split due to artistic differences, but I still send them a message asking if it's possible to buy an album of their work. You should always take every opportunity to widen your musical taste.

A thought occurs to me. Birmingham can rightly claim to be the birthplace of PRENDERGAST's style of music. In the late 1960s hugely influential bands, such as Black Sabbath and Judas Priest, came from there, and half of Led Zeppelin – including singer Robert 'Stairway to Heaven' Plant – were born in the Midlands. The legacy of these bands was the creation of heavy metal, guitar-based hard rock with lyrics that are often broodingly dark or aggressive.

Incidentally, the name heavy metal is of contested origin. In chemistry, the periodic table separates elements of light and heavy metals, and the American writer William Burroughs, whose books still remain inspirational and a source of band names for musicians, used the phrase in his 1961 cut-up novel *The Soft Machine* for a character called 'Uranian Willy, the Heavy Metal Kid' – and the phrase was used pejoratively and derogatorily by certain music critics of the time. But the name somehow fits the music forged in the factories and furnaces of the once aptly named Black Country, and it stuck.

My knowledge of contemporary Birmingham metal bands is non-existent, but a quick bit of research brings me to an expert who must be able to help me. *Kerrang!*, the alternative rock-music magazine, also has its own radio station, broadcasting 'rock music with attitude'. If anyone is going to be able to help me find out more about PRENDERGAST the band, it's one of Kerrang! Radio's regular DJs, Birmingham's own Johnny Doom.

Johnny Doom, it seems, took his surname from his former band Doom, who released the infamous guttural thrash of an EP *Police Bastard* back in 1989. Johnny's radio show is not only dedicated to celebrating the musical legacy of Birmingham and the Midlands, but to promoting and encouraging emerging local bands. That devotion to the area helped him win the coveted Brummie of the Year award in 2008.

I'm usually terrible at speaking on the phone, being acutely anxious about not knowing what I might be interrupting by calling and quickly becoming tongue-tied in the process. I just have to surprise myself into dialling, then it's not so much of a problem. I quickly call the radio station before reason can stop me, and ask the receptionist if I can be put through to Johnny Doom. Thirty seconds of alternative-rock hold music later the phone is answered.

'Hi, is that Johnny Doom?' I ask.

'Yeah, how can I help?' Johnny says in a soft, laid-back Birmingham drawl.

'I don't suppose you know anything about a band called Prendergast?'

'What have they released?' he asks.

'Nothing, as far as I know. They have a Myspace page.'

'Myspace?' Johnny laughs.

I give him the web address. At the other end of the line there is a silence for a moment that's broken only by the sound of typing.

'Hold the phone away from your ear, I'm just going to turn it up,' Johnny says.

The now familiar opening to 'Hate You' resounds around the Kerrang! Radio studio and out of my phone speaker.

'I don't know about Afrobeat,' Johnny says, turning the music off, and evidently reading PRENDERGAST's information page, 'but yeah, tell me about it.'

I begin to explain the story so far, the rational part of my mind finding it hard to believe my obsession has got to a stage where I'm telling a metal DJ called Johnny Doom about *Choose Your Own Adventure* books.

'Right, I remember those books,' Johnny says, reassuringly.

'They all belonged to one kid, and he also left four pages of a heartbreaking diary inside one of the books. And I'm attempting to find him, and return the diary to him.'

'Riiiiiight,' Johnny says, slowly drawing out his reply while his brain processes what I'm telling him.

'Do you mind if I read you a little bit of the diary?'

'No, I'd love to hear it. I'm quite intrigued.'

I read out a short extract from Terence's diary, hoping that Johnny, someone who obviously loves Birmingham and daily celebrates the influence of its creativity, will understand Terence's need to get away.

'Sounds like a lonely fellow,' Johnny comments. 'I can see why you're interested in this character, but how does that figure in with the band?'

'Terence is obviously angry with the world. I wondered if he'd channelled that anger into somehow forming a band.'

'Yeah, I see, maybe using his last name.'

'It seems like the kind of music that perhaps he'd be into.'

'Yeah, from his diary extract, definitely. I've played with a lot of bands like that, and there is a kind of, you know, just good aggression in it.'

'So that's why I'm trying to contact them. I thought you might be able to help me in some way.'

'Sure, if I can. What about labels? Were they on a label you could track down?'

'They were unsigned.'

'Oh, so their website's not working, either. I'm just digging around in their Myspace photos. There's a poster on here that looks like they're playing their home town. It seems that they're actually from Wedel. I don't know where that is, Germany. It might be worth getting in touch with some of the other bands who played with them – Overdose, Last Line of Defence, Metal Witch, Irate Architect – see if their websites are still going. But for some reason I've just got a feeling that the band has nothing to do with Terence.'

'You might be right,' I say, becoming resigned to the fact that I've been sidetracked on to the wrong path.

'He wrote that diary a while ago, and he may have reached some strange point in his life, I suppose, and then just stuck around Birmingham and be a fairly average guy . . . but he could be in prison,' Johnny said. 'You just don't know.'

I hadn't considered it before but Johnny might be right. It could be that Terence is in prison, particularly if he's been involved in drugs and guns. Maybe the *Choose Your Own Adventure* books were sold by his family because he was now on the inside. Despite Johnny's reasonable doubts about the band having anything to do with Terence, following Sherlock Holmes' advice I still need to eliminate them from my list entirely and to feel, without the slightest doubt, that this line of investigation has come to an end.

I trawl through years of the German metal scene, tracing a tangled family tree of band members and gig histories, trying to find a photo of PRENDERGAST playing live, or a mention of anyone called Terence. Eventually, I find myself out on a limb, an intimidating branch of the Hamburg music scene – an old-school, hardcore punk thrash four piece called Inside Job, formed of Hagi on vocals, Benni on guitar, Mazi on bass and Wallace on drums. It seems, if my research is right, that Wallace used to be the drummer of PRENDERGAST. I've found an email address for Hagi and send him a message, asking if he can pass my query on to Inside Job's drummer Wallace: did PRENDERGAST name themselves after Terence Prendergast from Birmingham?

It's now dark. I've spent the whole day in front of the computer searching for Terence Prendergast. My shoulders and back ache from the tension caused by typing. I try one final Google search, this time adding another key word from my most likely lead – Terence Prendergast Australia.

At the top of the list is an Australian memorial site. The implications of Terence's thoughts of suicide hit me with full force. I click the link with a knot of sadness in my stomach.

Terence Prendergast, aged 85, loving husband to Una for 60 years, sadly passed away on the 23rd December 2010.

He was too old to be my Terence, but the spectre of death suddenly looms over this whole search. I really don't know how I'd feel if Terence has died. I don't want to acknowledge his death as a possibility.

When Sarah comes home from work, I tell her about my quest, that I've finally set out on the path I should've started out on years ago. She looks at me quizzically.

'You mean the diary, right?'

'Of course, what else?'

'It's just . . .' she stops herself, 'just be careful.'

I laugh. Sarah scowls in a way that immediately makes me feel bad.

'I wasn't laughing at you,' I say. 'It's not like I'm fighting dragons or anything. I'm just sitting in front of the computer.'

'I know. I mean, just be careful with whatever it is you're trying to do or find out. I hate to sound like a cliché but sometimes the past should stay in the past.'

That night I dream of a room full of Terry Prendergasts. They are all having a party of some kind but they don't seem to be having any fun. I'm watching them through a window. I try knocking on the glass, but no one notices. All I can do is stand outside and observe.

I wake to a knock at the door. The postman is standing outside clutching two parcels.

'Morning,' he says with a grin. 'Looks like you've got plenty to keep you busy!' Little does he know he's holding six hours and twenty-nine minutes of made-for-TV drama featuring the handiwork of Terence Prendergast. As soon as the door is closed I rip open the packages, tripping over the cat in my haste to turn the DVD player on. There definitely is no point in opening the curtains today.

While I gather supplies from the kitchen and put the kettle on, I check my inbox in the hope that one of the Terry Prendergasts has replied. Nothing from Terry four, five or six. But there is a message from Terry Prendergast number three:

Sorry Nathan, I am not the Terry Prendergast you are looking for.

Cheers, Terry Prendergast

Short, friendly, abrupt. It's as if Terry Prendergast thought he was dealing with someone slightly unhinged, someone you don't want to start entering into a dialogue. But at least that's one Terry I can cross from the list.

There is also a reply from Hagi, the singer from Inside Job.

> I'm (hagi) writing to you in the name of Wallace because he is not that firm in wirting english.
>
> Prendergast was a concept band named after a charakter from the movie 'falling down' with Michael Douglas. The film is about a guy called D-Fens whos going to his daughter's birthday party. On his way he always crashs into situation that shows him social injustice. Step by step he gets more aggressiv. Martin Prendergast is a cop who tries to stop D-fens on his violent trip!
>
> Prendergast (the band) also used quotes from the movie as intro for their songs.
>
> The Mr Prendergast is not known by Wallace.

I can firmly cross PRENDERGAST the band from my enquiries, too, but at least I now know from where the samples on 'Hate You' were taken.

I decide to watch Terry Prendergast's films in chronological order, my obsessiveness allows for no other sequence. I'm excited – I'm a big fan of Jules Verne, the nineteenth-century French science-fiction writer, famous as the author of *Around the World in Eighty Days* and *Twenty Thousand Leagues Under The Sea*, books that I devoured as a teenager. I have even read some of his more obscure works, including *The Green Ray*, which concerns the hunt for a rare meteorological phenomenon, a green beam of light created as the sun sits just below the horizon: 'at its apparition all deceit and falsehood are done away, and he who has been fortunate enough once to behold it is enabled to see closely into his own heart and read the thoughts of others.' I hadn't thought about it before, but oddly, a lot of Jules Verne's central characters are focused on a mysterious obsession, which is generally misunderstood by others.

I'm not more than ten minutes into *Journey to the Centre of the*

Earth before I realise this is going to be an excruciating ordeal. The dialogue is wooden and lumpy, the acting is forced and laboured, and the set and props seem flimsier than an umbrella made of toilet roll in a tornado. By the time the characters arrive at the polystyrene caves, any normal person would give in, but the obsessive elements of my personality won't let me. Even though I'm starting to hate myself for doing it, I still sit through the drawn-out scenes with blue trees and latex lizard men who live underground, scenes that decimate the legacy of Jules Verne.

When the final credits roll I'm relieved I made it through, pleased I'll be able to tell Terence I've watched his work. It is a joy to see his name in the credits as they scroll up the screen; that one tiny moment fills me with the happiness the rest of the film ripped from my soul.

I put the DVD of *On the Beach* straight into the player, knowing I've got nearly four hours of everyone's worst apocalypse scenario to sit through before I'm allowed that tiny moment of happiness again. I don't think I've ever seen such a clean-looking aftermath of nuclear war, with characters who seem genuinely, psychotically unaffected by the events unfolding around them.

Over the next days, I watch the films over and over again, as if I might discern in them some clue to the current location of Terence Prendergast, or a hint of his past or personality. I play them in the background while I spend days trying to find out more information on the internet.

I make Sarah sit through the films, too, but time and again she drifts off. There are better things to do, it seems, like catch up on sleep, than indulge in terrible films, the props for which may or may not have been assisted by a man who may or may not have written a diary. Yet, doubt doesn't affect me, and Sarah's reaction to the films doesn't matter. All that matters is that I find him. As the credits roll yet again it suddenly dawns on me that the best hope of finding Terence Prendergast is through someone who might have known him – and a list of those people is scrolling right in front of me.

Through some more internet sleuthing I manage to track down the CV of Dean Sullivan, standby props for *On the Beach*, whose name appears just above Terence's on the credits.

Dean's CV is a little more promising than Terence Prendergast's. Since *On the Beach*, he has worked on a huge array of adverts and films, including the critically acclaimed *Rabbit Proof Fence*, a film about three mixed-race aboriginal girls who attempt to return to their families a 1,500-mile walk away, and their persecution by white Australians.

At the top of the page is his home phone number. I set my alarm for six o'clock the next morning, which, allowing for the time difference, would make it around four o'clock Sunday afternoon in Australia – hopefully the perfect time to catch Dean at home.

With tiredness eroding my nerves, I key in the numbers and wait while the phone makes an unfamiliar dialling tone. Thankfully, I don't have to wait long before my call is answered.

'Hello,' says a voice, deeply but cheerily Australian.

'Hi, is that Dean?' I ask.

'Yeah,' he says, seemingly thrown slightly by my British accent.

'Hello, this is Nathan Penlington, you don't know me. Are you the Dean Sullivan who worked on *On the Beach*?'

'Yes,' he answers, not surprisingly surprised.

'This is going to sound like a very strange question. I'm trying to contact someone called Terence Prendergast who also worked as props assistant on *On the Beach*. I just wondered if you still had any contact details for him?'

I explain to Dean about finding Terence's diary, the *Choose Your Own Adventure* books and my quest to return the pages to him. There is silence on the other end of the phone. I'm worried we've been cut off, or worse, that Dean's put the phone down.

'You won't believe this,' Dean says finally. His voice is quiet but excited. 'I did happen to find an old diary today.'

I can't tell if this is Australian humour and he's winding me up. 'Did you?!' I say, half question, half exclamation. A questlamation.

'Yeah, I was clearing out some old boxes,' Dean explains. 'Bear with me and I'll dig it out. Let's take a walk.'

I've never been invited to take a walk on the phone before. In the background I can now hear the sound of kids playing, and a woman asking, 'Who is it?' It is hard not to imagine this very moment as a scene from *Neighbours*, admittedly a scene from the later years when the viewing figures had plummeted and the original scriptwriters had left, but it seems too much like a story for it to be real life. I never imagined the path to Terence would be a series of stepping stones constructed from diaries found by chance.

'I have to say,' Dean says at last, now as animated as I am, 'this diary I did literally find today, is terribly, terribly old, ten years at least. I'm just looking through the contacts . . . here we go. I've got a mobile number if you want it?'

'That would be amazing,' I reply.

Dean reads out the number and I carefully write it down, triple checking every digit.

'Terence was a really funny guy, I really liked him,' Dean says, clearly happy at being reminded of someone he's lost contact with over the years. 'And if you do get in touch, say hello from me.'

'I will do. Thank you very much for your time.'

'Not at all mate. See ya.'

It seems luck isn't a button on the internet. It happens when people interact with the world, and with each other. Dean had found a diary today, and in the back of that diary is a phone number for Terence. If I'd called even a day earlier, the outcome of our conversation would have been entirely different. But, because of the choices I've made and the procrastination I've indulged, in moments I could actually be speaking to Terence Prendergast.

For the second time in my life I call an Australian phone. It produces another series of beeps that makes the whole world seem alien, and then nothing. It feels like the 10,266 miles between us are being measured out with silence.

The silence is finally interrupted, disappointingly not by the voice of Terence Prendergast but by an automated female voice pre-programmed with standard BBC English that's been given an Australian twang: 'The number you have called is not connected. Please check the number before calling again.'

I can't help but let out a loud shout of PRENDERGAST-style frustration. I really felt that I was on to something, but that something is just another dead-end.

That night I'm kept awake by images from *On the Beach* washing through my thoughts. I turn to Sarah for someone real to talk to, but she is half asleep and now is not the time for sympathy. I know enough to realise you don't get sympathy by waking someone up in the middle of the night. Sarah knows how much the diary haunts me, but she is pragmatic. As supportive and encouraging as she is, she doesn't understand why I can't face up to the fact there is still no evidence that it was the same Terence who helped make these films. After waking her up at six thirty this morning with my shout of frustration, she'd called me out on it. I responded by being defensive and retreating a little, but the reality is I'm still no closer to finding Terence than I ever was. From all the emails and messages I've sent to the unknown Prendergasts of the World Wide Web, I have had nothing but rejections.

To shake off the self-doubt that is starting to gnaw at me, I get up and tramp downstairs. I will lose myself for a while. I will do what I did as a boy. I will use books to escape.

The shelf of Terence Prendergast's *Choose Your Own Adventure* books, the long row of red and white spines neatly arranged in numerical order, are, to use a term taken from TV make-over shows, a focal point of the lounge. I close my eyes and pull a book off the shelf at random: number 29 *Trouble on Planet Earth*. The blurb on the back explains the plot and outlines the dilemma.

> You and your brother Ned have just taken on your toughest case: finding out why every drop of oil on the planet has disappeared.

Will you save the world? How does the story end? Only *you* can find out!

Even though it sounds like another end-of-the-world scenario, I hope *Trouble on Planet Earth* will take my mind off things for the time being, and I take the book back upstairs with me. Sarah must be heavily asleep because she doesn't turn over as I slide in gently beside her. I turn the bedside light on and settle back under the covers. Kook, our cat, making the sound of a mobile set to vibrate, pours herself over me like a Dali-esque phone. I open the book to the first page.

And there, staring me in the face, is the clue I need to find Terence Prendergast – the location in the universe where he used to live, his old Birmingham street address. When I couldn't find him using all the tools of the twenty-first century, Terence himself has told me where to start looking, his voice crying out to me from Christmas, 1988.

I have no other choice.

I am going to have to go to that address.

Chapter 4 – Life through a fish-eyed lens

Last night I was lying in bed, with Sarah half asleep at my side, poring over the pages of *Trouble on Planet Earth* when my eyes roamed for the hundredth time over the address Terence had written, back in 1988, of a house somewhere in Birmingham.

In that instant, I had the answer. It had been staring me in the face all along. I didn't have to prowl the darker recesses of the internet, the forums and chatrooms of dubious legality, or hire any private detectives to find out if the boy named Terence Prendergast was still alive. In the pages of the *Choose Your Own Adventure* books, he had been telling me where to find him all along. All I had to do was go to his old address. I turned and shook Sarah awake, excitedly showing her Terence's boyish scrawl. She gave me a look, half real-world exasperation, half dream-world confusion. The address, I implored her to see, was part of Terence's message-in-a-bottle. Not only was he telling me what had happened to him, all those private fears and emotions; he was telling me where to find him, where to go to rescue him from his prison.

'Uugghhufff,' Sarah said, in a language yet to be catalogued by linguists.

I sent my thoughts out into the ether, through *The Cave of Time*: Terence Prendergast, I'm coming to find you.

I slept soundly for the first time in what felt like for ever.

* * *

Now it is morning, the quest, like all late-night good ideas, doesn't seem so clear. In fact, in all honesty, it sounds a bit creepy. Perhaps I don't have the answer at all; perhaps I only have a signpost along the way, pointing in a vague direction. After all, there is no evidence to suggest that, after all these years, the Prendergasts still live in the same house. As I prowl the flat, making a breakfast I'm too anxious to eat, my head is obsessively listing a hundred and six things that could possibly go wrong: 1 Terence is dead; 2 the Prendergasts don't live at that address; 3 I find Terence but he doesn't want to talk to me; all the way down to 104 I get arrested for stalking; 105 the diary is all an elaborate hoax for a reality TV show; 106 the world ends just as I'm about to find out the truth about Terence.

I don't believe in fate, and in return fate doesn't believe in me, but even so I don't want to tempt it. There is safety in not knowing, in not facing reality. I don't want the quest to be over. I don't want to 'Go to Page 240' to be met with a *Choose Your Own Adventure* style 'The End' of untimely demise. Today is Monday, I need a few days to form a plan, and I need help.

I tend to overthink situations that I know I'm going to find awkward, planning them out in advance. I guess this is the residue of my childhood shyness. Unfortunately, this forward planning means that, when the moment arrives, there is always a time delay between what is actually happening and my response, like a poor satellite link-up on a live TV interview, while my brain processes the fact that reality is unfolding in a way I haven't prepared for. The delay leaves enough room for endless bloopers, or fails as the kids these days are calling people falling over their words or just falling over.

What will I say to whoever lives at that address now? How will I even begin to explain what I'm doing on their doorstep before they slam the door in my face? My usual behaviour while rehearsing what I'm going to say, is to pace up and down the kitchen making more tea than I can drink, and muttering to myself in a semi-whisper to play out what the conversation might sound like. I realise this is an annoying habit, a habit that close friends and girlfriends learn to tune out, but this morning that is definitely harder to do than usual.

'"Hi my name is Nathan, you don't know me." No, they don't. "I'm not selling anything." That seems like a good place to start. "I'm not selling anything, and I'm not religious." But what if they want to buy something, and they are religious?'

I should really just try and quickly communicate what I want to find out.

'"I'm looking for the Prendergasts." It could work, but if it doesn't, that would be my only path to Terence closed with a cold, hard door in the face.'

It's now 7.45 a.m. on Saturday morning and I've already spent an hour trying on different outfits and following Sarah around the flat to ask what she thinks. She gave up on having a lie-in at 6.46 a.m. and is now trying to use the unplanned early start to finish an article she is writing. While she is humouring me, I can tell that I'm close to overstepping the line. I stand pouting in the kitchen. 'What about this one?' I say, pulling my habitual mirror pose.

Sarah looks up from her laptop. 'Nathan, you look nice, smart, yet casual. Clean. Exactly like the last outfit . . .'

'Yes, but am I too smart, like in a religious way?'

'You need to relax. Whoever answers the door is not going to judge you on what you're wearing. Just be friendly and open. Imagine if it was you opening the door to a stranger. What would you do first? What would you want to know?'

'That's exactly my problem,' I reply, filling the kettle absentmindedly, even though it is already full. 'I'm imagining myself as the person opening the door, as well as the stranger on the doorstep. My brain hurts. I don't think I can go through with this . . .' Water sprays from the tap, soaking my carefully chosen shirt, half of the kitchen, Sarah's laptop and the cat. I've finally succeeded in annoying everyone.

'Nathan, stop it,' Sarah says firmly. 'You need to calm down, and then you need to make a decision about whether you can cope with never knowing about the diary all because you can't think of what to say to a stranger when they open a door. If you can't even do that, what did you think you were going to say to Terence if you ever found him?'

I have no answer, so I slink quietly upstairs to get changed into my second choice outfit – a knitted white-and-black check short-sleeved polo shirt, grey fitted jacket, black jeans – an outfit I hope makes me look friendly yet secular.

Sarah is right. As a grown man I should be able to simply knock on a door and ask a question. My obsession has become like a fish-eyed lens, magnifying everything in the centre, making it seem larger and more significant, and warping the rest of the world around me. If I ever expect to see the world clearly, and rationally, I need to go through with this.

Before I get a chance to change my mind about the whole quest, my friend Fernando, who has agreed to drive me to Birmingham, calls to say he is waiting outside. I shout my goodbyes. Sarah shouts back.

'Good luck. Remember, just be yourself!'

It is good advice, but not advice I'm sure I can follow.

The plan is to arrive at Terence's old address mid-morning, during the lull between breakfast and doing whatever it is people do on a Saturday when they are not driving halfway up the country to knock on a stranger's door because of a diary written twenty years ago. Fernando is a good-looking, flamboyant Spanish-American, Long Island-born – and, unlike me, he has an easy confident charm with everyone. More than that, he is always optimistic in any situation. He's the perfect person to keep me focused, and stop me from backing out. But, more importantly, he used to read *Choose Your Own Adventure* books as a child. 'I hated where I grew up. It's just a huge highway with mile after mile of strip malls,' he told me when I first spoke to him about the diary. 'I wanted adventure as much as anyone.'

For our trip Fernando has hired a big black car with blacked-out windows. It's the most conspicuous vehicle I've ever seen. It does nothing to help my nerves.

'It'll be good for spying from,' he says excitedly. 'We're like detectives.'

We hit terrible traffic and roadworks as soon as we leave London, and we're two hours behind schedule even before we reach the outskirts of Birmingham. The longer the journey takes, and the closer we get, the more nervous I become. It feels like the world has conspired to drag out my agony inch by tortuous inch.

'Last chance for a toilet break before Terence's old house,' announces Fernando as we pass a service-station sign, an unromantic wake-up call to the reality of adventure. I take the opportunity to relieve my nerves.

Back on the road we keep following the directions of the route planner, which now seem to be taking us away from the city, the grey confusion of Birmingham giving way to greenery.

'This isn't Birmingham. I thought you said we were going to Birmingham. This is like *Lord of the Rings* or something,' Fernando exclaims. 'No wonder he wanted to run away. There's nothing here.'

I look out through the window. We're now driving down a small country road, trees and fields scrolling past on either side of us. It reminds me of a place near my old house in Rhyl that we used to call The Bounds – a country lane that marked the old boundaries of the town. Now Rhyl sprawls out beyond those boundaries – flat-packed housing estates, supermarkets and fast-food drive-throughs, linked together with bypasses that make it hard to know what it is you are actually bypassing. One summer in particular I spent a lot of time cycling The Bounds. I used to know every curve and dip in the road. It was as far as I was allowed to ride my bike on my own. My mum and dad trusted me to stick to my word, and I used that trust to travel to the edge of the town – on those edges my imagination thrived. I wonder if Terence ever did the same with these fields?

We turn a corner. The road changes once again and we are now in a suburban housing estate.

We've got two instructions left on the print-out – a left turn, and then 500 yards before we're at Terence's old house. I begin to feel sick. I don't know if it's because of the nerves or because I haven't eaten all day.

'Fernando, do you mind stopping and pulling over for a couple of minutes. I need to get myself together . . .' I'm whimpering. There is no other way to describe it. I'm actually whimpering.

'Come on! This is an adventure!' Fernando says, ignoring my request as we pull into the final street on our directions.

This is Terence's street. It looks like any quiet, suburban neighbourhood. Neat red-brick semis and small gardens. Ordinary. I'd imagined this street so many times that I can't even remember what it was I expected, but stupidly I wasn't expecting the ordinary.

We pull up opposite Terence's old house and reverse a little so we can see the front door through our blacked-out windows. The garden is bordered by two well-trimmed hedges, in front of which is a small yellow car. In the drive, in front of the lean-to garage, is parked another car, a sign that even though it's early afternoon, there is likely to be someone at home. Fernando turns off the engine.

As the reality of the situation sinks in, the consequences of following obsession to the point of absurdity seem to be reflected by the dull Birmingham clouds. I sit for a moment, willing my hands to stop shaking.

'Look at me,' Fernando says. 'What are you worried for? All you're doing is knocking on the door and asking if the Prendergasts live there. If they do, you say hi, ask to speak to Terence, and there you go. And if they don't, well, we'll have to think of another plan. We've come all this way, Nathan, you've got to do it . . .'

He's right.

As I close the car door behind me, I catch a glimpse of myself reflected in the blacked-out windows, and wonder if I have made the right choice about what to wear. Perhaps I do look a little like a religious double-glazing salesman after all.

The only sound is the distant lapping of cars on a dual carriageway, which seems to magnify the birdsong and the sound of my shoes crunching up the drive. Everything suddenly seems ominous, in a Hitchcock kind of way.

The front door is the kind with a panel of frosted glass set into the middle. It's too dark to see into the hallway, so dark the window acts as a mirror, making it look as though my wispy-edged Doppelganger is standing on the other side of the door. This is it. I ring the bell. How long are you supposed to wait once you've rung a doorbell? I count to ten under my breath – one, two, three, four, five, six – I can't hear anyone on the other side of the door – seven, eight, nine, ten – nothing, and then add another five just in case someone is in the backroom or on the toilet – eleven, twelve, thirteen, fourteen, fifteen. Absolutely nothing. To the right side of the house is the garage, its doors also set with panes of frosted glass, and to the left the bay window of a room that is clearly a lounge. I peer through the window. No sign of any movement from there either. Despite the build-up, the tension, the nervous anticipation, I am instantly deflated by the crushing inevitability of simply no one being home.

I ring the bell again to make sure, and this time bravely count to twenty before taking a tiny, hesitant peak through the letter box. A gangly man arriving in a creepy blacked-out vehicle peering through the letter box is not something I want their neighbours to see, so I quickly make my way back to the safety of the car to work out what we should do next.

'Did you look through the front window?' Fernando asks.

'Yeah, there's definitely nobody in. They could have gone on holiday, of course. I think there's a photo of two children on the mantelpiece. There's a magazine on an armchair, I think somebody is . . .' I hesitate, not sure of what my brain is actually making my mouth say any more. 'What do we do now?'

'Well, I guess if we were actually detectives, we would carry out a stakeout. You know, wait here and see if someone comes home.'

A white van is driving slowly down the street towards us.

'What's this van doing?' I whisper in panic.

We both slink down in our seats, our heads level with the bottom of the windows. The van passes us, neither its driver nor passenger even notice we are there.

'So what *are* we going to do now?' Fernando asks. It's a good question, and if this really is a stakeout, we could be here for a while. Luckily, I happen to have brought the answer to our problem, just in case.

'Dinosaur Top Trumps!' Fernando says, incredulously. 'How old are you?'

'Thirty-five,' I state flatly. 'Why? I thought it would be a good way to pass the time if we needed to. And it turns out that we do.'

I shuffle the cards – a riffle and cascade, followed by two simultaneous one-handed cuts, finishing with a four-packet Sybil, which is an elaborate two-handed spin-cut. It's good to know my years of magician training haven't gone to waste. I deal and we draw our top cards.

'I want to compete with you in weight,' Fernando says, confidently.

'That's OK with me.'

'Two hundred.'

'Two hundred kilograms? Are you sure?' I ask, double-checking my card, a twenty-six-metre-long Barosaurus.

'Yeah,' Fernando says with premature triumph.

'Forty thousand kilograms.'

Fernando looks crushed for a second, before bouncing back, 'So, I win because I'm lighter.'

'No,' I say, trying to take the card that is rightfully mine. 'It's all about who has the highest number.'

'No, because in dinosaur terms I'm a light fish.'

'But I'm a bloody big one.'

'Wait,' says Fernando, turning to stare out of the rear window. 'There *is* someone in the house.'

It has got to be a joke. It all seems a bit too convenient. I'm positive no one was home a few minutes ago and, despite our messing around, I would certainly also have noticed someone returning home.

'There is someone in the house, definitely,' Fernando says, excitedly. 'Did you see something moving then in the garage part? Promise you, one hundred per cent.'

I turn to look. A person-shaped shadow passes behind the glass part of the garage doors. 'I can see them,' I shout. An edge of fear has crept into my voice.

'We've got a sighting! It looks like a guy in a hat. Are they coming through the garage part?'

'Wait there,' I say. Circumstances are spiralling out of my control. This is not how I've planned for things to happen. My whole body is shaking. I need a moment to focus.

'What are we doing? Are we going to go up to him? This is the whole point of the stakeout. Just don't think about it. Go. Go. GO!' Fernando shouts. 'We've got them now. This is our chance.'

'Look, we can't rush it.' I'm deliberately dawdling, scared to confront the inevitable, and if I'm honest, I'm just scared.

'Someone's coming out, someone's coming out! Go! You're set, this is it,' Fernando shouts, almost pushing me out of the car.

'Where is he?' I've lost sight of him but I want a clear path between us, a straight walk for my legs of jelly.

'He's going to get in his car.'

'I can't stop him getting in his car.' There is no way I can confront a man getting in his car. However you look at it, that would be a moment of potential aggression, and I'm not built for confrontation or aggression.

'What do we do then? Follow the car?' asks Fernando, an edge of panic in his voice now, too.

'Follow the car,' I say. It's the only response my scrambled brain can come up with.

'Follow the car? Follow the car?' Fernando's panic has become a loop of sound, replaying the same moment while his brain catches up with what's happening. 'Follow the car?' he says again, starting the engine and pulling off slowly behind the car that has just left the driveway. 'What are the rules of following? Is it illegal?'

'I've no idea,' I reply. I don't know. It could be. This is so far out of the realm of normal I have nothing to compare it to. The blue car is directly in front of us, weaving slowly through the residential streets.

'So what are we following him for?'

'We . . . we're finding out about them. Wherever he stops, I promise I'll go and talk to him.'

Car chases in film and TV are nothing like the one we are in. There are no explosions, no vehicles overturn, no roadworks block our path, no police cars are used as ramps, no prams or pushchairs roll into the road, forcing us to swerve at the last minute into a fruit and vegetable stall on the pavement. We keep to a steady 15 miles an hour. The driver of the car we are following obviously knows these back roads better than we do and drives with more confidence. He is steadily increasing the distance between us.

We reach a T-junction minutes after them, but I can't see the car in either direction.

'I can't believe we've lost them,' Fernando says in frustration.

I can't believe we've lost them, either. Despite the slowest car chase in history, we were still too inept to keep up. If only I'd been braver. If only I'd got out of the car to speak to him while I had a chance.

'Which way do you want to go now? Do you choose to turn left or right?' Fernando asks.

I laugh. Fernando never seems to get tired of this joke; it's precisely the kind of question the young Terence and I were always confronted with in every *Choose Your Own Adventure*, and in its way it has become part of this quest to find Terence.

'Turn right. I have a bad feeling about the other direction . . .' I say, all excitement drained from my voice.

Fernando senses it. 'Right it is. Look, don't worry about losing the car. We can work out another plan.'

We pass a short row of shops, a newsagent's, a Spar, a chippie, a tanning salon and a bookies. The road has turned into another row of houses, and on the right-hand side of the road is a school. As I look at the gates, a strange feeling of foreboding rises in my chest. I want to fold down the corner of a page, just so I can come back to this moment later and choose a different alternative.

'I know that school! It's the one Terence mentions in *Trouble on Planet Earth* when he writes "Thinking about St James' and my old mates who I never see any more." Pull over!'

Fernando swings the car into the school's empty car park. I jump out almost before he puts on the brake.

'This is the one, this is where he went to school! Those early entries about being bullied, this where it must have happened . . .'

The school buildings are low and flat, surrounded by green railings. A corner of the large playing field is occupied by wooden climbing frames, monkey bars and swings, all of which look recently installed. The innocuousness of the school grounds suddenly amplifies the fear that Terence must have felt every morning, the fear that he wouldn't get through the day without being called names, having his dinner money stolen, being tripped, punched, kicked or worse. With it comes the realisation that the school is so close to his home that he might never have been able to escape the things he felt in this playground, or between the school walls.

Are these the gates from which he set out one evening 'with the intention to kill myself?' I think of my own sheltered and isolated childhood, trapped at home, sick, without any friends. If Terence's world was that small, and hurt him so much, no wonder he seemed to be constantly seeking a way out. My fear is that he might have achieved that way out through suicide and not adventure. What if I arrive on the doorstep to be faced with parents who have been, in their quiet way, grieving for their lost son for two long decades? I don't want to be the person to remind his parents of that pain.

'Are you all right?' Fernando asks gently, coming to join me at the school gates.

'Yeah, I'm OK. I'm just wondering if I'm doing the right thing.'

'You are,' Fernando insists. 'I believe in this quest. It comes from a good place.'

'Thanks, Fernando.'

'I think we should go and talk to one of the neighbours, though, just to make sure we're not wasting our time,' he says as we get back in the car.

My mum and dad lived at our house in Rhyl for twenty-five years before moving to Essex. I doubt that any of their old neighbours would know where to find them now. Friendships of that kind are formed purely through proximity, and people lose touch, forget a birthday, miss a Christmas card. The same must be true for the Prendergasts. Suddenly, the 1980s, childhood, *Choose Your Own Adventures* themselves, feel so very far away.

I really don't want to waste our journey to Birmingham, and I know Fernando won't leave until I've knocked on the neighbour's door, and, if they're not in, every door in the street until we find someone who might remember the Prendergasts. We pull back into Terence's street, Fernando reverses the car a little until we're in front of the other half of the semi.

I haven't rehearsed for this moment, and quickly start running sentences through my head – 'Do they live next door?' 'Do they *still* live next door?' – forming a mantra that somehow gives me more confidence and purpose. The neighbour's driveway also has a car parked in it, but unlike next door, the front door is surrounded by a small glass porch. Hung in the corner of the porch are three wind-chimes that need moving three inches to the left if they are ever to experience even the slightest breeze. Maybe they've been hung there so they don't chime. I ring the bell and start to count. I'm at fourteen when the inner door is opened by a woman in her mid-fifties. She smiles. I relax a little.

'Hello,' she says, opening the porch door.

She seems friendly, but I'm not taking any chances. I manage to find my most polite talking-to-a-girlfriend's-parents voice.

'Hello, sorry to disturb you . . .'

'Shoes,' she says immediately.

That is exactly the kind of unpredictable reply rehearsal can't prepare you for. I'm instantly thrown off script.

'Shoes? What's wrong with my shoes?' I ask, looking down at my black-and-white bowling shoes. I guess, being in suburban Birmingham, it is a legitimate question.

'Oh, no, sorry I thought . . .'

I begin to laugh nervously. It's clear that this could become awkward for both of us, so I try to move the conversation on quickly.

'I'm just wondering if you can help? I'm trying to find the Prendergast family. Do you know if they live next door?'

'Next door, yes . . .'

Another moment I wasn't expecting. I reel backwards. 'They . . . still live next door?'

My evident surprise doesn't faze her.

'They still live next door. Are they not in? Because their yellow car is there . . .'

'It's just that I've found something that belongs to Terence. I'm just trying to return it to him, but they still live there, next door?'

'Yes, is there definitely no one in?'

'No, no one's answering the door.'

'If you wanted to try again, that would be good. But if not, leave it with me, and I'll pass whatever it is on to them.'

'Oh, it's no problem, I'll come back again. I just wanted to check. But thank you very much for your help.'

I start to walk back down the drive quickly, aware that she is watching me head toward the most suspicious-looking car in the street. She must think I'm the nerdy front-man for a seedy loan shark.

The neighbour has given me the first positive piece of information I've had. I feel sick again, sick and apprehensive.

'Are you OK? What happened?' asks an extremely concerned Fernando. I tell him exactly what the neighbour has just told me.

His face is a reflection of mine in negative, filled with elation, triumph and the joy of victory.

Fernando starts the engine, and we drive off, guessing our way through the odd curves and cul-de-sacs of 1960s suburban town planning. I cannot shake the image that beyond those brick walls is the bedroom where Terence used to hide, lost in his books, writing his diary. I don't want to go back to the house – now I know the Prendergasts live there part of me just wants to take the easy way out, go home and post a letter. But I know a larger part of me will always regret that I wasn't brave enough to try again.

'You know what this means,' I say to Fernando. 'We might just have chased Terence Prendergast through these very streets.'

Chapter 5 – Who isn't a geek?

It's now two in the afternoon, and we know no one's in at the Prendergast house. I also know that as much as I don't want to, I'm going to have to come back and knock on the door again later today. Rather than park our overtly suspicious car in the street outside the house to keep watch on the door for the next few hours, Fernando and I decide we should take advantage of our time. We are in Birmingham, the UK's second largest city. We must be able to find out something else about Terence Prendergast.

We park the car near the headquarters of Kerrang! Radio, where the friendly Johnny Doom is busy championing the darker musical expression of the human psyche, and wander through the maze of walkways and shopping centres that is Birmingham city centre. We soon find ourselves walking through Paradise Circus, which is a cross between a 1980s shopping centre and an indoor market.

Indoor markets are the last refuge of what makes town centres unique. They used to be the home of the specialist and collector. They are where you would find coins and stamps, cigarette cards and comics, haberdashery and sari fabrics, sweet stalls and tobacco sellers, tarot and palm readers. The fringe of small town exotica. Now the majority of indoor markets are half empty or closed for good. Birmingham's is no exception, and Paradise Circus is anything but a paradise or a circus. It's more of a dingy corridor containing more empty units than occupied ones. There's a shop selling crystal ornaments and incense, a tattoo parlour that I imagine doesn't have a waiting list, a newsagent's, a gun shop – I can't remember ever having seen a gun shop before – and a shop called Wayland's Forge.

Looking at the shop from the outside, I immediately feel brave. There is hope in the proud display of the Dungeons & Dragons logo next to the 'We accept credit cards' sticker in the window. There is strength in the broadsword emblazoned with the words 'Wayland's Forge' running along its length in medieval lettering. Where else would a 15-year-old fan of *Choose Your Own Adventure* books from Birmingham, a 15-year-old who was bullied, hang out after school?

Terence clearly loved the fantasy genre, and it would seem logical that perhaps he progressed from reading fantasy books to playing fantasy games. Dungeons & Dragons is the biggest fantasy game of them all. Created in the early 1970s by two American games designers, Gary Gygax and Dave Arneson, Dungeons & Dragons is a rule-based game set in a fantasy world, each player taking on a character with certain attributes, such as wizard, barbarian, elf or dwarf, and one player assuming the role of the Dungeon Master. The Dungeon Master is responsible for overseeing the complex labyrinthine rules, and, more importantly, creating the world, the action and the monsters through language. Essentially, Dungeons & Dragons is a rule-based group story-telling system in a fantasy setting. Within those rules, players can make their own decisions, testing them against random chance by rolling dice, often resulting in outcomes the Dungeon Master could never have predicted. Every choice takes the story in a new, unexpected direction. Some games can take days, weeks or even months to play. It is escape through collective imagination.

Role-playing games are now a huge industry and have developed a large dedicated following. It has become a hobby with many different elements in addition to the actual game playing. Many enthusiasts spend hundreds of hours painting the elaborate figures that are used to represent the heroes, the armies of undead or the tanks of space marines; adding details and insignia that mark the nuances between the evil Plague Drones of Nurgle and the fiery death machines known as the Burning Chariots of Tzeentch; or creating vast tabletop landscapes in intricate detail, right down to the putrefying skeleton of an orc lying in a swamp, or developing just the correct consistency of varnish for the murky ooze of a sewer grate.

I push open the door of Wayland's Forge with a confidence I've not felt all day. The shop is filled with a bewildering array of games, and the rule books, dice and models needed to play them. Into the remaining space is squeezed a table large enough to seat ten, covered in green baize. The top is strewn with trading cards and tea cups. I've clearly interrupted a game in progress, and the six middle-aged men who are playing it look at me accusingly. I feel immediately and acutely out of my depth. This must be what it's like to walk into an orc's lair.

'Can I, erm, I'd like to speak to the manager,' I sputter, not knowing who to address.

'That's me,' says a voice from behind. I turn to find a man sitting cross-legged on the sales counter. I'm sure he wasn't sitting there when I came in. His build is similar to mine, limbs slightly too long to move through space without awkwardness. His hair reaches halfway down his back and the fingernails of both hands are painted a deep red. 'I'm Roj,' says Rodger. 'How can I help?'

'I'm a huge fan of *Choose Your Own Adventure* books. I bought the first hundred and six in the series second-hand, and I'm trying to find the person who originally owned them. I know they lived in the Birmingham area. It was someone called Terence. I don't suppose you have any customers called Terence?'

'I know quite a few of my customers,' Roj replies, with an air of suspicion, 'but Terence doesn't ring any bells at all.'

'This person obviously got rid of the whole collection, but I wondered if he might be someone who's still into those kinds of things . . .' I say.

'Half the people in this hobby are collectors. They'll hoard everything. I'm assuming if he sold the whole collection,' Roj says nervously, 'he got out of it, grew up and moved on.'

There is silence from players at the table, and it feels like it's been years since a stranger has visited the shop. They are watching me with distrust. I'm a novelty and a potential threat. I try not to make it seem as though I've taken Roj's comment about growing up personally, even though I have.

'*Choose Your Own Adventure* books aren't really our thing,' says one guy with glasses, a heavy Birmingham accent and a bunched-up, orc-like face, rubbing it in. 'I've still got the *Warlock of Firetop Mountain*, the first *Fighting Fantasy* book. In the back is the full map I drew out by hand. I went through the whole book and worked out every little route. I never opened the second one or bothered with them after that. I didn't see the point.'

'They encouraged you to read, and that's a good thing I suppose,' says the guy next to him. He seems warmer, friendlier. I bet his regular Dungeons & Dragons character is a dwarf who spends most of his time in the taverns of the fantasy world, just enjoying being alive, but who is also a mean axe fighter if crossed.

I relax a little.

'I got fed up with them. I just found them boring,' the guy with glasses continues, disparagingly. 'You're not interacting with anybody, and it was so much hassle just sitting there doing the map. Or you'd get nearly to the end and you had to start again. And after you've done it once, you just cheat.'

'You did it once without cheating?' the friendly guy asks him knowingly, smiling at me.

Roj is still sat on top of the counter, like a Dungeon Master, overseeing everything.

'Game books are something we did in between role playing,' he says. 'They were ideal basically to spend some time on your own. There was a series of Dungeon & Dragon ones. You didn't need dice or anything, which made them easier to read on the bus. I even had a teacher grab some of my books to use with kids with learning difficulties who weren't reading very well. The books died away after a while, but they're making a bit of a comeback. The *Fighting Fantasy* books were re-released about four years ago.'

'Do you have any ideas about the kind of person who might have been really into *Choose Your Own Adventure*?' I ask him, and everyone in the shop who is still listening. I've lost the interest of a couple of the men, who have drifted to flicking through each other's card collector's albums waiting for the game to start again.

'A lot—' begins the man in glasses.

Roj interrupts quickly, clearly used to the personalities of his customers. 'One thing I've found in running the shop, and I've been running it for twenty years now, is the breadth of people that come in from students all the way up to lawyers, a total cross-section of the community. But they all have something in common – playing the games. They chat. It's a social thing. You can't really put all role players into a single category. The general public would view them as geeks, but then, who isn't a geek? Everyone's got a hobby. I wouldn't say role players fit into any niche or group at all.'

The man in glasses seizes the opportunity to finish his sentence. 'A lot of role-playing games are based on fiction, so a lot of role players are very literate.'

'It's a meeting of minds,' the friendly guy says. 'You can come and be geeky here with other geeks without getting beaten up on your way to school and having your dinner money taken off you.'

I wonder if this is the reason for the 'us-against-the-world' feeling I experienced when I first walked into the shop. Strong social bonds are an amazing thing, but if they reinforce any narrow world view then they also have disadvantages. It's easier to be prickly and self-defensive, rather than inquisitive and open.

'A lot of our customer base has grown up playing the games. A lot of our sales are to customers on nostalgia trips, certainly,' says Roj.

A man who has been standing in the far corner, seemingly uninterested in the whole conversation, suddenly speaks, shy and hesitant, 'From those days, they might have been in the local war-games clubs.'

'There are role-playing clubs, war-games clubs and Dungeons & Dragons meet-ups in Birmingham,' explains Roj, 'but *Choose Your Own Adventure* is very much a solo activity, so it's doubtful any of them would be very helpful.'

Roj is right. Terence and I both seem to have been loners as teenagers, either out of choice or by circumstance, I'm not sure which. But our attraction to *Choose Your Own Adventure*, for that very reason, is another thing we have in common.

I thank Roj and his customers for their time. They might not have known Terence, or even have read *Choose Your Own Adventure*, but by talking about what a solitary activity reading the books is, they've inadvertently confirmed the fact that perhaps Terence and I really did use the books for the same kind of escape, in exactly the same kind of way.

I'm not going to find the present-day Terence by spending the afternoon prowling what I had hoped were the haunts of his childhood. I've been thinking of Terence as a vision from the diary, or perhaps even a different iteration of me as a little boy. I have to start to confront the truth – Terence is not a projection of me. Terence is – or was – a real, living boy, and, as such, he deserves his own history, not one I've imagined for him.

I can't put it off any longer. I have to return to the address in the books.

Before we pull up, I ask Fernando to drive slowly past the Prendergast house. Three cars are parked outside. The blue car we chased through the back streets earlier is parked in the drive alongside another car, and the yellow car the neighbour mentioned is still parked outside the front. It's the night of the Eurovision song contest, and somehow I immediately manage to convince myself they are having a Eurovision party. Three cars equals, potentially, quite a lot of people. My brain starts to panic. My lips and mouth are suddenly incredibly dry.

'I don't know how I would feel if someone turned up on my doorstep on a Saturday night, when lots of friends were round, and presented me with a diary I wrote when I was fifteen. I don't know if I would be happy about that,' I gabble.

'Listen, if they're in a festive mood, they're going to want to meet people,' Fernando says with a logic as flawed as mine but from the opposite end of the social-interaction spectrum.

I start talking rapidly, not really to Fernando, but also not not to Fernando.

'I'll have to forget I've been stalking him, mentally, for years. Try and forget about the diary. OK, this is the way I'm going to do it. "This is going to sound odd, I called earlier on, no one was in. I've just been in the Birmingham area. Erm, I came earlier on" . . .'

'Deep breath,' Fernando says again, in a shout designed to bring me back to the moment. 'You can't put this off any more. This is the culmination of everything you've been building up to. You are going to do this.'

I take that deep breath, and hold it. A combination of obsession, compulsion and assumption has got me to this point, and now I have to face the consequences. I put my lips together and blow out a thin stream of air.

Fernando has driven around the block again, and we're now pulling up to where we parked the car earlier in the day. As soon as he stops I get out. It's not so much that I've tricked myself into self-confidence, but I've finally realised I've been tricking myself with self-doubt.

I squeeze past the cars in the drive, and ring the doorbell. I begin counting to ten again. One, two, I can hear someone on the other side of the door fumbling with the catch. This is it. Breathe. I force myself to remember to breathe. The door is opening slowly.

In the small gap between the door and the wall is an elderly man, at least in his seventies. Can this really be Terence's dad? I move slightly so I can see behind him. At the other end of the hallway is a kitchen. A woman, of a similar age to the man, sits at a table – Terence's mum? There is also clearly a third person but their head and body are obscured by the angle of the door. They are all in the middle of eating their tea.

I launch into my practised speech, my brain running too fast for my mouth, what emerges is a confused collage of sense and nonsense.

'Hello, sorry to disturb you. I'm not selling anything. I'm in the area, and I . . . I just wanted to ask you a question about some books I bought second-hand, *Choose Your Own Adventure* books. Some of them seem to have belonged to your son . . .'

'Belonged to my son?' the man asks, clearly confused. He has a slight Irish accent that catches mainly on the word 'son'.

'Yes, they were sold second-hand a while ago.'

'What's his name?' he asks, his suspicion clearly growing.

'Terence,' I reply, wondering how I'm going to explain why I want to contact him to this elderly and understandably bewildered man.

He turns slightly from the doorway. For a fraction of a second I think he's about to close the door on me but, leaning back into the hall, he shouts through to the kitchen.

'Terry, did you sell some books?'

I hear someone get up from the table. Suddenly, my heart drops in my chest.

'Years ago, yeah,' a voice comes from further down the hall, softly Brummie.

Is this him? Is this really the voice of Terence Prendergast, a voice I've imagined hearing for so long.

The narrowing gap of the front door has been left empty. The door is pulled open by a boyish-looking man, wearing a T-shirt and jeans, sockless. My heart dives. My heart soars. My heart begs for a thousand questions to be answered. I feel like a young girl at a Boyzone concert.

This is him. This is the boy in the book. This is Terence Prendergast as I never thought I would find him – thankfully alive, eating tea at his parents' house, on planet Earth, third planet from the sun.

He is exactly as I imagined him, and yet as far from my imagination as it's possible to be. This is the same face that peered into *The Cave of Time*; his hands, the same hands that wrote the diary that has driven me here. He has soft, gentle eyes. They flit from me, to the car over my shoulder, to his feet, to me again. He shuffles.

'*Choose Your Own Adventure* books?' I begin. There seems to be an insurmountable chasm between us, but at least I have our love of *Choose Your Own Adventure* as a bridge.

'Yeah, I used to love them many, many years ago,' he whispers. 'When I was a boy.'

I think of the diary and what it must have meant to this man when he was that boy. I think about how I would feel if, one Saturday evening, some stranger announced himself at my doorstep and began to unravel every last one of my childhood fears. I know that at times I am a coward. I came here with the intention of being honest but I look at Terence Prendergast and once again I shy from the truth. I scramble for a story to tell him. It feels like some defining moment in a *Choose Your Own Adventure*: do I go one way and confess everything to Terence, and risk an unseemly end? Or do I go another route, and delay telling the truth, spin him a lie instead, a vague half-truth.

'I'm writing a book about *Choose Your Own Adventure*,' I begin. 'I've been in the Birmingham area talking to some people . . .'

The best lies are the ones that are almost the truth, and this lie is more truth than fiction. Terence is friendly but nervous. I know I should be honest, but now I'm here face to face with him I know this isn't the time to talk about the diary. If I can get him to agree to an interview about *Choose Your Own Adventure* at another point, I can bring the conversation around to the diary then. He's pulled the door almost closed behind him, and is now standing on the step in bare feet. I look down at his toes.

'I know it's probably not a good time to catch you at the moment,' I say.

'No, don't worry . . .'

'I'm wondering if you'd be interested in being interviewed about *Choose Your Own Adventure*?'

He looks at me oddly, as if detecting that something is wrong. 'Yeah, yeah, sure . . .'

'We can arrange to meet anywhere at a time that's convenient for you.'

'Yeah, great. Will it be soon?' Terence pauses. 'It's just that . . . I'm moving to Austria.'

Austria? My stomach turns. I've finally found Terence Prendergast, more easily than I thought possible, but it seems I could lose him again just as easily. I wonder if saying I can interview him in Austria seems too creepy.

'Oh really, why Austria?' I ask, trying to underplay my concern.

'I'm starting up a gardening business with my partner,' Terence says shyly.

'Wow, that sounds great. We can make it as soon as possible, if that's OK with you?'

'Sure,' he pauses. 'Have you spoken to many people about *Choose Your Own Adventure* so far?'

It seems as if Terence knows, that he's seen through my story. 'Yes, quite a few . . .' I reply. This also isn't a complete lie, but I don't want to start down a path of constructing a whole series of them, backing myself into a corner in the process. It will make telling him the truth impossible.

Setting up a business in another country is no easy feat. It demands confidence and forthrightness, so perhaps those issues that tormented him in childhood are gone, like any old boyhood nightmare, and all of my fears about Terence are untrue. Then I look up and remember where I am: his parents' house. It just seems too easy to have found him. Has Terence ever moved away? Did he ever find his escape?

I give him my phone number and email address, and he writes his in my notebook, promising to be in touch soon.

Then we say our goodbyes. Terence Prendergast, the boy in the book, still seeming so young despite the advance of time – if the dates in the diary are true he must be nearly forty – closes the door on me, and I listen to his voice recede down the hall. I can't help but wonder what the Prendergast family are talking about as they finish eating their tea, if I've done what would have seemed impossible this morning and made it into their conversation.

Alone on the doorstep, I start to realise that although I've answered the most important question – Terence is still alive – finding him has resulted in hundreds more. Why wasn't he surprised when I knocked on the door? Does he remember leaving the diary in one of the books, and writing in some of the others? Does he still live with his parents? What about Karen, drugs, guns?

I open my notebook to the page on which Terence has just written his email address. I want to compare his current handwriting with that of the diary. I stare in confusion at what he has written – an email address that doesn't start with 'Terence' or 'Terry' or 'TJP', but one that starts 'James1415'. James? Who is James? His dad called him Terry, but was that even Terence that I just spoke to? The world wobbles for a second. I turn and walk slowly back to the car.

And then it clicks – eBay - littlejim75.

The person I bought the *Choose Your Own Adventure* books from was called James. And if I just spoke to James, he also answered to the name Terry. I haven't just found one person, I've found two – littlejim75 was Terence Prendergast himself acting under the name James Costello.

The question is why?

Chapter 6 – A dying species

I never expected finding Terence Prendergast would be this easy. It wasn't supposed to be this easy. That you can knock on the door of the address written by a boy in the margins of a book twenty-three years ago and find the boy as grown-up man standing in front of you is astonishing. It defies all the possibilities, all the choices, all the dead-ends, all the decisions made between then and now. Despite the places, the conversations, the thoughts imagined, all the things that have happened and been forgotten, the mundane and the monumental, all it took was a knock on the door.

Even so, I'll be honest, I wavered a few times. It's fine to have an idea for a long time, but when you push yourself over the edge into making it a real thing, it becomes scary. The Prendergasts weren't having a party; they were just eating their tea.

Now I'm back home in London, I'm still giddy with excitement. I tell Sarah about the momentous meeting. I recount it in detail, the ups, the downs, the revelations, the twists in the plot. It sounds like one of those stories people say is too good to be true, but unbelievably this story really is true.

This is, to me, the culmination of several years of persistence and heartache. To my friends and acquaintances, it seems a strange eccentricity, a pub story and nothing more. Although I can't talk freely to the majority of my friends about Terence, I can to Sarah – for her, my obsession with Terence's diary has always been a part of who I am, part of my story – but I wonder if she truly understands. I wonder if Fernando even, who watched the historic meeting from the car, and who has been a crucial part of this whole adventure, feels the same things I feel.

I don't want to seem too keen, so I leave it a few days before emailing Terence. The email itself is easy to write, partly because my anxiousness has been slightly relieved, purely through finding him alive and well, and also because it isn't entirely the truth. Knowing who to address the email to is a problem, though – Terence or Terry, James or Jim? I opt for the name his dad called him.

Hi Terry,

Great to meet you on Saturday. Sorry for just turning up on your doorstep but it was the only way I had of contacting you!

To give you some more information, the book is about *Choose Your Own Adventure* and the people who grew up reading them. As someone who was a big fan of these books it would be fantastic to have you involved. I was wondering what days and times are best for you? And we can work out when I can come back to Birmingham.

All the best,

speak soon,

Nathan

I don't have time to worry about whether he'll get back to me or not. A couple of hours later a reply is in my inbox.

Hi Nathan,

Don't worry about the turning up, lol, I was just a bit surprised because it was my parents' house and it was just a coincidence I was there. It would be great to do the interview. Date wise I know I cannot do 1–2 June, or 9–14 June, but I can do any other date. I can't wait to talk about *Choose Your Own Adventure*. I used to collect them from around 1984–1986. God, I used to love those books, lol! Just name a place and we'll try and do the interview asap.

His email is friendly and chatty and enthusiastic. This is going better than I ever could have imagined. Interestingly, though, he doesn't sign off with a name. It makes me wonder whether I was right to use Terry at all. Maybe I was too familiar too soon, too familiar with the wrong name.

I reply, arranging a date next month for me to travel to Birmingham for the interview. I count off the days on the calendar as I wait for the day of the meeting with Terence to arrive. I obsess endlessly over the questions I will ask him. The order of questions that will help lead from talking about *Choose Your Own Adventure* to talking about our childhoods, and ultimately, to his diary. I begin to think of us as two adventurers thrown together, without anybody else who can truly understand our entwined stories.

For our weekly date night, Sarah and I decide to go out for dinner. London spoils you with diversity, but once you've experienced diversity on a daily basis it becomes distinctly ordinary. We're stood outside two of the local restaurants, one Turkish and one Vietnamese. Although neighbours, they are worlds apart from each other, but the food is of equal quality. There is nothing to choose between them. Choice, while being a good thing, can sometimes be paralysing. We stand on the street, echoing the mantra of the indecisive to each other.

'You decide.'

'No, no, you decide.'

'I can't. Please, you decide.'

And so on. Etc x ∞. We'd still be there in an infinite deadlock if Sarah hadn't had the inspiration to pull a coin out of her pocket.

'Heads or tails,' she says, flipping the ten-pence piece into the air. The coin spins around its vertical axis, and at the peak of the throw looks momentarily like one of the ubiquitous tokens in a computer game, hanging miraculously in the air. I half expect a small Italian plumber to come bouncing down the street and grab the coin before Sarah can catch it, making the copyrighted two-note bleep of acknowledgement as he does so.

But gravity causes the coin to fall into Sarah's outstretched palm, and chance chooses Vietnamese.

While we are waiting for our food to arrive, we discuss the article Sarah is currently writing. It's about the first manned mission to Mars. For the first time in our generation there could be a genuine adventure large enough to capture the world's imagination. The psychological implications are incalculable.

I try to explain to Sarah the feeling I have about Terence and me as adventurers on a smaller scale, adventuring through time. Sarah looks at me curiously, and asks, 'What would Terence think if you told him that? You're so far from the truth that you make the Mars mission seem down to earth.' She laughs, jabbing me with her chopsticks.

Again, Sarah snaps me back to reality. I know Terence and I are still twenty thousand leagues apart, but I must look hurt because Sarah continues, 'I'm sorry, Nathan, but you have to face the facts. He has no idea about any of this – about your "adventure", about how much you've thought and worried about him. He still doesn't even know you have his diary.'

I know she's right, and that night, as I fall asleep in her arms, adrift in our own universe, I know she's only saying those things because she cares.

Slowly, the excitement of finding Terence wears off, and apprehension and confusion take its place. That he's still alive is, of course, a huge relief, but some of my other worries about him might still be true. Maybe he still lives at home and has always lived there, perhaps he hasn't overcome the feelings he had as a teenager and he still feels trapped and lonely. Although he claimed he is moving to Austria to start a business, something doesn't seem to sit right with his story. He doesn't appear to be the successful entrepreneur I liked to imagine he would be. It seems that perhaps this story won't have a happy ending after all.

But the meeting on the doorstep was so brief I couldn't really tell anything about the man who stood before me. Was he still anything like the Terence Prendergast I'd found in the diary? Or anything like the Terence Prendergast my obsession had created from those words and phrases? I'm beginning to feel out of my depth. I might have found the boy in the book but I still don't know anything about either the boy or the man he became.

In the following days thoughts about the impending conversation consume me. I become distracted and distant. I go to a friend's birthday party. I'm there but not there – locked in a room puzzle of my own creation but without any clues on how to escape, no one to turn to for a walkthrough. Friends come and knock on the door, strangers post notes under it, but no one and nothing is capable of breaking through and commanding my full attention. I know I'm coming across as rude and aloof, and I hate myself for that. If I'm not careful, my obsession will lose me the few good friends I do have.

My friend Fuchsia is strong-willed, confident and gentle, and has a genuine love of people and of difference. She's a good talker and a good listener. She suggests I should meet her from work and we can catch-up over a drink. Her plan, as I now know, is to try coaxing me out of myself in a different way, not by distraction but by encouraging me to talk about Terence and the problems I face now that meeting him properly is a reality. Her hope is that it will help me find the clues I need to escape from the room in which my obsession has locked me.

Fuchsia works in an antiquarian and rare bookshop in Mayfair, one of the oldest book sellers in the world. The shop itself is alleged to be the most haunted house in London. When I visit I'm usually shown some of the latest treasures – the complete works of Walt Whitman signed by Walt Whitman, a screen-printed poster advertising an early reading by Allen Ginsberg, Jack Kerouac and other Beat writers, a first American edition of *Moby Dick* dated 1851. Recently, Fuchsia has been cataloguing a collection of esoterica – books on drugs and death, bound beautifully in leather and embossed with skulls. Today, though, she is most excited about a small black-and-white photograph she's found tucked inside one of the books. The back of the photo is inscribed and dated in pencil – 'Hairless Horse which I handled in Melbourne knew the owner. A remarkable Freak not a trace of hair even as an eyelash – 1873'. Standing alongside the bald animal is a man looking very pleased with himself. Luckily, my obsession lies firmly with Terence and his diary, so there is no danger of me trying to travel back in time to discover what became of this fabulous glabrous beast.

The bookshop staff often find letters and photos left forgotten between the pages of old books, so while showing me around, Fuchsia explains to her boss about my consuming obsession with Terence's diary.

'Have you spoken to Dr Irving Finkel?' he asks.

'No. That's an amazing name, who is he?' It's the first time I've been excited for days.

'Dr Finkel collects people's diaries, he has hundreds. He's trying to set up a national diary archive.' He scribbles Irving Finkel's name on a scrap of paper and hands it to me. 'Definitely someone you should talk to.'

'Thank you, I will,' I say, clutching the piece of paper tightly. This could be the clue I've been looking for.

Fuchsia and I walk up to The Windsor Castle, a pub tucked in a side street behind Edgware Road station. The pub turns out to be the meeting place for the Handlebar Moustache Club, an international club for men with, as their website states, 'a hirsute appendage of the upper lip with graspable extremities'. The pub walls and ceiling are covered with photographs of members past and present, displaying a huge variety of moustaches – the Dali, the Stalin, the Nietzsche, the Pringles Guy. Looking around, I discover, hanging opposite the door of the pub, is a pencil drawing of the Handlebar Moustache Club's 1963 Christmas card. It depicts thirty-two members of the club gathered around a Christmas pudding wearing glasses and a moustache and topped with a sprig of holly. There are thirty-two pairs of shoulders but only thirty-one of them have heads – mysteriously one of the men's heads is missing. The mystery pierces the bubble I've been living in. Who is the missing man? Why has he been rubbed out? Is it because of a facial-hair misdemeanour? Perhaps he grew a beard, or even worse – shaved. Or is it because of something more sinister?

Terence Prendergast isn't the only mystery in the world, and I know it's impossible to solve every question that comes to me unanswered. Meeting up with Fuchsia has been the perfect antidote to my obsessive despondency, and more than that, I also have a way forward to a closer understanding of Terence.

The following morning I Google 'Dr Irving Finkel'. He is a very easy man to find. Dr Finkel works at the British Museum as the Assistant Keeper of the Middle East department, a specialist in Ancient Mesopotamian, that is Sumerian, Babylonian and Assyrian script, languages and cultures. I send him an email outlining the story so far. Minutes later my phone rings. It's Dr Finkel. He is excited, intrigued, and wants to know more. We arrange to meet the following afternoon at the information desk of the British Museum.

I squeeze past rival London tour parties crowding around the burger van parked outside the gates of the museum, and walk up the stairs of the main entrance. The towering Greek-revival-style colonnade still inspiring the awe it was designed to do when the building opened a hundred and sixty years ago. Once I'm past the bag check, I make my way to the information desk and ask for Dr Irving Finkel.

'Oh, you're here to see Dr Finkel, are you?' the girl behind the counter asks cryptically while picking up the phone. She makes him sound like someone to be afraid of, the thought must be reflected on my face, because she quickly covers the mouthpiece with her hand and smiles at me. 'You're in for a treat,' she whispers.

From our short conversation I have formed a distinct image of what Dr Irving Finkel looks like, and he doesn't disappoint. A shaggy outline of a man is moving towards me. I imagine him playing an obscure hopscotch of his own devising with the triangular shadows as he walks through the spectacular great court. The first thing you notice about Dr Finkel is his beard, a white curly scribble that reaches the middle of his chest. The second thing you notice about Dr Finkel is also his beard. He waves as his sees me looking at him.

'Hello, I'm glad you are here. We are going to talk about diaries I believe.' Dr Finkel is friendly and witty, like Father Christmas if he'd gone to university, grown his hair into a long white ponytail, and followed his passion for ancient history. 'For my living I have to read ancient inscriptions from Babylonia, cuneiform tablets, that's what I really do, but in a way they are just like diaries,' he says, leading me through the impressive statues of the Egyptian hall, dodging the hordes of Italian exchange students crowding into self-shot group photographs alongside the Rosetta Stone. We walk up the stairs and down a series of corridors marked Staff Only that lead finally to a cramped room at the side of the building.

A small desk sits alongside a windowless wall. Surrounding it are piles of books, papers and boxes.

'My office is somewhat chaotic as it contains a semi-secret collection, which are the fruits of my hunting for diaries for the last fifteen years.' Dr Finkel points to one of the other walls, along which stands a glass-fronted cupboard containing small leather-bound volumes, some tied together carefully with what look like narrow strips of bandage.

'I fell into collecting diaries by accident. I bought some off a friend of mine who wanted to get rid of them; they were someone else's diaries. I started reading them, deciphering this immaculate handwriting, and suddenly became very interested. I began poking around and discovered that they are a sort of dying species, and you have to go round with a butterfly net and scoop them up wherever you can. These are just a few examples of my collection. In total there are about two thousand"

'That's incredible,' I say, trying to imagine the weight and space of those thoughts and lives converted into words and ink.

Irving reaches into a box and hands me a large leather-bound volume with a bone of a rabbit or fox stitched into the cover.

'Where do you find them all?' I ask, rubbing my fingers over the bone, worn smooth no doubt by someone else repeatedly doing the same thing.

'The funny thing about diaries is that they are in lots of people's families. Lots of relatives have them, your aunt writes one, or your sister writes one, so they exist in people's families but they are not talked about very much. One of the consequences is that when people die, their diaries are usually cast on the waters. No one cares about them or makes provision for them, and they very often get thrown away. Take a seat,' he says, offering me a stool he's just cleared of papers.

'The diary you are holding was written by a teenager in the 1960s. It's actually one of the least interesting ones in the collection because it is so self-obsessed, more so even than the introspective trend of ordinary diaries.' I hand the bone-adorned diary back to him and it disappears back into a box.

'Because of the work that I do here, which is reading inscriptions from four thousand years ago, I've long been used to the idea of a bit of writing surviving from the past which you can take and squeeze out like a sponge in order to find out everything that's in it . . .' Irving looks around the office for a place to put the papers he removed from my stool, shrugs, and places them on top of another pile of papers. 'The same is true with diaries. You might think one is boring, about waiting for a bus or shopping, or something of this kind, but when you read it carefully, and give it the sponge treatment, you will find that diaries as a species are very, very interesting human documents.' He takes a seat next to me, near the desk.

'What do you think it is about diaries that makes them so compelling to read?' I ask, gazing at the diary-filled cabinet.

'If you have a consecutive run of diaries written by one person that might go from boyhood, or adolescence, to old age, when you start to read, you get swept into the story, in the same way you do when you are reading a Dickens novel. The first chapter is heavy going, but when you get to know who is who, it's as absorbing as a work of fiction, and diaries in many ways are much more interesting.'

'Do you feel that by reading other people's diaries you're prying into their lives?'

'It is true that in a diary one writes things that you wouldn't wish others to read. Often they are full of hatred for people at work, or slanderous remarks about neighbours, all sorts of things, as people often use their diary to get rid of their animosity. It is a healthy way of doing it. But with the passage of time, these documents, written by one person in their own life for their own needs, achieve a different value. Instead of being one person's private thoughts, they become an individual voice from a certain time period.'

'So, is it acceptable to make those private thoughts public?' I ask. It's a question that's the crux of my situation, and the moral conundrum inherent in making any private correspondence or journal public.

"This question as to whether things are private or not is a very valid query, because when people write their own diaries during their own lives, perhaps the most significant thing about them is that they're very private. Schoolgirls hide them in their shoes at the bottom of the wardrobe. People take all sorts of steps to make sure no one ever sees their diary, sometimes even writing curses on the front, just in case someone inadvertently finds it. Many diarists I know would rather die than have somebody read their diary – not literally, but it would fill them with horror. I'm sympathetic to this because it seems to be an intrinsic part of diaries in general, but the passage of time has an effect of making this privacy less crucial.

'For example, if you read medieval inscriptions, you don't feel you are prying into the private life of someone who has been dead for centuries. It seems to me an interesting idea that there is no problem with reading something written in the seventeenth and eighteenth centuries, and the nineteenth century's fine of course – they were only Victorians. In the twentieth century, if a diary was written before the war, that's no problem, and if it was after that war it is before the other war, so that is OK, too. The 1950s are fine, likewise the sixties. Maybe the seventies are a bit close. I think this can certainly be respected, but where on one hand 1970 is only forty years ago, it won't be very long before it is eighty years, and one thing you can be sure of is that time marches on relentlessly.'

I'm enjoying hearing Irving talk at length; he's knowledgeable, astute, hirsute. I don't know if I'm looking for endorsement for my obsession or criticism of my actions. Either way, Dr Irving Finkel is a man whose opinion, in regards to the moral questions surrounding other people's diaries, is to be respected. But now's the time to find out what his years of experience, enquiry and understanding can bring to Terence's diary and my situation.

'As I explained to you on the phone, I found a diary that was left inside a book. The diary was written just over twenty years ago.'

'Ah ha, I see.' Irving raises his eyebrows. I can't tell if it's due to surprise or intrigue. 'Was the diary hidden by the diarist in the books inadvertently?'

'I'm not entirely sure. This was the book I found it in.' I rummage in my bag and pull out my copy of *The Cave of Time.*

'Oh yes, ha.' Irving's eyes sparkle with curiosity.

'It is only four pages long, but it touched something in me and really spoke to me, which is what has compelled me to start all of this.'

'Absolutely.' Irving nods a nod of complete understanding. I couldn't have found anybody more sympathetic to my obsession.

'Do you mind if I read it to you?' I ask.

'Please do. I can't tell you how interested I am.'

I read out loud through the list of school years and the speed of light equation. Dr Finkel strokes his beard thoughtfully.

'The diarist was how old do you calculate?'

'About fifteen at this time, I think.'

He nods again, this time a nod of contemplation.

'The next page is a list of things that the writer of the diary wants to improve about themselves' I begin to read Terence's list, looking up from time to time to glance at Dr Finkel. He sits still, intense, absorbing every word. By the time I read out the last two words, 'Mirror . . . Report,' there is complete quiet. I turn to Terence's catalogue of years and continue reading. Throughout, Dr Finkel remains silent, but leans forward in his chair. I imagine him with his butterfly net, catching every word, absorbing and analysing every sentence, squeezing the diary for every drop of meaning. I reach the final words, '. . . Karen, drugs, guns,' and they too drop silently into Irving's butterfly net.

'Gosh,' he nods quietly, 'that is remarkable.' He takes the diary from me, holding it carefully like a rare and valuable ancient document and reads it to himself.

'Goodness, how interesting is that.' His chair creaks slightly as he leans back. This slightest of sounds is absorbed by the piles of documents and diaries, making the continuing silence feel acutely profound. 'So,' he says, breaking the spell. 'Tell me, what are you going to do with this treasure?'

'I'm trying to return it to Terence Prendergast,' I reply. As simple as it sounds, in essence that really is my quest.

He turns the diary over in his hands, removes his round, wire-rimmed glasses and holds the pages close to his face. Without looking up he throws question after question at me. 'Who sold the books on eBay?' 'Did they come in a box?' 'Have you scrutinised every volume?' 'What made you buy these books in the first place?' This must be what it was like to consult Sherlock Holmes, a thoroughness of questioning, being asked to describe the seemingly insignificant just in case a clue is revealed that solves the entire mystery. I answer every question in as much detail as I can – 'littlejim75'; 'an old crisp box, just for packaging'; 'yes, every page of every book'; 'I'm an obsessive nerd, I've loved these books since I was a child.'

'Hmmm. You can't be sure . . .' he mutters, turning the pages over once more. He looks up and replaces his glasses. 'I've never seen anything like this, it really is quite a curious matter.' He pauses slightly. 'But one thing I must say straight away is this. Most of my diaries belonged to people who are now dead, and this confers on one a rather comforting freedom from personal involvement, which on the whole is beneficial. When I've taken diaries that have belonged to the individuals themselves, it has always led to complications. So in my own work I have a horror of contaminating the existence of a manuscript diary with having to account for, or even meet, the person who wrote it. Your situation opens up a whole other range of possibilities, does it not? For example, the more you dig, you might find out things which are really rather horrible. Of course, there is another way of looking at it, that it is all a construction that has nothing to do with his real life at all. Maybe he wanted to be a novelist, maybe he had a fantasy that he'd write this and hide it in a book, like a message-in-a-bottle, in the hope that one day someone would find it and wonder, "What happened to this poor character?" Perhaps he just wrote for fun one afternoon at school. You never know with documents. All extremes between them are possible.'

Dr Finkel shakes his head. 'You can't be sure what it represents. Why should someone itemise the years of their life with a one-word or two-word description? And it is also strange at this age. A lot of diarists tend to think back over their lives on New Year's Eve, at all ages, and when they are old and figuring that one day soon they are going to be dead, and wonder "Did I do anything right?" All that kind of stuff. But for a fifteen-year-old, a psychologist would say that this document was a plea for help, would he not? It looks like a plea for help. If he was the sort of person to be sufficiently disturbed to be seriously thinking about suicide, in a way that provides a framework for thinking about one's life. I don't know much about such things, but to me it seems obvious that if someone is thinking about suicide, then what is very much at the forefront of their mind is how little they have accomplished with their life, and how little chance they have at doing anything better, and that appraisal involves a kind of survey of the past. Maybe it is a genuine document that reflects this kid's history and psychological world.'

If Dr Finkel is right, then the diary written by the boy in the book really was a message-in-a-bottle – I'm just twenty-one years late in answering that cry for help. At least I know I'm not too late, and that Terence is, thankfully, very much alive. Perhaps I should still find a psychologist who specialises in childhood depression to discuss Terence's writings. Irving puts the diary on his desk and leans back in his chair.

'But one of the curious things is that he steals money from his mum and dad, and he runs away to Scotland by plane and comes back the next day, and that's it. That is kind of odd,' he says, furrowing his brows while he eyes remain intently focused on me.

'I have wondered about how much of it is fiction, but then there are elements that are clearly true.'

'Exactly. No one would fictionalise wetting pants in that manner. It is those contradictory aspects which make the whole thing so intriguing.' He pauses again in contemplation. 'The power of stories is colossal. At that age it is possible to read a book that captures your imagination. There is something rather Holden Caulfield about it.'

Irving is referring to the seventeen-year-old protagonist of *Catcher in the Rye*, the novel written by J.D. Salinger. I hadn't thought about it before but perhaps Terence imagined writing a more modern-day Holden Caulfield character, with events transposed from 1940s New York to 1980s Birmingham, but with the same concerns and confusions of a teenager who has become detached from the world around him – being bullied, truancy from school, dreams of running away, thoughts of suicide. It is conceivable that what I've thought of as a diary is merely a character and plot outline. Or possibly Terence genuinely identified with the *Catcher in the Rye*, like generations of teenagers before him, particularly with the feelings of isolation and dislocation, and being unable to confide those feelings to anyone. One of the reasons the book has been, and continues to be, so popular is that everyone can read themselves in it as a teenager, and see Holden as someone who would understand.

Irving continues, 'Let's say this person had read *Catcher in the Rye* at school. It might have left a psychological deposit of the anti-hero teenager, which could generate something like this. I don't think that the drugs, guns stuff is real. People don't write year one, year two, year seven, drugs, heroin, needles, dealer, prison, rape, torture, farming, librarianship. Who does that? This is written at an age when kids fantasise like billy-o, and it is suspect as a really honest document that you can interpret in a direct way without stepping back from it. Unless of course it *is* a real thing. You can't be sure. I agree it is a very interesting thing, and touching. If it really is what it is, it is a very unusual thing for a person of that age to do. And if it *is* what it looks like, then the person who wrote it is a very unusual person, with conceivably a very unpredictable character.'

Irving rummages through the books on the shelf beside him, moving aside a small collection of knights from different chess sets, and pulls down a small, well-worn, hardbacked notebook, opens it to a page in the middle and hands it to me. It's a diary. The pages in front of me are filled with large, looping writing, but also crossings outs, scribbles, doodles. It's an unintelligible mess of ink.

'What you've shown me is something that doesn't measure up to normal diary material. For example, it is very neat and tidy. When people write diaries, one of the important things about them is that they never expect anyone is going to read them. So their handwriting, spelling and crossings out can be completely uninhibited,' Irving says, pointing at the book I'm holding. He picks up Terence's diary from the desk. 'But this isn't a diary in the normal sense because it includes summaries of his life. It is like a synthesis of his diary more than an actual diary.'

I'm instantly excited at the thought of what I've been calling Terence's diary being a synthesis of a larger diary. I can't help but wonder if he still has it and what secrets it contains.

'The reason this has spoken to me so much is that I can see bits of myself in the diary, the self I used to be when I was around the same age. I was cripplingly shy for example. I think it's perhaps one of those diaries that speaks to people.'

'I think that is true. Most boys are shy at that time in their lives, especially around girls, and people who aren't are usually jerks. Normal people are always like that, aren't they? It speaks to me in the same way. I remember acutely being like that. But I never went into drug and gun dealing, I have to say.'

Dr Finkel does his best Sigmund Freud/Kermit the frog impression. 'It zeems to me as a professional pzychologist, zhat you are interezted in your own childhood, zhat it rings a bell in your own inner zelf, and zhat you are hunting for zhis.'

Irving's parody of a psychologist is pretty spot on, and this search for Terence has started to become a search for myself. The question is how much of his childhood concerns are a mirror of my own?

'My collection is now at Bishopsgate Institute, where I have been collaborating to set up a permanent archive, a home for unwanted diaries. It is called The Great Diary Project. You're very welcome to visit and look at the collection. Since it was set up, we've been receiving hundreds of diaries, often rescued from skips, or bonfires, or house clearances. When they arrive, the librarians catalogue them, and then they do a lot of detective work, because they always want to find out who wrote the diaries, and sometimes the subtlest thing can be enough, especially with the internet, which can answer any question in the world.' Dr Finkel rolls his eyes. I laugh, knowing how useful the internet search was for Terence Prendergast, and how much time I wasted on made-for-TV films and German bands. 'So I'm very used to detective work where there is no possibility of somebody opening the door and that's the person. But it's really interesting for you to come and talk to me now you have found the person who wrote the diary, and are on the brink of talking to him at length. You will need to sort out very clearly why you are doing this, and be straightforward and honest with him. But he might not be very pleased to talk about it.'

'That is a worry, and the approach is going to have to be very sensitive.'

'What do you do if he says, "What the fuck do you want?" What do you answer? Because what *do* you want, actually?'

Dr Finkel is right. What the fuck *do* I want?

Irving's candour and earnestness have raised some difficult questions to add to my already lengthy list. The last one is the hardest to answer – what do I really want? How can I ever truthfully answer that question without a long, unflinching look at my own past? Some of my past, certain thoughts and feelings that I keep in a box at the back of my mind, I'd rather not explore. I know I need to open that box. If I expect Terence to answer the difficult questions I have for him, I need to be able to answer those questions for myself. But I'm not brave enough to face them just yet.

After saying goodbye to Dr Finkel, I climb the staircase that curves around the side of the original British Library reading room that now forms the centre of the museum's great court. On the third floor, in rooms 56 and 55, are artefacts from Mesopotamia dating from 6000 BC to 539 BC. The modestly arranged cases can't compete with the popular frenzy of the neighbouring Egyptian rooms, with their displays of sarcophagi and mummified animals. But it does mean you can view the contents of the display cases without anyone standing in the way. The cases contain small, unimpressive-looking, clay and stone tablets, some little more than fragments. They document the development of the greatest invention of mankind – writing. The tablets are inscribed with records of beer rations for workers, receipts for barley, instructions for dyeing wool blue and purple, recipes for making red glass, letters of advice, histories of ruling families, creation myths, and a fragment from the *Epic of Gilgamesh*. Seeing these tablets, many reconstructed from tiny sections of clay inscribed with minute symbols, I understand how Dr Irving Finkel's work blurs into his passion for more contemporary records of ordinary people's lives.

* * *

A week after my meeting with Dr Finkel I find myself in the library of the Bishopsgate Institute near London's Liverpool Street. I'm waiting for Luke, a young librarian, to find a colleague to cover for him on the research reception desk while he shows me the full extent of The Great Diary Project.

While I'm waiting, this seems to be the right time to admit to you that I've never kept a diary. Like many people, I've tried and failed a few times. My failure is due both to feeling I haven't got much of significance to write about every day, and then when I have felt that events perhaps are worth noting for posterity, not having the time to keep up to date with writing the entries. This seems to be the double-edged problem of the diarist throughout the ages.

The only way around this problem is to make writing a diary a habit, but habit flirts very closely with obsession, and as you'll have realised by now, obsession has its own catalogue of problems.

It is no surprise, then, that the most meticulous diarist in history is also the most obsessive. Although born in 1918, Robert Shields didn't start keeping a diary until 1972. For the next twenty-five years he kept a typewritten record of every minute of his life. Working with six electric typewriters arranged in a horseshoe, spreading the workload between them just in case one of them broke, Shields would spend at least four hours a day typing up his handwritten diary notes. His diary documents the time he spends going to the toilet, feeding the cat, the news headlines from the paper and the radio, the drugs and vitamins he takes, what food he eats and how much it costs, the household chores he has completed, the weight of the day's junk mail, and the amount of time it takes typing up his diary.

In essence, Robert Shields was a one man proto-Twitter.

After suffering from a stroke in 1997 he could no longer keep up with the constant demands of his obsession. Shields died in 2007, but had already bequeathed all eighty-one boxes of his single-spaced diary to Washington State University in 1999. A fifty-year ban has been placed on anyone being able to read his diary in full, apart from the six pages released to the public, so ultimately an actual word count is impossible to calculate. Estimates have totalled the number of words at over 37,000,000. To put that in perspective, it is approximately 35,075,000 more words than the world's most famous diarist Samuel Pepys, whose output consisted of a mere 1,025,000 words. But Robert Shields' diligence in attempting to document every minute of his life doesn't necessarily guarantee his place in history. His diary's façade of completeness just emphasises our inability to document everything. The power of Terence's diary to me is its sparseness, the lack of facts, the fragments. The personality of the diarist, the selection process, the filter of importance that the diarist places on his own life, are as crucial as the content.

Although I've never kept a diary, since I was seventeen, I have always kept a notebook. I use notebooks to jot down thoughts, sketch out ideas for poems and stories, write first drafts, record snatches of overheard conversations and things people have said to me, plus those rare flashes of inspiration and quotes from books I'm reading. In the back of each notebook are phone numbers and addresses of people important to me at that stage in my life, as well as lists of things to have been done, some of which are destined to remain forever undone.

I would say I'm a moderate but regular note taker. Keeping a useful notebook needs to become a habit, and I'd like to think it's definitely a habit, not an obsession – not something I need to think about doing, just something I do. Unlike Robert Shields that aspect of my life isn't ruled by a compulsion. But the line between habit and obsession is, once again, a question of definition.

Due to another unknown and unnameable obsessive compulsion, I always used the same type of A6 Daler Rowney spiral-bound sketchbook, containing twenty-five sheets of 150gsm blank cartridge paper, sandwiched between a piece of brown pulp board and the distinctive red and yellow cover. In a period of seventeen years I filled fifty-two of these notebooks, both sides of each page covered in my small, spidery writing. The first entry is dated May 1994, a month before my eighteenth birthday; the final entry in the last notebook was made in November 2011. Between 1998 and 2002 I also filled seven A5 hardback notebooks, containing sixty pages each, three A4 notebooks for the years 1995, 1998 and 2000, and one six-inch-square hardback notebook in 1997, consisting of a collage a day. Since 2011 my habits have changed and my note keeping has mainly become digital, but despite the technological shift, in addition I've filled two more sixty-page A5 hardback notebooks, and six twenty-page, soft-covered A5 books. That is a lot of notes.

A day or two before visiting the Bishopsgate Institute, I spread out all of those notebooks on the floor in front of me. I'm surprised at just how much of it there is, how much of my life is reflected in these scribbles. Together this sprawl of notes forms a catalogue of my failed relationships, the novelty of their beginnings and the emotion of their falling apart; they chart the rise and demise of various obsessions; they record friends I've made and lost, the films I've watched and books I've read, and moments of strangers' lives that have captured my imagination. They map the last twenty years of my life, from being an awkward teenager with an 'artistic temperament', writing terrible poems, to a man rapidly heading into middle age and still floundering around for meaning.

Although they might inadvertently resemble a diary, documenting some things that were significant at that time in my life, it's a version of my life filtered by a very particular thought process. The purpose of keeping notes is that they might be useful for something else in the future. A notebook is a halfway house, a shed of first drafts, a stockroom of ideas; a diary, even if it's kept with one eye on future publication, is the final document itself. Nowhere in my notes can I find anything that resembles Terence's diary, or anything that could be a key to unlock my obsession with his diary. Perhaps these notes are too self-consciously written for another purpose, or perhaps I was just slightly too old to be as honestly revealing as Terence.

During this digression, Luke has managed to find someone to cover for him, and he asks me to follow him down a steep, narrow staircase to the left of the Staff Only area near the research section. The windowless basement contains the special collections of the library related to the social and cultural history of London, as well as labour and socialist, and protest and campaigning, history. Every available inch of shelving and floor space is stacked with archive boxes containing pamphlets, posters, newspapers, periodicals, photographs, directories, guidebooks and maps. Luke leads me through the stacks to the back wall where the diaries are kept. Row upon row of floor-to-ceiling shelves are filled with neatly labelled boxes, each containing sets of diaries – larger diaries are kept singly, but some boxes contain as many as thirty smaller diaries. The diaries have been grouped by date or, where the run of diaries has been large enough, by individual author. I've asked Luke if I can look specifically at teenage diaries. I'm not allowed to view some of them due to a time sensitive 'lock' being placed on their contents – which means they are unavailable for public consultation until that length of time has expired – similar to the one placed on Robert Shields' mass of pages.

Luke pulls out seven large grey boxes, which I help him carry upstairs to the reading room. 'These are all the teenage diaries we've catalogued so far. But if you need anything else,' he says, 'just let me know.'

I arrange the boxes on the table in front of me in date order. Just under a hundred years separate the oldest from the most recent of the teenage diaries. I pull the first book out and open it carefully on the table, and before I realise it I've spent the rest of the day absorbed in these handwritten worlds in miniature, drawn into the concerns and characters played out page after page. By the time I have to pack up, I've managed to work my way through the collected work of only six separate diarists, a small handful of the volumes in front of me.

Surprisingly, or unsurprisingly, I can't decide which, the concerns expressed in the diaries remain consistent, regardless of the era – the fallings out, the fallings in love, the lists of things bought, presents received, clothes worn. The preoccupation with factual accounts of social visits and music recitals don't change between 1902 and 1995, just the manner and style of those friendships and events – everything from organised dances with elaborate invitations to the end-of-year school disco are events of huge significance. Throughout the years, the same kind of ephemera are stuck between the pages – menus, newspaper clippings, theatre and concert programmes, receipts, train and bus tickets, football programmes, Quasar scorecards, letters – keepsakes that elevate the everyday into something special, tiny mementoes that prove all our lives are something to be treasured.

The diaries do what all diaries through the ages have done. They record and reflect on the problems and concerns of the diarist, and in some way attempt to improve the life of the author through introspection.

The Great Diary Project, especially as the collection continues to grow, will undoubtedly be an invaluable resource for future historians. For now, I still hope that I can squeeze a little more information from the four pages of Terence's diary.

During our conversation, Dr Finkel touched on the subject of Terence's handwriting, how it was too neat for a normal diary, too considered to match up with the emotional aspects of some of the content. Now, during my examination of other diaries, I've been able to place that in context for myself, and I can see that Irving is definitely right.

There is a belief that handwriting holds the key to the personality and character traits of the writer. I'm not sure that I believe in it, but at this stage I'm still willing to try anything.

Chapter 7 – Inside a suit of armour

My interview with Terence is still more than two full weeks away. When the date arrives, I need to be ready, not only ready to tell the truth, but ready to face the facts and the fiction of his diary.

After talking to Dr Finkel, and examining the diaries in the Bishopsgate Institute, I realise that if I am to apply Irving's sponge treatment and squeeze any remaining information from Terence's pages, I have to consider having the handwriting analysed. And for that I need to find a graphologist.

Graphology is the study of handwriting shapes and patterns in an attempt to determine the personality traits and behaviour of the writer. It has a surprisingly long and, not surprisingly, controversial history. Camillo Baldi, an Italian doctor and professor of theoretical medicine at Bologna University, published the first book to examine the connection between personality and handwriting in 1622. But the modern school of handwriting analysis can be traced to a French Catholic priest, Jean-Hippolyte Michon, who not only coined the word 'graphology' but, in 1871, also founded the Society of Graphology in Paris. Since then, graphology has been used for forensic and criminal profiling, to examine fake signatures and forged documents, to assess applicant suitability for job vacancies, to offer relationship and compatibility advice, and to diagnose medical conditions.

It is the plausibility of graphology that has proved controversial. The rationale is that if handwriting is an idiosyncratic expressive behaviour, unique to every individual, then it should in some way reflect the character of the writer. Therefore the marks made by ink on paper could be subject to an objective scientific examination that links those marks to the individual's personality. But different graphologists, and competing graphology schools, offer conflicting interpretations of the same aspects of writing. This lack of scientific rigour in any results puts graphology in the same category as other forms of character divination that once claimed a scientific basis – astrology, palmistry, numerology and phrenology, that is personality divined from the position of the stars, the lines on your hand, significant numbers derived from your name, and the bumps and indentations of your skull.

But I'm willing to keep an open mind. Apart from a brief conversation with Terence I don't know anything about his personality, what inspires him, what emotional responses he might have to any given situation. And subjecting his handwriting to scrutiny might just help me form a greater understanding of him before we meet properly.

A search for a graphologist in London brings me to the website of Ruth Myers. She seems well qualified, judging by the string of letters that follows her name: Ruth Myers ABFHE WADE CGA MAQG – a sequence of acronyms that on first reading seem more like a cryptic cypher created by the Enigma machine than a series of qualifications. Thanks to the internet and the spirit of Alan Turing I manage to decode her credentials: American Board of Forensic Handwriting Examiners, World Association of Document Examiners, Certified Graphology Analyst, Member of the Association of Qualified Graphologists.

Not only are her graphology qualifications outstanding but she has also analysed Prince William and Kate Middleton's handwriting for the *Sun* newspaper, appeared on the BBC and Sky News, and analysed the handwriting of Charles Dickens, Albert Einstein and Lady Gaga for TV chat shows. She is definitely the person to tackle Terence Prendergast's handwriting.

I send her an email, outlining what I would like to be analysed, and asking how I would go about making it happen. I don't tell her who wrote the diary, or anything about already having found Terence. I just want a clear response to the actual handwriting, uncluttered by any external information.

My phone rings. It is Ruth. It seems that all experts prefer to speak in person rather than email. She clarifies what it is she does, and what it is she can't do – determine gender, age or the ethnicity of the writer. She asks questions that I try to answer without revealing too much. What do I do for a living? What is the analysis for? How did I find her? She asks me to email a scan of Terence's diary, and to give her a week to measure, chart and correlate.

Ruth lives at the far end of the Northern Line, at the point where the tube abruptly stops as if the map designer suddenly ran out of ink. The address is a brisk walk from the station, and although the sun is shining, the wind is unexpectedly cold, and by the time I get there my hands are freezing. The house is tucked at the end of a small side street. I ring the bell and Ruth answers the door immediately.

'Don't just stand there, come in, lovely to meet you,' she says with a slight dance in her step.

I'm never quite sure of the etiquette of meeting an older woman. I'm a hugger by nature, rather than a cheek kisser, but some people find it awkward, mainly me. We end up shaking hands.

'Gosh, you're frozen. Warm your hands on the radiator,' Ruth says.

She shows me into a lounge decorated in shades of white and cream. Portraits of animals and still-life prints cover every inch of available wall space. It's homely and comfortable. Ruth is not entirely as I imagined her, a little older, but she also has a little more sparkle behind the eyes, more artistic than scientific. Despite her age she is abundantly girlish, small, spritely, reminding me of Maude from the film *Harold & Maude*.

A quick side note: *Harold & Maude* is my favourite film. Released in 1971, it tells the story of a young man obsessed with death. He stages elaborate fake suicides, and attends strangers' funerals for fun.

That all changes when Harold meets 79-year-old Maude. It's an existential romantic comedy – a love story between two people whose ages are fifty-nine years apart. It demonstrates that the flipside of existential despair is a passionate celebration of life.

Ruth sits beside me on one of the two small, two-seater couches.

'How did you end up doing this?' I ask, knowing it's a question she must have been asked hundreds of times.

'I started life as a graphologist, well not really life as a graphologist . . .' she pulls herself upright and begins again. 'I trained originally to be a graphologist, and then I studied further for forensic work, which is forgery examination on disputed documents and also when people send the most awful things, despicable things, such as poisoned pen letters.'

At that moment a sound like a car alarm pierces the room. 'Oh, damn phone!' Ruth says, reaching for the handset on the coffee table to turn it off. She tuts loudly. 'It always rings when I have visitors.'

Ruth gives me the feeling that our conversation could veer off in any direction, so to try to keep her focused I immediately ask a question about graphology. 'What do you look for when you examine handwriting?'

'I look at the line, the slant, the depth – that means how hard you press. Where you place the handwriting on the paper, the margins, gives you an idea about a lot of things.' As she talks Ruth describes the words in the air with her hands. I feel myself becoming beguiled by her enthusiasm. 'The point is – most of the time, looking at the writing, you can see first of all your emotional foundation. For example, some people are very outgoing, some people are very difficult to get to know, very reserved, a lot of people are withdrawn, emotionally withdrawn, and some people are variable, which means you never know where you are with them. Sensuality you can see in writing,' she looks directly at me, 'but that doesn't always mean you're good in bed. Shall I turn that music down?'

Ruth stands up suddenly and walks into the dining room, turning off the radio, which is faintly playing gentle fifties rock and roll. 'It's distracting. I just always have it on in the background when I'm working.' Ruth comes back and sits next to me on the couch again.

'I find it an amazing science but unfortunately not a lot of people know what a graphologist even is. They know about an astrologer, and they know about silly old tarot cards, and all that rubbishy numerology, which I don't believe a word of. What annoys me most is if I've given a talk, someone at the end will always ask me, "Ruth, what star sign are you?" I think, for God's sake what has that got to do with what I'm telling you? First of all, I'm Aries. And secondly, I don't believe in astrology. It's just hocus pocus. If people were so clever as to forecast the future, look at what people would be doing – they would forecast the most wonderful and the most terrible things. But they can't! What is annoying is that every newspaper or magazine has these astrologers in there. What rubbish! Do you know what I really think about people in regards to tarot cards and astrology? Most people want to have a kind of reassurance. That's what they're seeking. They might be going through a bad patch now, but they want to be told that next week it's going to improve, you're going to meet someone, or your career is going to change. They never tell you bad things, do they? It is ambiguous, so vague that everyone can project into it something that will happen to them. Graphology is an absolute science. It has nothing to do with the future. Anyway, this is for you, all yours . . .' she says, picking up an envelope from the table with my name neatly calligraphed across the front. 'Do you want me to read it, what I saw?'

'Yes, please.'

She picks up a glasses case from the table, opens it, and ceremoniously puts her glasses on before taking her analysis out of the envelope.

'I don't know who it is,' Ruth says, pushing her glasses down her nose slightly to look at me over the top of the frames – a look that clearly means she thinks the diary is mine, and I'm trying to catch her out somehow. 'So, I've written here, "The writer has a pleasant disposition, objective in nature he tries to regulate his feelings and keeps them in perspective . . ."'

She begins to read out her analysis. Her voice is that of someone well practised in public speaking, clear, bright, engaging. She sounds like perhaps she once had elocution lessons but the results have been softened by time. This is her analysis in full:

Handwriting Consultants of London

CHARACTER ASSESSMENT

The writer has a pleasant disposition, objective in nature he tries to regulate his feelings and keeps them in perspective and can face problems and is rarely over enthusiastic. Naturally poised outwardly, he exercises a good sense of justice and can work well under pressure and will not get ruffled in tense and or tumultuous situations.

If temper is displayed it is deliberate and not impulsive. He maintains emotional balance between self-interest and interests of others. A mild temperament he finds it difficult to express personal warmth and may appear distant cool and a spectator of life. His mind controls his feelings, disciplined and rational he will respond with caution even though alert to the happenings at the moment. He is neither impulsive nor demonstrative nor open in expressing his feelings and could be prone to mood swings.

He has good logical thinking, accumulates and retaining information well, using controlled verified reasoning, the methodical approach that lends itself to creativity. His writing indicates a strong depth of emotion mental force and vitality which has a profound influence on his ideas and he will be affected by environmental circumstances and aesthetics. Sensuous, he will enjoy all that appeals to the senses, taste, fragrances, colour, harmony, or discord in music, all forms of beauty which could influence his surroundings and choice of wardrobe.

Experiences are felt deeply and are remembered and play a part on an unconscious level in affecting attitudes and decisions and once deeply touched the memory stays for ever whether sorrow or joy.

He is direct in approach but has learnt to withhold and maintain emotional poise buried deeply in his subconscious past experiences which may have been disturbing and unacceptable . These repressed inhibited feelings cause inner tensions and only on rare occasions will cause an eruption of pent-up release when his control system breaks down.

He has a need for social acceptance and wants to present a good image. Self-conscious, timid, prudent he tries to compensate by work and self-expression. He does not always face up to problems and unconsciously rationalizes his actions by avoiding true facts thus misleading himself and finding excuses that he may be reluctant to face. Fear of censure robs him of peace of mind and may result in his feeling inadequate within himself often interpreting criticism as dislike and can be easily irritated.

He has the ability to set his own goals and work without supervision, knowing what he wants he will be eager and optimistic at times to accomplish his efforts with reasonably good determination and firmness of purpose he has the capacity to keep moving forward in spite of fear and obstacles. When provoked can respond with caustic retorts.

The writer is an individualist, nonconforming he sets his own standards and does not always follow the conventional, idiosyncratic he could present himself, an idea or project in a singular and curious mode.

He is exacting liking order with good attention to details. Manual dexterity allows him to apply skill and ease with his hands even coordination actions with his feet. Intuitive he has quick insight and could interpret his emotions and feelings through the artistic media.

His writing indicates a supportive factor in cultivating any literary or musical aptitude and a keen sense of timing and versatility enables him to adapt easily to challenging situations and people and with cultural interests an emotional satisfaction in the need to express himself in the need to perform.

A good listener and will communicate but not overly, can be sociable but at heart he enjoys and is quite happy in his own company

Ruth Myers

Ruth Myers ABFHE WADE CGA

As Ruth reads out her analysis, I think about how any of it might apply to the grown-up man I met on the doorstep in Birmingham, how much she has just inferred from the content of the diary itself rather than the handwriting, and how much of it is just made from Barnum statements – sentences used by mediums, psychics and mind-readers that seem personal and perceptive, but are actually all-encompassing generalities. The term 'Barnum effect' was coined by psychologist Paul Meehl in 1956 as a backhanded compliment to the grand lover of the fraudulent, American showman, raconteur and circus owner P.T. Barnum, who, it is claimed, described his circus by saying 'We've got something for everyone!' The psychology of statements used by psychics and in character assessments is strong, and the effect is that the description is tailor-made for you, full of personal meaning that seems impossible to apply to anyone else.

'There's a lot to think about in that,' I say, using a non-committal generalisation of my own. 'Do you mind if I read it again?'

'No, not at all,' she says folding her glasses away.

I read through Ruth's descriptions of Terence's personality and characteristics. Contradictions jump out at me from the page: the writer is someone who will enjoy both 'harmony, or discord in music', 'can be sociable but . . . is quite happy in his own company'.

I can't help but wonder again whether, despite my assurances that the diary isn't mine, Ruth thinks I'm here to catch her out. If she really thinks the diary is mine, perhaps after our phone conversation she did some quick research into my career – evidence of my performances and writing litter the internet. That would explain 'an emotional satisfaction in the need to express himself in the need to perform'. The phrase 'could present himself, an idea or project in a singular and curious mode' would definitely apply to this whole endeavour. Maybe she was just trying to flatter my ego by referring to cultivation of any literary aptitude. I don't know if this is just my inherent scepticism, reading myself into Ruth's analysis, or she really has responded to believing the diary is mine.

Either way, I feel disappointed and let down. It's not Ruth's fault. I'm just desperate for help, obsessed with trying to find anything I can grasp hold of, the tiniest of hints to tell me what to do next, in which direction to go. I want to know that everything is going to be OK, this adventure won't end badly and I'm doing the right thing. I feel frustrated at myself for wasting everybody's time.

'Can I ask, why did you pick up this diary? And why did you like the idea of it?'

Ruth has asked questions guaranteed to bring me back to the moment, questions that make meeting Ruth immediately feel worthwhile, even if it's just for someone to discuss the diary with.

'I was drawn to it for some reason. It is just really evocative for me . . .'

'Well, I thought it was a bit odd.' Ruth leans back into the corner of the couch, folds her arms and pouts in a childlike way. 'On one side you have this light factor, light coming, and then all the zeros going millions and millions of miles away from the light. And then the precision of the actual writing going down to one side. It's all kept in order. It is exacting. You know the dots going over the "i"s – idiosyncrasy – it says that the writer is different. It's non-conformist. It is very clear, but on the other hand, it's someone who doesn't tell the truth all the time. He evades the truth, because the truth is too painful.' She pauses, and in that pause there seems to be a flicker in her eyes of something happening in her own life that she can't quite bring herself to use as an example. 'Sometimes people don't want to tell the truth because a problem is too painful. They mislead themselves, and in misleading themselves they are misleading others. They go for years and years and years suffering within themselves. It takes courage to face up to something ghastly.'

'Where do you see that he's deceiving himself in the writing?' I ask, thinking about the parts of the diary that seem to be fictional, creative inventions of a teenager fuelled by escapism.

'In some of the circles,' Ruth says with conviction.

'That *is* interesting, because in some of the content it seems that he's not telling the truth. I can't work out if it's truth or fiction,' I say, echoing Dr Finkel's concerns.

'It's a strange diary. For some years there is only one line. And it's so brief, so little innermost thoughts, because you've only sent four pages. Do you have the rest?'

'No, no, that's it. That's the whole thing.'

'I think the fact that he wrote some of those things, the fact that he stole money and ran away, was a cry for help. He's someone who has suffered a great deal. He got hit, didn't he? He tried to run away, and then he wants to kill himself. He had no friends. How sad is that? No friends! They are on the outside looking in all their lives.'

Ruth's reaction is more revealing than her analysis was. She's hit upon the power of the diary to capture elements of everyone's adolescence, and in doing so has unexpectedly revealed something very fragile about her own past.

'Remember this,' she continues, 'we are, all of us – what we are is what happened to us during our lifetime as a child, what happened to us at school, in our family, with our siblings, with our parents. A lot of people can't express themselves because they are too frightened to express themselves.'

Out of all Ruth's generalities, this is the thing that floors me. We are, she says, all of us, defined by what happened to us when we were children – for better, for worse, for absolute indifference. That is who we are, and we are limited and contained by those patterns, or we react against them, for the rest of our lives. Before I think of my own childhood, illnesses and isolation, I think of Terence, lost in a real cave of time, still living with his parents, even his desperation for escape destroyed.

'And so you were drawn to this diary because you felt some identification there?' Ruth asks, looking at me intently.

'Yes, particularly the list of things that he wants to improve about himself, the list that says "shy, no friends".'

'You mean that you can relate to that?'

'Some of that, yes, I was incredibly shy as a kid for example.'

'Well, I was shy . . . but I've come out of it now!' Ruth laughs, breaking the moment. I can't help but laugh, too. 'I was so shy!' She thinks for a moment before continuing. 'I can tell you this because it's the truth. I remember when my parents had friends over for dinner or anything, I was so shy I had to stand outside the door for a while to gain my strength of confidence to be able to open that door, because I felt everyone would drop everything and be staring at me. You imagine the response, you exaggerate in your mind the attention you will get, and no one is really taking the blindest bit of notice.'

'How did you overcome your shyness?'

'Shyness is something that you live with, I think. But I think over the years if people give you confidence, if they encourage you . . . most of us need warmth, praise, encouragement and a pat on the back. You know what? When you are given those things, you seem to blossom, you open up like a flower, your petals grow,' she says, pantomiming the motion of a flower opening. 'Receiving a compliment is very rare, and you are always listening for another one. They're like nectar, Ambrosia to the soul. You can look at someone and admire them, but never say anything. The British tend to be very reserved as a nation, we tend to put everyone down. But I'll tell you this. A little bit of praise opens doors.'

I'm warming to Ruth. I don't know if her reading of Terence's handwriting is accurate or genuine, but her strong empathy for people and their emotional problems is certainly making me consider my motivation for wanting to speak to him in a new light.

'Do you think he could have put the diary in the book because he wanted someone to find it? Perhaps as a cry for help?'

'I don't know about that, but I always find that people who write diaries can't relate to normal people, but they can relate by the pen. They feel release in putting their feelings down on paper. I find when I receive greetings cards, the more introverted a person is, the more the cards are overflowing with words. They read on for ever . . . and when you meet those people, they don't open their mouth!'

'People must be frightened to send you birthday and Christmas cards,' I say.

Ruth laughs, although it must be something else she's heard a hundred times. 'Of course I get cards.'

Despite my inclination to disbelieve Ruth's analysis, I can't help but ask her another question to prolong our conversation. 'Do you think I would get on with Terence?'

'It depends on some of the things you've told me. Get on with yourself if the diary is yours,' she gives me the over-the-glasses look again. 'You seem to be able to get on with people, but compatibility in terms of friendship is a different issue. The strangest thing I saw, talking about compatibility, is . . . you know the famous comedians Laurel and Hardy? I used to love Laurel and Hardy, I thought they were great, really unique. They had a great quality in their talent, which was a kind of gentleness. And then I looked at their writing and I could see why they got on. Because when I measured their signatures, the two of them were exactly the same. They both wrote at exactly the same angles,' Ruth places her hands palm to palm, opens her fingers, then interlocks them together tightly, 'which means they harmonised together. If you get on very, very well with someone, you'll find similar characteristics in the writing.'

I imagine me and Terence as the next Laurel and Hardy, buddies of the best kind, even in the most hapless of situations.

'If you give me your writing, I can point out why you may or may not get on,' she says.

Without hesitation, going against everything I said a page or two ago, I reach into my bag to find my notebook, the one that also contains Terence's email address. I open it to a page near the front and hand it to Ruth. She puts her glasses back on and studies my writing attentively.

'You press quite hard, don't you?' Ruth rests the notebook across her knees so she can use both hands to gesture. 'The deeper you press, the more emotional you are. You feel things quite deeply.

Often people who press very hard have an awful lot of stress in their lives. They know they feel life at a very strong ebb, so they have to control their feelings and not let other people know how much everything affects them. It's like you're riding a horse and pulling back on the reins.' I nod, trying not to give too much away, but encourage her to continue.

'And usually people who press very hard try and achieve more in life, and people who get to the top in life, who have achieved greatness, press very hard because everything is very meaningful to them, more so than to anyone else. Sometimes they succeed, but of course fate intervenes and luck plays a huge part in life. No matter how talented you are, it's a question of being at the right place at the right time. The more angular your writing, the more you want to know, the more you are searching, the more you are criticising, investigating, and the more you are not going just to be pleased with what anyone is saying to you.' She pulls her glasses down slightly and looks at me again. I can't help but feel like a schoolkid who has done something wrong.

'You've got a bit of drive here. Your thinking is quicker than your hand can relate. You are motivated, because you've crossed your "t"s and they extend out a bit, so you are optimistic. Can you see they go up in the air?' She indicates the crossbar of my "t"s – they really do rise slightly on the right-hand side. 'When they go up in the air, it means you've got an optimistic attitude, in your eyes, you hope that things will turn out all right.

'The willpower you've got is quite good, so you tend to be motivated. It's important for you to do things, but it is hard for you to express how you feel. You've closed up all your circle connection letters – the "o"s and "a"s are all shut. In fact, you haven't got anything open at all,' Ruth says, pointing at each word in turn. 'So you can probably only find expression by the pen. You are inside a suit of armour, and you've got all sorts of emotions going around inside there, but it's hard for you to let them out. You do so through the pen rather than talking. And that comes from your earliest childhood.

You are sensitive to criticism. It's like a stab wound. Whoever has made the criticism probably wouldn't know it, but inwardly you are deeply hurt – can you see the second stroke is slightly higher, only slightly. An ordinary person wouldn't notice, but you are self-conscious, shy, you feel ridicule. People go through life seeming supremely confident but inside they doubt themselves. Actors can be like that, for instance – and often the more inhibited they are as a person, the better the actor.'

While talking, Ruth has punctuated each sentence with hand gestures – the hard press of her thumb in the air, pulling back the reins of an imaginary horse, the rise of the lines, the locked-up loops, the emotions held tightly inside, a mime of graphology.

'Have you ever done any acting?' I ask.

'I wanted to be an actress, when I first started off. I give talks, and I find I'm better off giving talks than I am writing reports for hours on end. I feel I can tell people more about themselves when they can listen to what I say, not so much preaching but more on a friendly basis.'

'So, *do* you think Terence and I will get on?' I ask again, worried that Ruth has forgotten my question.

'It's impossible to say with certainty, but I would say you only seek friendships of a certain type or calibre. You wouldn't be friends with anybody. You would be highly selective in who is your friend.'

I think back to all the friendships I've made and lost, ones that have endured despite huge stretches of time or distance between meeting up, the friendships that were mistakes from the beginning, serious misjudgements of personality or a willing blindness to character flaws, the friends that were always fated to be fleeting, born of proximity, or mutual kindness. I think about how quick I can be to make judgements. Usually those judgements serve me well but sometimes I've been completely wrong. I like strangers, and I give a lot in friendship, but as soon as I feel betrayed, I'm quick to shut someone out.

As I say goodbye I give Ruth a quick hug. Whatever the truth about graphology I've been completely charmed by this funny, energetic, expressive woman. I'm intrigued by her past, how she's got to this point, what choices she's made in life to get here to this small, comfortable house, with a complete stranger asking the most abstract of questions about another stranger's diary.

On the walk back to the train station I find myself returning to Ruth's words: 'we are, all of us – what we are is what happened to us during our lifetime as a child.' I had known from the moment I first read his diary that I was like Terence in some inherent way. I loved books, I loved words, I sought means of escape in magic and fiction.

Stations at the end of a line are sad or magical places, depending on which way you are travelling. I'm travelling the magical way. I feel I'm slowly getting closer to the truth – to the truth of the diary, and to the truth of my obsession.

The train is waiting at the platform. I take a seat in an empty carriage, still thinking over everything Ruth has said, and at that moment I remember, starkly, that I was similar to Terence in other ways.

When I was a young teenager, I too wrote down what I thought and felt when I was isolated from the world. I have a sudden burning desire to find those words, and to place them alongside Terence's own. If I am going to excavate his past, it's only right that I also excavate my own.

Chapter 8 – The first love-letter I never sent

The following morning I wake up early and call my mum and dad to ask if I can come over to visit. Today is Sunday, which means I have only six days before my meeting with Terence. Luckily, the remnants of my childhood aren't hard to unearth.

When my mum and dad moved house ten years ago, a lot of things were thrown away, but just as much was kept to be sorted through later. The remains of my childhood are now contained in about a dozen crisp-box-shaped time capsules, dampening in the dark in the back of a garage in Essex, waiting patiently for me to sort through them. Lack of time and impetus has left the boxes stacked in precarious piles while other not-quite-yet-discarded objects have collected around them – a wicker couch, garden chairs, a sewing machine, suitcases of old clothes, half empty paint cans, and half full paint cans. The moment to open the boxes has finally arrived.

My parents' house is only a half-hour train ride from Liverpool Street station, out towards Romford. It's a journey I remember well from the time circumstances forced me to live with them a few years ago. Chadwell Heath is a nice enough place, a small high street on the way to and from somewhere else. Perfect for growing older, and perfect for my retired mum and dad. But it's not a place where I fit in.

Trying to get your life back together while you're living with your parents is difficult, especially if there's nowhere to escape to. It's hard to start a new relationship while recovering from the serious setback of a recurring illness, and while sleeping in a single bed in the box room while your mum and dad are asleep on the other side of the wall. In a way, I can understand how, during that time, I hid from myself, retreating a little into my teenage ways, reading more and playing computer games. Maybe even buying the *Choose Your Own Adventure* books was part of my desire to withdraw into something comfortable and childlike.

As the train pulls into Chadwell Heath I feel the half-familiar dread of the ten-minute walk to my parents' house. I don't look very different from the way I always have – I'm tall, I'm still thin despite the threat of the inevitable middle-aged fallout, I like clothes that fit me, I like colour, I wear glasses. Not so different from many men, but for some reason the combination of those things are justification enough for a few people to feel the need to point and comment. Essex is full of finger pointers. The predictable – 'Harry Potter, where's your broomstick?' 'Hey, Jarvis, show us yer arse,' 'Where did you park your TARDIS?' 'Oi, John Lennon, I thought you were dead' – I can usually live with, but sometimes it's worse. Once a man tried to stop me getting off the train at Chadwell Heath. I hadn't noticed him during the journey but he must have somehow taken offence to something about me. He held me up against the partition, his full body weight pressed against my chest. And with a straight face, inches away from mine, one grown-up man in his thirties to another, he spat the words 'Speccy four eyes'.

I'm not built for fighting or fighting back, but somehow I managed to wriggle free just before the doors closed. I escaped, a little shaken, with a few bruises. I hate intolerance, idiocy and violence. These are the same reasons I left Rhyl as a teenager. But those things still stalk the streets of small towns. I'm not sure what fuels them or where they're born, probably a combination of fear and unhappiness, but that is not an excuse. A bully is always a bully.

But bullies can't be allowed to win. You need to keep on, celebrate your passions and your difference. Next to Chadwell Heath station is a brilliant and unexpected treasure – a miniature steam railway. Kept by enthusiasts, it opens to the public on the first Sunday of every month during the summer, and for 50p you can actually ride the 7¼-inch gauge steam train. The Ilford & West Essex Model Railway Club is a rare and beautiful thing, flowering in the cracks alongside the railway tracks. We might have different obsessions but they are my kind of people.

Even with allies so close, it is with relief I find my mum waiting for me in the car outside the station. We stop by my dad's allotment to pick him up too. His allotment is how I imagine our post-apocalyptic future, if it doesn't contain only Australians and a sub-marine of Americans. A softer, friendly version of *Mad Max*, Mel Gibson's character replaced by *Last of the Summer Wine*'s Compo, violence replaced by lending a hand, and technology's cooling edges performing new functions – terraces of radiators, raised beds from roadwork fences, the greatest hits of Lady Gaga and Blu-ray box sets of *Lost* reduced to reflecting sunlight, spinning mirrors to frighten birds.

As always, my mum and dad are pleased to see me, and when we get to the house the kettle is on before I can take my coat off. We do the general catch-ups. How's Sarah? Have you seen your sister recently? Have you heard from your brother? They tell me about their day trips – the numbers of the roads they've travelled on, and detailed accounts of every meal they ate while away. I'm updated on my dad's vegetable growing and their health. My mum has recently had her knees replaced, and my dad has serious nerve damage to his spine, but since they've both retired they've taken up swimming, so I now also get the gossip on their fellow swimmers. My dad goes back into the kitchen to make the tea. I take the opportunity to plunge into the reason I'm here to my mum.

'Mum, you know when I was living here I bought some *Choose Your Own Adventure* books from eBay?'

'I remember yes, yet another box of stuff to be added to your collections,' my mum rolls her eyes.

'One of the books had a diary hidden inside . . .'

'What's this?' my dad shouts, coming through into the lounge, worried he's missing out on something. I explain to both of them about the diary, about actually finding Terence, and our imminent meeting. I describe my conversations with everyone I've met so far, particularly Dr Finkel and Ruth.

'The graphologist said, "What we are is what happened to us during our lifetime as a child." Would you say that was true or not?' I ask them.

'Not really I wouldn't, no,' my dad answers. 'Some people can have a terrible, terrible time as a child but get over their problems and have a great life. So, no, I wouldn't agree with that, not really . . .'

'I think it has to have a bearing on you,' my mum interrupts. 'I think it must do. Whether it strengthens you or weakens you, again it depends on what kind of personality you have. For some people who've had a particularly hellish childhood, they can fall by the wayside.'

'Terence's story is quite sad, really,' my dad says, 'realising, as most of us do, the teenage years are pretty traumatic anyway. If people live what I would call ordinary type lives, the teenage years are probably the hardest part of your life. Except when you get married and have children,' he says, looking at my mum, 'that's another hugely traumatic time in your life.' My mum and dad have been together for over forty-five years, so he is definitely half joking. 'Obviously, some people have terribly traumatic times in their life, but I would say on average, the teenage years are the most traumatic. They are a strange time. They can be good fun, but growing up is also very hard.'

'Do you think Terence will have got over those things?'

'All depends on the kind of person he is. He might not be the kind of person to get over them completely. He may try to forget about them for a while, but I think his mind might always go back to thinking about those times. It's hard to say, really. A lot of us went through terrible, traumatic times. Some people get over them, and some people don't.'

I'm thrown for a moment by my dad's half admission of his own terrible teenage years. 'Would you say you had a traumatic time in your teenage years?' I ask him.

'I wouldn't say it was fantastic.' He pauses, clearly remembering his youth. 'Not really it wasn't.' My dad has clammed up a little, and from experience, just pressing on with the same subject won't be any more revealing. My mum, used to our family's flow of conversation, fills the space.

'I must say I'm in two minds about whether talking to Terence about the diary is a good thing to do,' she says, pausing to sip her tea, 'because you don't know what has happened to him, but at the same time it's too tantalising to ignore.' My mum has hit upon my exact predicament, the tension I'm caught in, the opposite pull of caution and obsession.

'I think the reason you care so much about this Terence Prendergast,' my mum continues, 'is the hope that, even though you might suffer so much as a child, you can come out of it all right at the other end. You did. So, perhaps . . . perhaps it's what might have happened that scares you. If things had taken an alternative course. Not only for you, but for Terence, too.'

Just like in the *Choose Your Own Adventure* books that Terence, me, and millions of other children used to know and love, life can go one way and lead you to happiness and riches, but a single false decision can shape the rest of your life for the worse. My mum is right, of course, but how can I help Terence understand my reasons and motivations?

I know just the broad shape of a large part of my childhood. The details I don't remember, or perhaps they were never there at all. This is the point in my quest for honesty. And with my mum's help I try to piece together the details of my past, parts of which I might have forgotten for a reason.

* * *

I'd been an average, active, studious child. It was the last year of primary school and I was deputy head boy and school librarian. I was performing magic in the playground and sharing a marble collection with Lindsey Smith.

It was the autumn of 1986 and I'd been back at school two months when I caught a flu-type virus. I was never really fully well after that. I suffered from severe headaches, chronic joint and muscle pain, and repeated bouts of prolonged intense fatigue.

Over Christmas and New Year I caught another infection, this time of the chest and throat. At the end of January 1987 my GP sent me for consultation to the local hospital, by which time I was also suffering from excruciating stomach pains. The consultant admitted me to the hospital with suspected appendicitis. I was discharged but readmitted nine days later for further tests and examination – a series of ultrasounds, barium meal, CAT scan, and electroencephalograms – but still the doctors were unable to give a diagnosis. I was discharged again, even though my stomach was sore and swollen. By Easter, my bladder had stopped working. It was as if my muscles and nerves were unable to tell my brain to tell me that I needed to go to the toilet, but it would empty at night in my sleep. Bed-wetting when you're 11 is acutely embarrassing, so I can really sympathise with Terence when he worries about his 'wet pants x 2'. But if it was a bed-wetting contest, I'd have definitely won.

The doctors fitted a catheter through my stomach to the bladder, which was then attached by a small tube to a transparent bag. When the bag was full, it was emptied by using a small plastic tap. It's a very strange moment to see your internal processes externalised. The tests continued as the doctors tried to discover what was wrong. I half remember a strange test to see how much they could fill my bladder with sterile water, using the tube the doctors had already attached. I was made to stand over a small windmill-on-a-funnel type contraption and wait to see if I needed to urinate, while the doctors continued to fill my bladder through the tube. We all waited a very long time before they finally emptied it the way it had been filled, back through the small tube. I remember thinking that must be the way cyborgs have to drink.

The doctors also subjected me to a lumbar puncture, also known as a spinal tap, which is a way of collecting fluid by injecting a hollow needle into the spine. It's used to test for meningitis, among other things. As a writer, I'd like to make the description of the procedure as intense as possible, to summarise the process in detail, the fear of pain and discomfort. But thinking about the whole operation makes me feel faint even now. I am not scared of needles or blood necessarily, but the thought of those things, the graphic image constructed by my imagination, is the problem.

I first fainted in the first year of junior school. I can still picture the moment. It was Halloween. The teacher, Mrs Jones, was warning the class how dangerous it was to go trick-or-treating. As an example of the danger, she told us a story of a boy who went trick-or-treating the previous year. He'd dressed up as a ghost, using the classic white-sheet method. One of the corners of the sheet somehow caught a candle flame of a pumpkin lantern. At the conclusion of the story the boy ended up in hospital with third-degree burns over his face and body, and I ended up on the floor in the middle of the classroom. I was lying on my back, somehow still in the sitting position, my chair tipped back, feet in the air. I'd fainted. My imagination had joined the gaps in the story, and the realisation of the vivid fragility of the human body had tipped mine into unconsciousness. I must have been out for a few seconds only. In those moments when you first regain consciousness, your brain tries to make sense of the information gathered by your senses – like rebooting a computer. For some reason my brain was telling me I was curled up on the floor of our bathroom at home, using a towel for a pillow. The reality was I was being stared at by thirty pairs of eyes, my classmates having just witnessed powerful secondary proof of the dangers of fancy dress.

After that I not only fainted at every blood test, but in sixth-form assembly when a representative from Oxfam showed a film of starving

African children, at the cinema with a girlfriend during the part of the film *Face/Off* when Nicolas Cage and John Travolta's faces are swapped, at the 20-20 optical store when the optometrist described trying to scrape a small white fleck from the surface of my eye, and at my parents' house when I trapped my thumb in the folding mechanism of the sofa bed. In every instance, unconsciousness creeps up quickly, always the same dizzy feeling, a cold sick sweat, blurred vision. The triggers might be different but they always result in my brain constructing a vivid image of the soft machine of the body failing or being damaged. You could call it weakness or empathy.

Back on the hospital ward in the 1980s, the lumbar puncture aftercare procedure involved being tilted for six hours towards the feet, and then for six hours headwards, to minimise the possibility of air bubbles being trapped in the spinal fluid. That night I was a human spirit level, trying to get to sleep on an agonisingly slow see-saw.

After a fortnight, I was transferred to Alder Hey Children's Hospital in Liverpool for a further three weeks to be seen by a urology specialist, to try to discover the cause of my bladder problems. I have a vague recollection of all these ins and outs of hospital. Dates and places are blurred as they recede from importance in my life. But these are moments that shaped my childhood. At times I must have felt lonely and isolated, wondered if I'd ever be normal again, whether I'd have friends or be able to play out. I must have worried if I would have to catheterise myself for my whole life, and if that would stop me ever having a girlfriend.

I continued visiting Alder Hey and Glan Clwyd hospitals throughout 1988, before being referred to Great Ormond Street Children's Hospital in London. I was admitted as an in-patient for four weeks in September and October that year, while tests continued. Photos from that time show me flabby and fluid filled. My knees are still covered in stretch marks, patterned like camouflage on the ghost of an albino tiger.

While I was the one being prodded and probed, it is easy to forget that this isn't only my history. Listening to my mum and dad describing these years makes me realise it's theirs, too – having an ill child was their heartbreak and struggle, with the added expense of hospital visits and staying away from home, seeing how my health affected everyone in the family, my brother Neil and sister Nina too, who had their own individual needs and worries about the future.

Throughout this time I still suffered from chronic fatigue and severe joint pain, but during the first half of 1989 these symptoms began to improve, followed by the first signs of my bladder regaining normal function – I would wake at night instead of wetting the bed, and I'd be able to go to the toilet. After steady progress I started back at school full time.

I was 13, and back to being a normal healthy child. I was performing magic shows. I started a summer job. I was riding bikes and juggling. Just over a year later that was all taken away once again, as the pain and fatigue returned and with them more hospital visits.

I remained at home, too ill to go to school, until halfway through the final year of high school. My education was reduced to six hours a week of home tuition, half an hour of *Neighbours* and one and half hours a day of Richard and Judy's TV show *This Morning*. Without *This Morning* my day-to-day life would have been so much poorer. In that final year of high school I could sit just two exams, both in English. I can't remember much about *The Merchant of Venice* but I still know a lot about what clothes look best on which body type, advice I've given to friends in need has been due to osmosis from *This Morning*'s in-house agony aunt Denise Robertson, and I know how to bake a mean savoury scone.

The official diagnosis for my condition was myalgic encephalomyelitis or, to give it its common name, ME – post-viral fatigue syndrome. ME remains a controversial illness, debates are still being had about what it should be called, how it should be defined, and, more importantly, how it should be treated. But there is no question of it being a very real, debilitating condition for millions of sufferers around the world.

However, my diagnosis was wrong. For twenty years I'd been suffering from a completely different illness from the one I'd been told I had. I've had bouts of serious ill health throughout my adulthood, too. The last of these was at the beginning of my thirties, a recurrence of the severe fatigue and chronic joint pain of my childhood. This time I was referred directly to an ME specialist. All it took was a shake of the hand.

'I think you might have Ehlers-Danlos syndrome,' said the professor. 'Your symptoms are consistent with the condition, and from shaking your hand your joints certainly feel more flexible than average.'

After a referral to one of the world's leading specialists in Ehlers-Danlos syndrome, or EDS as it is commonly abbreviated, and twenty years after I first became ill, my condition was confirmed.

EDS is caused by alterations in certain genes that make collagen weaker. Collagen is the body's most abundant protein, a building block that strengthens and supports various body tissues. It's found in all the stuff that forms the body and helps it function – the tendons and ligaments, the skin and bone, the blood vessels and the spine, hair and nails. In essence, collagen is a glue that holds the body together. With EDS, the joints lack strength and support, and can be prone to being easily sprained or dislocated; skin is stretchier than normal and bruises and scars easily; there is a tendency to faint more easily; and the body is prone to fatigue and severe joint and muscle pain. EDS is not usually life threatening, but there is no cure, just supportive care.

The last few years have been a struggle, through both the pain and the continuing mental and physical exhaustion of trying to maintain a full, normal, active life without a total relapse into immobility. I haven't always been successful, but I've realised one thing – obsession holds fear at bay. If your mind is focused fully on one thing, it can't dwell on the shadows and storms the mind threatens to create.

A word about fatigue. Pain is exhausting. It puts demands on the processing power of your brain, like running a complete virus scan of your hard drive while you're using your laptop for something else, browsing the internet, word processing, watching a film. The body is the same. The more demands on your brain, the more your responses to other stimuli become sluggish, and the faster the drain on your energy. I am in pain constantly. It's there when I wake up. It's there when I go to sleep. Pain disrupts sleep, making the symptoms of fatigue worse – a vicious cycle that can escalate quickly.

I am likely to be in some pain for the rest of my life. I have things I do to cope with my condition. I'm on a series of pain-suppressing drugs, and I do physiotherapy exercises. I know that some things make the pain worse, including standing for long periods, carrying a bag, walking up hill or running. Despite the coping mechanisms I've learnt over the years, sometimes it is impossible to filter out the pain signal. That can make life difficult. People close to me have learnt to make allowances when I need them to be made – carrying bags for me, waiting at a bar so I don't have to stand for a long time, ensuring I have a seat, cancelling social engagements at the last minute if I'm too exhausted or in too much pain. Sometimes I do things even though I know it will make the pain worse, but I plan for that. Time becomes an extended commodity – a night out can necessitate a few days for recovery. Taken together, it's all very complicated to explain to a stranger, and generally I'd prefer for people not to know. I don't want special treatment when I don't always need it – I guess the problem can be admitting that sometimes I do.

It is hard not to be angry about my misdiagnosis. The symptoms were there all along – the joint and muscle pain, the easy bruising, the fainting, the abnormally stretchy soft skin and the fatigue. I can't help wondering what my life would have been like if I'd been given a correct diagnosis all those years ago? Would I be stronger and more resilient, with less pain and a better level of fitness? How would being fitter have altered my mental processes? Would I even be so obsessive?

* * *

My dad has never been entirely comfortable about sharing his emotions and feelings – he once gave me a cheery, 'Morning, love,' then after turning and seeing it was me, quickly followed it up with an embarrassed, 'Sorry, I thought you were your sister' – and while I've been talking to my mum, he has already started on the more practical route to understanding my childhood. It takes us half a day to clear a path to the boxes at the back of the garage. We carry them through into my parents' lounge, where four years ago I first laid out Terence Prendergast's *Choose Your Own Adventure* books and discovered the diary.

I stand back and survey the pile of crushed, damp, mouse-chewed boxes filling the room. This is it. This is my childhood, the things that were important to me. It was all emptied out of drawers and cupboards ten years ago, and nothing has been touched since. I rip the parcel tape from the first box. It feels like a cross between Christmas, an archaeological dig and an episode of *This Is Your Life* on which I am both host and special guest.

The first of the boxes contains a variety of collections I'd curated throughout my childhood. I've always been a collector and my childhood remains prove it. Inside an old Gino Ginelli ice-cream tub, sealed carefully around the rim with masking tape, are ninety-seven sew-on badges, souvenirs of childhood outings to the Welsh Mountain Zoo, Liverpool's Beatle City, The Museum of the Moving Image and Rhyl's lifeboat centre, among many others. Opening the box is like reading tiny fabric postcards sent from my past. One badge, picturing Alton Tower's iconic British roller-coaster the Corkscrew, summons a fact in my brain I never knew I knew, let alone had forgotten – that the roller-coaster had a top speed of forty miles an hour. Remembering a fact that insignificant gives me hope that I will be able to recall something more relevant to my quest, possibly the key to understanding my empathy with Terence.

Further down in the tub are a group of swimming awards, badges that were designed to sew on your trunks as a medal of honour, and with them another badge for the Lawn Tennis Association. They are a reminder that before my illness started I was an active child – swimming, cycling, running and playing just like any other kid. I feel suddenly saddened. I knew this was going to be hard, but the emotions I feel just seeing these badges surprises me. I learnt as a child to take each day at a time, to keep myself occupied and do what I could. My focus became smaller – what was on TV, what time Dad would be home from work with the post, whether my little sister Nina was coming back straight after school and would be able to keep me company. The worse my illness became, the smaller my focus. Keeping my focus narrowed to a smaller world meant I didn't feel I was missing out on all the things I could no longer do. If your world doesn't contain it, it ceases to be important. But looking back, I realise now just how much my choices were narrowed. If my life at that point had been a *Choose Your Own Adventure*, it would have lacked both adventure and choice. It's no surprise that I became obsessed with Edward Packard's books, stories in which I could actually live the adventure.

Among the souvenir and award badges are a set of cub-scout patches – the rank and file of Baden-Powell. Despite being the shyest cub in my pack, I was awarded merit badges for entertainment, book reading, collecting, first aid, athletics and camping. One is a commemorative badge, celebrating the 70th anniversary of cub scouts in 1986. That summer I turned ten, just five months before I first became ill. It's a summer, and a summer camp, I wish I could remember in detail; but all I can recall are vague memories of hiking, campfire singalongs, a rope swing over a river, cooking bread dough on a stick, and a boy whose name I can't remember being rushed to A & E after getting his leg caught on barbed wire. Ordinary boy stuff, but the last summer of ordinary boy stuff before my childhood changed. I put the badges back carefully in their now vintage ice-cream tub, and carry on with the trawl through my past.

Tucked in the corner of the box is a brown envelope addressed to Ward 1, Ysbyty Glan Clwyd, the hospital in North Wales where I was admitted when I was first ill. The envelope is full of handmade get well soon cards from everyone in my primary school class. Pictures of hospital beds and thermometers, top hats, rabbits and magic wands are drawn with felt tip on beige sugar paper. Made at an age when social anxiety hadn't taken over, the messages range from notes of concern and practicality and important school news to those featuring spelling mistakes that transform cracker jokes into absurdist language experiments:

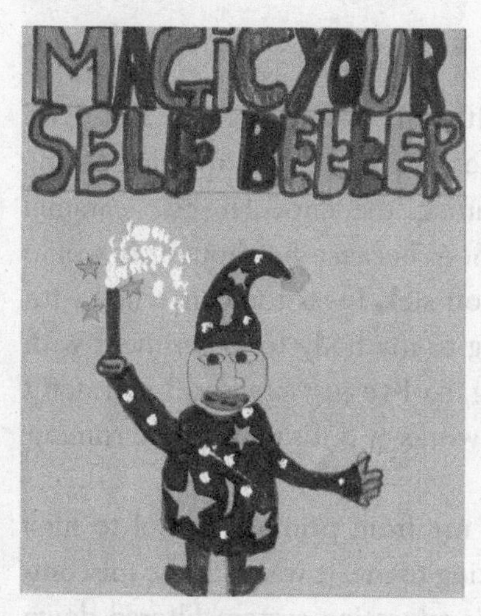

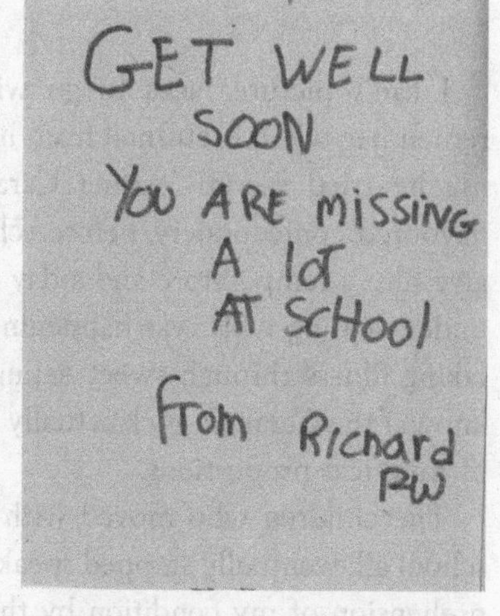

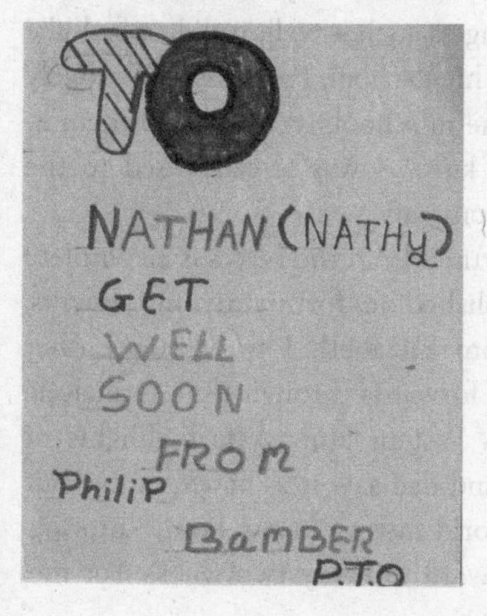

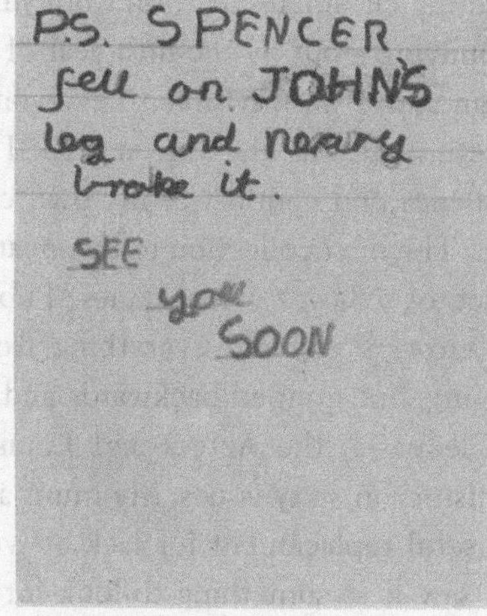

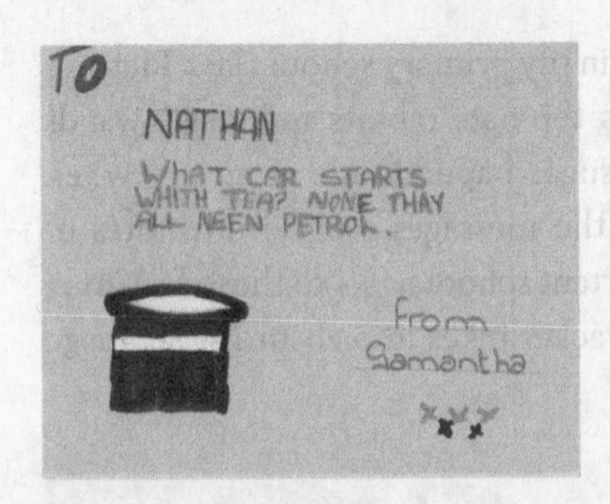

I can't picture faces to go with any of the names. But I do remember, when I returned from hospital, one boy in my class telling me he tried secretly eating Caramac, the chocolate-like caramel flavoured confectionery, before school because he thought it would give him a temperature and a day off sick. I was too concerned with understanding what was happening to my body to experiment with faking illness through sweet eating, so I've just realised I still don't know if the Caramac trick actually works or if it's playground rumour of mythical proportions.

The children who moved with me from primary school to high school all eventually stopped speaking to me. It was as if the miscomprehension of my condition by the education system filtered down to my classmates. It wasn't bullying as such – well, it didn't feel like bullying – but by the fifth year of high school, I was just collectively ignored. I was invisible to everyone in school, so I vanished them in return. It was the easiest trick I knew. I was already used to the silence and comfort of my own company.

The next collection to be unearthed from the boxes is a complete set of *Discovery* magazines. Published in fortnightly instalments, *Discovery* covered everything from Elizabeth I to Martin Luther King, but jumped backwards and forwards through time to include Cleopatra, the Aztecs and Louis Pasteur among its highlights of history in sixty issues. My mum and dad saw it as an expensive but useful replacement for lack of world history in my home tutoring. I saw it as something to look forward to every two weeks. For me, it was more than just a magazine. When *Discovery* day arrived, I savoured every moment. 'Travel back in time and bring the past to life' was the tag line. Even now, just smelling the ink of the pages brings back that same excitement. The folder of every issue also contained facsimile documents from history – a copy of Samuel Pepys' diary, important letters, early maps – but I was most excited about the models, elaborate and fiddly cardboard constructions that had to be painstakingly cut out and glued together. They included Shakespeare's Globe theatre, a Da Vinci flying machine and a fifteenth-century siege tower. It was the perfect thing for a bored and lonely child. I'd make slow progress, cutting and gluing a section when I was well enough, and usually by the end of the fourteen days between issues each model would be complete. My knowledge of history is vague, but my cutting-out skills are second to none.

I put world history away and carry on exploring my own.

Carefully wrapped in the next box are the first magic tricks I bought from a real magic shop. I'd had magic sets, plastic and card-board tricks that looked like the toys they were, but these were props designed for professionals. There was no magic shop in North Wales, and in the days before the internet, buying magic meant the wonder and joy of stamped addressed envelopes, postal orders, credit notes and catalogues. Magic was another world with its own language and secrets. I spent hours poring over catalogues from mysterious shops, with descriptions that sounded like miracles, illustrated by line drawings that bristled with exclamation marks and 'surprise lines'.

They were fantasies for a small boy, fantasies that could become a reality if I just saved my pocket money. Throughout the time I spent alone during my illness, I wanted magic in my life more than anything. I loved magic, and I still do, but for different reasons. As a child, magic was a way outside of myself, a bridge to other people. Now I'm older and more experienced, I understand that magic should be the opposite – a way to draw other people outside of themselves, to experience a rare moment of childlike wonder where the normal rules of reality don't apply.

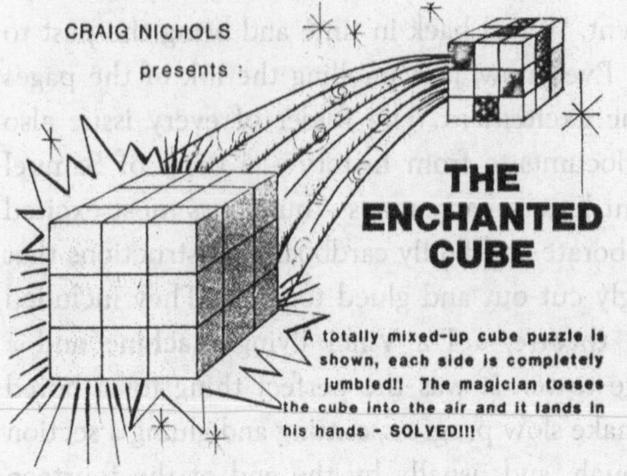

A Supreme British Exclusive!

Supreme Magic are happy and proud to have secured the Exclusive British Rights on what surely must be considered the greatest Cube trick of all time!

A thoroughly mixed-up cube puzzle is shown, each side is completely jumbled, - sure it can be given to a spectator to examine.

Further efforts to unscramble it only succeeds in jumbling it even more.
Magician simply takes the cube, TOSSES IT INTO THE AIR and it lands in his hands ... SOLVED!

you've ever seen. You'll enjoy presenting and mystifying with this.

The Enchanted Cube, complete with printed, illustrated routine. Price, £6.50, (U.S.A. $15.00).

IAN ADAIR–

Ian Adair has thought up many a book test and has had quite a few published in the pages of the New Pentagram magazine. This brainwave of his is NEW and is REVEALED for the first time. Just imagine this:
You could go into the biggest library of books in the world and ask someone to simply take one off the shelf for the experiment. Needless to say that half a dozen books displayed on stage would still be a nice selection. Use ANY BORROWED BOOK, any size, any number of pages. Ask someone to open the book at ANY PAGE, and remember the top words or bottom words of that page, and then to mark the place with a playing card acting as a bookmark, so the choice cannot be changed. The bookmark is casually removed and the pages are flicked through - IMMEDIATELY the performer is able to reel off the words remembered by the spectator.

Don't be misled by the low, low, price.

Price, £3.50, (U.S.A. $6.00

SKELETON IN THE CUPBOARD

Everybody has a skeleton in their cupboard - but mark our words, this skeleton won't remain in your cupboard for very long, it's an entertaining, amusing and mystifying effect that you can and will use and which will take its place amongst the winners!
A tube, 11" high, decorated to look like a cupboard - the cupboard of a **Haunted House** - is lifted to show a **skeleton** figure painted on three blocks. The skeleton is replaced correctly in the tube - **but** in some eerie and mysterious manner the blocks re-arrange themselves, they get "scrambled" and when the tube is lifted, there is the skeleton, "with his head tucked underneath his arm"!!
The fun waxes fast and furious, for this can be repeated again and again. Finally, the head is taken away altogether and "hidden" underneath a handkerchief. A flick and the block has **vanished** to appear in its place, back on the skeleton, in its proper order at last!
We supply everything complete, ready to work right away.
Now made better than ever, complete with cloth and everything you need.

Price, £25.00, U.S.A. $50.00.

No matter what type of act you do, THE END WAND is a perfect finish. Do it close-up, on platform or stage.
A transformation effect with the wand that you have been using all through your act. You hold the wand in full view and, while making your closing remarks the transformation takes place into a banner with a picture of a skeleton and the words "THE END".
The skeleton and wording are white against a black background making a striking picture.

Entirely self-contained. No refills necessary. Good for either patter or silent act. For "patter merchants" we include a good novelty presentation in the form of a neat little monologue. The transformation takes place on the last line and makes a wonderful surprise finish. Wand is black with white tips.

Price, £7.50, (U.S.A. $18.00).

BEND A 10p COIN

A REGULAR 10p. PIECE, yet taking it between the hands it suddenly becomes FLEXIBLE. You bend it this way and that, straightening it out once again!
DO IT ONCE MORE? You do, BUT this time you leave the 10p. piece for them to examine, BENT!

One of those quick little 'asides' that you'll enjoy performing. Great when used with your more profound mysteries, but it's a good 'talking point' any time.
Watch them try to straighten it out!

Price, £2.50, (U.S.A. $5.00).

The shop I most looked forward to visiting on my childhood holidays at my Auntie Avril's is still hidden in the unlikely depths of Charing Cross underground station, in the maze of exits and subways that sprawl under The Strand and St Martin-in-the-Fields. Opening the door of Davenports you enter into a dark, red-carpeted room, glass cases lining the walls on three sides, a long glass-topped counter on the other. It's like a set from a David Lynch film, or a museum of novelty curated by someone with deep reverence for fake dog poo and whoopee cushions. It was here I bought my first real magic tricks: Candle Through Arm, Zombie Ball, The Gungho Box. Real and solid, and made of wood and metal, they were a world away from the flimsy constructions of the magic sets I'd had up until then.

The tricks I bought from Davenports I used for a silent act I performed at old people's homes at Christmas the year I was well enough to return to school. In the box before me is that act – the feather flowers, a collapsible top-hat, glitter-covered wooden boxes with secret compartments and, buried under it all, an old VHS cassette. The label, carefully written in blue fountain pen, in handwriting that is unmistakably mine, reads: Nathan Penlington, magician (Age 13).

I'd forgotten this tape even existed. Luckily, despite having Sky+ and a touch-screen computer, my parents still have one toe in the 1980s. I take the video out of the box and carefully insert it into their VHS player. There is a tense moment as the machine makes an enormous clunking and whirring sound, a celebration of when technology told you it was doing something, and then the dreaded sound of the automatic rewind. It starts slowly, and as it speeds up we all cross our fingers in the hope that the tape doesn't get chewed up. The noise stops suddenly. There is a silence for a moment, which is when my dad always assumes something is broken. Then the TV produces two static lines that waver and quiver. An image appears on the screen. It wobbles slightly. The stage is set with a large box-like table that has the words 'It's Magic' written on it in red prismatic material. The top of the table is covered with a jumble of props: a stand holding three black records, a candle, a tube decorated in the same material as the front of the table, and a black cloth covering a mysterious object. The music starts and . . . it is me. A 13-year-old me, wearing black trousers, a white shirt, paisley tie and glasses that have finally become fashionable twenty years later. I burst in from the left, holding four small metal rings. I throw one into the air and catch it and start waving the others around in time to the music.

It is excruciating.

I force myself to watch the video all the way through – cards and flowers are produced from a hat; a candle vanishes and re-appears before it penetrates my arm, still lit; the records change colour to red, yellow and blue; the mysterious object under the black cloth is revealed to be a silver ball, which floats and levitates seemingly out of my control. It's all performed to a self-constructed soundtrack consisting of elements of the *Top of the Pops* theme, Jeff Wayne's musical version of *War of the Worlds*, and Richard Strauss's *Also Sprach Zarathustra*, which was the theme from *2001: A Space Odyssey* – a musical mash-up that was years ahead of its time.

I was performer, producer, choreographer, director and sound engineer of this video, but the performance must have been a practice session because there is no audience. Either that or no one wanted to come to watch. Despite that, it seems I am too shy to look at the camera even once. I'd clearly spent a lot of time rehearsing in front of a mirror, my bedroom-choreographed hand gestures are a testament to that, but I'd not had the opportunity to rehearse with a real audience.

Watching the video is an odd out-of-body experience. The boy in it is clearly me but also not me. Perhaps this is the way Terence will feel about his diary? I was once this kid, but I can't even begin to imagine how I really felt at that time. Was I proud of this performance? Embarrassed? Critical? How would I feel if a stranger had found this tape, knocked on my door one Saturday night and wanted to talk about it?

I eject the cassette and pick up the video box – it rattles. It seems I missed something when I took the video out of the case. Crumpled at the bottom of the box are two small folded squares of paper covered with a biro scrawl, also unmistakably my 13-year-old handwriting. The pages contain a list of things to improve about my act. These tiny pieces of paper take me completely by surprise. When I began looking for clues to why I'm so drawn to Terence's story, I never expected to find such an oddly striking similarity between us.

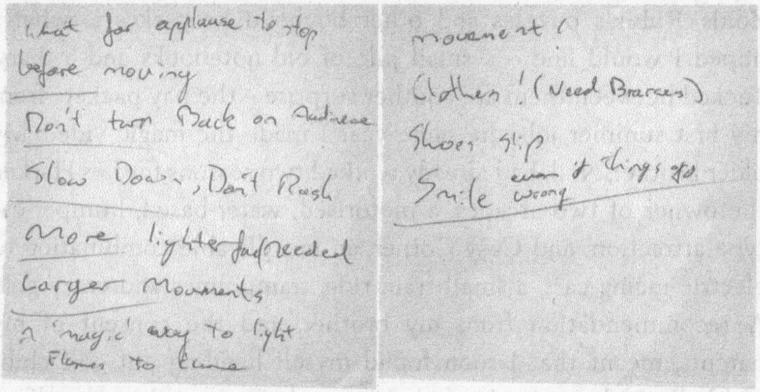

I know my handwriting is terrible, so if you can't read the scrawl, this is what it says:

Wait for applause to stop before moving
Don't turn back on audience
Slow down, don't rush
More lighter fuel needed
Larger movements
A 'magic' way to light flames to cane
Movement!
Clothes! (Need braces)
Shoes slip
Smile even if things go wrong

It sounds odd to say, but I sympathise with the boy who wrote this list. However, unlike Terence's list of things to improve, these things were in my control, abstractions that I could work on. Looking back, my focus on magic wasn't just about overcoming my shyness, although that certainly was a huge part of it; it was also about control, fantasy, distraction and escape – all of those things I needed to help me get through my illness, and a love of those elements has become a huge part of my personality as an adult.

I rip open the next box. Among the bits of Transformers, broken Zoids, Rubik's puzzles and other boyhood keepsakes is what I hoped I would find – a small pile of old notebooks and a diary. Tucked between them are another surprise – the pay packets from my first summer job, the same year I made the magic video. My older brother, Neil, had already worked two seasons for Les Harker, the owner of two arcades, a motorised, water-based, bumper-car type attraction, and Cosy Corner, an inexplicable combination of electric racing cars, a small train ride, trampolines and crazy golf. A recommendation from my brother, and the consent of my parents, meant that I soon found myself handing out golf clubs and balls, and monitoring kids not much younger than myself on the trampolines.

Each of the small brown envelopes has my name written across the top, and below the hours worked and the total wages for that week. The top envelope shows that one week I worked twenty and a half hours for a total of £13.35 – that's 65p per hour. An hour's work wouldn't even buy you an ice cream or a can of cherry coke from the stall near the arcade.

As interesting as the old pay packets might be, in my hands I have an old diary. I flick through the pages, but unfortunately, unlike Terence's diary, my entries rarely rise above the mundane.

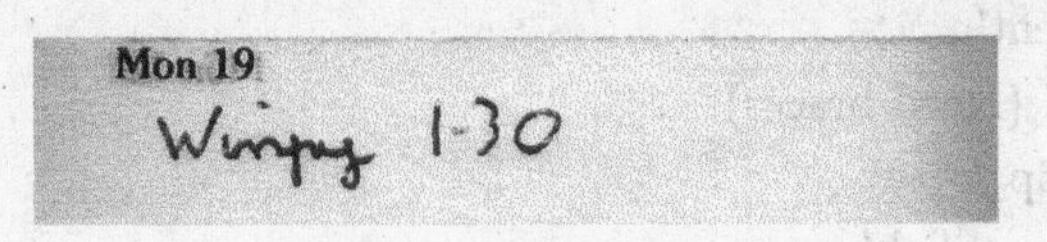
Mon 19
Wimpy 1·30

At the front is a list of my end-of-third-year exam results:

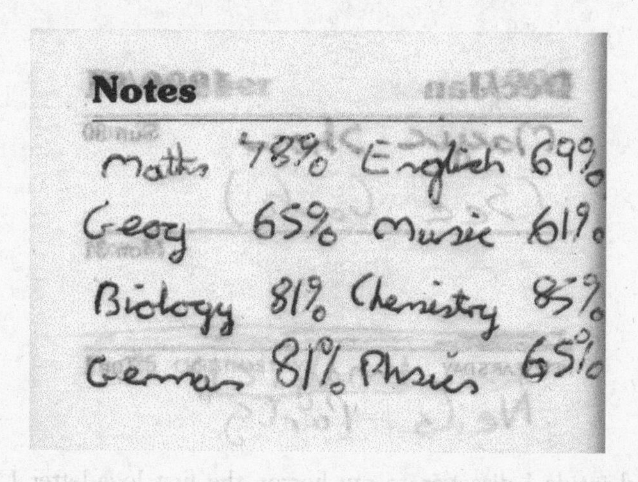

Notes

Maths 78% English 69%
Geog 65% Music 61%
Biology 81% Chemistry 85%
German 81% Phsics 65%

A set of results that aren't too bad, taking into consideration I'd spent two and a half years in and out of school, fairly low in half the subjects but surprisingly high in the sciences. To make it into the diary they must have been a proud achievement, or perhaps something I was concerned about. July and August list the work hours of my summer job, replaced later in the year by the times of hospital visits.

But on 19 December 1989 is a tantalising sentence that memorialises the stuff dreams are made of.

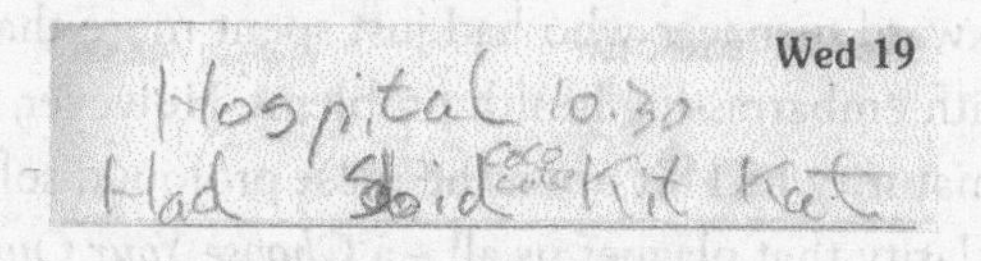

Wed 19
Hospital 10.30
Had Solid Kit Kat

I can feel your jealousy for the waferless KitKat from here.

I'd hoped for more, something that illustrated how I actually felt at the time. I'm about to start packing everything away, when I notice a plastic pocket at the back of the diary. Slipped into it is a piece of lined paper folded in half. On the front is written:

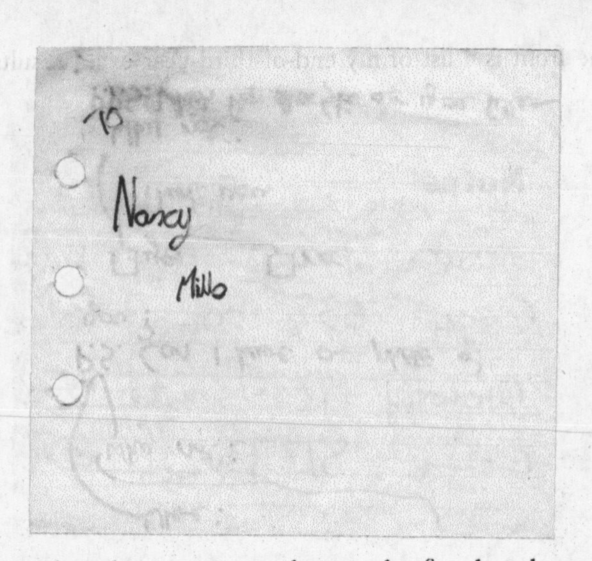
To

Nancy

Mills

And inside I discover, to my horror, the first love-letter I never sent.

I remember Nancy Mills as being best girl in school. She wasn't the most popular – in fact, she was shy and awkward – but she was funny and genuine. We were teenagers. I mean, I had turned 13 a month before; 13 years and one month meant I wasn't a child any more. This relationship, if it was going to happen, couldn't involve the childish things of tea parties and paddling pools; this was going to be an adult relationship, which meant it had to be started in an adult way – that much I knew from watching *This Morning*.

But adult relationships are complicated and confusing, especially to a shy, awkward teenager who had just spent more than two years off school with embarrassing health problems. However, it seems my new-found maturity had hit upon the most profound solution to the problem of clarity that plagues us all – a *Choose Your Own Adventure* style multiple-option love-letter:

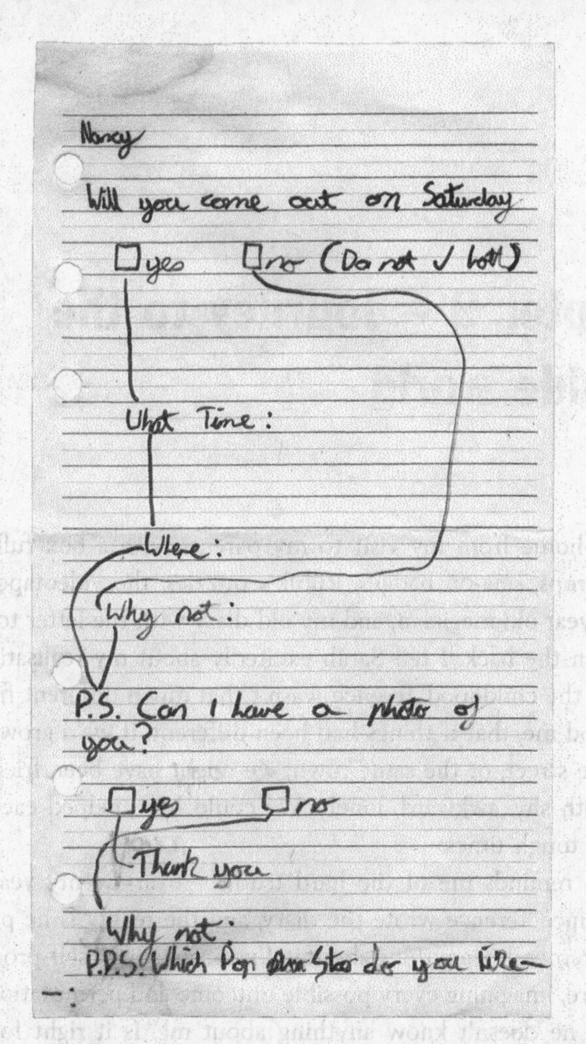

Nancy

Will you come out on Saturday

☐ yes ☐ no (Do not ✓ both)

What Time:

Where:

Why not:

P.S. Can I have a photo of you?

☐ yes ☐ no

Thank you

Why not:

P.P.S. Which Pop Star do you like —:

In the living room of my parents' house, an adult surrounded by the trinkets and treasures, souvenirs and scrawls of my own childhood, I think of the diary entries Terence cast out, a message-in-a-bottle, into the world. I look down again at the love-letter to Nancy. Then I break into a wide grin. Despite the emotion of trawling through my past, I can't help but laugh. The only redeeming thing about this love-letter is that I never sent it.

Chapter 9 – Journey to the outside world

I arrive home from my visit to my parents with a box full of old magic props, sew-on badges, Rubik's puzzles, the videotape of me as a 13-year-old magician, and my old diary with the letter to Nancy tucked in the back. I tell Sarah excitedly about my realisation that perhaps the childhood Terence wasn't that much different from the childhood me, that if things had been different, if we'd grown up in the same street, or the same town, we might have been friends. We were both shy, awkward, lonely. We could have helped each other through tough times.

Sarah reminds me of the hard truths – over twenty years have passed since Terence wrote the diary, and the reality is he probably doesn't remember anything about it. I've been living a self-proclaimed adventure, imagining every possible outcome and permutation of his life, but he doesn't know anything about me. Is it right for me, a complete stranger, to turn up on his doorstep and expect him to relive the emotional angst of his teenage years? I know why I want to find out, but why do I expect him to tell me? My mum was right when she said I want to know that Terence is OK, but is that all I really want from him?

Those are the thoughts turning over and over in the back of my mind as, day by day, the date of our meeting advances. At one point this moment seemed like a dream, a possibility of pure imagining, but after this interview there will be nothing left – no mystery, no unanswered questions and no quest. If I've been using Terence Prendergast as a way to direct my focus from my own existence, what will fill my life then?

There is one other avenue I should explore for advice. After another session of internet research I find child psychologist Dr Howard Fine – a man with a perfect name for his profession. Dr Fine has years of experience working with children with emotional and behavioural difficulties and their families. He also runs a company that helps rehabilitate children with brain injuries. Unfortunately, that means he is an extremely busy man. I try to explain my story over a quick telephone call, Dr Fine's confusion not helped by the constant interruption caused by the reception dropping in and out, and the fact I want to talk about the emotional problems of a child who exists only as fragments of an old diary. Even so, Dr Fine is intrigued enough to want to meet in person, but time isn't as flexible as it is in Edward Packard's stories and we're unable to squeeze in an appointment.

There is nothing else I can do. I've prepared for the interview with Terence as much as I can. Now I'm just going to have to hope the conversation comes naturally, and I'll instinctively know the right questions to ask. All I can do at this stage is buy some biscuits and some wine and see what happens.

I'm faced with a dizzying array of choice in the biscuit aisle of the nearest supermarket – new improved, retro limited edition, old-fashioned recipe, quality organic, gourmet luxury, extra crunchy, with milk, dark or white chocolate. Such a range of choices turns what should be an easy decision into a mind-numbing flowchart of complex possibility.

Studies have been done to assess how choice affects happiness. Common sense would say that more choice is good for us, freedom of choice makes us happier, a wider array means the more likely we are to find exactly the thing that suits us perfectly. But that isn't the case. The more alternatives we have to choose between, the more difficult the decision, which therefore takes more time and also results in us being less satisfied with our choice once we've made it. We can't help but compare our choice with the alternatives we didn't choose, becoming filled with regret at what could have been, and in the process reducing the pleasure we might have derived from our original choice.

This makes buying the right type of biscuit a huge problem. In addition, advertisers spend millions of pounds to try to ensure that different people take the 'meaning' of their product to be the same. In reality, it doesn't work. I want my biscuits to say friendly, fun, professional, trustworthy. To Terence the same biscuit might mean over-confident and old-fashioned, or they might remind Terence of someone he'd rather forget. He might also just not like biscuits.

The packets in front of me are seemingly arranged using a logic conceived by an algorithm designed specifically to make shoppers spend the most money. Without question, I immediately dismiss the rich tea and digestives. Even in the chocolate and caramel varieties they are too everyday, too normal. For the same reason I skip the Nice, Hobnobs, Bourbons and Custard Creams. I ignore anything with raisins or sultanas – not everyone likes eating dead grapes. I contemplate the nostalgia end of the biscuit spectrum, those glorious special occasions from our childhoods – Cadbury's fingers, Wagon Wheels, Tunnock's teacakes, animal crackers, jammie dodgers and party rings – but perhaps turning up with the equivalent of a five-year-old's birthday party would seem a little strange, like I'm forcing reminiscence. That leaves me with the middleground of cookies and shortbreads. As I hover indecisively around the shelves, flitting backwards and forwards, I attract the attention of the supermarket security guard, who is watching me carefully while he whispers into his walkie-talkie. Under this additional pressure I settle for the faux elegance of chocolate Viennese fingers.

The security guard follows me to the wine aisle. I don't feel comfortable contemplating the even more tangled semiotic ramifications of wine types under the steely gaze of the burly uniformed guard, so I grab the nearest bottle of red on special offer in a way that couldn't be less 'stealy', at arm's length and at finger tips. He follows me until I've paid and the sliding doors have closed behind me. Once outside I'm not convinced I've made the right choice.

I pull up outside the Prendergasts' house, parking where Fernando and I had carried out our stakeout on our last visit. The blue car is in the driveway, the one that Fernando and I followed around the backstreets. I wish I had someone to back me up this time, too, although I'm not as nervous as the first time I knocked on the door. Once you know the reality of a situation fear disappears. Now I'm nervous for a different reason – not because I don't know what is on the other side of the door, but because I do.

I'm not sure who is the most anxious as the door opens. This is the moment I'd obsessed over, the chance to speak to Terence Prendergast face to face in the house he grew up in. But obsession only prepares you for the *thought* of something, not the reality of it. He thinks I'm going to talk to him about *Choose Your Own Adventure*. He has no idea I have his diary. Even after the advice of everyone I've spoken to, especially Sarah, Dr Finkel and Ruth, I don't feel ready for this moment. I still have no idea about the best way to bring up the diary, and how to explain myself and the truth of this quest when I do. But it is too late for imagining alternative scenarios, reality is already unfolding around me. I'm here because of all the choices I've made in my entire life. In fact all of world history has conspired to make this moment happen, all possibility has narrowed to this point. That is a huge responsibility. We have that huge responsibility every moment of our lives.

In the hallway stands a man about my age, looking even more boyish than before, wearing blue-grey chinos, a white polo shirt under a maroon jumper, glasses. We simultaneously exchange clumsy hellos and fumble a handshake. I feel like the parody of a Mr Beanesque bumbling nerd.

'Hi,' says Terence.

I take a deep breath and pull myself together. 'Really good to meet you properly,' I say. Terence has no idea how much I mean it.

And, with one step, I am finally inside the house I have imagined hundreds of times, and hundreds of times I'd imagined it in different ways. In that tiny moment of walking through the door the flimsy constructs collapse with the weight of normality – the brown and beige tidiness of it. A heavily patterned carpet covers the hall floor and the stairs – stairs that lead inevitably to Terence's old bedroom, where he read and re-read *Trouble on Planet Earth* and felt the loneliness of regret. Loneliness created by regret is the worst kind of loneliness. His bedroom is where he ran to escape from the world, and where he tried to work through his problems.

Terence shows me into the front room, explaining that his mum and dad are out doing the shopping, so we can use the lounge. Babbling nervously about the traffic, the journey and the hire car being late, I scan the room looking for clues. Clues! In my mind I call them clues, but clues for what? I slap myself hard in my love of TV detectives and tell myself to calm down. I'm here. I'm finally here in the Prendergasts' lounge. I don't need clues. I just need to find out the truth and to do that I need to be honest.

The lounge is neat and unremarkable. A large, brown leather sofa fills the wall nearest the door and in the bay window opposite are two matching armchairs. At one end of the room is an imitation coal fire and at the other a small upright piano. I can't help noticing that all of the pot plants in the room have their own lace mats, and that among the row of framed photographs that stand on top of the piano is a graduation photo. Posed with customary awkwardness is someone who is clearly a slightly younger Terence wearing a mortarboard and holding a scroll. With him are his mum, dad, and a girl of about the same age.

I give Terence the bottle of Black Tower wine and the packet of chocolate Viennese biscuits. 'Thanks,' he says quietly, barely glancing at them before placing them on a small side table near the door.

I take a seat in one of the two leather armchairs in the bay window. Terence takes the other.

'Do you mind if I record our conversation?' I ask.

'No, not at all, go ahead.'

I set my phone to record, and place it on the coffee table. Now I'll have every moment of this conversation recorded for posterity. Terence is waiting for me to say something to explain myself, but now I'm here I don't know how to start the conversation. I'm still confused about what to call him after corresponding with someone whose email is james1415, and who hasn't signed off his emails with any name – either Terence or James.

'What do you prefer to be called?' I ask.

Terence looks at me shyly. 'Terry,' he says.

'Right, Terry,' I echo. He must think I'm acting oddly, or hopefully he might put it down to nerves. At that moment there is the sound of a key in the front door.

'Hellooo,' shouts a woman from the hallway.

'It's my mum and dad,' says Terry a little apologetically. 'They're supposed to be out doing the shopping.'

Terry's mum pops her head around the door. 'Sorry we're home early, we had to come back with the frozen food . . .' she says.

Terry's dad struggles past her with carrier bags from Morrisons. 'Don't worry, we'll sit in the back room,' he says.

'That's embarrassing, sorry,' Terry says.

'No, it's fine. We haven't really started anyway.'

'As I said . . .' I begin to say as Terence's mum knocks on the open door of the lounge.

'You've come a long way,' she begins. 'Would you like a cup of tea or something to eat before you start? I could do some sandwiches.'

We both reply with, 'No, thank you.'

'I'll do a pot of tea then,' she says going back through to the kitchen.

I try again. 'Like I said in my email, I'm a huge fan of *Choose Your Own Adventure* books, and I've been on a kind of adventure of my own,' I say, thinking of how nervous I was on the day I first knocked on the door of this very house, about the path linking Johnny Doom, Roj, Dr Finkel and Ruth, about trawling through my own past.

Terry nods.

'I've been a fan of the books since I was eight,' I continue. 'Weetabix had a promotion to give away *The Horror of High Ridge* and *Mountain Survival* if you collected enough tokens.' I'm hoping Terry was a Weetabix boy, too. 'Do you remember – it was around 1984 or so?'

'No, I don't, sorry,' he answers flatly.

'Do you remember when you read your first *Choose Your Own Adventure*?' I ask.

'I was nine,' Terry replies. 'I think,' he adds with the minimum of conversational elaboration. If I had imagined this meeting was suddenly going to blossom into friendship, I was wrong.

I try again. 'Where did you buy the books from?'

'I can't remember which one I bought first, but I got them anywhere, anywhere I went. On day trips, or whatever. When I was a kid, I was so obsessed with them I'd automatically look for them in WH Smiths and just buy one. Most of them are from Birmingham.' It's clear that talking about the books is making Terry a little more relaxed. 'I read them every night,' he says, 'each one over and over again, turning down the corners of the pages so that if I was killed, I could go back and try something else.'

Terry's mum knocks on the door again, this time using her foot. Her hands are full carrying a tray with a pot of tea, and a large plate of ham sandwiches, halves of pork pie, and quartered tomatoes. 'If you've come from London you should have something to eat . . .'

I respond with a polite, 'Thank you.'

'You're very welcome,' she says, closing the door behind her, finally leaving us to talk in private.

There is another awkward silence as we both stare at the plate for a few seconds, as if it's an object neither of us wants to touch.

'That's a lot of meat,' I say, trying to break the tension. I pick up the plate and offer Terry a ham sandwich.

Terry shakes his head and says, 'I don't eat my mum's food.'

I grin, 'Me neither.'

I would normally refuse a ham sandwich, too. I don't eat pork in any form, not for religious reasons, I just don't like it, but as Terry isn't eating I feel I should eat something out of excruciating politeness, so I take one – a small triangle of brown bread containing nothing but two layers of ham.

'She's got a bit better, but my mum used to be a terrible cook,' I say. 'Before I went to university she taught me how to cook basic things like stews, roasts, cottage pie. Her instructions for cottage pie were to boil the minced beef in a pan of water the day before you want to eat it. Then wait for it to go cold and skim the fat from the top. Crazy. I was in the halls of residence cooking like it was the forties and everything was rationed. My flatmates used to complain about the smell. It used to hang around for days. That kind of cooking can lose you a lot of friends very quickly. Luckily, I discovered you could fry mince in ten minutes.'

Terry laughs nervously. I take a bit of sandwich and chew slowly to stop myself from filling in the silence with more embarrassing anecdotes, and while I struggle to swallow, I ask another question.

'Why were you obsessed with the books?'

Terry shifts a bit in his seat, and starts a sentence that's broken by a quiver in his voice. 'They . . .' Terry's nerves have returned. I tell him to relax, we can take as many breaks as we need to. He pauses for a moment before starting again.

'They were exciting,' he says, 'a journey to the outside world. At the time I preferred the fantasy ones because I wanted to escape. Most people played in the street or watched TV after school. I just wanted to get out of Birmingham.' As he speaks, the boy behind the man becomes clearer. Despite the nerves, he is funny, intelligent – and awkward. I think of the diary entry about stealing money from his parents and running away to Scotland. Did he really go? Or was his escape just restricted to escapism?

Terry continues, 'No one else in my school read *Choose Your Own Adventure*, as far as I knew. I kept reading a secret because I worried the other kids would think I was a little strange and just walk off.'

My heart breaks a little at the thought of someone keeping reading a secret in case another kid just walks off; it's so tiny in its significance. But as we talk it turns out he did share the secret with someone else.

'When I was ten, I wrote to Bantam Books in America,' he tells me. 'My letter just said how I was really interested in *Choose Your Own Adventure* books. I even took a photo of my collection to send them. I don't know why, just because I was ten I suppose.'

Terry continues, 'I thought Bantam Books would come and visit me in Birmingham, but of course they didn't. They sent back a standard reply that said, "Thank you for your letter, yours sincerely," and that was it,' he says sadly.

In the front of every book was a set of quotes written by children who loved *Choose Your Own Adventure*, for example: 'It's great fun! I like the idea of making my own decisions' – Anthony Ziccardi, age 11. My favourite was: '*Choose Your Own Adventure* is the best thing that has come along since books themselves' – by the always understated Alysha Beyer, age 11. Perhaps all Terry hoped to achieve was to see his name alongside those of the other children: 'I love these books' – Terence Prendergast, age 10. It seems that, in Terry's eyes, the rejection was like another kid just walking off.

The conversation fades to silence again. I've touched on something sensitive, and I need to proceed with care. I try to change the subject for a while, a tentative questioning for common ground.

'What kind of music do you like? Were you into music as a kid?' I ask.

'As I kid I liked Duran Duran and the Thompson Twins, things that were in the charts. Now I listen to jazz, like Miles Davis. I also listen to a lot of elevator music, Mantovani and James Last, because it's relaxing.'

I've *never* heard anyone name elevator music as a genre of music they liked. It's more of a niche than the work of PRENDERGAST, whose songs I've been listening to in the car. I look over at the piano.

'Do you play any instruments?' I ask Terry.

'No, I couldn't get the hang of it. I tried the piano and the guitar. I just couldn't do it.'

'Me neither. I really, really like music, but I can't ever imagine myself playing it.'

This is turning very quickly into an extremely awkward conversation between two very nervous men. I know what the problem is – the diary is spreading its shadow over every question. Even if Terry can't put his finger on the problem exactly, the whole set-up must seem strange. He must be wondering what I actually want from him.

I ask Terry if we can take a short break. I need a moment to get myself together and think through my next series of questions. So far the questions are leading nowhere. It feels like the diary has become the planet Ultima, the illusory utopia of Edward Packard's book *Inside UFO 54-40*. In the story, your aim is to reach the planet of paradise, but it's cut off from the usual logic of *Choose Your Own Adventure*. You can reach it only by breaking the rules, by not following the directions laid out before you. But like Ultima exists, the diary exists. I just have to find the right way to reach it.

'The bathroom is through the kitchen, at the back of the garage,' Terry explains. 'You need to use the sink in the kitchen to wash your hands. The toilet only has cold water.'

The layout of the house isn't very different from my old house in Rhyl, another small semi-detached of a similar period, and I find my way around easily. I wonder if I could pretend I've got lost, sneak upstairs and take a look at Terry's old bedroom. How would I explain myself if I got caught?

I slide the lock of the toilet closed behind me, lean my back against the door. The palms of my hands have become cold with sweat. The words of advice from everyone I've spoken to are whirling around my brain in a conflicting chorus.

'Sometimes the past should stay in the past,' Sarah says, as Ruth interrupts in her bright, public-speaking voice, 'We are – all of us – what we are is what happened to us during our lifetime as a child.' Dr Finkel leans forward in his creaking office chair, stroking his beard. 'The diary is a construction that has nothing to do with his real life at all.' His brows suddenly knit together in thought. 'What the fuck *do* you want?'

I run the cold tap, splash water in my face and stare at myself in the mirror. 'Relax,' I say to my dripping reflection. I dry my face, take a deep breath and walk back through to the lounge. By the time I sit back down in the armchair I'm still wondering how to take the conversation forward. I'll be honest, it hasn't been the best start, more hesitant and uncomfortable than I ever imagined our meeting would be. Only I know the real reason for that – the diary.

'Are you OK?' Terry asks. 'You look a bit pale.'

'Yes, I'm fine,' I answer. 'I'm just a bit tired. I haven't really been sleeping very well recently.' I try to start the conversation again. 'I used to read a lot as a child, too. As a way of escape really,' I say, pouring myself some more tea. 'My favourite *Choose Your Own Adventure* was number twenty-one, *Hyperspace,* because you got to travel to the fifth dimension and actually meet Edward Packard inside his own book. I used to think that was the most amazing thing. In fact, I still do.'

'My favourite was *Sugarcane Island,* because it was just about a nice peaceful island in the tropical regions that existed only in my imagination in those days,' Terry says.

Sugarcane Island is a great book. It's about going on an expedition to study rare turtles but ending up shipwrecked on an isolated and deserted island. It's number 62 in the *Choose Your Own Adventure* series, but it was actually the first book that Edward Packard wrote back in 1968 while telling bedtime stories to his children. The book remained unpublished for nearly ten years.

I see *Sugarcane Island* as a book about overcoming misfortune and having faith in your abilities. Terry's reason for liking the book seems to be his constant desire for escape, for solitude, for calm. But maybe leaving the diary in *The Cave of Time* was Terry sending a message-in-a-bottle from that island?

'I also liked the one about the Maya,' Terry continues, becoming animated, 'because we didn't learn about things like that in school. We only learnt about European history. No one in my school had heard about the Maya. I suddenly found out about them and that was exciting. I also remember one about being a spy, in the Cold War. I remember one of the endings said something like, "Somebody shoots you, and he can't really expect to make a shot like that but he makes it. The end." I remember thinking that was quite funny.'

I laugh. It feels like our conversation is back on track.

'I have a few favourite deaths,' I tell Terry, 'but I really love the one in *The Race Forever* where you're taking part in an African road rally. Your lights go out as you make a right-hand turn, your experience as a driver means you still manage to keep the car on the road, then it says, "But no experience in the world will help get that elephant out of the way." You crash into the elephant, not only causing your death, but starting a grassland fire that kills hundreds of animals.'

It's Terry's turn to laugh. 'I was so obsessed,' he says. 'I had over a hundred of them before I gave up reading them, because I thought they were running out of ideas.'

'Did you read any of the *Fighting Fantasy* books?' I ask.

'Yeah, a few, when I was a bit older, in secondary school. But I preferred the original *Choose Your Own Adventure* ones because they weren't all about elves and pixies and things like that.'

It's a damning assessment of the core of the Wayland's Forge gaming community.

'I never really got the *Fighting Fantasy* ones either,' I admit to Terry. 'All that fighting of orcs and rolling dice I find really tedious.' I think back to that summer holiday in Rhyl when I first read *The*

Warlock of Firetop Mountain, and how exciting playing a book seemed, but also how anything would have been a welcome distraction from the constant rain and biting wind blowing in from the Irish Sea, anything that is except yet another visit to Rhyl lifeboat centre.

'I was more into the books set in space and based on history. *Underground Kingdom* was as far as I'd go into the fantasy genre.'

This is my chance. I'm still hoping that the man sat before me is the prop-maker responsible for *Journey to the Centre of the Earth* and *On the Beach*. The fact he's moved back to Birmingham would perhaps explain why his list of film credits is so short. It might freak Terry out to know I've watched his films, but it's definitely a topic of conversation that will open doors to the diary. I take yet another deep breath.

'I'm a big fan of Jules Verne,' I say. 'I think a lot of the ideas for *Choose Your Own Adventure* come from the early sci-fi writers like Jules Verne, H.G. Wells, people like that. Have you ever read any Jules Verne?' I ask.

'No, no, I haven't read any. He's not really for me,' Terry answers solemnly, without a flicker of recognition.

I feel crushed. I was convinced this Terence Prendergast and the prop-maker Terence Prendergast were the same person. Not only had I been following another false trail, but now I need to work towards another conversational opening.

'Did you read any other authors who weren't *Choose Your Own Adventure*? Do you remember any other books you were reading around that time?'

'Encyclopaedias for some reason. I was trying to improve myself so I used to read encyclopaedias. But I'd only get as far as the first few pages . . .' Terry laughs, shaking his head.

'So, you've got a really good knowledge of aardvarks.'

'And abacus,' he adds.

We're getting on well, but it seems we're circling around the diary, never really getting any closer. Every time I promise myself I will mention it with the next question Terry says something that stops that line of conversation cold, or reminds me of what he had written in his diary and I shy away from continuing. Now I imagine Terry as the teenaged boy who has not only written a list of things to improve about himself, but a boy who also keeps reading a secret, sitting upstairs in his room after school, working his way through a set of encyclopaedias in the hope that knowledge and education would be a shortcut out of there.

I know we are talking about something we both obsessed over as children, but outside of that focus, Terry seems ordinarily to filter everything through his past. I've got no sense of how he sees the future, and how you imagine your future is a measure of your present. I have a small idea about who Terry was in his past, but an even smaller one about who Terry is now.

'If your life was a *Choose Your Own Adventure*, where would you go next?' I ask. 'If nothing was out of bounds, anything was possible . . .'

Terry looks down at his hands for a moment. What am I thinking? Have I gone too far? He thinks I'm here to interview him about his childhood passion, but now I'm asking an understandably nervous and anxious man strange, abstract, philosophical questions. It's a question I'd find difficult to answer. I wouldn't blame him if he asked me to pack up and leave immediately.

Terry looks up again before speaking. 'I'd like to go to a monastery, not for religious reasons, just to hide for a bit, and take stock of my life. Retreat somewhere, make a plan and play it safe. But that's not *Choose Your Own Adventure* is it?'

I think for a moment. 'Life is about making decisions you think are right, whether other people agree with them or not. That's definitely also a key part of adventure. Those decisions don't necessarily have to be risks.'

'I think I'd rather play it safe and explore the world through my own mind, spiritually or philosophically, and try to find some meaning to this vast world. I think security gives you time out to think about adventures and consequences of things. I think you should get your own house in order and then take risks.'

Terry is right. To make the best decisions, important decisions that can affect your whole life – whether to buy a house or travel the world, whether to study or look for a new job, whether to settle down and start a family – you first need the security to be able to buy the time to consider all options equally, time to weigh the pros and cons of each possible choice. Without security, you risk the possibility of making one rash choice after another, while you chase short-term needs and fulfilment. I can't help but read myself into Terry's statement – is he saying I need to look at my own life before I take the risk of talking about someone else's? Is my obsession distracting me from making those huge, grown-up decisions?

There is another awkward pause. But this time it's Terry who breaks the silence, and snaps me out of my self-questioning. 'Have you re-bought all the *Choose Your Own Adventure* books?' he asks.

Terry hasn't expressed surprise at me finding him or being here, and I've begun to think that he knows about the diary and has been waiting for me to confront him with it. 'Well . . .' I begin nervously, 'I bought the first hundred and six from eBay a few years ago. Did you sell yours?'

'Yeah, but I can't remember who to because I think I sold them all to different people,' he says.

I can't tell if he's lying, trying to provoke the truth from me, or genuinely can't remember. If he really can't remember selling them, then I really have been building this moment up from nothing. But if he is lying and I am lying, then . . . my head begins to spin.

'But did you sell most of them as one lot?' I ask, my hands are trembling slightly.

'I . . . I can't remember,' Terry says again.

Here it is. My heart is pounding. I can feel the blood pulsing in my ears again. I summon the courage.

'I bought the first hundred and six from eBay, in one auction. They all belonged to . . . to you . . .' I say, the words tumbling from my mouth in a stream.

A guardedness has appeared on Terence's face now. Something ghosts across it that I can't quite see.

'Really?' he says with a nervous half laugh. 'I hope I didn't rip you off . . .'

And with those seven words there is suddenly no mystery. '*I* hope *I* didn't rip you off.' I now know for certain Terry sold the books himself on eBay under a different name.

I can't help but grin. Maybe the mysteries of the diary will be this easy to solve, too. Perhaps Irving Finkel was right and the diary is just the fantasy of a young boy playing out his imagination.

'No, you definitely didn't rip me off. I paid forty one pounds and a penny,' I say, laughing. 'I was thrilled to have won the auction because I had already collected a lot of *Choose Your Own Adventure* but I wasn't even close to owning a complete set . . .'

'The postage must have been a lot,' Terry says, pragmatically.

'Eleven pounds. It was worth every penny, though!' I can't help but think what would have happened if I hadn't won the bid. I wouldn't be on this adventure. I wouldn't have found the video of me performing magic, or that embarrassing love-letter. I wouldn't be here now. All of that really has been worth the price I paid for the books. 'Do you still sell a lot of stuff on eBay?' I ask.

'No, not at all,' Terry says. He pauses, clearly distracted by something for a moment.

'So, why did you sell all the books?'

Terry shifts in his seat, looks down at his hands again, becomes silent. I wait for him to reply, letting the silence grow more awkward with every tick of the clock on the mantelpiece. I can't help but feel like I'm a school bully, perhaps the kind with which Terry used to contend, pinning him down in the playground with the sole of my shoe, refusing to let him stand until he's answered. I know I need to take responsibility but maybe obsession is the bully of us both.

'Because I'd grown up, and the stress of life meant that I couldn't, didn't have the time to read old books again really. I just wanted to get rid of everything from my childhood. I sold toys and everything as well.' He repeats the words again, his voice almost quivering. 'Everything from my childhood . . .'

I stop dead. Any questions I have left to ask Terry have died on my tongue.

What am I doing here? I've got no right to be here, in this lounge, with this man who sold his childhood because he wanted to get rid of it. I've got no right to bring it back to him by surprising him with his teenage diary.

All of the lies I've been telling myself have suddenly been exposed – and Terence doesn't even know it. Had I really thought that meeting Terry would be a conversation about *Choose Your Own Adventure* books, about the past, how things used to be and how things have changed? That we'd be able to talk openly about the diary, about how bullying, illness or despair can seriously affect your life, but that you can overcome it? That this would be a story of triumph over adversity? And more importantly, we'd be able to laugh together in the face of that adversity? Did I really think that we'd become buddies, avoiding the pratfalls of life together?

In that second, the guilt I feel is overpowering. I have turned Terence Prendergast into my own story. I have tried to commandeer him without ever knowing a single thing about the real boy behind the books. I feel foolish for my naivety. It doesn't matter what choices I've made on this adventure, who I've spoken to, what I've found out – Terence has made his own choices and I can't remake them for him. If he sold his books to bury his childhood, what kind of a man would it make me to dredge it all back up, just to satisfy my own curiosity and obsession? Sarah was right, sometimes the past should stay in the past.

I gather my things and start to say my goodbyes. I thank Terry for his time and thank his mum for the sandwiches. As I button up my jacket my eyes linger on the photographs on the top of the piano. I can't help but ask Terry just one more question. I promise myself this really will be the last.

'Is that you graduating . . .' I say, pointing at the photograph.

'Yeah, it must have been 1998. I was a bit fatter then,' Terry replies, apologetically.

'Who's the girl with you?' I ask.

'That,' Terry says, as if stating the obvious, 'is my sister, Karen.'

Chapter 10 – Found and lost

Karen.

Karen is the girl mentioned in the diary.

The hint of knowing that I've solved one mystery – that Karen is Terence's sister – is enough to kick my obsession with the diary into mania.

I know that not mentioning the diary to Terry was the right decision, but it's not the best decision for me. I've missed my chance to talk about the diary because I was too scared to bring it up, and I was too scared because I didn't know how he would react. And now I'm torn between realising I should let go of the diary and desperately needing to know more, torn between *imagining* what is the right thing to do and *knowing* what is the right thing to do.

But what about Coulson? What about Kenny? I'll never find out who those bullies were. I'll never know what 'back of knee' actually refers to, or if he really did run away to Scotland on an airplane and fly back to Birmingham the next day.

I spend the drive back home, and the rest of the weekend, mulling it over. Just as I was forcing myself to admit my obsession with Terry's childhood verged on the unhealthy, and was literally and actually saying goodbye, my compulsion to find out the truth has been forced up a notch. And I'm helpless to do anything about it.

* * *

It is now Monday morning. Two days have passed since interviewing Terry at his parents' house, two long, agonising days in which I've done nothing but mope around the house, berating myself for not asking Terry better questions. I was so focused on maintaining the *Choose Your Own Adventure* book writing bluff I even forgot to ask any ordinary questions like 'Where do you live?' or 'What do you do for a living?' I've come away still knowing nothing about him.

I boot up my computer, and while I wait, start composing a thank-you email to Terry in my head, but when I open my inbox, it seems that he has actually beaten me to it.

Hi Nathan,

I just wanted to say how nice it was to meet you to talk about *Choose Your Own Adventure* books. It was good of you to come all this way.

During the interview, I kept repeating myself. I do this a lot, due to worrying about other things, and not being able to get my brain in gear! And I should have said more when you asked about my reading . . . but I suffered from spontaneous tongue-tied syndrome . . . 'Arnold Rimmer style'!

Oh and I have to ask, about those *Choose Your Own Adventure* books I sold you . . . did I write or scribble things in them? I have a feeling I used to do that with books I owned . . . I was a weird kid!!

I also forgot to ask about you when you mentioned Rhyl, why did you want to leave?

The sensation that hits me is a heady concoction: relief that I have not pushed Terry too far away, heartache that he still obsesses over worrying, but, most of all, a strange kind of triumph – it seems Terry really does remember writing in the books, and perhaps he sensed an ulterior motive for my wanting to meet him. So perhaps it won't be too difficult to ask him, one day, about the diary pages and everything that they contain. It seems, too, that Terry suffers from the same tongue-tied awkwardness as I do at times. He doesn't know it, but I was tongue-tied for most of our meeting. I don't know who or what Arnold Rimmer refers to, but a quick internet search reveals him to be a character in the late 1980s sci-fi sitcom *Red Dwarf*.

Wikipedia has a whole page devoted to the character's fictional background and personality, filled out, no doubt, by obsessive fans who have documented and cross-referenced every episode of all ten series. I skim-read, looking for specific mentions of speech difficulties, but while doing so, a darker similarity emerges. Wikipedia says that Arnold Rimmer 'suffered an unhappy childhood . . . was also bullied by other children at school . . . had a deep-seated sense of self-loathing . . . his personality flaws are in fact almost completely a result of his hang-ups'. In this oblique reference, is Terry hinting at his childhood and the kind of person he has become, or is it just me projecting the aspects I know about him onto anything that comes within range?

I show Sarah the email from Terry. Perhaps I consider it a kind of vindication of all I have been doing these last few months. It's a good sign, I explain, that Terence is asking me questions, especially questions that are personal and revealing – the more honest I am about my past, the easier it will be for Terry to understand why I've been obsessed with finding out about him if I finally get the chance to tell him the truth.

It is now the middle of the summer. Terry and I send each other a few friendly emails; it feels like we're getting to know each other – and, the more I get to know, the more I like Terry.

We begin to make plans to meet again, and this time I feel that now I understand him a little more I will be able talk about the diary openly, and now he understands me, it will be easier for Terry to feel he can confide in me. I've been feeling dishonest and deceitful. I hope coming clean and talking about the diary will be cathartic for both of us.

I send Terry another email, this time suggesting a date to meet up again, perhaps for a friendly drink. I check my inbox regularly over the next few days for a reply. Days turn to weeks. Weeks turn to months. Nothing. For a reason I can't understand Terence Prendergast has stopped responding.

I send a few more emails, each a combination of nostalgia, questions and reminiscences about *Choose Your Own Adventure.* He doesn't reply to any of them. Every time I think of him, every time I think of the diary, I wonder if I have made things worse – if I have opened a real-life Pandora's box-like chest from *Mystery of the Secret Room*, a box better left sealed. Would Terence have been better off without ever meeting me? Maybe I've been too revealing, and maybe by trying to get closer to him all I've done is push him away.

But I have an idea that will hopefully ease my concerns. I search the internet using the email address Terry's been using to correspond with – it turns up a Facebook account under James Costello, the name under which he sold the books on eBay. I tell myself I just want to check if he's OK, but as the Facebook page slowly loads I know that I'm half-lying to myself. In truth, I want to see if there are any clues about where or what he has been doing, and why he might be ignoring me.

The privacy of James Costello's Facebook is set so I can't see his profile picture, activity, photos, or status, but I can still see his favourite quotes, and a list of his likes and interests.

Favourite quotes:

'A man who claims to have no conscience, is a liar' – Oscar Wilde

'A man's real possession is his memory; in nothing else is he rich, nor is he poor' – Alexander Smith

'You can't protect anyone in this world, the sooner you realise that, the better' – Carver, Seraphim Falls

Likes:

'The Six Million Dollar Man', 'Manimal', 'Different Strokes', 'The Littlest Hobo', 'Police Squad!', Theatre of the Absurd, Dutch colonial architecture, German beer, Pearl & Dean, Richard Pryor, Charles Bronson, Charles Dickens, Charlie Sheen, Magic Johnson, Evel Knievel, STOP BULLYING!!, Mike Reid, 'Red Dwarf', University of North London, Stephen Hawking, Chris Morris, Nell Gwyn, Lewis

Carroll, Woody Harrelson, Margaret Nolan, Joan Sims, Percy Thrower, Henrik Ibsen, Richard Brinsley Sheridan, 'Kojak', Sophia Coppola, Chevy Chase, Sid James, Petrarch, Daniel Defoe, Henry Fielding, The Old Vic Theatre, John Osborne, James Booth, Benny Hill, Lee Majors, Archimedes, Dick Mann, Victor French, Chuck Norris, Burt Reynolds, William Holden, Telly Savalas, Hippasus, Lonely, Pythagoras.

It is a bewildering list of art, theatre and pop culture, with a cut-off point that seems to have been drawn in the mid-1980s. It's partly a list of the favourite things of a child growing up in that era, combined with actors known for films liked by an older generation, a sprinkling of university reading and cult comedians. Two things, however, jump out immediately – 'Stop bullying' and 'lonely'. Not for the first time, my heart wrenches. This is not just a list of likes but another time capsule, just like the diary.

I watched a lot of daytime TV in my teenage years when I was ill. After *This Morning* and *Neighbours,* afternoons mainly consisted of reruns of 1970s detective and cop dramas – *Columbo, Ironside, Hawaii Five-O, The Six Million Dollar Man, Kojak, Starsky and Hutch, The Magician*. The residue of such idiosyncratic personalities must have imprinted itself on my youthful imagination.

I looked forward to the school holidays because, while not changing anything about my circumstances, it altered the TV schedule. Death, murder and revenge gave way to intelligent animals helping humans in distress – *The Littlest Hobo, Gentle Ben* and *Flipper*. I watched these programmes just as avidly, but with the company of my sister Nina. Whatever was on telly, they were all a way out of my reality, something to look forward to on a daily basis, something to fill the hundreds of hours I had been forced to spend alone. As much as those programmes were part of my childhood, and I look back on them with fondness, they are part of a different time and place, another era, another me. But does Terry/James still enjoy watching those films and those TV shows? Is it nostalgia? Or is it that he still measures himself by that time, still feels trapped by it?

His favourite film list consists mainly of classic seventies and eighties comedies, and a handful of other films from the same era, many of which I've not seen – *Cannonball Run, Viva Knievel!, Twilight Zone – The Movie, Holiday on the Buses, Airplane!, Mary Poppins, The Taking of Pelham One Two Three*. So, in an attempt to understand Terry, or at least to have a shared ground to talk about if he does finally get back in touch with me, I need to rectify that situation.

I've agreed to spend Friday having a quiet night in with Sarah. She said recently that I've been distant and aloof again, as if my thoughts are constantly elsewhere. I apologised and explained that there isn't anything wrong; it's just that I'm worried about the whole Terry situation and that I don't know where to turn and what else to try.

When she gets home from work she immediately spots the pile of DVDs on the coffee table.

'What are these?' she asks, picking them up and flicking through them, 'They're not your usual type of film . . .'

'Oh,' I say quickly, desperately trying to come up with a plausible explanation, 'I just haven't seen any of them. I thought we could watch one tonight?'

Sarah considers me closely. Something is troubling her. 'Sure, sure,' she begins. 'But is there something you want to tell me first?'

I don't want to start keeping any more secrets, so I tell her the truth about James Costello's Facebook page, the list of his favourite TV shows and films. She looks at me with an expression of disappointment, sadness and genuine concern that I have not yet been able to shake my obsession, like it's slipped beyond a personality quirk into becoming a serious psychological issue.

'Nathan,' she says gently. 'This has to stop. It isn't healthy – not for you, not for us . . . I'm worried about you. This man, this Terence, this James Costello, he's all you ever talk about.'

She's right. There's no denying she's right. And yet, even so, I know I can't resist.

'I promise,' I say, 'once I've watched these films, and if I don't hear from him by Christmas, I'll . . .'

'You'll what?'

'I'll . . . give in.'

She scrunches her face up in a way that I know means she doesn't believe me, folds her arms and drops into the armchair. 'Listen to yourself! It isn't giving in! It's doing the right thing. This has gone too far already. Seriously, what do you really hope to gain by watching any of these films?' she asks, waving a copy of *Holiday on the Buses* at me accusingly.

With bawdy/sexist cartoon representations of busty women staring me in the face I have to admit I don't know.

'I really don't know, I just feel that I have to . . .' I say. I can't explain the compulsion in a way that makes sense. All I know is I can't not.

For our weekly date night we end up watching *Cannonball Run* – a light-hearted buddy movie based on an illegal coast-to-coast, cross-country car race, like a live action *Wacky Races* – in a cold, cold silence, which makes the confused plot even more bewildering and the forced script even more leaden. It is the worst ninety-five minutes of our relationship.

30 October

Inspired by Dr Finkel, and after consulting the teenage diaries at the Bishopsgate Institute, I've decided to start keeping my own diary. Forcing Sarah to watch *Cannonball Run* has finally managed to alienate her. I need to have someone to talk to about all of this, even if it is only myself.

This diary will not only help me keep a record, but also help me feel closer to Terence, and to make me feel that something is actually happening.

1 November

Last night Terence featured really heavily in my dreams again. He was wearing a sailor's outfit, one of the old-fashioned kind that flairs out at the bottom of the leg, but it was purple instead of navy. He didn't say why he was wearing it, and I didn't feel I could ask him. But as we spoke he began telling me he'd been learning magic from some of my favourite magicians. That left me feeling really annoyed, that he'd gone away and done this without telling me, like he was using everything I'd said to him against me. I'm not a psychologist, but I think a lot of dreams are your brain storing stuff away, getting rid of things that aren't important. In this dream, though, there are elements of pure anxiousness, I guess from wanting to know what Terence is doing, and where he is, and also from wondering whether the things that I am doing are really right.

14 November

It has been two weeks or so since I last made a diary entry. I still haven't heard from Terence.

I could try to phone him, I do have his mobile phone number, but if he's not answering emails, then he's less likely to answer his mobile phone. I don't want to go behind Terence's back but I also have his mum and dad's phone number. I've got no reason to believe he isn't OK, but it could be good to make sure. Maybe I could ask Fernando to call Terence's mum for me. He has a good rapport with people, especially mums. If Terry doesn't respond soon, I will have to do one of those two things.

22 November

It's been another couple of weeks and Terry still hasn't got back to me.

I'm not writing any more entries until I have something to say other than I still haven't heard from him.

23 November

I've just finished reading Edward Packard's new book. It's a memoir-of-sorts called *All It Takes*, in which he describes the three keys to making good decisions and how to avoid making bad ones.

Key 1: Be in the right state of mind.

Key 2: Think clearly.

Key 3: Keep your decisions under surveillance.
I think the book is something Terry would appreciate.

8 December

Christmas is only seventeen days away. Sarah has made it clear that, if I want our relationship to continue, then I have to stick to my promise. I have watched nearly all of James Costello's favourite films – on my own – and I still haven't heard from Terry. I don't want to give up Sarah, or for Sarah to give up on me, but I think of that message-in-a-bottle and something compels me. I still check the junk box of my email every morning, just in case a message has slipped through. Still nothing.

10 December

I've got some good news! Just when I'd finally given up all hope of Terry ever getting back in touch, possibly the best Christmas present I could ask for has arrived – an email from Terry!

> Hello Nathan,
> I just arrived home for a couple of days, and got your email. It was great to hear from you. I'm staying in Bleiberg at the moment. It is very easy going, you can have a Finnish massage every morning, have schnapps and then cycle around the lakes and look at the mountains, eat dinner and have another sauna in the evening! It is very invigorating and takes your mind away from all worries.

After my conversations with Sarah, it feels as if communicating with Terry is now a shameful thing, illicit, wrong – as if I'm betraying Sarah, or betraying myself. I've been reading the email over and over to myself for the past half an hour.

I'm just really pleased he has got back in touch with me. Maybe his silence is just because he's been abroad and not checking emails, getting on with having a good relaxing time while getting away from it all. Taken at face value, it seems Terry really has achieved exactly what he told me on his doorstep, and fulfilled his aim of moving to a new country to start a business with his partner.

But something about the email makes it sound like a fantasy, like the running away to Scotland. It just doesn't seem true – the kind of detail he goes into, the massage every morning, the schnapps and then cycling around the mountains. Perhaps part of me is just jealous – it does sound idyllic. Maybe it's me who needs to get away from it all. But the other part of me thinks that if this isn't true, maybe he just wants to sound like he's done what he said he was going to do, which was move away.

I have no reason to doubt him, nothing to base my hunch on, and if I look at this situation objectively, *I'm* the one not telling the truth – to Terry about his diary, to Sarah about this diary. Things are turned upside down in my own head. I need a release. I need to talk to Terry to set things straight.

His message is friendly and open, and it is nice to say that it was great to hear from me. I really would like to speak to him. But I'm going to send him a reply now, and fingers crossed I get a chance to speak to him before Christmas.

This is what I'm going to say:

Hi Terry,

Really good to hear from you. Wow, Bleiberg sounds fantastic, very jealous! Maybe if I save some money I could come and interview you again there – perfect excuse for a short getaway!

I would really like to talk to you again – do you know when you might be back in UK/Birmingham in the new year? It would be great if we could work something out.

speak soon,

Nathan

PS. I have something to send you that I think you'd really enjoy reading – what's the best place to send it? I can post it to your parents if that is easiest, and they can pass it on.

13 December

I've found some internet activity I haven't seen before from the James Costello email address that Terence gave me when we first met. There are now websites that allow you to sign petitions online. Petitions can be started for anything, and then forwarded to the relevant organisation. James Costello has signed this petition to Paramount Pictures:

Sign this petition to request a Planes, Trains and Automobiles Special Edition DVD be released, with new and old behind-the-scenes, DELETED SCENES, COMMENTARY BY JOHN HUGHES AND STEVE MARTIN, THE THREE-HOUR VERSION OF THE FILM, AND TRAILER(S).

By signing the following form, you are requesting that Paramount Pictures create this DVD for us, the fans, who will be sure to spend our hard-earned cash on it.

You are saying, "Paramount, listen up, MAKE THIS DVD

Because, remember, Paramount: If you treat your fans with respect, they will come. Or, in this case, they will buy. Either way works.

So why are you people still reading? Sign the petition already!

James Costello has signed his name and commented:

The original version is three hours, why not release it?!

Only 837 other people seem to agree with him.

I've not seen *Planes, Trains and Automobiles*, and the problem is . . . I now feel the compulsion to watch the film. But there is no point. The rational part of me knows I don't need to watch the film. I don't need to watch *any* version of that film. I've not seen it, and I've probably not seen it for a reason. I've not been interested. I might be missing out. This is the problem – because James/Terence likes it I feel I should at least experience it in some way. But why? Why? That is a question I can't answer. I better do some research on Amazon. I can only hope they haven't released the three-hour special edition yet.

19 December

Today's date is very significant – twenty-three years ago, Terence Prendergast wrote his address in *Trouble on Planet Earth*, the book that eventually led me to him.

I mentioned in my last email to Terry that I've bought a present for him. As I don't know where he is at the moment I'm going to post it to his mum and dad's address. There is something amazing about sending a book that is also *Choose Your Own Adventure* related back to that house.

I'm going to put it in the post today, so maybe he'll get it before Christmas. If he is in Austria, hopefully his mum and dad will pass it along next time they see him, or if he's in Birmingham, I hope he'll read it soon and get some use out of it.

23 December

I'm at my mum and dad's house for Christmas.

James Costello has posted a Facebook update that may corroborate what he has said about being away:

> Off work for xmas, so got 2 brits & some dutchies comin round for a weekend of German lager, weisswurst, a sofa and Mike Reid stand-up videos; best comedian eva!

It's another significant day. Up until now I haven't been able to see any of his photos, but now he has a face, and it is his own! The face, the profile picture of James Costello, is the face of the person I've met, who has been called Terry by his family. So, I now know definitively that they are the same person. That is now one truth I can grasp hold of, but it doesn't answer any of the other questions I have about the diary, or the question of why Terence Prendergast changed his name to James Costello.

I hope the status update is true, and he's going to be hanging out with friends, watching Mike Reid stand-up videos. I've never seen Mike Reid doing stand-up. All I know is he was on *EastEnders*. I've never watched *EastEnders* – but I know he was famous for saying things like 'Wotcha doing, Pat?' in a gravelly voice. But unfortunately, it means I now have to watch at least one Mike Reid stand-up video, especially as, according to Terry, he is the 'best comedian eva'. The status update might also mean that Terry is back in Birmingham. Either way, I hope he gets my present and that he has a good Christmas.

6 January

It's now the beginning of January, and I've still not heard anything from Terry, not even an email to say thank you for the present. I hope that it got there OK. It should have arrived before Christmas. I posted it on the twentieth, which was the last day of first-class postage. If he didn't get it before Christmas, it definitely would have arrived by now.

Terry said in his email that he'd been away and that he couldn't check his emails until he was back in Birmingham, which would mean he's got no internet access. But James Costello, who has got the same face as Terence – is Terence – has changed his Facebook profile picture. So clearly he *has* got internet access.

Today, *Mike Reid: the guvnor's last stand* DVD arrived. It contains two live shows, including the never before seen on DVD last-ever gig. The blurb reads: 'Join the greatest adult comedian of all time, Mike Reid . . .' – sixty minutes, and a special feature of eight minutes. Sixty-eight minutes of a performer James Costello considers the best comedian ever. Russ Abbot, again another fine comedian, said this: 'A very, very funny man' and 'A great deliverer of great, great jokes'. Not to critique a quote from the great Russ Abbot, but what did they have to cut out of one small sentence to make it two quotes?

Sarah is out tonight, so this is what I am going to spend my night watching. I don't know what to expect, but I can guess. If my guess is right, it's not going to be a fun evening.

20 January

The most significant sporting event of the year is over once again. I held my annual nine-day-long, fancy-dress world darts championship in miniature in honour of the British Darts Organisation Lakeside World Darts Championship. At the real championship my favourite player – Tony 'The Silverback' O'Shea – made it all the way through to the final, and then let himself and everyone else down by playing badly. It was a crushing disappointment.

There were two trophies at Mini-Lakeside this year, one for the Ultimate Mini-Lakeside Champion and one for the Best Costume/Character/Walk-on. The Best Costume trophy was won by Double T'win, the world's first-ever conjoined twin dart players – Alex and Sarah. Well-deserved winners. And the Ultimate Champion was Llama Karma, a Peruvian panpipe-playing darts player – aka Tom Bell. It came down to a final between Llama Karma and Farmhand Jenkins – aka Sarah. At one set each, the third and deciding set went all the way to the wire, down to madhouse, double one. Very emotional scenes followed the final dart. So, a great start to the year. It felt good to allow another of my obsessions to consume me and take over my life for a while. It's also amazing to be reminded annually of just how great my friends are.

But throughout the darts, there was a kind of sadness, caused by not hearing from Terence. This is not how I hoped it would be. I hoped we could be friends, too, and he could take part in Mini-Lakeside.

Perhaps I could go to Austria, but until I hear back from him there's not a lot I can do. I've still got to watch the Mike Reid DVD. I did try to watch the first ten minutes – I mean I tried to watch the whole thing, but only managed the first ten minutes.

I've got to watch it. Tonight. I'm going to do it. It's a promise. I don't know who to, but it's a promise.

21 January

Last night, as promised, I finally got round to watching Mike Reid. The whole thing, all because James Costello said he was the best comedian ever. I don't know where to begin to explain the experience.

I had thought after fifteen minutes in, when he tells a joke where the punch line is the spoonerism Cooking Socks, that I would turn it off. But I carried on. It was awful. The jokes are old, the punch lines are obvious, the delivery is terrible. Mike Reid says at one point, 'We all 'ave different senses of 'umours.' Yeah, we do, we do, and that's what makes performance and comedy brilliant. And we do all have different senses of humour. But the best comedian ever? No, no, he is not. It feels like a bit of me has died inside. I can't help but think what the hell have I been doing to get to this point – spending sixty-eight minutes of my life watching Mike Reid? I've chosen to watch this as part of my quest to understanding Terence Prendergast. In *Choose Your Own Adventure* books you die if you don't choose carefully and this is definitely a death. There was no way I was going to find out anything, it was not going to tell me anything, it was not going to progress me in any way, it was not going to help me understand Terence.

Have I gone too far?

There is nowhere to go from here.

4 February

I have just tried to phone Terry. All I got was his voicemail. I then called his mum and dad's home phone number. I spoke to his mum. She said he'd just popped out. I explained who I was, and asked if she would pass on my phone number. She was very polite, if a little distant. So, it would seem Terry is actually in Birmingham, not Austria.

6 February

It's Monday morning and has been snowing heavily for the past two days, making it hard to go out. So on top of everything I'm getting a bit of cabin fever. To back up what I said on the phone, I sent Terry an email; also, really, to make him feel not so bad about me phoning his mum and dad.

I'm getting desperate, but I've also been feeling sick for the last forty-eight hours. An anxious sick. It's lunchtime. I'm going to phone him now . . .

. . . at least the phone rang, even if it did go to voicemail. Maybe that means he saw my number and didn't want to answer. This is the worst bit about this whole quest so far, it really is. I don't know what to do. I just don't know what to do. Part of me wonders why should he care? Why does he care? He doesn't care. He's scared perhaps. I'm scared. This whole thing is ridiculous. I don't know what to do next. I can't do anything else. I can't even think straight. I just want to be able to speak to him.

8 February

It's two days after I last tried to phone Terry. This will be the fourth phone call that I've made to him.

His phone rang seven times. A voice answered.

'Hello,'

'Hello, is that Terry?'

The voice at the other end hung up.

It was answered but he hung up. It isn't a good sign. I don't want to seem like I'm harassing him. I'm not. If he doesn't phone me back today, maybe I'll try sending him an email or something tomorrow. There is nothing else I can do today.

27 February

In an effort to cheer myself up I've had a T-shirt made with the logo of *Choose Your Own Adventure* on it.

Perhaps I should have made a matching one for Terry.

16 March

It's now the middle of March and three months since I last heard from Terry. I'm seriously considering going to Austria to find him. I've looked up Bleiberg – it's a small town near the southern Austrian border with Slovakia, well off the main tourist routes. The official Bleiberg website has a tag line that reads: 'A landscape that creates friendships'. Friendship is exactly what Terry and I need to create. Bleiberg could be the place to make that happen.

I've plotted a potential journey on a map, a kind of European *Planes, Trains & Automobiles*: Eurostar to Brussels, sleeper train from Brussels to Munich, drive from Munich to Bleiberg, meet Terry, he's surprised to see me, I make some kind of excuse about being in the area again, he laughs, we go for a drink of schnapps, I tell him the truth about the diary, we become friends, I drive to Vienna to take a flight back to London. I've consulted timetables, ticket availability and hostels. My bank account won't take the strain of the trip, neither will my relationship with Sarah. But if it gives me some resolution, some closure, it will be worth a punishing overdraft and the desperate pleading for forgiveness when I return.

30 March

A photo has appeared on James Costello's Facebook. It shows him in a garden. The caption says: 'Inspecting the orangery'. Maybe that's where I should leave him. He's always been an enigma, and perhaps he's best left as one. I like to imagine that inspecting the orangery makes him happy. Perhaps I've got to come to accept that this is 'The End'.

2 April

Fernando called today. He said that he's worried about me, not only him but Sarah, too. Fernando and Sarah both think I need to get some distance, refocus and move on. Meeting Terry obviously wasn't enough. Fernando might be right. Sarah might be right.

This isn't a healthy mental state to be in permanently.

It really does seem I've reached the end with Terry – my emails, my calls, my gifts have come to nothing. And the despair I've felt has been made worse because I know I've brought it upon myself, and caught up Sarah, Fernando, Johnny Doom, Roj, my mum and dad, Dr Finkel and Ruth with it, and I feel guilty for that. This all started with *Choose Your Own Adventure* number 1 *The Cave of Time*, and now here I am, metaphorically, at the other end of my collection, number 106 *Hijacked!*, with no more options and no more pages to turn.

Everything I've researched, every lead I've followed up has hit a dead-end because Terry has chosen simply to not want to talk to me.

This isn't an adventure any more. I've done exactly the opposite of what I'd hoped the teenaged Terence had done – to realise there are always other choices, other options. I haven't. Obsession has narrowed my focus so tightly it's impossible to see the whole picture.

I *need* to go away, somewhere calm, quiet, contemplative. Hopefully, I'll find some peace within myself to forget Terence and resolve things in my own life. I *have* to work out why I am so obsessive and break its grip on me. Like Terry himself said, 'hide for a bit, take stock of my life, think of a plan'. I can't go on like this. If I do, I'll lose everything.

I need somewhere closer to home than Bleiberg for my escape, somewhere fairly remote, easy to travel to, preferably on the coast. Somewhere I can leave behind my obsession with Terence for good. There is only one place I can think of that meets my requirements – a caravan park I remember reading about in South Wales.

Chapter 11 – My own private Sugarcane Island

I almost miss the tiny, hand-painted sign that says 'Prendergast Caravan Park' while concentrating on the narrow road that turns abruptly uphill towards the village. I pull into the driveway. 'Park' seems an extravagant way to describe a small field with twelve static caravans. I'm a few hours later than I expected, and the owner is waiting anxiously for me in the doorway of his office.

'I'm Alan, good to see you,' he says. 'Let me grab the keys, and I'll show you to your caravan. You've booked a two-bed 2006 Torino with double-glazing.'

Despite it being the first week of May, it seems I'm the only person to be staying this week. The constant rain and the low cloud that hung over me for the entire drive might be the reason why.

'It's a bit quiet this week,' Alan continues, pushing his cap up his forehead. 'I guess people are waiting for it to warm up a bit. But the weather is supposed to be good for the next few days.' He unlocks the caravan. 'After you.'

The inside of the caravan, like the rest of the park, is immaculate. I could almost be the first person ever to stay, and if not, I'm definitely the first person of the new holiday season. Shades of beige and dappled magnolia wrap themselves around me; the imitation wood and laminate flooring shine in the glow of the light from the kitchenette. There is enough seating for ten and beds to sleep four. I feel relaxed immediately.

'Are you here for the walking? Or a bit of both?' Alan asks, handing me the key.

I have no idea what he means by a bit of both. ''Erm, a little bit of walking, but mainly quiet. Things have been a bit, what can I say . . . stressful . . . recently.'

'Oh, you'll get plenty of quiet, that's for sure. If you do want to go out, pop to the laundry room. You'll find lots of leaflets with ideas about where to visit. But if you want to stay in – the TV, he's also a DVD player. Any questions, just come and find me.'

As I close the door behind him, I'm left with the profound silence of an empty caravan park.

I unpack my bags, using the second bedroom as a walk-in wardrobe, and place the books and DVDs I've brought on the shelf in the lounge area – a selection of the best *Choose Your Own Adventure* books I'd bought from Terence: obviously *The Cave of Time*, but also *Return to the Cave of Time, Through the Black Hole, The Third Planet from Altair, You Are a Monster, You Are a Superstar, Inside UFO 54-40, The Worst Day of Your Life*, my favourite *Hyperspace*, and of course Terry's favourite, *Sugarcane Island*. I've also brought Edward Packard's self-help book *All It Takes*, photocopies of my medical records, my old diary I'd found in my parents' garage and the last of Terry's favourite films I haven't yet watched, *Viva Knievel*. If I'm going to find answers, surely I'm going to find them somewhere in this combination of books, personal records and solitude.

On the kitchen counter I find an obsessive laminated inventory of equipment provided for my stay.

4 mugs.	4 small plates.
4 cups.	4 large plates.
4 saucers.	4 water glasses.

4 egg cups.
4 fruit dishes.
1 large fruit dish.
1 milk jug.
1 sugar basin.
1 butter dish.
1 bread plate.
1 tray.
1 vinigar bottle.
1 cruet.
1 measuring jug.
2 veg dishes.
1 teapot.
1 teapot stand.
1 mixing bowl.
1 bread bin.
1 chopping board.
1 veg grater.
1 colonder.
1 trivet.
1 casserole dish.
1 frying pan.
1 oven tray.
3 sauspans & lids.
1 plastic pail.
1 plastic pan.
1 soap dish.
1 dust pan & hand brush.
1 floor brush.
1 toilet brush & holder.
16 coat hangers.
18 pegs in bag.
1 grill pan.
1 oven glove.

1 dish cloth.
1 dish brush.
2 dusters.
1 dust bin & lid.
1 cutlery box.
4 knives.
4 forks.
4 desert spoons.
4 tea spoons.
2 table spoons.
1 bread knife.
1 sharp knife.
1 tin opener.
1 bottle opener.
1 potatoe masher.
1 potatoe peeler.
1 ladle.
1 veg spoon.
1 mixing spoon.
1 kitchen scissors.

1 colour television.
1 microwave oven.
1 electric cordless kettle.
1 toaster.

2 single quilted mattress covers.
2 single duvets.
4 pillows & protectors.

1 fire extinguisher.
2 small stools.

4 tablemats.	1 cushion for extra bed.
4 coasters.	1 television mat.
1 draining pan.	2 doormat.

Reading the list, I realise how peculiar other people's obsessiveness can seem to anyone outside of that obsession, but my obsessiveness can't help but find fault with the faulty obsessiveness of Alan's list. What is a 'colonder'? The misspelling makes it sound more medical than household. Why would anyone put their television on a special television mat? And who would want to steal one?

The question is, if Alan Jenkins' obsessiveness seems this peculiar to me, how must my obsession seem to strangers? I don't want to think about such huge mysteries of the cosmos yet. I need sleep. I'm exhausted by the drive, and by the mental and emotional exertion of recent months. Even though it's only nine o'clock I decide to have an early night. As I lie in the dark I'm rocked slowly to sleep by the creak of the wind and the babble of the brook outside the window, punctuated by the hoot of an owl, like the start of a clichéd horror film. It's an ominous omen to the start of my week in Prendergast Caravan Park.

I awake early, my breath forming clouds of condensation in the dissipated light shining through the net curtains. I get dressed quickly, trying not to let my feet touch the searing cold of the laminate floor. Alan was right. Outside the dark rain clouds of yesterday have been replaced by a clear blue sky, a light frost covers the neatly clipped grass, the sun is rising slowly over the roofs of the caravans, and apart from the sound of birds, silence.

Trefin is a small village, halfway between St Davids and Fishguard, so small it has just one pub and a café geared towards rambling tourists. I walk up to the town square, actually an outcrop of rock, where a water pump installed in 1906 still stands. An old man is leaning on the wall outside his house, one of a row of squat terraces painted in bright shades of pastel pink, blue and yellow. He's wearing a set of overalls and has started poking a long-handled, two-pointed rake between the edge of his garden wall and the tarmac. Seeing me walk up the hill, he looks up. I'm prepared to say hello in the non-committal way you greet anyone who passes by in the countryside, and perhaps answer a polite question about being on holiday.

'The weeds know it's spring don't they?' he says in a soft Welsh accent, sounding like a character from Dylan Thomas's *Under Milk Wood*.

I can't tell if the question is purely rhetorical, or actually botanical, so I smile, mumble a 'Yes, yes they do,' and carry on walking quickly, following a sign for the coastal path.

The village gives way to a short field filled with grazing sheep, the edge of which ends in a sheer drop of forty feet, a cliff face eroded by time. The waves of St George's channel batter the rocks below, churning the sea into white foam, excited swallows swoop and chatter over the yellow-flowered gorse bushes, while the wind seems desperate to catch me off guard. This is a landscape that makes you feel dramatic and poetic, filled with caves and castles, stone circles and lighthouses, ruined churches and burial mounds – a landscape designed for imaginary adventures.

A sign on a wooden post offers a warning in Welsh and English: 'Mae clogwyni'n lladd cadwch at y llwybr – cliffs kill keep to the path'. I sit carefully on the edge of the cliff, soothed by the sound of the sea crashing against the rocks below. The horizon stretches unbroken and seems to curve slightly, a line that represents the essence of possibility. If I can't find distance from my obsession here, I'll never find it.

I hadn't planned for the village not to have a small corner shop of some sort from which to buy essential supplies, and a retreat is not really a retreat if I have to eat at the café or pub every day and actually converse with people. I need to make one trip to the supermarket, stock the fridge with food, and then I'll be free to revel in tranquillity and isolation.

About eighteen miles from Prendergast Caravan Park is

Haverfordwest, an old market town, now filled with pound shops and discount stores, ringed by a series of retail parks and home to the nearest large supermarket in South Pembrokeshire. It is also the hub of all the main roads in the area. I follow the road into town, spending the time mentally creating and memorising a lengthy shopping list.

Memorisation of long lists is a task that I find focuses the mind like a meditation mantra. It's a habit I formed just a few years ago, after seeing an advert in an old copy of the *Fortean Times*, a magazine dedicated to strange and unusual phenomena, which was named in tribute to the early twentieth-century writer and obsessive collector of unexplained data, Charles Fort. The advert featured a man wearing a blindfold and tuxedo, his hands pressed to his temples in concentration, the capitalised words 'YOU CAN REMEMBER!' shouting from the page beside him. It was advertising a 'home-study course in memory and concentration' by Dr Bruno Furst, first published in 1939. Dr Furst was described as 'probably the best all-round mental athlete of the century' by the *New Yorker*. With most of the century to go, the *New Yorker* was carefully covering its back by the use of the word 'probably'. The magazine was so old the advert was the now extinct reply-by-coupon kind, but a quick search on eBay found me the complete course for the grand total of 1p.

The twelve-part course teaches a comprehensive range of memorisation techniques, including the peg system. The peg system, which has a history going back to the late fifteenth century, allows you to remember long lists of unrelated items without repetition, and to recall them instantly both in and out of sequence. The most astounding thing is the course actually works. I can now remember lists of fifty or more objects in minutes. The basic principle is that each number has a permanent word and image associated with it, a peg on which to hang the new temporary list you want to remember. For example, the first ten pegs in Dr Furst's system are:

1 = tea
2 = Noah
3 = may(pole)
4 = ray (of light)
5 = law (represented by a policeman)
6 = jaw
7 = key
8 = fee
9 = pea
10 = toes
and so on.

Once you have the pegs stored in your permanent memory, you only need to combine the image of the word or item on your list with its corresponding peg image. For example, if the first item on your list is dog food, you might visualise stirring a cup of tea with a huge Alsatian. Animal cruelty aside, it's not an image you'll forget quickly.

I'm only on the seventh item of my shopping list, mentally trying to use a packet of butter to open the door of my caravan, when I see a road sign that says: Prendergast. I almost crash into the car in front of me in shock.

I'm too far away for the sign to refer to the caravan park. I'm either misreading a Welsh word or hallucinating. I do a circuit of the roundabout to double check. Without a doubt it definitely says Prendergast. I make the turning, and drive up an old street lined with terraced houses on each side, at the end of which are a row of small local shops. I pull up outside the launderette, named after the pantomime-dame character in *Aladdin* who runs a Chinese laundry: Widow Twankey's – Prendergast Launderette.

How did I get *here* from *The Cave of Time*?

As soon as I get back to the caravan park, I dump the shopping and stroll across the little bridge over the brook to try to find Alan, the owner. I have one question for him – why the name Prendergast?

I ring the bell on the door of the outhouse that Alan uses as an office. This is a door that doesn't make me nervous. He seemed friendly on my arrival, and it's not such an unusual question for a holidaymaker to ask. No one answers the door. He must be somewhere else on site, probably strimming a hedge or raking gravel into a millimetre of feng-shui-like precision. I'm just about to cross back over the bridge when the door opens.

'Sorry about that, I was just making some lunch,' Alan says, finishing a bite of sandwich.

'That's OK, it's not a very urgent enquiry. I was in Haverfordwest this morning, and I noticed an area called Prendergast . . .'

'Yes, it means entrance to a village or town.'

'Does it?' I ask, trying to conceal my excitement and failing. 'I wondered why the caravan park was called Prendergast. I wondered at first whether it was a local name.'

'Not so much, just the way into a village. That's what it's associated with anyway. As well as the one in Haverfordwest, there's one in Solva, just down from St Davids.'

'I haven't seen that one.'

Alan looks at me strangely. He must be wondering what kind of weird tourist I am.

'It's nice down there.' He pauses. We've clearly exhausted the etymological aspects of our conversation. He pulls his cap back from his eyes and contemplates the sky. 'Lovely day again isn't it, though? Later on there might be a bit of rain, you know, that's what the forecast said, but it's supposed to be grand again after that.'

Less than twenty minutes later I pull into the car park in Solva, which is half full of dog walkers, ramblers and holidaymakers. The car-park attendant walks over before I have the chance to park the car.

'Lovely day isn't it? How long do you want?' he asks sternly.

'I'm not sure. How much is it?'

'One pound twenty for an hour, three pounds for three hours.'

'Two hours would be enough. I'm just here to . . .'

He cuts me off mid-sentence. 'We don't do two hours. Just one *or* three. It *is* a *lovely* day. You can walk up to the harbour, have a coffee, or cross the bridge and walk up to the beach. The tide's right out. The village is nice, too. You could have a pint, relax in the sun. It is *really* lovely today – you don't get many days like this.'

The car-park attendant is right – it really is a lovely day – but I don't want to see the harbour or walk on the beach. I just want to do what I came here for – to walk up Prendergast and leave. I feel bullied into paying for three hours, not through aggression but through persistence. Maybe this is the kind of job that Coulson or Kenny could have ended up doing. The question I've thought about many times flashes through my mind again – what do bullies actually end up doing with their lives? I guess there are hundreds of jobs that attract small-minded bullies – traffic wardens, call-centre managers, bouncers.

Following the map I walk the opposite way to everyone else who has just arrived, away from the coast and up the short main street – a row of shops selling local crafts and antiques, a tea room and gallery. The street is sandwiched by a pub at either end, both running a fish-and-chip night, and one in the middle boasting 'Live music with Matt and Angie'. Choice is clearly not the main currency of small villages.

At the point where the main street ends and Prendergast begins the river is just six or seven feet wide, crossed by a narrow stone bridge. At one corner of the intersection is a sign that makes me feel a sudden rush of excitement. Below the bilingual 'Anaddas i gerbydau hir – unsuitable for long vehicles' in the simultaneously distinctive and indiscernible black-and-white Transport font, is just one word – PRENDERGAST.

Prendergast winds up the left bank of the river, flanked by a series of holiday cottages before thinning out into trees and grass banks. Opposite the last of the houses is an enclosure of stubby, curly-haired llamas. A few metres away Prendergast stops at an old water mill.

Built in 1907, the mill still produces rugs and carpets but the old engine rooms and weaving shed are now a tea room and gift shop.

I stand on the bridge that crosses the River Solva, exactly halfway between Prendergast and the water mill. At this point the river is barely four-foot wide, and the water trickles slowly down towards the sea. To my left a sign sternly requests 'Please do not throw stones into the river'.

As I stand on the bridge, watching the river pass under my feet, it feels like I'm finally letting go a little. I've been sidetracking myself. I'm not going to find whatever it is I'm looking for by visiting places just because they're called Prendergast. I'm fooling myself into thinking I'm finding answers when all I'm doing is constructing dead-ends, delaying the inevitable, refusing to accept reality.

Perhaps this quest hasn't been about Terence at all but about me – my love of the books, the difficulties of my childhood, the kind of person I have become in the process of growing-up. But now it is finally time to move on.

I'm tempted to drop the pages of Terence's diary into the river, let them be pushed and pulled towards the sea, where they will be lost for ever. An old couple look at me suspiciously as they pass me on the bridge on their way to the tea room. Involuntarily, I raise my hands to prove I'm not holding any pebbles.

I feel lighter, more relaxed, and decide that since I've already paid for it, I should make the most of the remaining car-parking time.

Back in the village, I walk past a converted church. Bright blue and red signs shout ART, CAFE, GALLERY in capital letters. A patio with rickety looking chairs and tables and painted fish has a garden area abundant with herbs and flowers. I place my order with a woman who is busy shouting at two cats, and sit outside on an old church pew in the last of the sun. I spread the map out on the table as the waitress brings over a pot of tea. I have an idea.

'Can I borrow a pencil, please?' I ask.

Unfazed, she pulls out a stub of a pencil from her apron. I mark the three Prendergasts I've visited on the map – Prendergast caravan park, Prendergast in Haverfordwest, Prendergast in Solva. Amazingly, they form the points of a neat scalene triangle. Suddenly it occurs to me that maybe the clues are here but I've been looking in the wrong place yet again. I rummage in my bag, and pull out my battered copy of *The Cave of Time*. Using it as a straight edge, I join the three dots. Then, marking the centre of each edge and joining them to the opposite corner, I locate the centre of the triangle of Prendergasts – itself a triangle of small unnamed roads between two farms. It doesn't look like a promising site of revelation and resolve, but Pembrokeshire has been the site of thousands of obscure pilgrimages over the centuries. It is said that two visits to St Davids are worth one to Rome. Maybe one visit to the centre of the Prendergast Triangle is worth two to Birmingham. I feel energised about my pilgrimage. It might be absurd, but this is one final symbolic act to rid myself of my obsession. I'm finally going to leave behind, not only my obsession, but my childhood.

This is the first pilgrimage I've ever been on, and I'm not sure of the correct protocol. Do I leave a sacrifice? An offering? Perhaps something that represents the journey I've been on and something of myself, a symbol of how I have ended up in this place. I have Terence's diary with me, but that, quite rightly, still needs somehow to be returned to Terry. I also have the copy of *The Cave of Time* in my bag. It's not the original copy that I bought from eBay, but an extra copy I bought as a back-up, just in case. *The Cave of Time* started this whole quest. This is what I should leave at the centre of the Prendergast Triangle for someone else to find. My life has been enriched by the joy of finding on so many occasions; it's time for me finally to be the leaver.

I stop at the nearest petrol station that also sells groceries. I need a clear plastic bag to wrap the book in so it's rainproof. It doesn't feel right just to take one from the roll hanging from the fruit and vegetable containers without buying anything, so I grab the nearest thing to me, a lemon, and tie it gently into its own contribution to our landfill problem. As I'm paying for my solitary lemon and a roll of gaffer tape, I notice on the counter a pile of guide booklets about Trefin called *Five circular walks and a guide to the village.* I buy a copy, hoping it might contain a little history, or a least a reference, to the caravan park.

Back in the car, I replace the lemon with *The Cave of Time*, including a note that reads: 'If you have found this book, please enjoy! It has led me on many adventures. Please let me know it has found a good home', adding my email address on the reverse. I don't expect, or even want, to hear back. I just want someone to find it and wonder why an old children's book from the 1980s has been securely gaffer taped to a signpost on an obscure back road in Wales. Clouds suddenly darken the sky. It looks like Alan's weather prediction is coming true. I hope that my knots are waterproof.

I still have six nights left of my retreat and I'm already feeling a kind of Terence Prendergast cold turkey. I know I've been pushing myself to the edges of absurdity and madness, but before I finally say goodbye to Terence, I have one more film to watch.

Viva Knievel! is the one DVD on James Costello's favourites list that I always moved to the bottom of the pile. It stars Evel Knievel as himself – an all-American, death-defying daredevil, famous for jumping huge obstacles on a motorbike. By the time the film was made in 1977, he had already made it into the *Guinness Book of Records* for having the most broken bones in a lifetime. The count in 1975 was 433 separate bone fractures. Evel Knievel was the biggest human jigsaw in history.

I pull the caravan curtains closed against the dark and light the gas fire.

The film starts with a mysterious man carrying a box into an orphanage late at night, long after lights out. The man turns out to be Evel Knievel, and in the box are the latest Evel Knievel toys to hit the market. They are gifts to the children of the orphanage from a 1970s Father Christmas, distributing branded merchandise of himself. While Evel wakes the boys up from their sleep to hand out the toys, a boy on crutches walks across from the farthest bed.

'Evel, look! Look at me! When I saw you walk away from that crash in England,' he throws one of the crutches away with a flourish, 'I figured I could do it, too.' The boy drops the other crutch to the floor with a clatter. He continues walking, holding on to the foot of the nearest bed for support. 'You're the reason I'm walking, Evel! You're the reason!'

'Oh, Wally! That's great! I knew you could do it. I'm so proud,' says Evel.

Within minutes we know that Evel is a good guy, a figure of inspiration, courage and strength, a fighter against adversity. I know instinctively that Terence saw this film as offering hope. I feel that hope myself.

Halfway through the film Evel is lying in hospital following another non-fatal but severe accident, suffered while trying to jump a cage of hungry lions and tigers. The troubled son of Evel's friend Will brings in a pile of telegrams, get-well-soon wishes for America's hero. The boy walks over to the hospital bed and sighs a sigh of concern and of existential questioning, as the bruised and bandaged Knievel opens his eyes.

'It sure is good to wake up in a hospital,' he croaks, 'at least I know I'm alive. Tommy, I'm sorry, this is sure turning out to be a bum vacation for you.'

'Evel, mind if I ask you a question?' Tommy says, asking a question.

'As far as I'm concerned, there are no secrets in this room. What is it?'

'Have you changed your mind about never jumping again?'

Now it's Evel's turn to sigh. He reaches his hand out to Tommy. 'Tommy, in every person's life they have to come to grips with themselves. They have to know when they've gone far enough . . . you've got to know when it's time to quit.'

'But you're not just another person. You're Evel Knievel.'

'Yeah,' Evel pauses, 'I know.' And in that pause I can't help but feel the weight of his problem, the contradiction of his self-constructed situation – the essence of Evel Knievel, the thing that defines him, will also destroy him if he doesn't know when to stop.

I know now is the time to stop this quest, before I destroy everything good in my life. I'm scared that forcing myself to forget Terence will leave a hole in my life that will be filled with another obsession. I don't just need a distraction, I need a new focus, a whole new direction, a new way of thinking.

I need a figure like Evel to speak to, someone to confide in who won't be biased by knowing me, someone who will understand my quest and help suggest a new path. My eyes scan the caravan's bookshelf. The answer is before me yet again – a man outside of time, who has spent his life considering the nature of choice and the folly of bad decision making, someone who saved my childhood by allowing me to go on adventures I could never have in real life, someone who allowed me to feel I could be in charge of my own destiny. There, lined up along the bookshelf is a name I've been carrying with me constantly – Edward Packard.

Prendergast Caravan Park is an illusory retreat. For the new holiday season, Alan has installed wifi access for all the caravans. I immediately pull out my laptop, log on to the wifi connection and direct the browser to Edward Packard's home page. Among his blogs and book reviews are his contact details. I send him a short email explaining that I'm a huge fan of *Choose Your Own Adventure* books, that I've read all his books, including his latest self-help book *All It Takes*, and although he lives in America, ask if it would it be possible to speak to him.

I get up early the next morning, through the net curtains I can see Alan walking around checking off the laminated inventories for a couple of the other caravans. I'm worried that soon I'm going to be getting neighbours. An email from Edward Packard is waiting for me in my inbox.

Hi Nathan,

I'm glad you like my new book. I'd be glad to conduct a phone or Skype interview. I've done Skype before; just let me know when you'd like to set it up. I'm free almost any time your evening/my afternoon, except occasionally when traveling.

All best,

Edward

I send an excited and enthusiastic reply, arranging a time later in the day to Skype. It's at times like these I realise I'm actually living in a version of the future I'd imagined in my childhood.

The sky is bright and clear, Alan's forecast is right again, and I sit on the steps of the caravan with my copy of *Hyperspace* open to the illustration of the boy meeting Edward Packard inside his own book. It feels like I am now that boy, in the fifth dimension, just about to shake the author's outstretched hand.

Holding out a hand, he says, 'Glad to meet you.'

You shake hands and introduce yourself. Then you realise the absurdity of the situation.

'Tell me,' you demand, 'how can you be here?'

'It's not really that surprising,' he replies, 'anything can happen in hyperspace.'

I skip forward in the book, making my favourite bad decision in the whole series:

[Unfortunately, the author of this book, Edward Packard, never made it to the sixth dimension. For that reason he is unable to describe it. Maybe you can, or maybe it can never be described at all.]

The End

I can't remember how bewildering or brilliant this ending was when I first read it, but I've read it hundreds of times since. And now, now

I'm about to enter *Hyperspace* in real life in the hope I can keep from falling into the unknown and unknowable.

'Hello, hello?'

I'm staring at the screen of my laptop. It's exactly seven-thirty, and in front of a computer on the other side of the world is Edward Packard.

'Hello, can you see me?' comes a disembodied voice from my laptop speakers. Despite belonging to an 81-year-old man, the voice is surprisingly youthful, with a strong American drawl. 'I'm just going to get a friend to help me sort out my problem,' the voice says.

This is not entirely how I imagined my trip into the fifth dimension beginning, but as Edward himself wrote, 'anything can happen in hyperspace'.

A few minutes later my screen changes, and I see a shot of arm, a flash of T-shirt.

'Nathan, bear with me. My friend's over here with his kids using the swimming pool, so he's had to help me with this.'

'That's OK. No rush,' I reply, looking at an image of a blank wall. The wall wobbles as the camera turns, and I'm finally face to face with Edward Packard.

'Hello Nathan, delighted to see you. We had a little struggle getting started but we're in business now. Tell me what your questions are. I might not have the answers but I might have other questions for you to think about.'

That is how I imagined my trip into the fifth dimension beginning. He looks older than I'd imagined, but then I don't know many 81-year-old people, and he's framed by a webcam in a room that's clearly his office. I suddenly become aware of my own surroundings, the 1970s-style caravan curtains behind me, but this is not the time for those kind of explanations.

'I've got an easy question to start with. How did you come up with the *Choose Your Own Adventure* format?' I ask, half knowing the answer, half wanting to hear it from the man himself.

'I first thought of this when I had two girls who were about nine and five. I used to tell them stories after getting home from work. I was telling them a story about a boy named Pete, who was washed up on a desert island, shipwrecked, and I really couldn't think of what would happen next in the story. I'd run out of steam, so I asked, "What do you think Pete should do?" Really, it was as easy as that.

'I was commuting at the time, and the next day on the train I began writing down the beginning of this story, except I changed Pete to "you" because I was asking the girls, "What would you do?" So, the story became about *you* the reader. I continued branching out the multiple storylines and multiple endings and sometimes one storyline would merge with another. I finally figured out you had to make a chart, like a tree lying on its side with its trunk and branches and twigs. Then I could keep track of things and preserve the continuity. That was the genesis.'

'Do you think *Choose Your Own Adventure* books attracted certain kinds of readers?' I'm thinking of the similarities between Terry and me, about the kinds of children who were drawn to the books.

'When we first released these books, it was before the computer age. So there wasn't competition with video games. The world has since become much more interactive,' Edward answers.

Terence was born three years after Pong, one of the earliest arcade games, was released by Atari – a two-dimensional tennis game, formed by two lines that could move vertically to hit a square pixelated ball across the screen. I was born two years before Space Invaders changed gaming history – you had to shoot at rows of alien figures that were descending at increasing speed from the top of the screen.

'I think at that point *Choose Your Own Adventure* attracted a great many people,' Edward continues. 'Not only was it a novelty, but instead of reading about someone else, you were reading about yourself in a way. I think for shy kids who might be nervous about adventures, about doing things, this was a way to do it safely – really be reckless and do bold things. So there's a reason why kids who are a little shy or introverted might like something like this.'

'Would you say you were a bold person, or a shy person?'

'I would say I'm a bit of both. I'm somewhat introverted, but I've sometimes swum to an island when I've been warned not to.' He pauses as if he's cataloguing a new plot for a future book. 'As a teenager, I was of a somewhat reckless disposition, but I didn't single myself out as being particularly bold or scared. Please excuse me, I'm going off camera for a second because I have to sneeze. I have a little hay fever.'

As suddenly as he appeared Edward Packard disappears from my screen. I hear a sneeze off camera. A virtual sneeze has never felt so human.

'Sorry, I'm back,' he says. 'Where were we? At the beginning of the books it always says, "Warning, do not read straight through, follow these instructions." One kid had been brought up in a Christian Fundamentalist, very strict way, with strong moral principles.' He laughs gently. 'Not that I'm against strong moral principles but not perhaps too rigid. So this kid cried and confessed to his mother that he hadn't observed the warning and had read the book straight through and he was afraid he might be punished by his god, I guess because it said "Warning!" So his mother sent me a letter and asked me to write him, and assure him it was all right to do that, so I did. There may be some kids who have taken the books too literally, but many of them like the terrible scenes, they like to die, because they don't die, they can turn back and try the other path.'

'There are so many deaths in the books, I think that death is one of the major themes of the series. They have an existential element to them . . .'

Edward laughs.

I continue, 'How do you think these books make children think about death?'

'I don't think they think about it a great deal. I tell you something, when I was a kid, about ten years old, or a little younger even, my brother and I each had these little toy pistols, like western six-shooters. We used to practise our quick draw, as though we were cowboys on the range, like John Wayne having a face-off, you know – one guy draws and the other guy draws, and pchhhcuuchch, one of us would fall down, because he'd been shot first. It was always more fun to be shot and writhe terribly on the ground than be the one who did the shooting. I think my brother felt the same way, that it was more fun to actually do the dying – of course, it wouldn't be more fun in actuality.

'It's like children with fairytales. Is it Hansel and Gretel where the children are put in the oven or something terrible? In one of his books, Bruno Bettelheim, who's a child psychologist, said something like imagining the worst and fantasising about it dispels, rather than reinforces, primal fears of that nature. I'm not sure if that's true or not, but I always tried to approach death humorously. For example, in *Sugarcane Island* you can end up in quicksand. There are various things you can do to try and escape, such as lie down so you're flat and roll out, rather than stand up and struggle, but if you pick the wrong choice, the ending simply said, "glug glug glug." So it was death in a very humorous vein.'

In a sense, this trip to Prendergast Caravan Park is my *Sugarcane Island*, and talking to Edward Packard is my attempt to roll out free of the glug glug glug of my obsession.

'You must have written hundreds of deaths. If you could choose which way to go, which one would it be?'

Edward laughs again. 'I'd just as sooner not know about it, rather than have it lingering,' he says, smiling.

The fan in me has one question I'd be foolish not to allow myself to ask. 'Out of all your books, which one are you the most proud of?'

'Well, I guess the first one, the one that was originally called *Adventures of You on Sugarcane Island*. It was kind of naive in a way, but it has a certain charm and sweetness to it. There are certain features about a number of books that I'm delighted with. In *Hyperspace* I appear as a character . . .'

'I've got the book with me!' I lift up the illustration to my webcam. 'In case I didn't recognise you.'

Edward Packard leans forward to look at his screen, the top of his head coming sharply into focus, and laughs.

'Even though that was published back in 1983, I could still recognise you,' I say.

There are a thousand questions I could ask about *Choose Your Own Adventure*, about the stories, about the endings, but it's Edward's experience of thinking about making decisions that I really want to talk to him about.

'What would you say is the key to making good decisions?'

'As I look back over life, I thought it's really amazing how many stupid decisions I've made and how many smart or wise decisions I've made, and I tried to figure out why some were so smart and some were so bad. I wondered, "What is it that causes us to act the way we do?"' He sneezes. 'Excuse me. I don't know what's causing this hay fever. Maybe it's the fan I have on.' Edward disappears once more and I'm left with the wall for a moment. He sneezes again.

'Bless you.'

'I haven't had this all day,' he snuffles. 'Hay-fever season is usually June. Sorry, as I was saying, there is no magic formula for living, but there are some principles for living a better life. Be kind, be firm, be strong, be honest – this list could go on a little bit longer – but I also have a principle that harder is easier. If you work to your best, follow your interests, study – all of this is very hard work. Life is easier if you are engaged like that than if you slouch on the couch, which sounds easy, but life gets harder and harder because you are such a slouch.'

'When you've made a bad choice, how have you realised you've made a bad choice?'

'That's an interesting question. Sometimes you know very quickly. Other times you don't know right away, and if you make a really bad choice, you may not want to admit it to yourself. Then your subconscious concocts a story in your mind, and thinks up a rationale so you can say, "Well, that wasn't such a bad choice." But eventually, the defences between your bad decision and the reality of your situation are broken down, and you have a sort of mini epiphany – "Oh my God, that was a terrible choice" – and admit it to yourself.

'Of course, sometimes a bad choice can work out well, because there's a certain amount of luck in life. To put it in a mathematical way, if you're playing a card game, like bridge, the percentages might suggest that leaving the king of spades will give you a better chance, but the cards might be positioned so that the thirty per cent chance wins out over the seventy per cent, and in that instance the bad choice wins out. But you can't go through life thinking, "Oh, the bad choice sometimes works out, so it doesn't matter."

'There's also this problem. Choices in life usually aren't as simple as they are in *Choose Your Own Adventure* books – do you choose A or B? There are all kinds of complexities and variables. So, living is not that easy.' He laughs his kind but knowing laugh.

'In your book you hint at some bad decisions you've made. What would you say was the worst choice you've ever made?'

'Well, I didn't want to make *All It Takes* into a confessional, and I also didn't want to bring in the names of people who were still alive. But I think it's no secret to my children – I have three children by my first marriage, and none otherwise – that my first marriage was a disaster. They've asked me themselves, "How did you two ever get together?" The funny thing about life is sometimes you make a terrible decision but you wouldn't want to reverse it because of things that happened afterwards, that exude from it and wouldn't have happened otherwise. And you wouldn't want to lose that. I think my kids are great, and I love them, so I can't exactly say that it was a terrible decision. But looking back, at the time it certainly was.'

'Would you say choice is liberating then?'

'I'm not a psychologist. I don't know the answer to some of these questions. I can only give you my impression. If you think of choices you can make, rather than relentlessly ploughing ahead in one track the way many people seem to do, like I seemed to do when I was younger, then it is liberating, and you can consider more options. In that sense, sure.'

Our conversation has come to an end and I hang up the Skype connection. It takes a moment to sink in that I've actually just spoken to Edward Packard. I feel like emailing Terry to tell him my news, to let him know that two of Edward's favourite books are mine and Terry's favourite books! But I'm now on the path to letting go and moving forward.

I've been relentlessly ploughing ahead, and as Edward warned, that isn't a healthy way to live; nor is worrying about things I haven't done.

I guess it's obvious now but this quest was never really about Terence, or at least not only about Terence. It was about me and my need to face up to issues from my own childhood. I found meaning in Terence's diary because I could see so much of myself reflected in his writing. My obsessiveness does seem to stem from my childhood and my teenage years. To move on, to finally let go, I need to resolve things in my own past, come to terms with things that I never did because of the kind of child that I was.

It's time to forget my search for answers to my questions about Terence's childhood, and instead starting looking for some answers of my own.

Chapter 12 – Russell Grant and the voice of god

After my epiphany in Prendergast Caravan Park it seems one of the questions that has remained unanswered throughout my life is: what would Nancy Mills have said if I'd been brave enough to give her that *Choose Your Own Adventure* style love-letter when I was 13? Would she have given me a photo, and would I know who her favourite pop star is?

I know it might sound strange, and perhaps it's not the solution I thought I would find on my retreat, but maybe I can end my obsession with my past by finding Nancy and finally being brave enough to deliver the letter in person.

Unfortunately, Nancy is someone who doesn't want to be found. I can't find anything about her on the internet, or where she lives now. The only clue I have to finding Nancy is her parents' old address in Rhyl. The name of her childhood street is, not surprisingly, etched into my memory from all the times I cycled past that summer, a long detour on the way to The Bounds, perhaps with the letter burning in the pocket of my shorts. As I think about writing to her now as an adult, it dawns on me that this is exactly the way I found Terence Prendergast – a grown-up child at their parents' house. I can't possibly be that lucky twice.

Back in London, I compose a carefully worded letter, asking Nancy if she remembers me from school. While I'm writing, the shy child I used to be tries his best to raise his voice. I can hear him quietly whispering in my inner ear, 'Of course she won't remember. Why would she?' However, the grown-up me is saying, with defensive confidence, 'It doesn't matter if she doesn't remember, but she might.' The ins and outs of my school history are perhaps enough for me to be at least remembered as the odd kid, the ill kid, the strange kid – and 'might' is as close to hope as I've got. I explain to Nancy that I'm writing a book about my childhood, I am planning to come to Rhyl in a few weeks' time and if she stills lives there, would she be interested in meeting up. I try to keep it chatty and friendly by asking if she'd like to meet for a cup of tea and a catch-up. It takes me three drafts to get it right. The first draft, despite the chattiness, is still a bit clinical and emotionless, the second a bit too over-friendly, the third I hope has the correct kind of balance. I include my address, my email and my phone number but to dispel the impression that I'm an obsessive serial killer, I don't mention the love-letter I never gave her but have kept for the last twenty-three years.

I just hope that Nancy's parents still live at their old address and, if they do, that they will pass my letter on, and I hope that Nancy will respond to my unusual request. There is a lot of hope in that one small envelope.

I rummage through my wallet and find one solitary Christmas stamp. Its images of the Virgin Mary and baby Jesus seem to be smiling dolefully, a reminder of the last thing I posted – a parcel to Terence back in December. It's now April, but a stamp is a stamp, so I stick it on the envelope and before I can stop myself I'm whistling Wizzard's 'I Wish It Could Be Christmas Everyday' as I walk to the corner of the street. It's been a long time since I've felt this positive and this petrified.

I pause at the postbox, the letter half in the slot but still held by my hand. I still have a choice – to remain true to my 13-year-old self and not post the letter, or to let go and let chance take over.

I watch the street around me – an old couple walk past and smile, a mother shouts at a toddler rummaging in an Iceland carrier bag hanging on the back of its pushchair, a boy wearing a Spiderman outfit cycles past on a small BMX.

'What am I doing?' I mutter out loud as I let the envelope fall into the dark cylindrical silence of the postbox. Looking around, the world hasn't come to an end, the old couple are now sat on a bench at the bus stop, the mother is still shouting at the toddler, and the boy has just executed a neat bunny-hop off the kerb, but the future is now actually and metaphorically out of my hands.

The following morning I'm working quietly from home, when my phone makes the piercing bleep bleep of a text arriving. It's from a mobile number I don't know: *my word talk about blast from the past. its great that you done so well. nancy x*

I don't know how efficient Royal Mail is. Even with a first-class stamp I still expect a letter to take a couple of days to arrive, and with a Christmas stamp even longer, so this reply seems too fast to be genuine. It could be somebody winding me up. Fernando? Sarah even, for jealousy's sake? My paranoia is that somebody who lives at that address has opened up the letter and is . . . oh, I don't know. My mind imagines a hundred different scenarios, almost all of them involving someone pointing and laughing. I want to believe my letter has miraculously reached Nancy, that this isn't a hoax and it really is her. Despite my paranoia, my face breaks into a smile. If it is genuine, this is the most amazing and positive thing that has happened to me for a while. I immediately start to compose a reply: *Hi Nancy, thank you so much for getting back to me so quickly, wasn't sure the letter would reach you! Hope everything is good with you. Are you around the weekend I'm in rhyl? Be great to see you x*

It has taken me an hour to write those thirty-nine words. I've agonised over every keystroke. It is only a text, and these days a text is the least frightening but most direct way to send a message to someone. But that doesn't stop my heart from pounding as I press send. A few minutes later my phone beep beeps in reply: *yh i only live a few doors down from my parents. i am around at the weekend.*

This is going better than I could ever have imagined – not only have I found Nancy, but she still lives in the same street! I'm another step closer to delivering that letter to her, another step closer to resolving those things in my past and so achieving closure. Then maybe I can stop dwelling on things that are out of my control. But to actually make it happen I need to keep the channels of communication open, and not spend hours composing each message while our conversation dissolves into nothingness. Texts are supposed to be quick and instant. I look at the clock and give myself five minutes in which to send a response: *Great, I'll send you a message that week and we can work when is best for you. x*

I put my phone on the desk, and go downstairs to put the kettle on, to give myself a moment to try to calm my excitement. By the time I've made a cup of tea Nancy has sent another message: *Txt me anytime hun. x What do you look like now?*

How do you answer a question like that honestly? It's impossible for me to know what she thought I looked like then. What *do* I look like now? Taller. Older. Just as nerdy. That's all I can reply. It's true. But I still don't know if this whole thing is a joke. It could still be Fernando. Truthfully, I could be messaging anybody. Whoever it is responds straight away: *ahhh, I never thought you were geeky.*

If this *is* the real Nancy, our text conversation has taken a turn for the sweet. If we do meet up, then reminiscing about our childhoods will be fun and talking about the letter perhaps won't be so difficult.

The difficult thing will be explaining all of this to Sarah. Under normal circumstances, sending a letter and texting an unknown woman would be a justifiable case for instant dismissal. I'm hoping that she'll be understanding enough to offer me extenuating circumstances in this instance. I'm not naive enough to dismiss her concerns. I really do understand them, and if this situation was reversed and

Sarah was about to meet up with a guy she had a crush on as a teenager, I know I would be jealous. Who knows what might happen if youthful yearnings are rekindled, if perhaps all the right moments align in two different lives for those feelings to take hold. What would that mean for current relationships?

'I can't say I'm happy about it,' Sarah says, fiercely popping the foil seal of the coffee.

I thought the after-work catch-up would be the time to get everything out in the open. But it seems my explanations haven't been convincing enough. I still have my phone in my hand after showing Sarah Nancy's texts and my replies.

'What if you fall in love with her?' It's a question from the heart of the problem.

'I won't.'

'How do you know?'

'I don't, but I won't. Don't be so silly. We live very different lives. I live with you. She has her own life and loves, too.'

'But Nancy doesn't know about the letter yet.' Sarah's pinpointed the loophole in my entire argument.

'No, no she doesn't.'

'People have got together in not dissimilar ways. After their marriage fell apart, my uncle got divorced from my auntie, and then got together with his childhood sweetheart when he was in his sixties, probably in a similar situation to this.'

'What do you mean? He found a letter in a garage that he'd written to a girl but never gave her?'

'Stop being facetious, you know what I mean,' Sarah says. 'It's like the Terence situation all over again. I don't know how much more I can take of this. I never told you to give up Terence. I was just concerned for you. I could see how much that meant to you. But Nancy? Seriously, what do you really expect to come of it?'

'I, I . . .' I find myself faltering. Sarah has supported me through situations that would cause many girlfriends to give up the relationship rather than continue dealing with the problem. I really appreciate the support and understanding that she's given me, but this could be our breaking point. 'It's you I care about,' I say, 'you I'm in a relationship with. If . . .'

At that moment my phone signals that a text has arrived. Never have two high-pitched beeps sounded so ominous.

'You better get that,' Sarah snarls, glaring at my phone. 'It could be your girlfriend.' She leaves the room and stomps upstairs.

That wasn't the way the conversation was supposed to go.

I glance down at my phone. It's a text from T-Mobile saying my phone bill is ready to view online.

It takes an evening together, a couple of drinks, and a long conversation with my phone on silent before I can convince Sarah that the situation with Nancy isn't about the future, but the past. It's as if all this time our relationship has involved a third party – not Terence, not even Nancy, but my obsession. This is a twist in my quest I wasn't expecting. My quest is now about resolving those things in my past that will help me confront the origins of my obsessional nature. Understanding the differences between the kind of child I was and the person I've become I hope will also help me forget Terence, and finally let me move on.

The following morning I check my phone. Another virtual closed envelope is waiting for me, another message from Nancy. I open it excitedly: *have u married, kids??*

That's not a question I was expecting. It's a question made larger by it being formed of cold hard words on a screen. If we were having a catch-up in a café and the same question was asked, perhaps it wouldn't seem so huge. And perhaps in conversation I wouldn't feel so unadult in my reply: *No, never been married, close once. No kids either, though i do have a cat. You? x*

Nancy responds in seconds: *I was married divorced three kids two dogs two cats four kittens two hamsters fish and a frog.*

It sounds like Nancy is the keeper of a menagerie, or a mini Noah's ark. It's my turn for the instant reply: *Wow that is a houseful! How do you keep them all from fighting?! x*

Without missing a beat, my phone bleeps again: *ive got a referee outfit and whistle.*

Nancy seems to be exactly the kind of person I'd want to hang out with; she's funny, and she's not afraid of being revealing. A few days later I text her again, just to check she is definitely still able to meet up the weekend I'm planning to be in Rhyl. She responds with: *i am indeedy.*

'Indeedy' is an amazing word – 'indeed', which is affirmatively positive, plus the 'dy' is like a great big smiley face stuck on the end. I'm just hoping our face-to-face conversation will be just as positive and free-flowing and smiley.

I won't lie, I'm nervous about staying in Rhyl. It's been so long since I've lived there, but memories of being beaten up on nights out, ending up with a broken nose and collarbone, make my face and shoulder twitch with pain like it was only yesterday.

But I've always wanted to stay on the promenade – an overnight holiday in my home town, rather than the day trips of my childhood – to wake up with the sea in front of me and hear the waves crashing and the seagulls barking overhead. That wish is enough to drive me forward, and as an adult it's easy to make those kind of wishes come true. A quick Google search finds a hotel with non-smoking rooms situated directly opposite the beach. The website states that it is 'Gay and Theatre friendly'. I'm not gay, but I am involved in theatre. It sounds like the least threatening hotel in North Wales, which is perfect. I book a room for two nights. The 'Adult Only' notice on the email receipt does worry me slightly. I hope it refers to the fact they don't allow children, but I'm not so sure. The tag line 'Arrive a guest and leave a friend . . .' does nothing to ease my concerns.

It takes me eight hours to get to Rhyl from London. Everything is delayed or cancelled. By the time I arrive at the hotel I'm tired, hungry and grouchy.

'Hi, I booked a room for two nights in the name of Penlington,' I say, putting my bags down at the reception.

'Ah, I've been waiting for you,' says the man behind the check-in desk, who is clearly the owner. 'Are you with the ballet?'

'Me? No.'

'Oh, I thought you were with the National Ballet at the theatre, you know, coming from London.' The corners of his mouth lose his professional smile. 'I've upgraded you to our best suite with our compliments.'

I can tell he is more than a little disappointed, especially when we pass through the hallway to my room. 'I'm very proud of this wall,' he says. I can see why. The wall is covered with signed photos from every celebrity, and near celebrity, to pass through the hotel – astrologer Russell Grant, eighties pop sensation Sonia, Sinbad from *Brookside*, *Hi-De-Hi* actresses Su Pollard and Ruth Madoc, a handful of people who star in *Emmerdale* and *Coronation Street*, and a dozen or so of those who didn't win *Big Brother* or *The X Factor*. I think he hoped I would be another photo to add to his collection.

My mistaken upgrade really is to a premium suite, complete with separate dressing room and bathroom tastefully decorated in shades of seaside blue and sand. The window of the main bedroom looks over the Events Arena where I used to hang out with my friends from the sixth form of Emrys Ap Iwan when we were still too young to drink in pubs legally. We'd drink cheap cider and make plans, gossip and tell stories, talk about our pasts and imagine the future. One future I never imagined is that I'd be staying in a hotel over the road, remembering the moment I imagined the future. My head hurts at that thought, or with tiredness, I can't be sure which. Regaining my focus about why I am here, I sit down on the edge of the bed and text Nancy: *Hello. After an epic 8 hour journey I'm finally in Rhyl. Just making plans for tomorrow morning. Where is best to meet you?*

That was 8.43 p.m., and by the time I take off my glasses to go to sleep I still don't have a reply.

* * *

I'm awake by eight, and check my phone for messages before I even put on my glasses – one message from Sarah asking if I'm OK, but nothing from Nancy. I tell myself that it's fine. I'll leave it for a couple of hours to give her a chance to reply before I text again. It gives me plenty of time for a leisurely breakfast and a quiet read in my room before heading out to meet her.

I was too tired to eat last night and now I realise how hungry I actually am. I get dressed quickly, and give a quick good morning to the wall of fame on my way downstairs. Strangely, Russell Grant seems to be missing, just a hook and an empty space where his beaming, cherubic face hung the night before.

The hotel dining room is empty. On the nearest table is an envelope with my name on it. Inside there is a five-pound note and a message that reads: 'Due to personal reasons there will be no breakfast served in the hotel today. Please find a £5 refund to purchase breakfast elsewhere.' The note is intriguing, puzzling, and somehow fitting for this adventure. But perhaps it's another mystery too many, especially when combined with the missing photo of the famous astrologer, and certainly a mystery not to be pursued on an empty stomach.

A cold drizzle is blowing in from the coast, and the sky is the colour of Airfix kits. By the time I get to the centre of town my jacket is soaked through. All the shutters of cafés on the high street are still closed, so I make my way back to the promenade. The dragon of Knight's Caverns arcade looms overhead, making an electronic growl, its long tongue looping through the neon circle that surrounds its body. Next to me on the pavement stands a knight that looks uncannily like the one on the battered cover of *The Cave of Time* I left at the centre of the Prendergast Triangle, except more weatherworn and with a hole where the right side of his face should be. A neon arrow points in to the smell of cooking fat. I've found breakfast.

The owner looks surprised and pleased to find me in his café. He says that *anything* is available from the extensive menu. It's too early for roast chicken and two veg, so I settle for a mug of tea and a sausage sandwich. The café is empty. The oddness of the enforced solitariness is making me doubt my reasons for coming back, and the reason for wanting to give the letter to Nancy in the first place.

I eat the sausage sandwich in silence. The owner of the café seems to be sitting in a back room, watching a muffled TV. I compose another text, one I hope doesn't make me seem too desperate, which is difficult when you're trying to meet up with someone you haven't seen for twenty-three years, who is no longer replying to you: *Hi Nancy, just wondering when is good for you? I have a couple of things to do this morning, but I'm pretty flexible*.

I have to be honest, I lied to Nancy in that last text. I have nothing to do this morning.

Staring distractedly around the café, I notice on the wall beside me is a canvas print of a painting, a sea scene of a small boat moored to a cluster of rocks on which two boys are standing. The sheen from years of chip grease gives the painting a heat haze, opalescent almost. There is a slit running up the centre of the canvas, I imagine as the result of a waitress tripping on the lino, smashing cutlery, crockery and the remains of an all-day breakfast against the wall. The boy on the right is either flying a kite or a triangular smear of ketchup. The boy on the left looks distractedly through the hole in the middle of the painting, a tear that seems to offer a way out, a glimpse of the bright beyond of the unfaded wall behind. I find it hard not to think of the boys as Terry and me. It is an image of hope, and I need all the hope I can get right now.

I finish my tea quickly, burning the top of my mouth in my haste to leave the emptiness of the café behind me. At the top of the stairs I can hear the distinctive sound of the wind blowing through the rusting metal cables of the Sky Tower – a two hundred and fifty foot tower that used to offer rides to the top in a doughnut-shaped gondola. It has now fallen into a state beyond repair, but when it worked, and the weather was right, it offered an aerial view of the entire town, the silhouette of the Blackpool Tower in one direction and the coast of Ireland in the other. Now it just stands making a staccato metallic buzz, the sound of a robot from the future with bad mobile phone reception. At least it has stopped raining.

I find my way along the prom as the last of the arcades are opening their shutters, my feet leading me to the flashing red lights of Les Harker's Amusements, the familiar sound of the bingo caller carried towards me on the wind like the song of a siren – 'Green line, it's retirement age, six and five, sixty-five. It's on the yellow, one and seven, seventeen.'

In the box in which I discovered the letter to Nancy, I also found the pay packets from my first summer job. I've brought one of them with me, as a totem of my childhood, a totem of the year I was well enough not only to go to school, but also ride a bike, and work for some extra pocket money. The pay packet shows I worked twenty and a half hours in a week for £13.35p, which means I was paid 65p an hour. Sixty-five pence seems a lot of money when you're 13, when just three hours work could buy you the latest *Choose Your Own Adventure* book. Cosy Corner, where I used to work, was knocked down in the early 1990s to make way for an underground car park and Disney-style Children's Village. It was part of what could be described as a friendly and mildly exploitative family-run business that prided itself on looking after its employees and providing harmless family entertainment with the aim of making a lot of money. At that time, it was run by father and son, Old Les and Big Les. Big Les took charge of the arcades while Old Les, a man in his seventies, took the comparatively more sedate role of managing Cosy Corner.

Cosy Corner was just across the road from the arcade, between the prom and the beach, a self-contained outdoor mini-amusements that included trampolines, crazy golf, mini go-carts, a train ride with a simulacrum/rip-off of Thomas the Tank Engine's face that went round a small circular track, and a space-rocket ride that did the same but a few feet in the air.

Working on any of the attractions had its own pros and cons. The trampolines were the most undemanding to be in charge of first thing in the day and towards the evening. Each child had ten minutes in which to jump up and down as much as they liked. If time was on your side, you could look busy without actually doing much, but if you were unfortunate enough to be working when it was really busy, you'd have a temporal logistical nightmare combined with aggressive scousers complaining you weren't doing your job properly and kids who were so excited about jumping that they'd sometimes accidently urinate in the middle of the trampoline. You'd be responsible for the cleaning up.

The crazy golf was straightforward, and you could even sit down to hand out the clubs and the balls. Unfortunately, it meant you were positioned next to Old Les's booth, where a woman called Beryl, who looked like the schoolboy/female dwarf cross-dresser from the Krankies, also worked and so you were subject to both of their nagging.

Working the go-carts had an element of danger. They were powered by car batteries that were recharged overnight, and at full speed they could drive at six miles an hour. Children aren't meant to travel that fast unattended, especially if they aren't tall enough to reach the brake pedal without a wooden block to make up for the difference in height. I still have a scar where a four year old in a mock Ferrari crashed into my right knee. I'll come clean – I've told more than one person that scar was from a racing-car accident. It's not entirely a lie.

The remaining two rides were thoroughly undemanding to work. Once children had climbed on-board, and had their tickets collected, you just turned a dial to start the rides in motion. I remember a trick an older boy had shown me that involved gaffer-taping the clanger of the train's bell to the side, so the bell-pull no longer worked. While writing that sentence I've only just realised how mean it was – denying a child on holiday the momentary pleasure of the joyous enacting of being a train driver from the end of the nineteenth century – but a full range of hearing is the thankful gift of that treacherous act of sabotage.

The biggest downside to working anywhere on Cosy Corner was that we all had to listen to Old Les playing the twenty greatest hit songs of World Wars I and II on repeat, every hour, every day of the summer, through the tinny holiday-camp speakers that were dotted around the amusements. Even now I can still sing every word to '(There'll Be Bluebirds Over) The White Cliffs of Dover' and 'It's a Long Way to Tipperary', a talent that is of very limited practical advantage.

A teenager wearing a bright red Les Harker's Amusements branded sweatshirt is just finishing filling one of a row of fruit machines with money. I wait until he's locked the small door on the back of the machine.

'I wonder if you could help me, is Les around?' I ask.

'Do you mean Big Les?' he says, spinning his large bunch of keys absentmindedly around his finger.

'Yeah,' I answer.

'He's just over by the bingo,' he says, pointing deeper into the arcade.

I walk towards the bank of bingo machines, the same machines I remember vividly from when I worked here. The only difference is that, due to the smoking ban, the ashtrays have been removed from the front, leaving behind two small holes and a bright patch of the original lurid orange Formica – the ghosts of thousands of cigarettes. Next to them, standing underneath the pink neon of the flashing Prize Bingo sign, is the unmistakable outline of Big Les. He must now be as old as Old Les was back when I worked here, but he still cuts an impressive figure on the arcade floor. He's still clearly someone only a fool would want to get on the wrong side of.

'Excuse me, Les? My name's Nathan. I used to work for you a long time ago.'

'I was just going to say. As soon as I saw you, I thought, I know that face . . . Christ, you have shot up, haven't you?' he smiles. 'I remember you used to be down here,' he says, putting his hand halfway down his chest.

I haven't been in an arcade for so long that I'm finding it hard to tune out the bingo caller, who is seated on a high stool in a raised booth, using a microphone that seems to be turned to a 'voice of god' setting – 'Red line, all the beans, five and seven, fifty-seven. White line, five and one, fifty-one.'

'I worked on Cosy Corner with your dad,' I shout, trying to make myself heard over the electronic blur of 'Rule Britannia' that has just started blaring out of a two-pence coin waterfall to my right.

'That's a long while ago, Christ almighty. Cosy Corner, that's got to be twenty-odd years ago, at least. The children's village has been up about eighteen years.' Les's cheerful reminiscence drops suddenly. 'My mum and dad are both sadly gone now.'

'I'm really sorry to hear that,' I say. 'I liked working over there. I even liked listening to "Pack up your troubles in your old kitbag and smile, smile, smile" ten times a day.'

Les laughs, a big, full-muscled laugh, then quickly becomes serious. 'You're catching us at a downwards point. When you was with us, Rhyl was vibrant. We've had a downwards spiral for the past nine or ten years, and we're just on the upwards surge now. With a bit of luck we might get an upwards surge for the next nine or ten years. I hope I'm here to see it . . . I'm seventy plus now.'

'Wow! You're looking really well. But, apart from you being here, it has all changed,' I say, indicating the vast space of the arcade, a space that has tripled in size since I worked for the Harkers.

'For our sins, we've inched along and finished up with the whole block. You'll remember we had the small arcade at one end, the Monty Carlo at the other and in the middle was the Silver Dollar. When we bought the middle bit, we knocked through, now we've got the block. I stand across the road some nights,' he steps back, arms crossed in front of his chest, 'and think to myself, "My dad would be proud of me now."'

'I brought something to show you.' I pull the small brown envelope out of my pocket. 'I found it in a pile of my old stuff in my mum and dad's garage. It's one of your old pay packets, look at this . . .'

I point out the neat handwriting on the front of the envelope, which I assume, thinking about it, belongs to Big Les's mum. He laughs, taking the envelope from my hands and reads aloud, '. . . twenty and a half hours for thirteen pounds thirty-five pence. It was hard work that, moving those trampolines. I still remember how we had to get them in, four of us, one on each corner and lift them in the shed. If you had any bad memories, apart from working in the rain when we had to shut things down, you wouldn't have come back to say hello.'

I guess Big Les is right. I don't really have any bad memories of that summer, just one regret, that I didn't give Nancy that letter.

Big Les continues, sounding like he's giving me one of the hundreds of references he must have written over the years for boys who used to work here, 'I remember you were hard-working, prompt, and would take anything on, and as a team guy, you were very good. 'Cos if you weren't a team guy over there, you didn't fit, and you became an outcast, and anybody who can't get on with the public or staff . . .' Les forms his hand into a fist and extends his thumb as he points it over his shoulder, '. . . phhft, out the window. I mean for the money we gave you for twenty hours, you must have enjoyed working here.' He laughs again, his eyes twinkle. 'I could do with a few more like you now, on the same wage.'

'That's how you saved enough money to buy the whole block,' I reply.

Les's laugh booms around the arcade this time, momentarily causing the bingo caller to look up from the microphone. He looks disgruntled, like we'd ruined the punch line to a very long joke. He uses this moment to sip tea from a glass mug, before he pushes his glasses up his nose and continues pulling the numbered balls out of the machine. He looks like me. In fact, it's so uncanny it's like peering through a wormhole to a parallel world in which I never left Rhyl – 'Last one for this game, it's yellow again, two and four, two dozen eggs, twenty-four. There we are ladies, don't move them, wait while we check the board. Only one winner this time, two prizes there for that one, though.'

But this is Big Les's turf and it's clear to see that not only does he own it, in all senses of the phrase, but he enjoys it. It's his world, and it has always been his world.

'It's lovely to get a blast from the past. In fact, wait there a moment.' Les disappears behind the bingo caller into the Staff Only room, guarded with CCTV and a one-way mirror. Minutes later he's back.

'This is a little bit of this,' he says, handing me a plastic pot branded with Harker Leisure and full of two-pence pieces. 'Look around, have a play, enjoy yourself, and remember when,' he says, pointing to the back of a boy working the floor whose sweatshirt has the word STAFF printed in large black letters.

'Thank you, Les, that's very kind.'

Looking around this side of the arcade, most of the machines are the classic coin-waterfall type of various designs, but they all work in the same way. Coins cover a number of shelves that constantly move backwards and forwards. After you feed a coin into a slot, a chute drops it on to the top shelf. If you time it right, and the coin ends up in the right place, your coin will sometimes push a few coins from the upper shelf to the lower shelf. If you're lucky, these fallen coins might then push a few coins from the lower shelf into the pay-out funnel. It sounds and looks simple, but the psychology behind these machines means they can be extremely addictive. The combination of lights and sounds, the piles of coins teetering suggestively over the edge of the pay-out funnel, the bonus tokens scrolling out of the machine, the extra prizes resting on the coins inching slowly forward every time a new coin is put in the slot, and the fact that you are playing with two-pence pieces means that, even if you do win, you are likely to keep playing until you completely run out of change. Despite knowing all of that, I've always enjoyed playing them. It's fun. You should always keep your fun gain and cash loss in balance.

I head straight for the machine decorated with a red-nosed, orange-haired clown looming down between two anatomically incorrect elephants. I pull up a stool and begin carefully timing the dropping of two-pence pieces into the slot of the Big Top Circus.

I've never seriously gambled, not any more than a few pounds. If you've worked in an arcade, I guess you understand the futility of it. Even if a fruit machine claims to pay out 95 per cent, and to pay out that highly would be unusual, it means the game is still paying out less than it takes in and it's making 5 per cent profit every day. You know the odds are weighed against you, and you have no chance of improving them. Even the coin waterfalls aren't as innocent as they look. Quite often the machines are designed to push the coins to the side where 'overflow' house funnels claim back pure profit. The extra prizes resting on the coins are not there because the owner of the arcade is feeling generous; they are there to help weigh down the coins to make them harder to dislodge, and if you do eventually win one of the prizes, you are likely to have paid for it four times over. Like I said, the odds in an arcade are stacked against you.

But in real life you do have a chance to improve your odds and you've got to try things in life to get the most out of it. Maybe that's what this whole adventure has been about. Maybe I should be content with having tried. People always say if you don't try, you'll never know, and if you do try, and it turns out that you'll still never know, at least you tried, right? I've tried with Terence. And I've tried with Nancy.

When I worked for the Harkers, I was definitely as shy as perhaps Terence worried that he was as a 13-year-old. The work was hard, but it really helped me come out of myself, forcing me to talk to people I wouldn't ordinarily have come into contact with, not least Old Les and Big Les. But it didn't push me far enough to put that letter through Nancy's front door. Maybe if I'd been well enough to work another season, I'd have worked off my shyness and things would have been very different.

It's now over twenty years later, and if she doesn't reply to my texts today, I should put the letter in an envelope with a note explaining what it is, address it to her and pop it through the letter box of her parents' house. At least then I've succeeded in doing what I've come back to Rhyl to do. I'll have tried.

I've been feeding coins into the slot without thinking, scooping out my winnings and reinvesting them immediately. Coin after coin has been fed into the slot, while paper tokens have been scrolling out of the top of the machine. I'm not sure what I'm doing to trigger it but I've won so many they are now spooling onto the carpet.

Suddenly, the game changes. A blue-and-white wristband is teetering on the end of the shelf, directly above the pay-out chute. Every coin nudges it forward a few millimetres. It's the most positive wristband I've ever seen, inscribed with words like 'Inspire', 'Wish' and 'Believe'. This has to be a sign. I wish my remaining few coins luck, inspiring them with belief as they travel down the chute to the first shelf. A couple fall by the wayside, but most hit the target and send five coins over the ledge on to the second self. As the shelf travels inwards I hold my breath, the wristband is pushed forward ever so slightly and wobbles a wobble that seems to contain the whole of time. Time stops for the most minute of fractions. I dare not breathe. I imagine all the old ladies leaving their seats at the bingo machines and crowding around behind me in anticipation. The bingo caller has even muted the voice of god out of respect for the moment. Time starts again. The wristband wobbles over the chasm of fate before falling into the pay-out chute . . . I've won! I've only gone and achieved the impossible. For a fraction of a second I'm invincible, no one can take this moment away from me. I reach down and pull the rubber bracelet from the pay-out slot, place it around my wrist and punch my fist in the air in triumph. I. am. a. winner. And judging by the name printed on the wristband, I am now also called Amanda.

On top of this big win I have also collected one hundred and seven paper tokens. Behind the bingo is an Aladdin's Cave of amusement-arcade treasure, glass-fronted cabinets that glitter with prizes. You can exchange your tokens for anything from fortune-telling fish valued at twenty-five tokens to toasted-sandwich makers and electric kettles for ten thousand tokens. In between the two extremes are an assortment of money boxes, glow-stick bracelets, swimming goggles, plastic swords filled with sweets, folding kites, *I ♥ Mum* mugs, miniature bingo games, eight-piece cappuccino sets, Angry Bird stress balls, and hand-painted metal Admiral figures. In the middle of one cabinet is a small gold-painted figurine of a laughing Buddha. A sign next to it reads 'Lucky Buddha – one hundred points'. Despite my win, luck is something I definitely need, and luckily I have a hundred points. I hand over my tokens to the guy behind the counter and he solemnly hands me a golden Buddha as though it's the most precious thing on earth – and at that moment, it is.

I walk over to Big Les who is talking to a member of staff next to the tea and coffee machine.

'I just wanted to say goodbye and thanks again for the two pences. I won a wristband . . .' I say, showing Les the inspiring side of my bracelet.

'So they call you Phillip now do they?' He turns my wrist over to look at the name printed on the other side. 'Amanda.' He laughs his infectious laugh.

As I step out on to the pavement, I can hear the voice of god intoning with infinite finality – 'There's no rush to exchange your tokens, they never, ever go out of date.'

It's still too early to try Nancy again, and it feels wrong to waste my time in the hotel. I start walking back through the town towards Vale Road bridge and the railway station. Since my parents moved away, I've been back in these streets once, for the funeral of my friend Kriston.

Our friendship began in Emrys Ap Iwan, not long after I'd started sixth form. I'd been at the school for just a few weeks, and was still very much the new guy. I was playing catch-up with all the years of education I'd missed by squeezing in two GCSEs with four

A-Levels. To make everything fit in the timetable, for some classes I was made to sit in with students who were a year younger, taking their GCSEs for the first time.

So, not only was I the new guy in my year, I was also a new guy in other years. It was a lot to cope with, not only educationally but socially. At first I thought I was going to have to sit in silence again for the whole term.

One of those classes was art. One morning I was quietly drawing a still life from a ram's skull sat on the desk in front of me. I was listening to The Doors on my Walkman to drown out the rest of the class, and to soak up my interior monologue. When the teacher left the room, a guy with long hair, wearing cowboy boots, came over and tapped me on the shoulder.

'What are you listening to, Buster?' he asked.

'The Doors,' I replied, expecting some kind of put down.

'Well, fucking aye chief, turn it up.' That was my first encounter with Kriston. We became friends immediately.

I'd not only found a friend, but an ally. Kriston had also missed years of school through ill health; he suffered from cystic fibrosis, a genetic disorder that affects the lungs, liver and pancreas. While my illness wasn't life-threatening like Kriston's disease, we both suffered from the side effects of childhood illness – long stretches of time in hospital, isolation, obsessive and existential tendencies. Kriston's obsessiveness took a different route from mine, forming itself into irrational counting routines of door locking, turning plug sockets on and off, and a germ-based fear of the telephone. He was loud. He was unpredictable. He loved the blues, partly for the romance of the mournful songs of the old bluesmen, forgetting their troubles with booze, women and song, but mainly for the music. He loved life, and I loved him for that.

Kriston's death hit me sideways. We were still good friends, but living in different places meant we didn't keep in touch as much as we should have. His death wasn't a surprise. Given his condition, a young death had been predicted by doctors since his teenage years. I just wasn't ready for it.

And now here I am again in Rhyl, my only visit since his death, on a fool's mission, but one that Kriston would have understood without question. Once he sent a Valentine's card to a girl, but became obsessively paranoid that it wouldn't be delivered. To make sure it was, he got up early and sat for an hour in his car next to the post box, waiting for the first post to be collected at 6 a.m., so that he could ask the postman if he could take the card back and deliver it himself. The postman, of course, said no. We never knew if the card was received or not, and Kriston was too scared to ask the girl in question to find out.

The day Kriston died I lost one of the first real friends I ever made, and I lost my ally, someone who could understand quirks of my personality and not hold them against me. I miss him madly.

On the day of his funeral I walked out of the crematorium on to a patio filled with grown-ups who were once teenagers I went to school with. Some of them had been my friends. Most of them I hadn't seen since I left Rhyl. I was crying. It started snowing. Then someone spoke to me, someone I hadn't spoken to for years. The first thing he said was, 'All right, Harry Potter.' If I'd been a fighter, I would've punched him.

My brain seems to have engaged a faulty homing mechanism, and before I realise it I'm on the corner of my old street, in the car park of the British Legion. When I say street, I mean cul-de-sac. There is no short cut through a cul-de-sac, which, by definition, means a dead-end. I always used to think of our street, not as a dead-end, but as a road that only led outwards.

Our cul-de-sac didn't end in a T-shape, but in more of an oval loop with a teardrop island. The island used to be overgrown with bushes and twelve-foot pine trees. When I was a child, the island held many mysteries, mainly because we were not allowed to play on it. When my sister and I felt especially brave, we'd sneak around the opposite side from our house, crawl under one of the bushes, carefully avoiding the dog poo, used condoms and broken glass. Once inside the centre of the island we were in another world – a kingdom of dinosaurs, the middle of the Amazon, a sailboat on a voyage around the world, a spaceship in an alien universe. But all adventures have to end. The council came one day to level the island and concrete it over. They hacked back the bushes and were about to chop down the trees when my mum and a neighbour ran out to form a human barrier to try to protect them. The council won of course, and our illicit adventures were over.

It is small changes that make a place feel different. Now I'm in my old street I feel taller. The paving slabs that I once mapped out on squared paper, with Xs marking imaginary booby-trapped squares you couldn't stand on for fear of falling to your death, were tarmacked over. The concrete lampposts I used to imagine were one-legged tripods, after first listening to Jeff Wayne's musical version of *War of the Worlds* with my dad, have all been replaced with newer, energy-efficient models. The high walls of the neighbours' gardens now are only waist height.

The most unrecognisable thing in the street is our old garden. They've ripped out all of the trees and bushes, and they've taken down the gate. The gate, wrought iron with the perfect curls for footholds, used to have a certain squeak. No matter how many times it was oiled, you would always know if it was being opened. My brother, sister and I used that squeak as an early warning system to indicate that Mum or Dad were coming home and we should stop doing the thing we shouldn't be doing. For a well-rounded upbringing every child should have the equivalent of a squeaky gate.

I take a deep breath and walk up the path to the front door. I ring the bell without counting. I don't know what I'm going to say. I haven't prepared for this, but I don't need to. I'm a grown man, I'm brave, I'm fearless, and, as my wrist proves, I'm a winner.

And once again no one is at home. I stand for a couple of seconds staring at the closed door, the surrounding pebble dash still missing the pebbles where I pulled them off in boredom the times no one was home after school. I don't know what I hoped to learn by coming back here, but in a way it is good that no one answered. You can't really revisit the past; you can only visit the current version of it. I didn't really want to sit in my old bedroom in a house that is now someone else's home, full of different furniture, different possessions. In the future I would have always remembered my bedroom overlaid with those differences. Our family grew up here, but it is best to let those moments be memories. This visit to Rhyl isn't only about trying, but also about saying goodbye, finally allowing myself to move on.

Back at the hotel the owner is managing the bar. I say hello as I pass by the open door.

'Sorry about this morning,' he says, walking though into the hallway. 'We just had a bit of a situation to deal with.'

'That's OK, I found breakfast in town,' I reply.

'The noise didn't keep you awake did it?' he asks.

'The noise?' I remember waking briefly in the early hours of the morning to shouting from the street. I assumed it was just people on the way home from a Friday night out. 'No, not really.'

'It's just that a friend got himself into a terrible state, threatened to kill himself. He'd been drinking all day, absolutely half cut. He was out there effing and blinding, calling everyone all sorts of names. We eventually got him in and calmed him down. He knocked my precious photographs off the wall, too, while we were trying to carry him to bed. So, that's why there was no breakfast, we were up all night sitting with him.'

'I'm really sorry to hear that. Is he OK?'

'Yes, yes, he's fine. Nothing a bit of sleep and a few days off the beer won't cure. The thing is it has happened before. He won't remember any of it, or how horrible he was to all of us. Sorry again if the fuss kept you awake.'

'Don't worry at all, I slept through.'

Upstairs in my premier suite I put my Lucky Buddha on the bedside table, and look out over the Events Arena.. I'm lucky I found my way out of this town. Of course, many people don't want to leave, and have made very happy lives here. But there are those who do want to find a way out, who want an opportunity to live a different life, who need a challenge or a chance. If you don't find that opening, then you can end up feeling even more trapped. It's very easy to bury those feelings, but the risk you face in ignoring them is that they can take you by surprise and overwhelm you. If I hadn't been able to move away from here, I wouldn't like to think what would have happened to me.

It's now six-thirty and I'm lying on the hotel bed. I've half snoozed half read the rest of the afternoon away. I've tried and failed with Terence, and I've tried and failed with Nancy. Now I'm just wondering what my next step should be, how I can find closure to my question without talking to her.

Suddenly my mobile buzzes. Unbelievably, it's a text from Nancy: *sorry couldn't answer earlier. I'm free this evening if u are. Come to mine for 8 so dont have to get babysitter.*

Just when I'd given up hope, possibility drops down the winning chute.

Chapter 13 - Love is all around

Nancy lives six doors down from her parents' house, in the same street she grew up in, the street I cycled down many times as a 13-year-old boy – a calculated diversion on the way to The Bounds in the hope of an accidental glimpse of her. As I approach the door a boy, only a little younger than I was then, walks down the street to greet me.

'Are you Nathan?' he asks.

'You're not Nancy,' I reply in surprise.

'No, my mum told me you were coming.'

'Yes, I'm Nathan. What's your name?' I ask, stretching my arm out to shake his hand. He glances at my Amanda bracelet. I pull my sleeve down quickly, hopefully managing to hide it in time.

'I'm Ryan, nice to meet you.'

The front door of the house is open, and a menagerie of children and animals pour out into the garden.

'Are you famous?' one of the children asks. There are so many of them I'm not sure which one.

'No, I'm not famous,' I laugh.

'I told them you did magic,' Nancy says from the doorstep.

Nancy is just as I remember her, obviously a little older, but now, if I remember her text correctly, 'a single mother of three, two dogs, two cats, four kittens, two hamsters, fish and a frog'. Around me the menagerie seems to be bigger than that, and Nancy senses my confusion.

'These aren't mine,' she says, circling the air above the heads of two of the youngest children. 'These ones are. Katie who's thirteen, Ryan who's ten, and Reece who's six next week.'

A toddler shows me his toy car, a welcome distraction from my bumbling nerves. 'It changes colour,' he says excitedly.

'Come in,' Nancy says, showing me into the living room. Two sprawling couches face each other over a low table. The room feels comfortable and inviting, paintings of roses decorate the walls and the mantelpiece is adorned with candles. It's the lounge of a warm heart.

'Sit down. How have you been?' Nancy asks. I sit on one of the couches. A cat immediately starts nuzzling itself into my lap. On the top of a bookshelf beside me is a fish tank. I begin mentally counting off the pets and children I've seen so far, like an *I-Spy Guide To The House And Family Of A Girl You Used To Go To School With But Is Now A Fully Grown Woman*.

'I'm good thanks. I've just spent the day in town, and in the arcades.'

'Sorry about earlier,' she says. 'Things were a little . . . err, a little hectic.'

Mutual surprise is easing the first few minutes of conversation, but I know it will soon wear off and I'll have to start explaining what I'm really doing in Rhyl, and more importantly what I'm really doing in her lounge. Nancy shoos the youngest children away into another room, before sitting on the couch on the opposite side of the coffee table.

'It was a bit of a bolt out of the blue hearing from you. My mum and dad called and said, "There's a letter here for you." "Is there? Why would anybody write to me there? Right, I'll come and get it." I was reading it thinking, "Nathan? Do I know a Nathan? Ooooh! I know who he is!" I couldn't believe it!'

'Sorry about that. I didn't know how else to get hold of you,' I say.

'Oh no, it's fine. It's really nice to hear from you. It was just a shock, you know.'

Already Nancy seems open and friendly, and I can now understand the honesty of her texts. My frustration at not hearing from her today and yesterday is totally forgiven. I need to redeem myself from my failure to tell Terence the truth, and I know from past experience the longer I leave it the harder the truth will be. I can't say goodbye to Nancy with the letter still in my pocket and a string of lies hanging in the air between us. I take a deep breath and just hope I don't blurt everything out in an unintelligible babble. This is not something I want to repeat.

'I was trying to find a guy who had written a diary that I found in an old book,' I begin. Nancy is leaning forward, trying to make sense of what I'm telling her. It's not a promising start. 'I found him, but I lost him again.'

'Right,' she says, unsure of how anything I've just said relates to her. Confusion settles in across her forehead and makes itself comfortable.

I take another breath. 'But as part of this journey I found something I wrote to you but never gave you.'

A flicker of fear passes through her eyes, her smile becoming tighter at the corners of her mouth from which escapes an involuntary, 'Oh, no.'

I pull the piece of folded paper from my pocket with a magical flourish and show Nancy her name written across the front. 'Oh no!' Nancy squeals again, covering her mouth with her hands.

'When did you write that?' she laughs.

'I'd just turned thirteen.'

Her eyes widen. 'No way!'

Not for the first time in this adventure I've managed to time travel. It feels like I've gone back in time, and then skipped forward to this point in an alternate reality. If Zemeckis made *Back to the Future 4* and set it in North Wales, in a small semi-detached house, starring an awkward nerd and really shy girl, this would be the crucial scene.

'Imagine the year is 1989,' I say, 'and I was brave enough to come round to your mum and dad's house and knock on the door. Your big brother isn't there to scare me away, and I'm courageous enough to deliver my letter in person.'

Nancy is actually sat on the edge of her seat. I'm trying not to let my nerves derail me.

'And it says,' I continue, hardly daring to look up, '"Nancy, will you come out on Saturday?" There are two little boxes – yes or no – and the letter says "do not tick both" . . .'

Nancy laughs again. There is something reassuring about that. Ryan and Katie are both sat on the arm of the couch, smiling. There is something reassuring about that, too.

'I guess I couldn't have any ambiguity,' I continue, 'so is it yes or no?'

'OK,' Nancy says, ambiguously and in a non-committal way. But I don't let her vague response put me off. I'm on a roll of sorts, and I have to keep going.

'I'll take that as a yes. So, "If yes, what time? Where?" Where would we have gone?'

'Probably the coronation gardens, because that's where we all used to hang out, wasn't it, on a Saturday or whatever. It would have been the coronation gardens.'

The coronation gardens were just over the road from Rhyl High School, a small park of formal gardens, football fields, tennis courts, crown-green bowling, swings and slides. A place for fights and first kisses.

'Are the coronation gardens still there?' I ask.

'Yeah, that place hasn't changed at all.'

'So, that's good, we're going to the coronation gardens. And then there's a PS. "PS can I have a photo of you?"'

'I would probably have given you one of my terrible school photos!' Nancy laughs and pulls a mock disgusted face at her kids.

'I can't believe I was so forward,' I say, feeling myself flushing a little. 'Well, I would have been forward. In my mind I was forward. I don't know what I was thinking. And then it says, "Thank you", so at least I was polite.'

Nancy laughs again.

'The letter ends with "PPS – which pop star do you like?"'

'Oh God! I was a big Wet Wet Wet fan. A huge Wet Wet Wet fan. I couldn't get enough of Marti Pellow!'

I can't remember any of Wet Wet Wet's songs, apart from their cover of 'Love Is All Around', originally by sixties band The Troggs, for the film *Four Weddings and a Funeral*, one of those annoying songs that spent months at the top of the charts. I fold up the letter and slide it across the coffee table.

'That's for you.'

'Aw, bless. Thank you. Can I keep it?'

'Of course you can.'

Nancy picks up the letter and reads it silently to herself. Despite the time delay of nearly twenty-three years it is still a love-letter, and love-letters make eyes sparkle in the most amazing of ways.

'Ah, it's so cute . . . your handwriting is appalling though!'

'Thanks!' I say, thinking back to the graphologist's comments about my closed circle connection letters, my suit of armour. 'Sorry it's taken so long, but I'm glad that I got to deliver it in person.'

'I can't believe you kept it! You're the last person I expected to hear from after twenty years . . .'

I still don't really understand why I kept it, either. Was it because one day I hoped to be fearless enough actually to deliver it? Or so I could read it and wonder 'what if?' – a kind of self-provocation to be braver.

Perhaps now is that time to be braver. Nancy has put me so much at ease that I'm compelled to test the past, to see if I was right or wrong not to give her the letter.

'Can I ask . . . if I had made a different choice at the time and given you that letter, would you have gone on a date with me?'

Nancy looks down at her hands. Oddly, for a second, she seems to be that 13-year-old girl again. Then the stronger, more confident woman is back in control. She looks me straight in the eye.

'Yes, definitely,' she says. 'I had a right crush on you.'

My heart drops like it did when I first met Terence.

'You were my first crush,' she says again, quietly, once more becoming that 13-year-old girl. 'I think I've gone red,' she laughs, putting up her hands to feel her cheeks. 'You should have given it me,' Nancy whispers.

It feels like a lift full of stones has just plummeted a hundred and six floors through the bottom of my stomach, the elevator music reduced to a squeal of regret.

'I wish I had,' I say.

Knowing that Nancy's answer would have been 'Yes' makes the realisation that I made the wrong choice, by being cautious and not taking a chance, hard to swallow.

'You should have given it me,' she says again.

As she repeats those words the full weight of the implication hits me. There is always someone else affected by every choice you don't make, as much as the choices you do make. My decision not to give Nancy the letter affected her life as much as mine.

'I would have if I'd been a little bit braver,' I stammer.

'Was I that scary?' Nancy laughs.

'Not at all!'

'It's the fear of rejection, isn't it?'

'It's the fear, but if you don't act, the moment passes. The thing is, you realise so much more about yourself as you get older. I'm not that shy boy any more.'

'I was also very shy, wasn't I? Very quiet . . .'

Nancy stands and passes the letter to Ryan and Katie, who are still sat on the arm of the couch, then comes and sits beside me.

'I always wondered what happened to you,' she says. 'I see quite a few around that were in school with us. It's funny, you remember all the cliques that were in school, the "successful ones", the "athletic ones", but there are no groups when you get older. Now, though, some people want to get back in touch through Facebook and things, but I always think, "Why do you want to talk to me now? You never spoke to me. How can you remember me from school? You never spoke to me."'

'I know exactly what you mean,' I say, thinking about the Facebook friend requests I've had from those who collectively ignored me in school. In return, I've left them waiting in endless digital purgatory, neither accepted or rejected.

'Rhyl High hasn't changed you know. I had to take Katie for an open evening before she moved from primary school. It was like walking into a time warp. They've still got the old tiled floors and the wooden partitions in the English block. Nothing's changed, absolutely nothing's changed. Even some of the teachers are still there. That was a real shocker. Mr Williams the science teacher was looking at me for a while before he said, "I know you don't I?"'

'One of the teachers called me Nancy the other day,' Katie says in a mock tragic way. 'How bad is that?'

Nancy rolls her eyes.

'What clique would you say you used to be in?' I ask Nancy.

'Oh, I was in the swotty clique, the quiet clique that just got on with the work. I was quite shy, very quiet. I thought if I just sit and get on with the work, no one will bother me.'

'I was like that, too, but more of a loner . . . sometimes out of choice but not always.'

'You were really shy, bless you. I remember you used to get really poorly, too. You'd not appear at school for a few weeks and we'd wonder what had happened. But I always thought you were a really nice lad. You were really shy, but shyness is related to confidence, isn't it. I left school without much confidence, but I went to Llandrillo College and my confidence level shot up. Definitely came out of myself. My dad says I'm now a wild child. I say to him, "I'm thirty six, I've got three kids, I'm not that wild, trust me."'

'It really helped me to get away from Rhyl High, too, and make a new start. I went to Abergele to do A-Levels, somewhere people didn't know me as the kid who had something wrong with him. Then I went to London to university. My mum and dad moved away about ten years ago, so I don't really come back.'

'Well, whenever you fancy coming to visit I've got a spare room. Free of charge, love. I'll even feed you.'

'That's an amazing offer. I'd really love to,' I reply.

As we talk, we reminisce about other places in Rhyl. I tell her about knocking on the front door of my old house, visiting Les Harker, winning on the arcade machines. I even proudly show them all my new name. I really like Nancy and her family. You can see that they've had to cope with some tough times, but they're strong and loving. An idea is forming in my head. It might be one step too far, but I'm enjoying catching up and part of me wants it to continue, to time travel one more time.

'What are you up to tomorrow?' I ask.

'Not a lot,' Nancy says. 'Why?'

I take another deep breath. 'Do you want to come to the coronation gardens?'

Nancy looks me in the eyes again. 'Are you finally asking me on the date we never had?' she gently elbows me in the ribs.

'Yes, I am.' I elbow her back.

'Of course it's a yes. Are you actually going to pick me up from the door?'

I nod. I hadn't planned any of this, so I'm thinking on my feet.

'Wow!' says Nancy. 'If you want me to get my big brother down, just say.'

I laugh. 'It's taken this long, so I guess I better make it special.'

'You better had!'

Katie and Ryan are sniggering and whispering to themselves. It's my turn for the mock tragic. 'Hey, you better not be making fun of us. Is there anything you think I should bring on the date to make it special for your mum?' I ask.

Without pause, they yell simultaneously.

'Flowers,' shouts Ryan.

'Chocolate,' shouts Katie.

Ryan thinks for a moment then adds '. . . and special biscuits from Home Bargains.'

Nancy puts her head in her hands, 'Oh, no.'

'Special biscuits?' I ask. 'What are they?'

Nancy lifts her head up. 'You'll remember these. They have a soft biscuit base with two lines of marshmallow. Well, Home Bargains sell them. As a kid I always used to eat them. They've brought them out again, and I can still finish a packet at a time! I tell the kids they're my special biscuits so they don't eat them. God, kids are embarrassing at times.'

We make final arrangements for the morning before I leave in a whirl of goodbyes and see you tomorrows. As she closes the door behind me I find myself feeling a huge combination of emotions. If they were a list of words, they would be things like: overwhelming, bewildering, sweet, embarrassing, nerve-racking. But as you can't feel words themselves, I just find myself standing in the street in a daze. At that moment the streetlamps turn themselves on, a moment that has always been magical, and tonight it seems more magical than ever. This has been an amazing day. And it's a rare and beautiful thing that has just happened.

If I went straight back to the hotel, I'd end up pacing my premier suite, restless with excitement. I call my friends Gary and James, who live in a village just outside Rhyl, to see if they fancy a pint and a catch-up. Thankfully, they do.

I know Gary and James from sixth form. When we were 17, Gary used to play bass, and James the drums, in a band called Red Drum Head. The name of the band came from a type of cabbage or lettuce seed found while browsing in Mr Bevan's home and garden store in Abergele one lunch break. They were a band who pushed boundaries, playing infamous lunchtime gigs in the school hall with songs like 'Kitsch Laden' and 'Popcorn Groove for the Bathroom Queen'. They even went as far as reversing both 'e's in their name – Rɘd Drum Hɘad. Once I was invited to guest vocal on a cover of Blur's 'Girls & Boys'. After that gig we were all given a serious talking to by the head of sixth form. That was my first and, for a while, my only time in a band.

I've been thinking about Rǝd Drum Hǝad all the way to the pub, and by the time I see the lights of The Plough another idea is beginning to form in my mind. I buy the first round to soften Gary and James up a little, and before any of us know what's happening words have arranged themselves together in a sentence I never ever thought I'd hear coming out of my mouth.

'Do you know any Wet Wet Wet songs?' I ask.

'What?' says Gary. James looks too stunned to speak.

'Wet Wet Wet, you know, the band. I was thinking because you were both in Rǝd Drum Hǝad you'd know . . .'

'Nathan!' Gary exclaims. 'We were a grunge band. A GRUNGE band. If you wanted me to play Nirvana or Smashing Pumpkins it would be no problem, but Wet Wet Wet?'

I explain to them the full story about Terence, about the diary, about the love-letter, about the adventure, about the elation I've felt, and the despair I've been through. I explain about my date with Nancy, and my idea.

'We haven't played together for years,' James says, finally snapping out of his speechlessness, 'and even if we were still in a band, it's a bit late notice. I've promised the wife I'd take her somewhere tomorrow morning.'

It's a blow to my plan, but it's another indication that I've got to realise we're not teenagers any more. People have commitments and families.

'And it's fucking Wet Wet Wet,' Gary says.

'Pleeeeeeease Gary!' I beg in the most pitiful voice I can manage. 'This is really important.'

'Damn you, Nath. You are mad, clearly mad, but I love you for it.' He looks at his watch. 'I can't promise anything, but I'll do my best. When I get home, I'll see if I can find the chords on the internet.'

We have a few more pints and catch up on the local gossip. It's like I've never been away. In less than two pints I know all the scandal. I leave before last orders. I have to get up early to prepare for my date, a date I've been waiting for for most of my life.

It's the day I never imagined would ever happen. I'm going on a date with Nancy Mills.

I slept soundly through the night, although anticipation wakes me up before the alarm clock goes off. The sun is streaming through the curtains and the screech of seagulls seems to have been miraculously transformed into a joyous seaside serenade. I shower and dress quickly. This morning I can actually smell breakfast cooking downstairs. I know I should eat, but I don't know if my nerves will let me.

'Mooorrrnnnning,' the hotel landlord trills. I take a seat near the window. Two of the other tables are occupied by middle-aged couples. 'Sorry again about yesterday,' he says.

'Please don't worry about it. You have bigger concerns. Is everything OK?' I ask.

'Oh yes, we're making sure everybody is being looked after. Full English?'

'I'm not sure I can eat that much, just some fruit would be fine.'

'Are you sure I can't tempt you?' he asks, punctuating the end of the question with a wink.

'No, thank you, though.'

'What have you got planned for today? Anything interesting?'

'Yes, actually. I'm going on a date,' I say excitedly, glancing at the clock over the bar to check the time.

'A date? With anyone I know?' He winks again.

'I don't think so, but you might. It's with a girl I used to go to school with called Nancy.'

He lets out a sigh. 'Oh, a girl.' I've clearly disappointed him for the second time in two days, but not for long, as minutes later he comes back with a fruit salad beautifully arranged into a star. 'I hope it goes well!'

'Me too! I'm trying to arrange a surprise. I don't suppose you can sing?'

'Me? Oh, I wish!' he says with a shrug. 'Sorry, there aren't any singers staying here this weekend, either.'

While I'm eating the star of fruit, I text Gary to check he hasn't slept through his alarm. Getting up at eight is a lot to ask of anyone on a Sunday. When I rush upstairs to grab my jacket, it's good to see Russell Grant is back on the wall – it seems all the stars are aligned in the hotel today. I dash across town. Before I meet Gary at the coronation gardens, I have to pick up the chocolates, flowers and special biscuits.

I think I know what Nancy means by special biscuits. I hope they're what used to be called Jamboree biscuits. They consisted of a biscuit base covered with jam sandwiched between two knobbly marshmallow fingers sprinkled with coconut. They were so special we only had them at birthday parties, hence they were known as Party Biscuits in our house.

I'm standing bemused in the middle of Home Bargains. It's the second time on this quest that I've been bewildered buying biscuits.

'Can I help you, sir?' asks a friendly shelf stacker in the distinctive, homely Welsh-Scouse accent that sends my nerves up a notch. I try to explain what I'm looking for. I get as far as Party Biscuits.

'Err, ah yeah, come with me,' she says, leaving her stock check of washing-up liquid. 'Are these they?'

She hands me a packet of Jam Mallows. Through the clear section of the wrapper I can see the distinctive pink bobbly strips of foamy marshmallow. 'Special occasion then is it?' she asks. It seems everyone reveres these biscuits.

'Yeah, really special. I'm going on a date I never had twenty-three years ago.'

It's her turn to look bemused. 'Good luck,' she says, 'although you won't need it with those,' she adds, pointing at the Jam Mallows. She turns and disappears down another aisle, a fairy godmother of the discount supermarket.

* * *

As I pull up in the car I'm relieved to see Gary standing at the gates, clutching his guitar. I'm not so relieved to see he's clearly hungover.

'I'm feeling really, really fragile, Nathan,' he croaks.

'I know this was an alcohol-induced agreement, but I really appreciate it.'

'Just don't expect greatness,' he replies.

We walk off quickly across the football field, heading for the other side of the park. Nancy is right, it hasn't changed since my childhood. My feet follow the familiar paths around the gardens and lily pond, trying to find the best place for Gary to sit out of sight until he sees Nancy and me turning the corner. At that moment, according to our ill-formed plan, he is to burst into song. We try a bench near the bowling greens or leaning near a large wooden statue of a bear, before finally settling for him sitting on one of the large stones of a less than impressive rockery.

Gary looks around at the place he has to spend the next half an hour. 'I've rented worse,' he says sardonically. 'At least I'll have time to learn the lyrics.'

'Are you going to be OK here? I'll be as quick as I can.'

Gary's managed to get to the park early on a Sunday morning with a print-out of the chords and the lyrics of a Wet Wet Wet song. Considering it was such a last-minute idea, I can't really be disappointed, whatever happens. Finally, I'm ready to take Nancy on the date we should have had all those years ago.

I stop the car a couple of houses down the street from where Nancy lives. To say I'm nervous would be an understatement. I'm more anxious than I was when I knocked on Terence's door for the first time.

Suddenly there is a small tap on the passenger window. Ryan is on the street to meet me again. I open the door so we can talk.

'Hi, you all right?' he asks.

'I'm OK. How's your mum?'

'She's very nervous, because she hasn't had a date in a while and because you're one of her old school friends,' he says. His honesty puts me at ease instantly.

'I'm really nervous, too. I think I've got everything, though, the flowers, chocolates and special biscuits . . . are these the ones?' I ask, holding up the Jam Mallows.

He grins. 'Yeah, she loves them.'

'Do you have any advice for me?'

Ryan fiddles with the opening tab of his can of Coke, and then looks up at me.

'Just be gentle,' he says softly.

My heart breaks at the thoughtful tenderness of this little boy, his understanding of his mum's relationships, and his love and care for her.

'Don't worry, I will,' I say, trying to sound reassuring. 'It's going to be really nice.'

'Yeah, the coronation gardens is nice.'

I gather my things together and take a deep breath.

'Are you ready?' Ryan asks.

I nod. 'I guess so.'

Ryan leads the way into the house. I follow behind, clutching my gifts like a liferaft. Nancy is waiting in the lounge with her coat on.

'Hello, sorry I'm so late,' I say, trying to hold everything behind my back without dropping anything. 'I've bought you a couple of gifts, flowers . . .' I clumsily produce the bouquet of white and orange calendula and hand them to Nancy.

'Aww, look at that,' she laughs, a brilliant, warm, infectious laugh.

'. . . chocolates . . .'

'Oh bless, thank you,' she says.

'. . . and the special biscuits.' I hand them over with a slight bow and the reverence they deserve.

'Nobody touches these,' Nancy says, pointing at the biscuits and then at each of the children in turn. 'They're mine. And be good for your nana, she'll be here in a minute. I'll be back in two hours.'

We drive in the direction of Rhyl High School, Nancy pointing out places that have changed or are no longer there along the way – a tour of invisible history too small for any guidebooks, of corner shops and shortcuts. I park the car on a side street opposite the coronation gardens. I've been longer than I thought I'd be, and I'm hoping that Gary is still sat in the right place, hasn't fallen asleep, gone to the toilet, or given in and gone home.

We cross the road near our old school, the pebble-dashed walls and iron gates of the park, like the gardens of my old street, seeming smaller than I remember them.

'This place hasn't changed at all,' Nancy says. She doesn't know I was here less than an hour ago, so I can answer truthfully.

'No, it doesn't look like it has.'

'We used to have PE here, do you remember?' she begins to ask, then catches herself. 'Sorry, I wasn't thinking.'

'That's OK. I did do some PE. I mainly played tennis here when I was still in primary school. I wasn't particularly very good, but I enjoyed it. I remember the tennis coach was mean about my cheap racket, though,' I pause in thought. 'It's strange how moments like that can stay with you.'

We turn the corner, away from the bowling greens, towards the carving of a bear and a path lined with cherry-blossom trees. Out of the corner of my eye I can see Gary is still sitting casually on the large boulder where I left him. He must have heard us coming as he's already strumming quietly, but as he sees us he bursts into a deep, rumbling, broken singing voice, Tom Waits after smoking two packets of cigarettes and downing a bottle of whiskey.

'I feel it in my fingers
I feel it in my toes . . .'

It takes a fraction of a second, a fraction in which you can tell Nancy thinks it's some kind of old drunk park guy with a guitar, before she recognises the song. But with that recognition Nancy immediately starts laughing, doubles up, and puts her hand to her mouth in shock.

'How the hell did you do that?'

> '. . . *Love is all around me*
> *and so the feeling grows* . . .'

Gary now sounds more like Darth Vader eating gravel while playing Nirvana, but it doesn't matter. I can't help but laugh with her. Surprise is an incredible, joyous thing to give to anyone – and this is the best surprise I've ever organised.

'How did you do that?' Nancy punches me lightly on the arm.

'It's magic,' I say, pulling one of my finest magical ta-da gestures. 'It's the only thing that was missing from your list. I'm sorry it's not Marti Pellow. This was the nearest I could get.'

Nancy hugs me gently, 'Thank you.'

'I'm getting wet now,' Gary shouts, but he carries on playing regardless. It's drizzling heavily, but in the laughter I hadn't noticed.

'It was a very last minute arrangement. This is my friend Gary. I met up with him in the pub last night and he kindly agreed to get up this morning . . .' the end of my sentence is drowned out as Gary raises his performance despite the rain.

> '. . . *You know I love you*
> *I always will* . . . Sorry, I think that should be a D minor there
> . . . *my mind's made up*
> *by the way that I feel*. . . Can I stop?'

Gary is trying to pull his hood up with one hand and still play his guitar with the other.

'Thank you so much, Gary. I'll call you later. Nancy, do you want to get out of the rain?'

We walk towards the redbrick toilet block, where the roof overhangs the edge of the deserted bowling green, leaving a narrow strip of shelter.

'I still can't believe you did that. I'm in total shock. I don't think anyone's done anything like that for me ever. It's lovely,' Nancy says.

I give her a hug, hoping that isn't true. Part of me wishes I was 13 again, and in a way we are teenagers again, but neither of us is naive enough to take this moment for more than it is. We're two adults whose paths have gone separate ways – I have a happy life with Sarah in London – but we're two adults who have been lucky enough to have travelled through time. It's hard to know what would have been, and we can always regret and wonder, but this moment is special. It's special because it shouldn't have happened. I found *The Cave of Time* and stepped through it – that kind of time travel is supposed to exist in stories only, not in real life. My brain is in a whirl. I can only assume Nancy's is too.

'It's taken a long time, though, for that to happen,' I say.

'Twenty-three years. I mean, there's taking your time and taking your time. Do you know what I mean?' she elbows me in the ribs.

I laugh, and that 13-year-old boy I once was laughs, too. 'I hope it was worth the wait.'

'Definitely. You so better not lose touch now.'

'I won't. I promise.'

It's now the end of May. It's been over a year since I first knocked on the front door of Terence's old address. The last time I tried to contact him was three months ago.

Visiting Rhyl, and seeing Nancy again, has helped me come to terms with the fact that in order to live a full life I've got to learn to let things go, allow for the unknown, not to be in control. I have to take Edward Packard's advice and learn to be kinder, firmer, stronger and more honest – with myself as well as other people.

This whole quest started out as a kind of nostalgia for *Choose Your Own Adventure* books, but following its twists and turns has always led back to me. I've revisited my own childhood, faced some of my demons and realised the things I've overcome to be the person I am now. It's time to move on and face responsibility.

I just need to send Terry one more email to wrap everything up. In it I outline some of the things I've learnt from my conversations with Dr Finkel and Ruth the graphologist. I mention about digging up some old things from my childhood, and the *Choose Your Own Adventure* style love-letter to Nancy. I tell him about speaking to Edward Packard. I still don't mention the diary, so although it's not quite the whole truth, it's close enough.

I send the email before I can change my mind. I haven't written to Terry with the expectation of ever hearing back from him. It's just my way of saying that this is. . .

The End

Chapter 14 – Falling into place

Real life isn't usually so dramatic or final as the two ominous words that threatened to cut the story short in every *Choose Your Own Adventure* book. Of course it can be, but not as often as *Choose Your Own Adventure* would have you believe. Life generally has a way of continuing, despite all the accidents, wars and diseases working against it every second of every minute of every day. Life changes, often in unexpected, surprising ways.

It has been nearly a year since I last spoke to Terry face to face, and five months since his last email. Less than twenty-four hours after I sent my goodbye, finally putting my obsession to rest, Terry breaks his unfathomable silence.

Hi Nathan,

Thank you for your email. If you'd like to, I'm happy to meet up. I was thinking of coming to London next weekend.

And in breaking his silence, he once again kick-starts my obsession. This time there is no other choice. I *have* to come clean.

I arrange to meet Terry at the Royal Festival Hall, the modernist, reinforced-concrete building on London's South Bank – not the best looking building in town, but one of the best for meeting people because of its central location without necessarily being on the tourist route.

I walk over the footbridge from Embankment station, running the gauntlet of buskers spread at even distances across the river – saxophone rock, a steel-drum rumba, modern classic violin, and mariachi – a confused soundtrack to add to my already overcrowded thoughts.

My best friend Guy used to busk along here, too, not with an instrument, just speaking. On a daily basis, people would hurl abuse at him, thinking he was a religious or political cultist, while all he doing was bringing beautiful, unexpected stories into the world. Guy suffers from acute OCD, the constant need to check and to count and to worry, which eats into his life. The day he left the UK to return to America he came over to my flat to say goodbye. It was an emotional farewell, and as Guy cycled off, disappearing into the traffic at the corner of my street, I immediately felt the loss of a good friend. Five minutes later my phone rang. It was Guy, asking me to go and stand outside the front of my house. He had cycled around the block, constantly worrying he hadn't made the most of our goodbye and wouldn't remember the details. His OCD had returned him to say goodbye all over again. Goodbyes are harder the second time.

Guy would understand my quest, and that I would never be able truly to rest until I'd found Terence. But Terry still has no idea this started with his diary and that's how I managed to find him, and it's been the underlying focus of my quest all along. In fact, he has no idea that this is a quest at all. This journey has been about the adventure, but it involves real people and I don't want to hurt anybody in any way. I have no idea how Terry is going to respond. I couldn't imagine any one of the hundred and six different possible outcomes. For him to come out and talk about those things in the diary I've been obsessed over, that would be the ideal situation, but I'm aware that he might just say, 'No, I'm not interested.'

As I walk towards the doors of the Festival Hall, a toddler runs towards me. I wonder at what age it becomes unacceptable to break into a sudden run, a dance or a tantrum to illustrate your mood, or just because you want to. If I could translate my feelings into movement, this moment would look like an agitated piece of physical theatre, performed at breakneck speed, by a man running very fast away from here.

Pushing through into the terrace-level café, I realise I've made a mistake. There are so many people, and so many café and bar areas, Terry and I could easily miss each other. I curse myself for not having been more specific. I was so concerned to get Terry to agree on a time and place that I didn't take time to contemplate the logistics of our meeting.

Faces blur in and out of focus as I scan the tables, the queue for coffee, the bar near the ballroom, the couches, the benches, the upstairs balcony, the members area. If I had to give a photofit description of Terry, I don't think I would remember how to describe him – boyish, mid-thirties, nothing useful or helpful. I just hope he hasn't stood me up. I lost Terry once and that caused me so much anguish and despair, I wouldn't be able to cope with going through those emotions again.

I walk back towards the way I came in, glancing at every man in his thirties that I pass, hoping one of them holds the answer to my questions. I decide to do another sweep of the entire building, starting where I began at the front doors. Once again I scan the café queue and tables. No one fits the faulty, flickering image I have of Terry in my head.

Suddenly, through the windows that run along the entire length of the river side of the building, I see a large group of people leaving an outside table they've been occupying on the terrace. Behind them is a man, sitting alone. He's in profile, facing away from me. I can't tell from where I'm standing if it's Terry or not. I move towards the doors, trying to keep one eye on him at the same time as not tripping over anyone. I manage only one of those things. I look away for a fraction of a second to apologise to the mother of a small child, and when I look back, the man has turned his head slightly. It is him. It's definitely Terry.

I rush out through the glass doors and squeeze my way through the sprawl of tables and chairs towards him. Seeing Terry more closely, the absurdity of my quest hits me once again. Away from his parents' house Terry immediately seems more confident, outgoing, relaxed. He's leaning back eating a sandwich and sipping a beer. He's swapped the trousers, jumper and glasses for a white T-shirt, chinos and canvas pumps. Like the first time I met him, he's wearing no socks, but this time it's a conscious fashion decision. It's almost as if the last time he was the teenaged Terence Prendergast, and now he's the person I found on Facebook. Now he is James Costello.

'Terry,' I say automatically, reaching out my hand.

'Nathan,' Terry exclaims, gripping my hand firmly. 'Hello.'

As we shake hands, I notice a tattoo of what looks like the bottom of an anchor on his upper arm. I make a mental note to ask him about it.

'Are you well?' I ask.

'Very well, thank you,' he says.

'Really nice to see you. Thank you so much for coming down to speak to me . . . you've got pigeons eating your sandwich, though,' I say, pointing at three pigeons who've taken advantage of Terry's distraction by landing on the table, and in a flurry of wings and feathers have started to peck apart his sandwich. 'I think we should find a quieter place.'

I buy a couple of beers from the bar, and we find a quiet corner on one of the upper floors, where we won't be disturbed.

'I have something important to tell you,' I begin. 'I didn't quite tell you the truth the first time we met. I *am* now writing a book about *Choose Your Own Adventure,* but it all began when I found four pages of a diary that you'd left inside one of the books.'

Terry's face blanches. 'Really?' he laughs nervously, taking a sip of his pint.

'I wasn't brave enough to be honest with you, because I wasn't sure how you would take it, or how that would make you feel.'

'Nathan, I can't have been much more than thirteen . . .' he begins as a way to excuse whatever it is I'm going to say next.

I reach into my bag and pull out a few of Terry's creased and well-worn *Choose Your Own Adventure* books, opening *Trouble on Planet Earth* to the page where Terry had written his name.

'Yeah, that's definitely me. I used to write my name in all my books,' Terry laughs nervously.

'*Trouble on Planet Earth*,' I say, trying to get straight to the heart of our meeting. 'This is how I found you. You'd written your old address and I knocked on the door in the hope that I'd find someone who would remember you, or know your family. I really didn't think I'd find your mum and dad still living there. You'd written in some of your other books, too.'

I produce other books from my bag – *You Are a Shark*, *Space Patrol* and our favourites *Sugarcane Island* and *Hyperspace*. Terence flicks through the pages, his eyes seemingly glassy at the memory of writing those childish words.

'I remember I used to write in all my books,' he says again.

I open *Space Patrol* and show Terry the words written inside the cover – 'Telbot's Book. Dimples is a fat prune'.

Terry laughs. 'There was a character on TV called "Delbot Wilkins" played by Lenny Henry. I thought he was quite funny at the time, so I must have given myself a stupid name because of that. I used to call my sister "Dimples".'

I feel encouraged by his memory of his writing. 'I've brought the diary with me, too,' I say, pulling out Terry's original copy of *The Cave of Time*.

'This is the diary.' I pull out the four small pages from inside the book. Those pages have come a long way, a journey that they were never intended to be on – both a message-in-a-bottle and a catalyst for adventure.

I put the diary on the table between us, but Terry doesn't reach to pick it up. It seems neither of us is really sure who it belongs to any more.

'Shall I read it out?' I ask.

'Sure,' Terry says.

As I read out the speed of light equation, time seems to slow down. I'm reading out the words in front of me, words I've read hundreds of times before, but it also feels like I'm standing outside of myself for a moment, observing the scene in slow motion, seeing in detail Terry fidgeting slightly with the beer mat, peeling the top layer backwards from the corner, and how I'm nervously flicking through the pages of *The Cave of Time* with my other hand – the comforting gestures of two men in an awkward situation. As I get towards the neat row of 0s travelling millions of miles into the distance, time returns to normal speed.

'I don't remember writing that.' Terry looks confused. 'I think it was probably a phase I went through. I failed GCSE science.'

'Me too,' I say, thinking back to my third-year exam results written in the back of my diary. I could have taken a scientific path if chance and circumstance hadn't intervened.

'I wish I could have concentrated on one idea or obsession and studied harder rather than moving from one thing to another. Maybe I would have a successful job. I just got distracted a lot.'

'That's something I do a lot, too,' I say. 'I get really obsessed with one idea, and then I'm compelled to move on to the next thing.'

'If you can find an obsession, and concentrate just on that one thing, you could make a very successful career out of it. Like playing music for example, or sports.'

'You're right, but I don't have the brain for that kind of narrow focus. There are too many things in the world I want to find out about. You're one of them,' I say, perhaps a bit too honestly. Thankfully, Terry laughs.

I turn the diary over to the list of years that starts '1975 born' and runs all the way through to '1990 3rd year'.

'I guess this is a list of your school years, but do you remember what they were for?' I ask, pointing to the list of numbers down the side.

'I've no idea, honestly.'

'When I first read it, I thought that, well, perhaps something I would have done is to mark something out as my favourite years, a top ten almost. Top eleven, in this case.'

Terry seems not to remember writing this page, either. I begin to think that I've built this whole moment up to a significance that the reality can't live up to. He seems to have no recollection of writing these things, or what they refer to. I turn to the list of things the teenaged Terence wanted to improve about himself.

'We can stop at any point if there's something you don't want to talk about,' I tell Terry.

'OK, sure,' he replies, almost dismissively. After all, he hasn't remembered the previous two pages.

'This page is a list,' I say, holding it up to show Terry. 'It starts "Fat, carry on exercise, don't eat cake etc".' An immediate look of recognition crosses his face.

'I do remember this. I used to write things down to try to organise my thoughts, rather than keep them in my head,' Terry says. 'When I was about eight, I started to become overweight. I don't know why. I was teased about it at school. It wasn't as if I started eating loads more sweets and crisps and things, but I suddenly became very fat and I was very self-conscious about it.'

Terry looks in fairly good shape, muscles bulge a little under the sleeves of his T-shirt and I catch a flash of tattoo on both biceps, too fleeting to see fully.

'How do you feel about your body now?' I ask, instantly realising that it's a difficult, demanding question. 'Sorry, you don't have to answer that.'

'I care what women think about my body, and I need constant reassurance. I'm still very insecure,' Terry answers.

I admire his honesty. 'I hate showing my body in public. I'm too gangly for shorts or swimming trunks. I've got terrible knees, too.' I carry on reading. 'The next line is "brace, voice, practice speaking" . . .'

'When I was ten I had a metal brace on my teeth,' Terry says.

'You wouldn't think so if you look at my teeth now,' I grin

awkwardly, showing Terry my wonky smile and chipped tooth, the result of a fight with a pavement, 'but I had a brace as well. One of those ones that you wear at night that go over your head, really uncomfortable and painful.'

'Yeah, I had to wear one of those, too. Horrible. I used to think that a lot of kids didn't really mind, but I was self-conscious anyway, so it made it worse. I also had a plastic jaw that I was supposed to wear during the day in Junior Three, but it gave me a lisp, so I didn't wear it, just kept it in my pocket. I remember I used to sit by a girl called Anthea Lee. One day, I looked up during class and saw her standing next to the teacher, saying, "I found this thing on the floor," and putting it on his desk. It had obviously fallen out of my pocket when I was sitting at my desk, and she had quietly picked it up and taken it over to Mr Kenny. I could feel myself burning with embarrassment. He asked if it was mine and I said it wasn't. I was so embarrassed. He said, "I don't care if it's yours or not, just come and take it off my desk!" The whole class was watching. I had to get up, walk to the front of the class and get it.'

'That sounds terrible,' I say. It really is the small moments that stay with you the longest. 'Do you mind me reading this list out?' I ask Terry, still worried that reading through his diary might not be the right thing to do.

'Not at all. I'm happy to go through each one,' Terry answers.

'Only if you're sure,' I reply.

'What's next?' Terry asks.

'"Stutter, practice speaking".'

'Again when I was about ten I developed a stutter from complete nervousness. I still have a bit of a stutter now.'

'The next line says "Posture – walk properly when slim".'

'I developed bad posture due to a spinal problem, a twisted spine, which probably added to my nervousness. I suddenly found myself walking like I was falling over, and no one could work out why until a few years later. I was finally referred to a spinal specialist, and he told me I had scoliosis. I used to be the tallest kid in my class, and

I suddenly stopped growing, and even lost a bit of height. I used to be the big kid, the one who had to keep a low profile. I was always conscious of seeming like an ogre, and then everyone else overtook me in height.'

'"Hair" is the next thing on the list.'

'Really?' Terry asks, laughing.

'That's what it says.' I show him the word, unmistakable in his neat handwriting.

'Maybe that was when I was in Junior Three, aged ten. I remember after the Christmas holidays, Daniel Bridger came in with a really trendy haircut, spiky hair I think it was at that time. Before that, we all had our hair combed by our mums. I thought, "I'm going to have to try that," thought it might help with my confidence or something. I wanted to try and make girls like me.'

'I remember experimenting with hair conditioner, leaving it in until it dried. I remember thinking it looked good, kept my hair shiny and styled, until it rained that is, when I just turned into a foamy mess.'

Terry laughs.

'"No friends",' I say quietly, thinking back to my own teenage years. I feel torn between wanting Terry to know I understand completely how he feels and not wanting to interrupt him now that he's opened up.

'When I was at primary school,' he says, 'I was always trying to be a clown. Saying things out loud that I thought were funny, but other kids didn't. The rest of the class seemed to be athletic and good at sport. I wasn't, I was just tall and awkward. I felt really lonely, and I just wanted to get out of that area even if that was into a make-believe world. I was lonely, I had no friends, I didn't know what I was doing. That's probably why I wrote all this stuff down.'

'"Shy",' I whisper. It feels as if I'm reading out a list of my own childhood things to improve.

'I was terribly shy as a kid, terribly shy. No confidence whatsoever. Instead of talking to people in a normal fashion, I would either just shy away or blurt things out that I thought were funny or witty but weren't. I never knew how to act or socialise around people. I knew it was a problem. I think it's something you just pick up off your parents. My parents weren't particularly extroverted . . .'

'It can be quite crippling, can't it, if you're in a social situation,' I say, thinking of all the moments I've wished I could be abducted by a race of timid aliens who communicate their thoughts purely through telepathy.

'Definitely, yes. If you're shy, that's one of the most crippling positions there is. It really holds you back in life.'

'I was incredibly shy as a kid, too. I can still be quite shy in some social situations even now, but as a kid I got into magic. The thing with magic is that it's quite nerdy, so you have to spend a lot of time on your own, learning how to do the tricks, but obviously it's a performance art so you have to perform. You have to force yourself to not be shy. I think that's what happened to me. Do you think you're still shy now, or have you managed to come out of that?'

'I'm not introverted, because I like meeting people, but I am still a shy person. I still tend to have to think about what I'm going to say before I meet people, or think about the consequences of doing something, which I think holds me back. It's the same for other shy people I've met.'

'Next on the list is "self-conscious".'

'I think the thing for me, when I was young, I was the tallest in the class until I was about eleven. In junior school I remember being held back from playing with the other kids because a teacher thought I was older than they were, even though I was in the same class. I think since then I've had this self-consciousness of "don't stick out". It's never gone away, really. I have social anxiety in just wanting to fit in.'

'"PE, if I get slim do it".'

'I hated PE – because of being tall, worrying about being fat and sticking out. I hated it, but I thought, "If I want to be slim, I have to do it."'

I think back to the graduation photo on the top of the piano, the moment this one piece fell into place, the tiny piece of knowledge that kicked my obsession into mania. 'The next entry is "Karen".'

'Oh, that's my sister. I don't know why I wrote about her.'

'Did you get on with your sister?'

'Yeah, I liked her. I knew some kids who hated their brothers and sisters, but yeah, we got on.'

'But if this is a list of things that were worrying you, to organise your thoughts, do you think she might have done something at that time?' I ask.

'I thought that she'd grown up too quickly. She used to copy pop stars when she was too young. She dressed promiscuously.'

I imagine a room wallpapered with posters of Madonna and Cher, a change of uniform hidden in her school bag.

Terry continues, 'My mum used to go on about it all the time, saying she got too much attention from boys, that kind of thing. It was probably a source of worry for me because I cared about her, and added stress at home.'

'"Laugh, practice laugh".'

'I thought that by practising laughing I would be more spontaneous and not so self-conscious, and I'd get on better with people if I could laugh.'

'Did that come out of being shy?'

'That's exactly right. I thought that by practising laughing, it would come out more naturally, rather than a forced smile or something.'

My heart breaks for the young Terence, practising his laugh in the mirror, and even if he was happy to be somewhere, finding it hard to show that happiness because he was so anxious about it.

'The next sentence is "Being left out". . .'

Terry looks at me, but not in sadness. I don't have to drag the words out of him. Somehow, he feels compelled to let it all out. I had been beginning to think that there really was no message-in-a-bottle – that, in fact, this quest really had been about me all this time, that I needed the connection, not Terence. Yet, sitting with him now, the words he wants to share are almost palpable in the space between us. It's clear Terry finds it reassuring to be finally talking about these things after all this time.

'I always felt left out. I didn't fit in and I wanted to be somewhere else. I was always worried about what my position in life would be, and wondering if I would ever find it. When we left primary school, I remember worrying, "What am I going to do when I'm twenty, thirty, forty? I can't think of any job I can do." Most people get sentimental when they get to adulthood but I remember being sentimental from a very young age, from eight or something, thinking back to when I was five, four, three. I thought back to the age before I started school, the age of having no worries, not having to go to school, family outings all the time, at home all day watching children's TV. When I started school, I hated it.'

'Why did you think school was so terrible?'

'I think I was agoraphobic – just chronic shyness, fear of being in the same environment as other people. It started the first day of primary school. I still remember that first day of primary school. I remember thinking I just wanted to be in that world with my parents, free of school, being free of having to be in a room of structured order, other kids running around, rules, teachers and discipline. I hated it. I was a nervous wreck. I was depressed. I just didn't want to go to school. That's why I started reading those *Choose Your Own Adventure* books, just to imagine another world, and what the rest of the world was like without school, where you could just wander around on your own. I just wanted to get away from everything. Get away from my parents maybe and that school, and just explore the world on my own. And be free of everything.'

'It's a pretty big awareness when you're that young, to know . . .'

'. . . that I hated school,' Terry says, finishing my sentence. 'I don't know why I did, I just did. I hated school, I feared school, other kids my age. I wasn't ready for it. I felt low and unhappy. I wouldn't have used the word depressed, it would have been too big a word. I would have used unhappy or sad.'

I take a deep breath. Now is the time for me to be completely honest with Terry, not just about the diary, or the adventure, but about me, about my life.

'The period of time between finishing primary school and starting high school was when I became really ill for the first time. And I had similar thoughts, really. I spent a lot of time on my own at home because I was so ill. I remember thinking, "What am I going to do? It can't be like this for ever."'

For the first time, a slight smile creeps across Terence's features.

'I thought it was just me,' he says quickly. 'I thought that there was something wrong with me because I was having these thoughts and everybody else seemed to have no cares in the world. I was nervous, sweating and worried all the time. Now you've told me other children felt the same, and I wasn't alone at all. If I'd known that at the time, I wouldn't have stuttered, and sweated and worried, I would have relaxed and been more laid-back. Maybe things would have fallen into place a bit more.'

'Those feelings are more common than you think. The interesting thing about talking to various people on my quest . . .' I stop myself, and then continue, '. . . along the way to meeting you – Dr Irving Finkel, Ruth who's a graphologist, Sarah, Nancy, Fernando – they're all really similar in quite a few ways . . . even my dad. They were either shy or had tough teenage years.'

'It makes me feel better knowing I wasn't the only one.'

'I also think your story will inspire people to come out and be honest about how they felt, and how they feel now. That's an incredibly valuable thing.'

Terry squirms. I mean every word that I'm saying, but perhaps it's too much to hear, too soon. I turn my attention back to the list – just one word left.

'The final word is "report".'

'Really? I don't know what that means,' Terry says immediately, seemingly on the defensive. Then he nods slowly. 'Maybe it's report to myself.'

'What do you mean by that?' I ask, confused.

'Report back if any of the above entries aren't working at all. Writing things down was a way to cope because I didn't really have much help. I thought, rather than keep it in my own head, I'd just write it down. On the list of things to help myself, improve myself, the last entry, report, is to report back to myself – which I never did . . .' Terry lets the end of his sentence trail off.

A thought occurs to me. 'Well, this is a kind of report back now,' I say, 'and you've improved all of those things.'

Terry is silent for a moment. 'Yes,' he whispers. 'I suppose I have.'

We've been talking for over an hour. Terry has been completely open and honest about issues that clearly had a huge impact on his childhood, and our conversation has been emotionally draining for both of us. Terry goes outside for a cigarette, as a lifelong non-smoker I can't say well deserved, but in this instance it seems like the right thing to say.

So far everything Terry has said seems to be true, believable and heartbreaking in its ordinariness. I don't mean ordinary in that Terry's hurts are not unique and deeply felt, but ordinary in that they are hurts and concerns shared by millions of children all over the world.

His smoking seems to take longer than it should. I can't help but feel a momentarily paranoid thought – perhaps he's gone home? What if he's decided it's all been too much? He's taken his phone and wallet from the table, and he didn't have a jacket. Apart from the two empty glasses, there is no indication Terry's ever been here. How long should I wait for him to return?

It's with a huge feeling of relief that I see Terry climbing back up the stairs.

'Sorry I was so long,' Terry says. 'It took forever at the bar. I thought we would need these.' He hands me another drink.

'Thank you,' I reply, trying to avoid spilling anything on the diary. It would be one of the worst things to happen at this moment, to come face to face with Terence Prendergast, to talk to him about my obsession with a soggy inky mess.

'By the way, can I ask what tattoos you have?'

'I'm only going to show you one of them,' he says, rolling down the right arm of his T-shirt, suddenly extremely self-conscious. 'One of them is of an ex-girlfriend. The other one I don't mind showing you, but it's stupid.'

He pushes up his left sleeve to show me a colourful tattoo of a plant scrolling up his arm.

'I had it done while I was travelling,' says Terry, laughing. 'It's of a palm tree, but the tattooist was so bad it looks more like a cannabis leaf. I don't even smoke marijuana. I only smoke cigarettes.'

We both laugh.

'I'm glad I asked,' I say.

We both take a sip of our drinks, before I turn over the diary to the final page.

'There's one more page. If you want to stop, or there's anything you don't want to talk about, please tell me,' I say to Terry. 'The remaining page is a list of years, and each year has an entry. "Eighty-one, met Ada".'

'Ada – that was my friend at school, Adrian Jones. My parents were friends with his parents, and they took turns to pick us up from school, so we became friends. He was bullied by the teachers at school, so maybe I felt sorry for him.'

'What do you mean, bullied by the teachers?' I ask, shocked.

'The teachers used to hit the kids. I know you're not allowed to now, but in those days they did. He wasn't really naughty, just hyperactive or something. I guess they'd call it ADHD now.'

'"Nineteen-eighty-three, got smacked by Coulson times two, communion, confession" . . .'

'Communion, that's embarrassing,' he smiles. 'It was a Catholic school, my parents brought me up Catholic. At that time I didn't know any better. We didn't even learn science in school.' Terry is silent for a moment. 'Coulson was the headmaster.'

'Coulson was the headmaster.' I repeat his words in shock. 'And he hit you two times that year? What for? Do you remember?'

'One of the times, yes. We weren't allowed to lie down on the school playground. We had to stand up all the time. And one time during a game we were playing I did lie down. And I was hit for that.'

'They used to have the slipper in my primary school,' I say, pulling out a memory I didn't know existed from somewhere – a line of ten boys in front of the blackboard, each of us slapped on the hand. 'If you were bad, they would hit you with the slipper.'

Thinking about it now, a slipper seems such an odd choice for a weapon of corporal punishment, particularly in a non-boarding state school. The teacher must have looked down at his feet one evening as his imagination weaponised home comfort, and then brought one of the pair into school alongside his marking and sandwiches with the specific intention of inflicting pain on small hands. It's an evil thought.

'Yeah, it was like that in those days,' Terry says with an air of resigned acceptance.

'You were brought up Catholic, but what do you think about religion now? Are you religious?'

'I'm not religious, no, but if it keeps people happy or stops them worrying, I'm all for it.'

I don't entirely agree, but now isn't the time for in-depth religious argument.

The next entry also resonates strongly with my teenage years and the struggle with my health. '"Nineteen-eighty-four – wet pants times two".'

'I used to wet my pants, probably because of my nervousness and my depression as a kid,' Terry explains. 'Seeking attention probably. I used to wet my pants until I was about ten or so.'

It's my turn to shift a bit in my seat. I know how that feels – the embarrassment of it, the insecurities it breeds.

'I had serious bladder problems until I was about thirteen. It was a really difficult time, thinking back. You don't really want people poking and prodding you during puberty when you're at your most self-conscious. That same entry also says "realised about back of knee"'.

My conclusions about what Terry meant by this line have varied over the years, everything from a playground fighting tactic, to a supposed sexual turn-on.

'That was just tight hamstrings', Terry says as another mystery evaporates. 'I couldn't bend forward and touch my toes like all the other kids in PE could do'.

'I have similar issues because of my joint problems. If I'm lying down I can only get my legs to seventy-five degrees, I can't straighten them. Physiotherapy has helped a little though.'

'The next entry is "Eighty-five stroke eight-six – bullied by Kenny, crouched times three, PE worse".'

'Teacher,' Terry says flatly.

I'm shocked again. 'Another teacher?'

'Mr Kenny again, the one with my brace. He used to make you crouch down, holding books out for ten or fifteen minutes.'

Terry stands up and walks around to the other side of the table. He squats, the top of the legs taking the strain, holding both arms out straight in front of him, the palms of both hands facing towards the floor. A couple at a nearby table turn to look, but without hearing Terry's explanation you would think he was demonstrating a tough gym exercise.

'Mr Kenny would then put a pile of books on the backs of your hands. You'd have to stay like that in front of the class. If you dropped them before your time was up, he'd make you do it again.' Terry says, struggling to maintain his balance.

With every one of Terry's revelations, I have a hundred more questions.

'Was he the PE teacher?' I ask, hoping for some logical explanation to his punishment.

'No, he was the form tutor. The teachers didn't pick on me

specifically, just all the kids. They were particularly nasty to a couple of kids, though.'

These are the bullies I've thought about for so long – Coulson and Kenny. I'd imagined them as kids, nasty little kids with a grudge and power issues, pushing around those who were less able or willing to fight back. I had never, ever, imagined them as teachers, adults who should have been encouraging the less able, the shy, the timid. It's no wonder Terence didn't seem to have found anyone to confide in and tell his problems to. Where would you turn?

'Do they still work in that school now?' I ask.

'All the teachers I knew left just after I changed school. It was so long ago. It just seems like a dream or something, like it didn't really happen.'

'"Nineteen-eighty-seven – confirmation, WRGS, Karen ran away".'

'That was just another Catholic thing. By then I'd realised there was no such thing as a God. It was just seen as a social event – we all went to the church for the confirmation, and afterwards there was a disco. No one cared about the God bit, we were all just looking forward to the disco afterwards,' Terry laughs. 'I changed school, too – WRGS is Worcester Royal Grammar School.'

Another mystery is solved. 'Do you remember Karen running away?' I ask.

'She ran away a couple of times,' Terry answers, matter of factly.

'What was that like at home? Where did she go?'

'Liverpool. She was like me in a lot of ways. She used to want to escape and watched a lot of TV soap operas to help escape into fantasy worlds. I guess she thought after watching *Brookside* that people in Liverpool were more laid-back than the people we knew. And funnily enough, when we went to Liverpool the next day to collect her from the social services, they actually *were* more laid-back.'

'Were your parents quite strict?'

'No, just old-fashioned, fuddy-duddy, introverted. I'm still close to them. I'm still fond of them, but they didn't understand us, couldn't relate to us. I've never talked to them about my feelings ever.'

'"Nineteen-eighty-nine – skived day times four, smoking, caught first day after Easter".'

'I used to skive all the time from school because I hated it. I just didn't want to be there. I started smoking because I thought it was cool. When I first started, I just put it in my mouth, I didn't realise you had to inhale,' he laughs. 'But I still smoke now, of course. I like the taste of tobacco.'

It's time, at last, for one of the big mysteries of Terence's diary. I brood over the page for a moment before reading it aloud. Terry senses my apprehension.

'Go on, it's OK,' he says.

'The next entry . . . "two days before summer holiday, stole money from parents, bought airline ticket, ran away to Scotland, came back next day".'

'When I was fourteen or something, I put on my dad's tweed jacket so I looked older, stole his wallet, and went to Birmingham airport. I managed to buy a ticket to Spain, but they cottoned on somehow that I wasn't old enough. The receptionist chased me around the airport, but she never caught me. So I just got on the train to Glasgow, which was the furthest place I could get to, away from Birmingham. I was really scared when I arrived in Scotland – I was only fourteen – so I called my parents, well, my mum. She was in tears. I just went back the next day. That was two days before I had to go back to that school – Worcester Royal – a fate worse than hell, because I just wanted to be somewhere else, anywhere else. I hated it. I'd been going through this hell of going to school every day, and I didn't know what else to do.'

'What was it that made you hate school so much?'

'Fear. Mainly fear, but I was also really depressed. I didn't like myself. I didn't have any close friends, or anyone to talk to about my feelings and problems. I was facing two more years of school, and I just wanted to get away from that.'

'Was it the only time you ran away?' I don't know what else to ask. As much as I'd imagined this conversation, it seems I wasn't really ready for the emotional reality of it. I'd always assumed that Terence had made up running away, that it wasn't possible for him to run away to Scotland on an airplane. It seems I was right – it wasn't possible to get to Scotland on an airplane. But all this time, I'd been reading it wrongly – he'd bought an airline ticket to Spain, and a train ticket to Scotland. It wasn't one diary entry, it was a sequence of entries, all of them telling parts of a more complex truth.

'There was another time I got the ferry to Dún Laoghaire in Ireland. I had a sick feeling in my stomach, so I phoned my mum again. I took the next ferry back, and then the train from Wales.'

'What did your mum say?' I ask.

'Oh, she shouted, just got really mad.'

'What did your dad say about it all?' I ask, noticing that Terry never mentions his dad.

'He was always quiet. My mum was always head of the household.'

It's a serious thing, running away, especially as a child. Terry was lucky not to get into a terrible situation. It's a desperate attempt for attention, a frustrated cry for help. But no one answered it. I don't know how to say the next sentence.

'"Left school with intention to kill myself".'

Terence drains his pint. He's silent for a moment. I think he might be about to shut down completely, but he puts down his glass and faces me evenly.

'I thought about suicide all the time,' he admits, 'but I just didn't have the guts. I didn't know how to do it. I realised I was too scared and didn't really know how to do it, so running away was the only other thing to do.'

'Didn't you tell anybody how you felt?'

'No, no,' Terence shakes his head. 'I couldn't tell anyone at school and my parents wouldn't have understood. And I didn't tell Karen because she was depressed, too. She had no power to change anything. It might have made her feel worse. I knew how she felt, but she didn't know how I felt. We were in hell. We never asked to be born. But we were born and living and hating it. If you're chronically shy in this world, it's hard to survive. I just hated life. I was terrified of other people – the fear that someone is going to attack you or beat you up for no reason. My parents were older when they had me, I think they were thirty-nine or something, which isn't that old, but they just seemed older, like grandparents rather than parents. When I was at school, everyone else's parents were laid-back, going to Spain on holiday, smoking, going to the pub, watching the latest things on TV. My parents had cobwebs on them. It was like they lived in the nineteen-forties or something. So, my sister and me were just totally alone, and left to work out things by ourselves.'

'The next entry is "Stole, suspended and expelled".'

'After I ran away I went back to school and fell in with the same people. I didn't really like them. We were allowed out at lunchtimes to go into the city centre, and we just went out and nicked things from shops, and then tried to sell them to other pupils. I got caught and expelled.'

I try to imagine the path of this child, who loved the innocent stories of *Choose Your Own Adventure*, who wanted to escape from school and from being bullied by teachers, his downward spiral into depression, running away and suicidal thoughts, and then rebelling as an attempt to gain attention or acceptance.

'"Stopped smoking, language".'

'Maybe stopped smoking is because I stopped hanging around with those people in Worcester, in that school, who started me on it. I didn't see them again because I got expelled. And maybe I thought I wanted to learn a new language, once again to try and improve myself, like I did with the encyclopaedias.'

We are nearly at the end of the diary. 'This is the last set of entries,' I say. 'We're at 1990 – "slimmed, more likeable".'

'When I got expelled from that school, I slimmed before starting at the next school. I felt more confident, and I noticed then that the girls were more into me.' Terry laughs a little, and smiles awkwardly.

My eyes hover over the last three words, those words that first gripped me that night, four years ago, when I held the diary pages for the very first time. I gather my thoughts before I read them. I look Terry in the eyes, eager to register every infinitesimal twitch of his features.

'The last entry,' I begin, 'is "Karen – drugs, guns". . .'

Terry's face twists suddenly in shock, which is partly bewilderment. He laughs.

'What?! Karen – drugs, guns,' he repeats, reading the words out loud. He turns suddenly serious. 'Drugs? I don't know. She might have tried drugs later on, but I'm not really sure. When I was at university, I remember she called me up and said, "The lights, the lights are all on." That's all she said. But maybe she had tried drugs earlier on.'

It's strange how the things that mean most to us as children evaporate when we're adults. I am certain, now, that Terry is being completely honest and not hiding a single thing. The 15-year-old Terence was petrified that his sister was being sucked into a world of drugs he could not comprehend; the adult Terry dismisses it as any other childhood fancy.

'What about the guns?' I ask.

Terry's face changes again. He gazes into the distance. The guns Terry does remember clearly. He looks me in the eyes again and tells me this story.

It was just another regular Saturday morning. Terence lay in bed letting the sounds of the weekend wash over him – the radio, the indistinct voice of a newscaster, the dog next door, the muffled clatter of plates in the kitchen, a shout. Not sure who. He let his thoughts gather, tried to put them in order and then to drain the emotion from each one, to dispel the blackness. People might not understand why a 14-year-old would do what he was about to do, but it wasn't about them.

Terence listed his failures.

The time he took a knife from the kitchen at breakfast, hid it under the jumper of his school uniform while his mum wasn't looking, and sneaked it upstairs while he pretended to finish getting ready for school. He'd locked the bathroom door behind him, and pulled out the knife. Felt the blade, warm from its hiding place, small, but deceptively sharp. There were bigger knives in the kitchen, he'd just grabbed the first one, hoping it would do the job. He'd taken a breath, felt his heart pounding in his chest, imagined the blood. 'What would the pain be like?' he'd asked himself. He'd sat on the floor, gathered the towels in front of him. Blackness versus the knife. Pain of living or pain of death. 'Where do you stab yourself?' he'd thought. He didn't know. He'd thought of his mum, too, the mess he'd make.

'Terence, are you ready yet?' his mum had called up the stairs.

'Nearly,' he'd replied, straightening the bathroom, throwing the towels back on the rail, wiping his eyes, putting the knife back under his jumper, the blade tucked securely under his belt. He'd wait until break time at school and do it then.

The second plan seemed easy. The lesson before break, geography, was on the second floor. He'd get out of class first and run down the stairs, holding the knife under his school blazer, the blade pointing towards his chest, and jump off the balcony. The impact of his body on the banister or the floor would do the stabbing for him.

He'd sat near the door during the lesson. He liked geography, imagining what it would be like to live in different parts of the world, the calmness of colouring in landmass, but today he was too distracted to think about the movement of tectonic plates, and the effects of continental drift. Luckily, the teacher hadn't asked him any questions. He hated being asked questions in class, even if he knew the answer – if he got it wrong, he'd be laughed at; if he got it right, he'd be a swot. He'd kept his hands under the desk because they were shaking so much, every now and then feeling the ridges of the knife handle. Every time he touched the knife it stopped feeling like a dream and he started sweating again.

Time went so slow that morning, making a single lesson feel like a double. When the bell for break finally went he was ready. He'd grabbed his pencil case and exercise book from the desk, threw them into his bag and was first out of the door. He walked down the hall as fast as he could – he didn't want to get stopped for running in the corridor. At the top of the stairs, fear took over again. He was shaking. He couldn't face the pain, scared of how much it would hurt, the worry that it might not work, that he wouldn't die, just be injured, and he'd have to explain how he felt to the teachers, and the school, and his parents. He'd put the knife back in his pocket and went into the quad to get some air. Now he had the worry of carrying a knife around school all day.

There had been other times, when he'd hoarded pills – tubs of paracetamol and aspirin. Other mornings before school, always before school, handful after handful, gulping water from the running tap, and instantly vomiting them back up. And the other mornings, other years, the same – a hoard of pills, the failure and the fear of death.

This time he wouldn't fail.

Terence got up and pulled on his school trousers. He always wore them, even on weekends. He no longer let his mum and dad buy clothes for him, and fashion was just something else to worry about. He put on a T-shirt, then squirted gel across a comb and pulled it through his hair. It was the best way for instant spikes – a tip he'd got from Ada.

He'd have to tell his parents where he was going, so they wouldn't worry.

'Mum, I'm just off to Worcester for a bit,' Terence shouted down the hall. 'Have you got my pocket money?'

'You haven't had breakfast yet,' his mum shouted from the kitchen.

'I'll buy a sandwich while I'm out,' Terence replied.

'What time will you be back?' his mum asked, now standing in the doorway.

Terence looked at his watch, a Casio digital he'd been given for his last birthday. 'I'll be no later than three.'

'Pass me my purse,' she said. 'Me and your dad might still be shopping, so make sure you have your key, and take your coat, it's going to rain.'

Terence took his mum's handbag from the coat hooks near the door, and passed it to her, then pulled on his jacket and trainers, the well-worn comfort of black adidas three stripe. His mum counted the money in her purse.

'Don't spend it all at once,' she said, handing it to him.

'Thank you,' he replied, picked up his school bag and slammed the front door closed behind him.

The bus ride from his house to Worcester would take about fifty minutes, a ride he made every day to school. The boredom of it – the same streets, the same houses. At least he'd get to read the football magazine he'd bought with his dinner money. He took the longer way round to the bus stop, avoiding the possibility of running into the older boys who lived at the top of the road. Hopefully, it was still too early for them to be prowling around on their bikes. As he reached the bus stop the sky darkened dramatically, a bit like it does in *Ghostbusters* Terence thought, maybe not quite as dramatic. It is Birmingham, after all.

The bus arrived just as it started raining. Terence got on and sat downstairs, sitting upstairs wasn't worth the risk – you never knew who would be up there. He'd be sat with the mums and grannies, but it wouldn't matter today if anyone saw him. He pulled out his magazine and looked at the photo highlights of the summer's World Cup in Italy – Gazza crying on the cover, a feature on the penalty shoot-out between England and West Germany.

The shop was a short walk from Worcester bus station, tucked away on a street in the quieter part of town. Terence hoped he wouldn't bump into friends of his parents on the way. Luckily, the streets were a little emptier than usual because of the rain. He crossed the road on the opposite side to the cinema, just to be careful. He stopped in the doorway of the vacuum cleaner repair shop next door to check he had both the money he'd saved and his pocket money.

He couldn't tell if he was sweating or if he was just wet from the rain. He wished he still smoked.

Terence pushed open the door of the toy shop. He knew where on the shelves he'd find it. He'd been before, after school a couple of weeks ago, to check the price. He hadn't dared to ask for a closer look, but he'd been thinking about it constantly since then. Now he had enough money. He squeezed past the girls' stuff at the front of the shop, the My Little Ponies and Sylvanian Families, past the He-man, Star Wars and Teenage Mutant Ninja Turtles action figures, past the board games and Airfix kits, and past the toy guns – guns that fired a reel of red paper caps, cowboy guns with plastic sheriff badges, Rambo rip-offs that came with a headband and a plastic hand grenade.

He felt himself shaking a little as he asked the guy who ran the shop if he could have a look at the box. Terence hoped he hadn't noticed.

'It's a good little gun for the price,' the guy said. 'You'll have a lot of fun.'

Terence pretended to read the back of the box, the words and the warnings a haze in his anxiousness to pay for it and get out of the shop.

'It comes with a target, but you'll have to buy a tub of pellets,' the guy continued, 'fires about twenty-five feet.'

'I'll have it,' Terence said, tipping the money onto the counter, too nervous to count it.

Outside the shop, Terry unzipped his school bag and put the carrier from the toy shop into it. The box was a little too long for it to close completely. If his parents were in, he'd have to hide it with his coat.

The bus ride home was different. He kept his bag out of sight under the seat, beneath his legs. He was too nervous to read his magazine. Terence felt underneath his T-shirt. He'd definitely broken out in a cold sweat, worrying that someone would ask what he had in his bag, and he'd have to think up an excuse. He looked at his watch again. The bus was being so slow. It had started raining again. A low, grey drizzle. He had questions he was finding it hard to answer. Should he write a note? Should he switch on the TV to cover the noise? Then he thought of the mess again. His mum finding his body. It was his stop.

Terence walked quickly, hoping that people would think he was just rushing because of the rain. Two o'clock. He would have an hour or so before anyone should be home, but he wouldn't need that long. He just hoped they were still out doing the shopping. Today would be the best day to do it, there would be someone around all day tomorrow, and he'd have to live through the fear of school that Sunday always brought with it.

He opened the front door as quietly as he could, ran upstairs, closed the door of his bedroom and sat on the floor behind it. He pulled the carrier out from his school bag and shoved it under his bed.

Then he went downstairs again, pulled off his trainers in the hall and hung up his jacket. 'Mum, are you home? Dad?' he shouted. No answer.

Terence checked the lounge and the kitchen just to make sure. No one.

He went back upstairs to his bedroom and pulled out the carrier bag from under the bed. The drawing on the front of the box was of a small pistol. He opened it carefully and pulled out the gun. It was lighter than he thought it would be, and smelt strongly of new plastic. He pulled back on the trigger, and aimed across the room at the poster of Steve Austin – the Six Million Dollar Man. There was a solid click, the recoil of the strong spring, he felt the gun slip slightly in his hand. He'd have to remember to grip it tightly, he thought.

Terence opened the tub of plastic pellets and poured some into his hand. They were small, hard and bright yellow. He pressed the loading chamber open and filled it with pellets from his hand. He worried if he tested the gun, someone would hear him, or he'd lose his confidence, or he'd damage something.

He wrapped the gun in a T-shirt and opened his door a little. From here he could see down the landing past his sister's door, which always remained closed now she was away, past the open door of his parents' bedroom, to the bathroom. He ran down the landing, and locked the bathroom door quickly behind him. He unlocked it again, worried that his mum and dad would have to break the door down, and pulled the washing basket to hold it closed instead. He lent over the bath. If there was anything to clean up it would be easier this way.

Terence placed the barrel of the gun in his mouth. There was no panic on his face, or in his hands, no second thoughts, just a cold calm as his finger squeezed the trigger. The tension of the spring coiled tighter, and with a click released sending the pellet firing out of the barrel.

Terry pauses a moment.

'The pellet must have hit my tongue or something, because it bounced straight out and landed in the bath.' He shakes his head and laughs. 'Tragic.'

Chapter 15 – A half-solved puzzle

I don't know whether to laugh or cry at Terry's story. This is the truth I've been obsessed over, and the truth is that a young boy hated his life so much that he wanted to end it, and it was spared only by a slapstick moment of cosmic proportions.

Terry picks up *The Cave of Time* from the table.

'I really loved these books,' Terry whispers. 'They were a place to be. A place that wasn't school, a place that wasn't home, either. In *The Cave of Time* you just walk into a cave and you're somewhere else. I don't really know why but as a child I just had an instant dislike of the area I was brought up in. I wanted something better and I discovered these books. I wanted to be somewhere else in my own head rather than living in that small area and having to cope with everything at school. I couldn't rest until I had the second one. I even stole money from my mum's purse to get them.'

'Did you?' I ask, incredulous.

'Yeah, I even stole them from the shop.'

'You stole one of these books from the shop?'

'Two or three, I think . . .'

'So, I actually own stolen property?'

'I think they were seventy-five pence, so only two pounds twenty-five's worth!'

We both laugh.

'When you sold these I thought I bought the books from someone called James Costello, so I was surprised it was you.'

'Yeah, there's something I haven't told you.' Terry shifts uncomfortably again. 'I changed my name when I was seventeen because I was always teased about the name Terence Prendergast. I wanted to change it to something cooler. I wanted another Irish surname, out of sentimentality I guess, because my dad is Irish. I liked the sound of Costello. I was sick of being teased for being called Terence, so I wanted the most conventional name ever. I chose James. John was already my middle name. I changed it by deed poll to James John Costello.'

I think back to that moment on the doorstep. 'But your mum and dad still call you Terry? Do they know you changed your name?'

'Yeah,' Terry laughs, 'of course they do.'

'What did they say about it?'

'They didn't like it,' Terry says.

'So you're not called Terry any more?'

'No, but I thought I would let you keep calling me Terry because I didn't think it would make any difference. My parents and my relatives still call me Terry.'

'Do you feel that Terence Prendergast is a different part of your life?'

'It hasn't really made me a different person, but Terence Prendergast was who I was before I went to university. All of that is a different period, of hating my life and wanting to get out of Birmingham. When I was eighteen and came to London, that was stage two of my life,' James says, becoming animated. 'I felt my dream had come true, after all those years of wanting to get out of that area of Birmingham. I loved it at university. I met the exciting people I had always wanted to meet, these people from all over the country, from all these little villages and towns. I was just so happy. I went travelling around the world as well, America, Mexico, Brazil, Thailand, Australia, South Africa, Japan, China, and a few places in Europe. I had some lovely times, and discovered the world. I thought this is what life is really like. It's beautiful.'

This is the real story of the boy in the book, the real diary of Terence Prendergast. It's the story of a man who has been open, honest and brave, a man I'd be proud to call a new friend, a man called James Costello.

After we go our separate ways, I can't stop thinking through everything James has told me about his life. Now all ambiguity has been taken away from the diary pages I realise how wrong many of my assumptions were. The entries had always led me to believe that Terence was somewhat of a fantasist, and some of his notes were purely the imaginings of a teenager, but they were all true, and all the more heartbreaking for that. Over the next days I find myself returning again and again to our conversation, surprised by how many moments of our teenage lives and concerns overlapped. The real Terence was closer to me than I'd imagined.

When we talked about his childhood feelings of depression and suicide, he said he felt trapped, bullied and lonely, and there was no one he could talk to who would understand his feelings. His parents didn't understand, and his sister had already left home. Those feelings still seemed to haunt him. Being able to talk through the diary seems to have been as cathartic for James as finding Terence seems to have been cathartic for me. It's beginning to feel like, finally, I've found the friend that both the teenaged Terence and the teenaged me wanted, and despite all the years and all the differences between us, perhaps we could even become friends now we are adults.

Two weeks after meeting up with James I once again find myself on the south bank of the Thames. After finding out the truth about the diary, my concerns about Terence Prendergast are still troubling me. I've arranged a consultation with Dr Fine, the child psychologist and expert in childhood depression who was intrigued by my story. He has kindly agreed to give me an hour of his time to talk through those concerns.

Dr Fine lives a short train ride from Waterloo. I arrive at the station during rush hour in a cold drizzle, the time of day and the kind of weather designed to show London at its worst. I find myself getting on the train as the commuters get off, my departure point their final destination, and I'm greeted with a barrage of folding bikes and damp umbrellas. The train carriage is littered with newspapers and coffee cups.

The train line leads out from the grey glass, grey sky and grey river of Waterloo, a wet Rothko in grey, through the tower blocks and offices of south-west London towards Richmond. The train passes behind the MI6 building, the headquarters of the British Secret Service. If I'd really needed a spy to find Terence Prendergast, that would have been the place to ask. After my stakeout experience, maybe I should offer my services in the future. I leave the train at Barnes. The station is situated on the fringe of a wood, and now it has stopped raining the air is heavy with oxygen. Inversely, it seems hard to breath after the stale, damp, commuter sweat of the train.

Dr Fine runs consultations from home. I arrive fifteen minutes too early, and take a seat in the waiting area, which consists of two small armchairs in the hallway, a table with a vase of yellow roses sandwiched between them. A concealed door under the stairs leads to his office. Hearing the hushed conversation on the other side of the door brings back familiar memories of my childhood visits to various psychologists as part of my hospital care.

I can recall one of those incidents with clarity. The psychologist was running late with her appointments. I'd been waiting an hour longer than expected, and had a desperate thirst. I'd just returned with a can of Lilt from the hospital vending machine as my mum and I were called in for my appointment. The psychologist was a whispering woman in her thirties. Something about her over-earnest way of speaking made her instantly insincere and untrustworthy. I sat fiddling with the ring pull of my can, my throat drier than before, now a means to quench my thirst was literally so close to hand, not sure of the protocol about drinking pop in the middle of a hospital appointment and too shy to ask. The psychologist asked my mum to sit outside for a few minutes while she spoke with me in private. As soon as we were alone the psychologist said, 'I could tell from the way you were playing with the ring pull of your can that you have a bad relationship with your mother.' She couldn't have been further from the truth. I didn't correct her, but totally withdrew myself. How can you reveal aspects of yourself to someone who is wilfully going to misread everything you say? The same is true in any aspect of your life. I've had a latent disregard for psychologists ever since.

Now, sitting outside Dr Fine's secret consulting room, I'm feeling acutely anxious. The hidden door opens and a boy in school uniform is led out by his mother. I smile at him. He returns my smile solemnly. Dr Fine shows them both to the front door before he turns to greet me. He appears to be ten years or so older than James is or I am, instantly friendly and confident, professionally relaxed, certain aspects of his manner clearly honed from his TV and media work.

He leads me through into his consulting room, a comfortable office lined with books and films, toys and games. Immediately, I notice on one of the shelves a Rubik's cube abandoned halfway through being solved, one layer in perfect order, the rest a jumble of colour. I can't help but wonder whether someone had given up solving the cube in frustration or if it's an ornament designed to be a metaphor for psychology. I take a seat on the couch, while Dr Fine takes up the office chair at a desk on which the evidence of work, a laptop and piles of papers, wrestle for space with a Lego model of a fairground funhouse.

Dr Fine checks the time, a reflex action from marking a day in forty-five-minute blocks, before swinging round on his chair to face me.

'So, how can I help you?' he asks cheerfully.

I'd already explained a little about the diary on the phone, but I remind Dr Fine about my story as I pull Terence's pages from *The Cave of Time*.

'Is that all you've got from the diary?' He is evidently disappointed. 'Can I have a look at the writing?' he asks, taking the diary from me. He examines the pages quickly, scanning them line by line. 'Well, it's nice clear writing. What is interesting is that it's not pressured writing, which is telling you something about the potential mood state of this individual.'

I wasn't expecting another graphology assessment.

Dr Fine continues, 'To me, this is not particularly worrying. It's thought out. I know there are a few scribbles on there, but it's considered pieces rather than a few throwaway remarks. Yes, you see the words "drugs" and "guns" and "intention to kill myself", if it was a long diary and pressured handwriting, I would be a lot more worried.' Dr Fine has immediately disarmed the words that had haunted me for years. 'This is this person's individual life review. And some years after having the worst cases. It seems like he's been through something and he's come to the end of it. Things are better. Teenagers generally do go through a period of this aspect of suicidal ideation, almost like a fantasy – if I was going to do it, how would I do it? There's a whole internet forum based on suicidal ideation. Having ideas about doing it is not such a worry. When there has been actual intent and attempt, it's more of a concern.'

We've jumped straight into the area I find difficult to articulate. I'm here for Dr Fine's professional advice, so, putting my thoughts in order, I explain about Terence's contemplation of suicide and his attempts to end his life with paracetamol, kitchen knife and toy gun.

'I'd imagine these were all superficial efforts. A lot of teenagers go through that phase, girls certainly more than boys. And girls express it more than boys, so the attempts, even though they are superficial, will be more overtly superficial, whereas with boys, that phase is more likely to be supressed, it doesn't jump out at you, so you would expect it to be kept secret. If I was to read that diary, on reflection, I wouldn't be too concerned by it necessarily. You can see there has been a history of bullying, that he's had periods when he's been quite conscious of himself, for example with this PE business.'

I think back to James's demonstration of how Mr Kenny had humiliated children in front of the class by making them crouch with books on the backs of their outstretched hands. 'Coulson and Kenny actually turned out to be his teachers, which was a bit of a shock,' I say.

'Maybe not. It depends on how you perceive things, where you are in your life. Sometimes our harshest critics are going to be teachers, they're going to be the people who have got it in for us.' Dr Fine is more matter of fact than unsympathetic. He reads through the list of years again. 'Did he get to Scotland?'

I tell him about how Terence had stolen his dad's wallet and coat, his attempt to fly to Spain and how he ended up phoning his mum from Glasgow. 'It was a genuine but flawed attempt to run away,' I say. 'One thing he has expressed quite clearly is that he hated the area he was in, and that he wanted to escape. Finding him in that same house over twenty years later was a surprise, especially because of the things I'd imagined before I met him, and especially what I now know after speaking to him. It doesn't seem like he's moved on necessarily, psychologically I mean. I think a lot of the same issues might still trouble him in similar ways. He seems to be incredibly anxious, for example.'

Dr Fine leans back in his chair. 'Let's go back to the bullying. Even if it's done by teachers, it does have a long-term impact. For the majority of people who have had some degree of bullying at school, it affects their perception of the world around them. It stops victims of bullying taking risks. Yes, you might go to university, and have a great time, but it's very easy to fall back once you go home. Your surroundings are the same and you return to your default position. It does stop you taking chances for fear of being trodden down by other people.'

'He said he felt depressed as a child, and now, as an adult, he can express what that feeling was. He also said that when he first started school, he already felt nostalgic for his pre-school years. And that was the feeling he'd had all the way through his teenage years, too.'

'That would be very typical low confidence, low self-esteem. You look back at your pictures and you see "I was a happy kid, I was a smiley kid, everything was happy and easy" – and that's what might be interesting about those books – because you're holding on to that. You might not want to grow up. It's not necessarily Peter Pan, but a sense that things were safer, things were better. "I've now got all these pressures of school, I know it's going to get harder with social pressures, peer pressure. I'm not quite ready for that." So having all of these books is a bit of that fantasy, holding on to this more juvenile behaviour, juvenile ideas, which is why, not just the books, but what Terence wrote in them might seem to make sense.'

I can't tell if Dr Fine is referring to Terence as a teenager or me now as Peter Pan. I know my retreat into the world of *Choose Your Own Adventure* that started this story was because it was a safe place. I used the books as an adult in the same way I had used them as a child, a comfortable realm of adventure without risk. I don't think that the desire to retreat is so unusual. Nostalgia, the longing to revisit our own recent past, is a cultural epidemic. It's almost as if no one is quite ready for the future.

I explain to Dr Fine why I identify with Terence's diary, about my visits in and out of hospital, the physical complications and misdiagnosis, the years of missed schooling.

'That's a tough one. You missed out on growing up with your peers, so were somewhat socially isolated, unless you had good enough friendships for your friends still to visit you and be very much part of it. But nine months, in five years . . .' Dr Fine shakes his head, 'that's a tough one.'

'Would you say that my obsessiveness could potentially have roots in that kind of childhood?' I ask.

'There are lots of different ways to look at it. For some people it might be neurodevelopmental. In other words, it's more to do with how the brain is functioning: "I need order, I need control." That's more for people who might be on the autistic spectrum for example, where there's more rigidity in thinking. That need for control is about a part of the brain called the amygdala, which often "overfies" – it's overly anxious. The way you can help contain that anxiety is to have orderliness.

'For other people, it might be more about life experiences, but there's a difference between being obsessive about certain things and having obsessive compulsive type ideas, particularly around counting. I think that's the most damaging, because everything has to be done in a certain way, three times or five times, or jumping on one leg on a Tuesday. Those are probably the most destructive and hardest to deal with. Real OCD cannot be easily fixed. It's really difficult to manage and is often better addressed with the aid of medication. OCD, or any sort of obsessiveness or orderliness, if it's not impacting on your life – in other words, if it's not interfering with your ability to function socially in a normal working life – is fine.'

As Dr Fine speaks I think back, first to my friend Kriston, then my friend Guy's second goodbye, then to my recent secret diary keeping. My obsessiveness really was verging on the destructive end of the spectrum, and if I hadn't gone away to Prendergast Caravan Park to find peace, my life could be very different now. I don't know if I'll ever find out why James Costello stopped responding to my emails. Maybe he was right to be scared by an over-keen obsessive who'd tracked him down to his parents' house because he sold some books he once owned as a child. Looking back, I would have been scared of me at that point.

'As part of the digging around in my past, I found a diary I kept when I was well enough to go to school. And in the back of it I found a note.' I show Dr Fine a copy of the letter I wrote to Nancy.

He laughs, a genuine, understanding laugh. '"Can I have a photo of you?" That's really creepy, but at least you were thinking about doing something about your crush. Most people don't do anything at all. At least you had a plan.'

'I had a plan but I didn't go through with it, that is until a few months ago. I went to find Nancy as a grown woman, to give her the letter.' The words to 'Love Is All Around' immediately fill my head. Unfortunately, they are sung by Gary.

Dr Fine laughs again. 'And she said?'

'She said, "I wish you *had* asked me then, because you were my first crush at school."'

Dr Fine makes the sound a coffee morning would make after a hundred kittens, blow dried and dressed in bows, are released into a crèche – a long-drawn-out 'Ahhhhhhhh.'

'The worst thing was I never knew.'

'You know, I have to teach that to a lot of kids,' he says emphatically. 'You've got nothing to lose. If they say no, you're in no worse position than you were beforehand. And if they say yes, brilliant. But either way, you've not lost anything.'

'The most important thing I've realised throughout this adventure is that regret is the worst kind of feeling to sustain.'

'Yes, completely. The one thing that exacerbates depression and anxiety is regret, because you're living with things that you can't change. They've happened. You can't do anything about it. They've happened, but try to learn the lesson from it. People who suffer from trauma, for example road traffic accidents, often think, "What could I have done differently? If only I'd turned left instead of right. If only I hadn't had that argument before I left home, maybe I wouldn't have had that accident." It's happened. It's history. If you hold by those regrets, that rumination is the kind of thing that grinds you down, eats away at you. You end up in a downward cycle. The idea is to seize every new day. Let's make amends, and deal with what I've got now to make sure I'm not living by the same regrets now and in the future about things that have passed.'

I look down at *The Cave of Time*, which I'm absentmindedly still holding. 'Do you think that *Choose Your Own Adventure* books are good for allowing you to play out various options, to see what would have happened if you'd made a different decision?'

'We know that, unlike in *Choose Your Own Adventure*, there aren't always two options. Life isn't that simple. Within each option there are always other parameters. As a psychologist I can't always be that pragmatic. We're always trying to discover and interpret the meaning behind certain behaviour. On different days you might behave differently – "There's too much risk," or "We might fail." Those are the boundaries we set up for ourselves. People *do* stop themselves from acting because of these fears, but really, you've got a broken arm – so what? You've still got another arm, and you'll get a bit of sympathy for it. OK, so you've got a puncture. It's going to make you a little bit late, but you know what? You're still alive, you didn't die. It's important to have a little bit of optimism, to reframe the situation. Yes, it looks bleak, but if you reframe it, actually you realise it's all relative, and it's not as bad as you think.'

'Looking back at my childhood, I think, yes, I missed a lot of school, but I still went to university and I've got a master's degree. You can still succeed in education without traditional schooling.'

'It didn't hold you back too much then.'

'I've not only been looking at Terence's, and my own, teenage years, I've also examined teenage diaries stretching back a hundred years,' I say, briefly explaining about Dr Irving Finkel's Great Diary Project. 'What I found most interesting was that the concerns of teenagers always seem to be the same, and are mainly about social anxiety.'

'People don't generally keep diaries as much these days. It's all Facebook. It's very social, and more judgemental. I've certainly seen a change in the last few years. I think this is the worst time to be a teenager. It *is* bleak. Even while they're going through the schooling system, they're being told – the media is telling them, the news is telling them – "You know what? There are no jobs out there, you're going to be screwed, there's going to be no financial prosperity or security. You're screwed, so why try any harder?" You have that mixed in with all the social-networking pressures – you've got to be online, you've got to be reactive. That's a lot of pressure. It's awful. And on top of that, you are constantly being academically tested and scrutinised. It's the worst time to be a teenager.'

'Have you seen a rise in teenage depression or anxiety?'

'Well, I'm very busy, so I'd say yes. But I've also seen a very big rise in bullying, because of cyber bullying. The cyber bullies themselves feel quite protected because they have the idea that "I'm not hurting you, I'm just saying bad things about you." Actually, the whole phrase "Sticks and stones may break my bones, but words will never hurt me" is wrong. No, words hold. You know what? Physical wounds heal, but emotional wounds hold for a lot longer and are more damaging.'

Dr Fine is right. Even for adults, cruel and cowardly comments can be difficult to overcome, the anonymity of the internet allowing people to say things they wouldn't have the guts to say to someone's face. For teenagers trying to understand who they are, it can be devastating, and, as with Terence, quite often the true emotional impact can be hard to detect.

'Are there any signs that perhaps you should look out for with children that indicate the child is depressed?'

'In terms of signs of symptoms, it depends on the age of the child. Younger children tend almost to regress behaviourally. Children under five might regress developmentally and go back to bed-wetting, for example, or show more attachment to mother or loss of language skills, really regressing to that infantile, security-seeking behaviour. In older children, you'll see them choosing to become isolated, not going out as much, finding reasons not to mix with other people. If you think about level of activity, what they are doing is downward spiralling – doing less, and the less they do the less they want to do, so really becoming quite insular and living in the small world of their house. Sometimes you get more risk-taking behaviours because they feel they've got nothing to lose, sabotaging relationships, sabotaging school activities for example. So externally, those are the kinds of things you might be seeking – loss of appetite, for older kids loss of interest in sex, loss of interest in the things they used to enjoy doing, feeling they've got a bleak future, feeling there is no hope, feeling quite melancholic, potentially wanting to die, lots of different types of symptoms like that.

'Every child presents slightly differently, but we do have standardised assessment tools we use to recognise at what point a person meets the criteria for depression. For some people it might be more of a transient depression, and actually quite normal. They may be going through a difficult patch in their life or a difficult transition – changing schools, parents divorcing, something that's a single episode. The depression will pass once the episode has passed. And for some people, their depression is more about their way of seeing the world.'

I've never suffered from depression but I've definitely been at its borders. As a teenager, during the worst of my illness, in unhappy moments of isolation and loneliness, I had thoughts along the lines of 'Is this how it's going to be for ever?' 'Is this going to be my life?' I filled the empty hours that led to those feelings with obsessive thoughts about other things, to keep me occupied, to keep me distracted, to keep me happy. Depression could be understood as stemming from a feeling of lack of control, and obsession as about regaining control over your environment. For me, obsession was a preventative cure that has since become a personality trait.

Dr Fine's list of symptoms are immediately evident throughout Terence's diary, from the early entries – 'wet pants x 2' – right through to the sabotaging of school and social activities – 'stole, suspended and expelled'. I've been feeling the burden of James's admission that he had never told anyone as a child about the true nature of his feelings. I want to try to understand the root of that reluctance to find help. I have some final questions for Dr Fine.

'During the eighties and nineties when Terence was a child, would it have been harder for him to express his feelings than it might be now? Is there less of a stigma attached to childhood depression today? Is it more understood?'

'That's a controversial question. On one level you might say that depression is over-diagnosed, and that any mental-health issues are being over-diagnosed. We are more aware of it, so we are more likely to ask questions about it and therefore we are diagnosing more. Or are we over-diagnosing? ADHD, for example, is being over-diagnosed because parents are worried, and unfortunately GPs are more prone to offer medication than to ask if there's a behavioural route to managing difficult behaviour.

'Going back to the eighties, there were a lot less services available. People were less likely to recognise depression – maybe this child is just misbehaving, or maybe he's just troubled by something.' He pauses momentarily, scanning Terence's writing again. 'And for Terence there would also have been the fear of how his family would react – would they see him differently? Would they see him as a weaker person because he suffered from depression? Unfortunately, there's still a lot of stigma around mental health, even from health professionals, and if you come from a traditional family background, very much so. Mental-health difficulties are just like having a cold – they're there, they're symptomatic, they pass with good support. One in four people will have a mental-health difficulty at some point in their life.'

'As a teenager now, if you felt you were depressed and you didn't feel you had anyone to confide those thoughts to, is there a way to get help?'

'There's a lot of support out there. But I don't think kids necessarily know where to turn. Keeping a diary *is* really effective, keeping a proper diary,' Dr Fine says, putting the pages of Terence's diary on the arm of the couch, 'a thought and a mood journal, because it acts a bit like a brain dump. You've got all these ideas that are hassling you, bouncing around in your brain, and this jumble of ideas can be quite fatiguing – you're constantly thinking about them, they don't go away, and there's no order to the thoughts. By putting them down on paper, you start to process them and begin to create a narrative.

'Then there's a hierarchy of interventions. Ideally, you'd talk to your nearest and dearest, your family, your friends, people you can trust, if you can trust them. Of course, we don't always want to own up and say we've got a difficulty, so we might not go down that route. You might find a school counsellor, or your GP, is the person to talk to, or the Samaritans or Childline. As your degree of risk increases, you progress up the hierarchy, so if you're feeling quite suicidal or self-harming, you need to take yourself to A & E, where you'll be seen in the next couple of hours by a duty psychiatrist.

'Even when we know support is there, we question if it's really for us – "should I really be calling this number?" But if you've got a concern, it's not such a big deal to call NHS Direct or somebody to get advice. Often people feel they don't need support or don't want to ask for it, which is a shame because our teenage years can be our best years. We should be out there living them and enjoying them. We're allowed to take risks, and somehow society is more forgiving of teenagers' innocence, so it's a shame to be living under a cloud.'

Dr Fine has answered all of the concerns I had after talking to James Costello. Sadly, it seems that his childhood wasn't so different from many children's back in the 1980s, or even now. Bullying is still as pervasive as ever and can still lead to tragic ends, as is all too frequently reported in the media, but the current support networks are stronger if you reach out to them. Likewise, important progress is being made in understanding the causes of, and cures for, depression, and the stigma of suffering from mental-health issues is being confronted.

Talking to Dr Fine has also made me refine my thoughts about regret and what it means to choose. The person I am today is the product of all the choices I've made in the past. They have led me to this exact point, all the wrong decisions and the ones that turned out to be right. Who I am in the future depends on the choices I make today.

You can't regret every decision made in life because the other choices might have been better. Every time life forces you to make a choice you leave behind a trail of 'what ifs?' *Choose your Own*

Adventure allows you to play out those 'what ifs?' Real life just leaves you a trail of imagination and memory. The unknown is scary, but the known can be scarier still. No path in life is the right path. And if you don't like the one you're on, choose another one. To choose is to imagine the future, and no harm can come from imagining the future. It might just help you get one step closer to it.

Anyone who thinks about life will inevitably wonder at some point about what it all means. What is it for? What is the point? Those questions don't have to be frightening or destructive.

The hard answer is life doesn't *mean* anything. Life isn't *for* anything, either, which is the most liberating thing about it. It's not *for* anything, but it can *be* anything. Life is pointless, therefore we should sharpen it, poke it at things, wake them up. We should face the huge expanse of the universe and feel alive not despair, look in the direction of universes beyond our own and feel small. We are all tiny, insignificant beings, which doesn't give anyone the right to make themselves feel big by bullying all the other little people near them. We should feel big by giving others a hand up.

We all need that help from time to time.

Chapter 16 – Choose wisely

This quest has been full of surprises, but most surprising of all perhaps is that, against the odds, James Costello and I are actually becoming friends. I invite him to visit me in London and, surprising me again, he agrees.

The first night is understandably incredibly awkward for both of us. I meet James in a small Spanish bar off Oxford Street. Our mutual nervousness means we quickly find ourselves matching each other pint for pint, our conversation is an anxious replay of the small talk of our first meeting 'What have you been up to?' 'What films do you like?' 'What music are you into?' I'm worried he will well and truly drink me under the table before half past eight, even though I'm drinking shandy, and I'll have to make a blurred and hasty exit.

Thankfully, the intense pressure of conversation is relaxed as we're joined by Sarah, my sister Nina, and my friends Pete and Alex. I feel somewhat responsible for James, trying hard not to keep checking to see if he's OK. That comes partly from thinking of him as the child he used to be, not the man he has become, and partly the circumstances surrounding our embryonic friendship.

Sarah and James have found a shared passion for general knowledge and head to the pub quiz machine on the other side of the bar. Minutes later I can hear the cheers and groans of evident bonding. Soon James is in his element, chatting, laughing, telling jokes, sharing cigarettes with strangers. I can see the residual shyness of Terence Prendergast, but James Costello clearly loves people, and the pub is his natural social environment.

I wake early the next morning feeling like I've been dried out from the inside. Age is doing nothing to help my socialising recovery ability. I'm not entirely sure how it happened but, unbelievably, James is asleep downstairs on the couch, his old *Choose Your Own Adventure* books lined up neatly on the shelves beside him. Despite the rules of time and space of the physical world, it seems we've broken through into *The Cave of Time* yet again, collapsing the real into the fictional, history becoming the present.

I walk through into the kitchen to put the kettle on.

'Morning,' James shouts from the lounge. I put my head around the door to ask if he would like a drink. Kook has nestled herself onto James's chest, her nose two inches from his. He looks a little petrified.

'Are you OK with her asleep on you? Sorry, if she woke you up.'

'No, no, I like it. I was worried, though, when she started making a noise like a machine.'

'That just means she's happy,' I say.

'I've never had a pet,' James says, stroking Kook's head awkwardly. 'I couldn't stand the loss if it was run over or went missing.'

'No, I couldn't either. But worrying what might happen is no reason not to love and take care of something or someone.'

I make tea for everyone, taking Sarah's up to the bedroom.

'I know this must be really strange for you,' I say, sitting on the edge the bed. 'So thank you for agreeing James could stay over.'

'It's not a big deal. And anyway it was fun. I mean it was weird, but still fun. He was really up for the pub quiz machine. And I think that's one of the main qualities I look for in a friend.'

'You made a formidable team. You were robbed, those machines rarely let you win the big prize.'

'How's he doing down there with Kook? I get the feeling he

doesn't want to go back to Birmingham – do you think he's just going to move in?'

I laugh. 'They've become really good friends, too, but I don't think he's ready to move in yet. He's asked to borrow some socks, though. I'm not sure I have any that don't have holes in.'

It's a brisk late spring morning. We spend it walking up Holloway Road, from Highbury Corner towards Archway, past the places James used to frequent when he was studying at the University of North London – the old university buildings, the student union, the pubs he went to, and the pubs to be avoided. That was when he changed his name.

We turn off the main road into a side street. An old Irish bar on the corner of the road is in the middle of being refurbished, a new sign hung in expectancy. I can't help but think of the change between Terence Prendergast and James Costello, almost a refurbishment of personality.

'Did changing your name help you reinvent yourself?' I wonder.

'Oh yeah, definitely. It gave me a bit of confidence. It helped to get rid of the things that always depressed me about myself. I always hated having to introduce myself to anyone. I'd mumble, "Hi yeah, my name is Terence." I hated being in the doctor's waiting room when they would call for Terence Prendergast. I dreaded that. It was amazing how many teachers couldn't pronounce my surname, either. I'd get called Pentercost, Prentercast or something. No one ever took the piss out of James Costello.'

'So did that help the depression?'

'It changed because of the confidence going to university gave me. I went straight from my parents' house into halls of residence, and I wondered how I was going to cope with it because I was shy. You have to be really outgoing, a party animal, to survive in halls of residence. I turned to the student bar and made friends that way. I made a lot of really good friends.'

'I reinvented myself, too, really. Because I was ill I hadn't really been to school properly until I was sixteen and went to do A-Levels.

I didn't know who I was because I hadn't socialised in the same way as everyone else my age. I went to a completely different school, in a different town, so no one knew me or anything about me and I became more outgoing, more myself. Then, in the same way as you, I came to London as soon as I could. I was desperate to get out of Rhyl. It was too small for me. I always felt I was missing out on the world.'

We finally arrive at the address of his old flat-share, a small house at the end of a terrace. 'I loved living here,' he says with fondness. 'It used to be known as the party house.'

I know then that if we'd gone to the same university, if our paths had crossed, we would definitely have been friends. It could have happened. I was just the other side of London. James has lit a cigarette, lost in remembrance of things past.

'Are you still in contact with any of the people you lived with?' I ask.

'No, not really. Everybody moved on,' he says sadly.

'Where did you first live when you came to London?' James asks when we sit down for lunch.

'I moved into student halls in Bethnal Green for the first year. I've moved around quite a lot since then.'

'Do you want to go and have a look? I've never been to Bethnal Green.'

We catch a bus heading towards the city, and walk east through Liverpool Street and Brick Lane, and up the Bethnal Green Road towards my old block of flats. The area has changed beyond recognition in the last seventeen years. The burnt-out shell of a tower block that stood opposite my halls of residence has been converted into six-figure penthouse apartments. It seems strange walking these streets with someone who I'd imagined for so long, but who is now very much a flesh and blood reality beside me. We have a lifetime of history to catch up on.

Despite our brief time together, James knows my childhood in more detail than people who have been close to me for years, and I know the reality of his more than anyone. But it seems we've tacitly agreed that, if we're going to become friends now, as two men past the mid-point of their thirties, each other's university years are the best place to begin. In a way, we've missed out on sharing some of the good times, the fun stuff, the really late nights when you didn't have to worry about getting up the next day, when you could get up and just do it all again, when you could be reckless, drink and sing, and forget yourself.

That night we head to Camden, just the two of us, for a few drinks and to try to find a dart board, reliving our student years and the heady days of Brit Pop. We drink through a tour of The Good Mixer, The Hawley Arms and The Dublin Castle, the old haunts of Oasis, Blur and Pulp. I'm just about to order another drink from the bar when a section of The Dublin Castle's ceiling collapses, a dangerous mix of brick and skylight frame hitting the floor with a thud, narrowly missing James as he returns from the toilet.

'I'm glad I chose to check my phone on the stairs,' he jokes, standing bewildered in a cloud of plaster dust, 'or we'd be going to A & E.' We decide to find a more robust pub for the next round.

We're now sat in the window of The Elephant's Head, opposite the fringe theatre where Uri Geller first came to watch the show about my obsession with his life and merchandise. 'If someone asked you to do some magic now, could you do some?' James asks shyly.

'I could, yes,' I reply. I love magic, but it changes the moment, not always for the better.

'Go on then,' is his unintentionally curt provocation. It's like an exchange from the awkward playground of our imaginations.

Between us, in our pockets full of pub change, we manage to find four ten-pence pieces. James watches in silence as the coins disappear one at a time from my hand, hanging invisibly in the air for a moment, before landing with a clink on his open palm. It feels like this moment is the obsessiveness of my youth coming full circle – my boyhood obsession with magic, the repetition and loneliness of practice, performing tricks to someone who has become a new friend as a result of my obsessiveness with *Choose Your Own Adventure*.

'That was amazing,' James says. 'Can you do anything else?'

I ask him to make a simple drawing of anything that comes to mind, but nothing as obvious as a flower or smiley face. I turn my back, making sure I can't see what James is drawing.

'When you've finished, concentrate on that image,' I say. A blur of lines begin to form in my mind, a confused outline. I sketch the image on a separate piece of paper and place it face down beside his.

'It's strange,' I say. 'I'm not sure if I'm right, but I'm getting the image of water, but like a road.' I show James my drawing of two straight lines and something that looks like a pointy car driving between them.

'I don't believe it,' he says, turning over his drawing. 'I was thinking of a canal boat. How did you know? It's impossible. I need another drink to get my head around it.'

Magic is about these moments, when the world seems to wobble in a good way, where for a few minutes anything seems possible.

James comes back from the bar with two bottles of Hooch, alcoholic lemonade that became *the* drink of our teenage years. It tastes of the juice squeezed from the plastic lemons you only see in the shops around pancake day. He sits down just as Radiohead's song 'Creep' comes through the speakers. I burst out laughing.

'What are you laughing at?' James asks, suddenly seeming anxious.

'Don't worry, not you. One, the fact that we're two grown men drinking Hooch, and two this song. It feels like I've fallen through another wormhole in time,' I reply.

I think back to my precarious pile of fifty-two spiral-bound notebooks, the earliest ones full of terrible poems to my first real girlfriend, most of them probably written when I'd been drinking Hooch. One of the pages also has the lyrics to 'Creep' carefully written out in full.

'I once made a tape to send to a girl for Valentine's Day. All it contained was "Creep" copied obsessively on both sides. It was a C90, which means it must have been repeated at least twenty-two times.'

'What did she say?' James asks, sipping Hooch.

'Well, it must have worked. We went out together for years. She said she first listened to it all the way through thinking it must contain a secret message, which it didn't, just the continual whining of Thom Yorke. She had no idea who it was from. And after we got together she played it until the tape wore out.'

'She must really hate the song now,' James says.

'She must really hate me now,' I reply.

James laughs. 'What was the first single you ever bought?' he asks. 'Mine is really embarrassing – Sam Fox, "Touch Me I Want Your Body". I don't know what I was thinking.'

It's quite easy to work out what a young teenaged boy was thinking when he bought a single by the 1980s topless model, and it was certainly nothing to do with her singing ability.

'I was really into the Welsh Elvis, Shakin' Stevens. But I had a huge crush on Kylie Minogue as soon as she tried breaking into the Ramseys' house in *Neighbours*. It probably explains my taste in girlfriends ever since. They've all been tomboys.'

'For me, *Neighbours* and Bomb the Bass killed the nineteen-eighties,' James says, enigmatically.

I think it's the Hooch talking. We need food.

We stand out of the rain in the doorway of NatWest bank, eating chips bought from a tourist-trap chippy round the corner from The World's End. It's a pub that sounds like it was named after a *Choose Your Own Adventure* book, but the only adventure to be found inside is trying not to get your feet wet in the toilets.

'A guy used to busk every night in the doorway here,' I say. 'He'd set up a temporary drum kit of rubbish bins and boxes, and play along to whatever he was listening to on his Walkman. I would always give him money if I could.'

'Could you tell what songs he was playing?'

'Never.'

James laughs.

While we eat, a Cadillac painted like a Mexican Day of the Dead retablo pauses at the traffic lights, elaborate garlands of bright colours. A couple dressed in Victorian evening wear hurry past, his cane causing small ripples in the puddles that she is desperately trying not to drop her petticoats in, followed by a wet medley of beautiful French girls and Spanish punks. This was the vibrancy that we both always knew our home towns were missing, the acceptance and disregard only a city like London can give you.

'I'd like to move back, if I can,' James says, looking out into the rain.

'Yeah, that'd be good,' I say, prodding another chip onto the wooden chip fork.

Two weeks later, Fernando has gently strong-armed me into joining him on a last-minute trip back home to stay at his mum and dad's in Wantagh on Long Island, New York. Last time I took Fernando's advice to get away from it all I got as far as Prendergast Caravan Park, and he no longer seems to trust me to make holiday plans on my own. But having the chance to go to New York is an adventure I can't refuse.

I love flying.

I flew for the first time when I was 23. We visited an airport once when we were kids, a day trip into other people's holidays, to see up close the incredible size of airplanes, and hear deafening noise from the viewing platform. I think my mum and dad, who had never flown at this point in their lives, were also awed by them. I've flown many times since, but I still love every moment of the process of flying, including the bag checks and the travelators. That is I love the process apart from the last time I flew to America, when I was a victim of gender discrimination by the woman working the baggage check.

'Did you pack this bag yourself, sir?' she asked, emptying my carry-on luggage haphazardly into a tray.

'Yes, why?' I replied, watching the pile of carelessly dismissed books and toiletries with growing discomfort.

'It's just *very* neatly packed for a man,' she said.

On board the flight to New York I seem to be the only person taking an interest in the sick bags, duty free catalogues, and the socks, sleep-mask and miniature toothbrush in the seat pocket in front of me. I normally love the safety demonstration, but I'm a little disappointed by today's performance, the hand gestures suffering from the curse of over-rehearsal. I have a window seat and as we taxi onto the runway, I watch the flaps and panels of the wing make their surprisingly mechanical movements.

I still find it impossible to believe all this metal and wire and electronics and rubber and glass and plastic and people will actually fly. Everyone around me settles down to wait for the films to start playing, as if the only reason we are all here is to watch the latest Hollywood blockbusters, while outside on the runway a miracle or a disaster is about to happen.

We're lucky and it's a miracle. I can feel the throb of the engines through my forehead resting on the glass. Outside the clouds form an undulating landscape of rolling hills and fields, erasing the world below for a few hours. In this non-place I can't help but think back on my quest. This is as far away from my boyhood love for *Choose Your Own Adventure* books as I could be. I never imagined that collecting tokens from the back of a Weetabix box would lead me here. I've met and spoken to amazing people, I've made new friends, I've come to terms with my past, and, more importantly, I've begun to understand my future. It's two days before my thirty-sixth birthday. There are no dragons to be fought, but that doesn't mean life can't be full of adventure – you just have to be willing to take a risk.

A few hours later, as we make the final approach to JFK International, the clouds clear. We are flying over Long Island, the shadow of the plane outlined sharply on the ground below us, a phantom shadow plane full of passengers from an alternate dimension. Throughout this adventure I've felt as though I've been travelling through time, and flying somehow seems to be returning time to normal. As we descend, the phantom plane grows larger, flickering over swimming pools and shopping malls, and as our wheels touch down on the runway and the shadow attaches itself, it feels like I've finally caught up with myself.

On holiday, even the simplest of acts are rendered strange. Everything in America feels like an America constructed from film and TV sets a decade behind the present, a sluggish but comfortable dislocation of time. There also seems to be a trend in Wantagh to personalise businesses in the manner of *Sesame Street*. In a block of three shops, the practical Mr Vacuum and Mrs Sew live next door to the greedy Mr Pies.

I leave Fernando to catch up with his parents for the day and head into Manhattan on my own, taking the Babylon branch of the Long Island Rail Road to Penn station in the heart of New York.

The journey takes about an hour, the miles measured by the rotation of strip malls and roadside diners, punctuated with peculiarly predictable regularity by the mattress shop Sleepys. Judged by the shops alone, you would be forgiven for concluding that Americans are primarily interested in eating and sleeping, and that they did a lot of both.

There is a heatwave in New York. A film of sweat covers every inch of my body as soon as I climb the stairs of the subway. The streets are a maze of unforgiving thick sticky heat. I slowly wander eastwards, every turn dictated by the longest patch of unbroken shade.

Life is heightened by difference. You can feel life more acutely in unfamiliar surroundings. On holiday it's easy to feel part of the world, while at home it's just as easy to feel part of the scenery. You have to trick the novelty and wonder of travelling into your everyday life. I can understand James Costello's need for travel. You can be anyone or no one, you can feel connected or isolated, and you can see that people in every corner of the globe struggle with being human. People can be cruel and spiteful, but most people are genuinely good and kind in their own way. Travelling also reminds you that people can be brilliant and surprising.

At the corner of 23rd and 6th, the work of a street artist immediately catches my eye. His paintings are outlines of animals rendered from a thick layer of textured acrylic; his canvases are the opened covers of discarded hardbacked books.

I stand back to view the entire exhibition of his work. The paintings rest along a wall on the shadiest side of the street. The artist comes over and introduces himself as Teofilo Olivieri. As soon as I speak he realises from my accent I'm not local. He asks what I'm doing in New York, particularly at the permanent temporary exhibition of his work. I give him the short version of my adventure, and soon we're talking about how books have saved us, although in very different ways. For him, the outside of the book, the colour of the cover and the words and typeface of the title are his inspiration.

'Painting on book covers has changed my life,' he tells me earnestly.

I'm drawn to a blue silhouette of a horned goat, a full moon rising just behind him, the speckled white lettering of the spine just showing through the paint: *The Final Days*. The painting speaks to me, but not of pessimism. It speaks to me about the wonder of found things, of stubbornness and the strength of perseverance, of mystery and new beginnings, and the final days of this obsession.

I ask Teofilo to sign the back of the painting to Sarah. He asks who she is.

'A very patient and understanding girlfriend,' I explain.

He draws a heart surrounded with magic advert-style surprise lines.

* * *

I'm staying in a self-contained flat in the basement of Fernando's parents' house. It's cool, dark and quiet – a cave away from time. This is where I should have come to escape when I needed to. I'm woken by a Skype call from Sarah wishing me a happy birthday. The video keeps breaking up, but I'm happy just to see her face. It feels like I haven't been mentally committed to our relationship recently, but as she lifts Kook to wave hello at the camera, I'm overwhelmed by my feelings for them both. I've spent the last few years searching for something, and it seems I've found it without realising.

I get dressed and go upstairs for breakfast, the morning sun already fiercely hot in the few seconds it takes to cross the side of the house. Fernando's dad has made a trip over the road to the bagel shop, and a spread of fruit and pastries is already laid out on the table. Fernando's mum magically appears behind me, a genuinely fairy-like spirit with an artist's soul. She presents me with a small cotton bag, sewn together from T-shirt remnants. The bag is inscribed with a message in marker pen: 'Uncommon goods from the cave of time'. I pull off the ribbon and pour the contents into my hand – a pine-cone and four fruit stones, peach, avocado, plum and apricot. Alongside them is a note that reads: 'Seeds for bloom. The basement will remain Nathan's cave in honour of your birthday'.

It's a thoughtful, considered, sweet gift. I just hope US customs don't pull me in on my return flight for questioning over exporting seeds without adhering to the phytosanitation laws. I don't know where I'd even begin to explain the cave of time.

Fernando has organised a mystery birthday road trip by borrowing his dad's car. 'It's going to take a couple of hours,' he says, turning the air conditioning to full.

I don't know where we're going, but this road trip has an air of finality about it, perhaps a way to mark the end of this adventure. We're heading away from Manhattan. According to the map spread out in front of me, we're following the sunrise highway out towards Montauk, a small town at the end of Long Island, famous for its fishing and for a monster that washed up on the beach in the summer of 2008. I remember reading an article about it in the *Fortean Times*. It was a real-life monster, the hybrid corpse of a rodent-like animal the size of a small dog with a dinosaur beak, a fantastical creature straight out of Jules Verne, but a terrible Top Trump card. Before scientists could test the DNA of the animal to work out if the creature was a new species created by a medical experiment gone wrong, or just the bloated and decaying corpse of a raccoon, an old man made off with the remains. I'm convinced Montauk is our destination, a cryptozoological tourist trip to appeal to my sense of wonder.

We pass a sign near Farmingdale for a theme park called, appropriately, Adventureland. 'I used to work there!' says Fernando. You never know when people will surprise you. Once again it seems I've found a friend who is not entirely dissimilar to me.

We've been driving for over an hour and we're both getting restless, me with excitement, Fernando with anticipation.

'We're only halfway,' Fernando says, looking at his watch, 'but I need a coffee. We've got time.' We pull off the highway into the car park of a diner. In the relentless sun the bright neon, mirrors and polished chrome seem like a mirage of a mirage.

'A strawberry slushie, please,' I ask the girl behind the counter.

'Regular or large?' she asks with a smile as wide as her face, the perfect gleam of her teeth instantly making me feel self-conscious of my own wonky, chipped, British smile.

I look out of the window at the haze rising from the tarmac of the car park. The heat haze glazes everything with an opalescence that reminds me of the painting hanging on the wall of the café in Rhyl. That lonely breakfast feels so long ago.

'Large please,' I reply.

Minutes later I'm handed a bucket of luminous pink crushed ice laced with dangerous amounts of sugar.

Fernando laughs. 'You can tell you're British. We're in America now. Regular is large, and large is astronomical. And you definitely don't want an astronomical slushie.'

In Rhyl the scale of things made me feel taller. In America the scale of things makes me feel like I've been shrunk by the scientist's ray in Edward Packard's *You Are Microscopic*. I'm only a third of the way through the slushie when I sink into a hazy coma of cold and sugar crash. When I wake, Fernando is just turning off the highway at East Hampton.

'I thought we were going to visit the Montauk Monster,' I say groggily.

'Well, you're wrong,' Fernando replies.

The highway gives way to space, a green calm, large houses glimpsed at the end of long private drives, a millionaire's retreat full of private beaches.

'We're here!' Fernando announces moments later.

'Yes, but where?' I ask. We're parked in a driveway lined with trees in front of a large wooden-tiled house, like something an estranged uncle would live in if this was a *Choose Your Own Adventure* book.

Fernando reaches over and opens the door on my side of the car. I can instantly feel the heat fighting to get in. 'You should go first,' he says.

'Not another door knock, I really thought we'd finished with all that.' I don't really mean my protests. After all I've been through, facing strangers is easy, without counting and without rehearsal.

I get out of the car and walk up the short row of steps to a set of patio doors. The temperature, along with the sun, has been climbing steadily all morning and is just a couple of degrees from a hundred. The brightness makes it impossible for me to see anything but the squint of my own reflection. The glass slides open. It takes a moment for my eyes to adjust.

'Oh hi, Nathan, I've been expecting you,' says the voice of a man who is unmistakably Edward Packard.

'Hello . . . Edward,' I manage to reply.

Edward Packard walks towards me, extending his arm in exactly the same way as the illustration in my favourite book, *Hyperspace*.

* * *

It's my thirty-sixth birthday. Fernando has driven the length of Long Island, and now I'm sat in the summer-house kitchen of one of my boyhood heroes, the man whose writing helped to save my childhood, Edward Packard.

I'm stunned.

Out of all the twists and turns this adventure has taken, I did not see this one coming. I did not expect the originator of *Choose Your Own Adventure* to be my final destination.

Edward pours us each a Canada Dry ginger ale. 'Great to meet you finally, in person,' he says, adding ice and a slice of orange. It's exactly what I need after my slushie error. He introduces us to his daughter Andrea, whom is visiting with Edward's grandchildren. Andrea is one of the children to whom Edward first asked the question, 'What happens next?' all those years ago. I feel awed by literary history.

'I have a couple of things to give you,' Edward says, handing me a copy of the new edition of *Return to the Cave of Time*. 'Now it's even more challenging, and there are even more choices.'

I flick through the book, my eyes drawn to the words of an oracle in the cave of time:

> The Cave of Time has passageways that lead to places where you perceive others as they will be in the future, while they will perceive you as you were in your past, as well as places where you perceive others as they were in their past, while they perceive you as you will be in your future.

It's enough to make my head hurt.

Edward also gives me a copy of his latest book, his first non-interactive novel for adults, *Notes from the Afterlife*.

'It's just wild enough that I think you might like it,' he says laughing. 'The story follows a confirmed atheist called Jack who dies and finds himself in heaven. Not only does he have to come to terms with there being an afterlife, and having to consider all the bad choices he'd made in his life, but he also has to cope with the fact that the multi-faith divine being we know as God is thoroughly depressed.'

We talk about our journey to visit him and to America, and my journey to find Terence, and my friendship with James Costello. Edward listens attentively and lets me speak without interruption. When I'm finished telling the story you've been reading, like a sage, or the oracle in *The Cave of Time*, he says simply, in his soft American drawl, 'Sometimes a choice is no choice at all.'

While I was in Manhattan I picked up a postcard with a photograph of a confusion of signposts pointing in every direction. I was going to send it to James, it seemed fitting somehow. I ask Edward Packard to write the postcard for me, not to James Costello, but to the boy he once was, the boy in the book, Terence Prendergast. I wish I could send Edward Packard's words back in time to make things better for Terence, but even if I can't, it's the perfect advice for us all to follow in the future.

To Terrence

Choose wisely.

Edward Packard

Chapter 17 – Epilogue

Three weeks after I return home from New York a letter arrives in the morning post. I scan the envelope on the way back to the lounge. The postmark is smudged, and it's missing a return address. I rip open the envelope and pull out its contents.

No letter, no note, just a single photograph with the words 'Me, 1986' written across the back.

As I turn the photograph over between my fingers, I can't help but smile.

Afterword

Everything you have just read is true, but almost a lie.

In chapter five I wrote 'the best lies are the ones that are almost the truth.' The reverse of that sentence could also be said to be true – the best truth is the one that is almost a lie. That is how I would define this book.

To tell the story in the best way, the chronology of some moments has been altered, moved around in time from when they actually happened. But I really did find a diary in *The Cave of Time*, I really did become obsessed with finding Terence Prendergast. I also became obsessed, even before I started looking for him, with wanting to tell his story. That meant documenting everything.

The story that became this book started out as a live, interactive real-life theatre show called *Choose Your Own Documentary*. The show allows the audience to choose what happens next, in the manner of *Choose Your Own Adventure* books, by voting using small electronic keypads at important points in the story. There are 1,566 different possible versions of *Choose Your Own Documentary*, each one documenting my journey to find the boy in the book.

Everyone in this story is real too including Dr Irving Finkel, Ruth the graphologist, Roj, Johnny Doom and Edward Packard. All conversations are taken from actual filmed interviews.

Everyone is real that is apart from Fernando. In this story, Fernando is actually an amalgamation of three people – Fernando Gutierrez

De Jesus, Nick Watson and Sam Smaïl. They are my fellow adventurers, who accompanied me on every step of the quest to find Terence Prendergast. So although obsession genuinely is acutely isolating, there are moments in this book when I wasn't actually alone, even though being on the lens side of the camera can sometimes feel like it. While writing this book I've fretted and worried about offending people, that it would result in severed friendships and relationships, but the story won out. One is loneliness and four is a crowd.

I found Fernando through a film- and theatre-making friend, Dorna. He was a very lucky find. Fernando has a background in directing and editing, and has a huge list of television credits to his name. He brought that experience, combined with passion and imagination, to documenting the quest to find Terence.

Fernando quickly realised that if we were going to tell the best story, we would need a bigger team, and brought Sam and Nick on board. Both of them also have years of film, TV and documentary experience. Sam has an eye for detail that can sometimes easily be missed in the excitement of filming, and Nick's experience of filming real-life events means he's always ready to anticipate what might happen in a given situation and to capture it on camera. Together the four of us planned, filmed, plotted and created what would become *Choose Your Own Documentary*.

London's Southbank Centre co-commissioned the show and we performed a rough work in progress at the Festival Hall with additional support from Arts Council England. Those first two performances were not only nerve-racking due to their technical and narrative complexities, but in a replay of my experience with Uri Geller, they were also attended by James Costello.

Understandably, James Costello was more nervous than I was, and like a distorting fairground mirror, Nick was a blurry wobble of nervous energy greater than either of us. It is incredibly brave to allow a stranger to tell the story of your life; James watched those two shows with a combination of anxiousness and fear. One of the shows told the story of my letter to Nancy, and the other, due to some reckless decision making by the audience, ended in my virtual narrative death – the only fictional element in the show, a *Choose Your Own Adventure* style death specially written by Edward Packard. It was at that point that James understood why I wanted to tell his story.

Since those early performances, we have refined the show, increased the interactivity, heightened the emotional involvement, and raised the feelings of agency and responsibility. As a result, we were invited to preview the documentary at SXSW festival in Austin, Texas, in the spring of 2013. We followed this up with a month-long series of shows at the Edinburgh Fringe, the largest arts festival in the world. To our huge surprise, the show was featured in the *New York Times*, which was followed by an excited phone call from Fernando's mum and dad, our photograph spread before them in the daily newspaper of one of the world's biggest cities. They had supported the same intrepid band of adventurers, filling us with fruit and bagels every morning, while we were filming in New York. Those uncommon seeds from the cave of time seemed to have begun to bloom.

We were also awarded a *Scotsman* Fringe First, a prize given in recognition of 'innovation and outstanding new writing' in theatre. But more than this, I was most awed by the reaction of our audiences. As I hoped, Terence's story really does emotionally resonate with people of all ages, and the need for audiences to share similar experiences is the reward for persevering when perhaps I should have given up, let things go and moved on. I have obsession to thank for that obstinacy.

As I write this, we are about to embark on a two-week run at the Soho Theatre, in London's West End, followed by a tour of theatres across the UK. Each one of those shows is a tribute to a little boy who dreamed of adventure.

In a *Choose Your Own Adventure* book there is no true version of a story, no one correct path. *The Boy in the Book* is another path through the story of my friendship with James Costello. Is this story closer to the truth than any other version? The honest answer to that question is that there is both more truth and more fiction.

I think of the loneliness of that little boy sat in Birmingham, believing he has no friends in the world. How impossible it would be for him to imagine that his story would reach thousands of people, all of them, I hope, in adventuring through time, becoming a new friend in the process.

Nathan Penlington
January 2014

Acknowledgements

I would like to thank the following people:

James Costello for allowing me to tell the story of Terence Prendergast.

My fellow adventurers Fernando Gutierrez De Jesus, Nick Watson and Sam Smaïl, who were with me every step of this quest – without them, there wouldn't be a story.

Sarah Lester, who, it should be known, is edgier in real life than her fictional counterpart, for embracing my obsessions.

Mum, Dad and Nina, the most supportive family a writer and performer could wish for.

Auntie Avril, a patron of the arts in the truest sense.

Dorna, my favourite dude, for pointing me in the right direction.

My best buddy Guy J. Jackson for all the Parlour Games.

Gary Davies for the best cover version ever committed to film.

Sally Wagner for the regime.

Dr Irving Finkel; Ruth Myers; Nancy Mills and family; Dr Howard Fine; Johnny Doom and Kerrang! Radio; Hagi, Wallace and Inside Job; Dean Sullivan; Roj and the warriors of Wayland's Forge; Fuchsia Voremberg; the staff of the Bishopsgate Institute; James Davidson; Les Harker; Candy and Damian Gutierrez.

Everyone who has given their time to the filming or producing of *Choose Your Own Documentary*: all members of Out of Print for their early encouragement and support, especially Bea Colley and

Tom Chivers; Arts Council England; Sarah Sanders; David Cross; Southbank Centre London; Fay Woolven; Simon Oliver; Fiona Bartosch; Ruth Harrison; Elizabeth Lovius; Stuart Murdoch; Ann-Marie Soane; Kristina Kordiak; The Little Theatre, Rhyl; the music of Prendergast; Jacqui Thomas at Weetabix; Gordon Beswick; Social Media World Forum; Anthony Ziccardi; Brendan Davin; Kosta Efstathiou; Timmy Sullivan; Cary Romanos; Chris Brogan; P. Damian Gutierrez; Vic Latino and Miss Stacy at Party 105 FM; Brett Loudermilk.

Robert Dinsdale for believing in this story before it had been written.

Simon Thorogood, and all at Headline, for the opportunity.

And finally, to Edward Packard, whose stories planted the seed of adventure for millions of children all over the world.

Sources

Edward Packard is publishing revised and expanded versions of his classic *Choose Your Own Adventure* books, both in print and as iPhone apps, under the title U-Ventures: u-ventures.net For information about his other work: edwardpackard.com

R.A. Montgomery, Edward Packard's original publishing partner, maintained copyright on the title *Choose Your Own Adventure* and is republishing other books in the series under the Chooseco imprint: cyoa.com

All interviews were carried out as part of *Choose Your Own Documentary*. For tour dates and further information: chooseyourown documentary.com

The Great Diary Project, including a recording of the BBC Radio 4 programme *The Man Who Saves Life Stories* featuring Dr Finkel, can be found at: thegreatdiaryproject.co.uk

I first came across the obsessive diarist Robert Shields in Alexandra Johnson's *A Brief History of Diaries*, Hesperus Press, London, 2011.

To contact Ruth Myers about handwriting analysis: ruthmyers. com

The problem of choosing, and advice on how to choose well, is explored in: Barry Schwartz, *The Paradox of Choice*, HarperCollins, New York, 2004; and Sheena Iyengar, *The Art of Choosing*, Little, Brown, London, 2010.

An interesting and interdisciplinary examination of obsession:

Lennard J. Davis, *Obsession*, University of Chicago Press, 2008.

On the compulsion and practice of collecting: John Elsner and Roger Cardinal (eds.), *The Cultures of Collecting*, Reaktion Books, London, 1994.

Quote from Mark Setteducati, 'My life is an invention!', *M.U.M.*, Society of American Magicians, February 1994, Volume 83, Issue 9, page 10.

Magic advertisements reproduced from various issues of *Magigram*, the magazine of Supreme Magic, 1984–1987.

Excerpt of dialogue in Chapter 11 is from *Viva Knievel!*, 1977, Warner Bros Pictures.

For more about Dr Bruno Furst's memory course: youcanremember.com

Teofilo Olivieri can be found at the corner of 23rd and 6th in Manhattan, and at facebook.com/teofilo.olivieri

Lyrics to 'Love is all Around' are by Reg Presley, published by Universal Music.